Josephine Elizabeth Grey Butler

Catharine of Siena

A Biography

Josephine Elizabeth Grey Butler

Catharine of Siena
A Biography

ISBN/EAN: 9783337029760

Printed in Europe, USA, Canada, Australia, Japan

Cover: Foto ©Raphael Reischuk / pixelio.de

More available books at **www.hansebooks.com**

CATHARINE OF SIENA:

A BIOGRAPHY.

By JOSEPHINE E. BUTLER,

AUTHOR OF THE "MEMOIR OF JOHN GREY
OF DILSTON;" ETC.

(Third Edition).

LONDON:

HORACE MARSHALL & SON,

TEMPLE HOUSE, TEMPLE AVENUE, & 125, FLEET STREET.

1894.

$\mathfrak{Dedicated}$

TO

MY DEAR SONS.

LETTER FROM THE RT. HON. W. E. GLADSTONE.

———

When the first edition of "Catharine of Siena" appeared, Mr. Gladstone wrote as follows to Canon Butler:—

"*I received Mrs. Butler's kind gift yesterday morning and spent some time in reading the first three chapters with intense interest. It is evident that she is on the level of her subject, and it is a very high level. To say this is virtually saying all. Her reply (by anticipation) to those who scoff down the visions is, I think, admirable. It is interesting to divine the veins of sympathy which may have guided Mrs. Butler in the choice of her subject.* ✿ ✿ ✿ ✿

With many thanks,
Most faithfully yours,
W. E. GLADSTONE.

Hawarden,
October 14th, 1878.

PREFACE TO THE THIRD EDITION OF "CATHARINE OF SIENA."

There have been more than forty lives written of Catharine of Siena—in Latin, Italian, French, German, Dutch and Spanish.

Until recently her life and character have been very little known in England.

The principal chroniclers or historians who have been consulted in the following record are :—*Malavolti*, "Historia di Siena ;" *Tomasi*, "Historia di Siena;" *Muratori*, "Annali d'Italia ;" *Villani*, "Istorie;" *Machiavelli*, "Istorie Fioren ;" and *Sismondi*, "Histoire des Republiques Italiennes."

The most interesting details, however, of Catharine's inner life and active labours are drawn from the "Acta Sanctorum" and the annals kept by her friend, confessor, and companion in labours, Raimondo of Capua.

It is desired, by the publication of a less expensive edition of this book, which is continuously asked for, to place it more within the reach of persons who have hitherto only been able to obtain it from circulating libraries.

CATHARINE OF SIENA.

CHAPTER I.

IN order to be able to realize with greater clearness the character and career of the woman whom I desire to make better known among us in England, it is desirable to give some brief account of the principal events of the time in which she lived, and on some of which she exercised so great a moral influence.

Siena is situated in the undulating plains of Southern Tuscany, south of Florence, and between the Apennines and the sea.

This city is in many respects unique. The number of its inhabitants was about[1] 200,000 in the fourteenth century, when it ranked as the rival of Florence among the Italian Republics. Its population has slowly and gradually diminished since that time, and the city has not spread out one foot beyond its ancient walls. Its streets are narrow and steep; so steep in some cases that no carriage can ascend them, and sometimes resembling irregular stone staircases rather than streets. It had originally thirty-nine gates, of which all but nine

---

[1] Sismondi, "History of the Italian Republics."

are now closed. The city stands on the top of a hill of tertiary sandstone, and commands an extensive view. The citadel stands apart on the summit of another hill of the same range, with a small grassy valley dividing them.

The following sketch, written by an English lady in a letter to a friend in the winter of 1877, may give some idea to those who have not visited Siena of the scenery around the city :—

"Leaving the long narrow winding streets, we passed through one of the great gateways, and came direct out into the open country, where there are no straggling houses nor suburb of any kind. There is a wonderful charm about this sudden transition. The town stands on a hill, so that the country roads all lead up to its nine gates. One could imagine oneself in Palestine, near the 'city set upon an hill,' with the outer slopes covered with olive trees.

"The graceful, tender landscape stretches far away before you; hills crowned with ancient castles; the soil of a beautiful auburn or burnt-siena tint, and copses of oak, still covered with their russet autumn leaves. We went upon the ramparts of the citadel, upon which there are paths with tender green grass. There was a splendid winter sunset. Looking across the landscape, I could count nine or ten beautiful undulating lines, each like a horizon line, but always with one beyond it, and one beyond that again, and each distinguished from the one before it by showing fainter and fainter through a light haze, till the scene ended at last in a pale line of snow mountains. The shades were too delicate for any painter to have caught, and the haze only veiled without hiding the soft purples and mauves; while the visions of castles, convents, and campaniles varied and gave life to the undulating lines of each ridge.

"This part of Tuscany is sometimes described by travellers as desolate and bare; but I confess that I love the look of the country round Siena. There is something tender and warm and homelike in it. Certainly one may admire more the richer and grander features of other parts of Italy, but this country attracts me more as country to live in. One feels possessed by a wish to explore it, to visit the villas and castles which crown the tops of the low hills, to find out where every path leads to, and to ride about the tempting roads, which are open, with hedges studded with oaks as in England. The landscape is probably more tender and dreamlike in winter than in the glare of the summer light, when it appears more flat and uniform, and when you do not see one range of wave-like hills beyond another, as indicated by the lines of haze in autumn or winter.

"Down at our feet, as we looked from the ramparts, there were wooded valleys falling away from the city walls, before rising again into the opposite ridges, and close at our side was Siena itself, crowning the hill, all its towers and walls bathed on one side with the red glow of the winter sunset, and on the other in cobalt blue shade. There were sweet winding lanes with the long evening shadows cast across them, ascending the ridges, and then often following along the backbones of the little hills; many old fortified houses with olive-yards and cypresses around them, and sometimes even green lawns with sheep feeding—an uncommon sight in Italy.

"The people appear to live scattered about the country in single villas or castles, and not wedged into villages composed of a crowded street of tall houses, as is so common in Italy. These are signs of a very old-established civilization.

"Although the city itself is nothing in importance compared with what it once was, it is not ruinous or dilapidated. Everyone knows that it is in Siena that the purest Italian is spoken. The people are very proud of their fine old city and their past history. It offends them to say that this or that is like Florence, for they consider that Siena stands in the front rank among Italian cities.

"A little valley lies between the ancient city and a low hill to the west, on which stands the great church of St. Dominic. In this depression there was formerly the old district inhabited by the poor people of Siena, and known as the Contrada d'Oca. This was the birthplace of Catharine. Her father's house still stands there, also his workshop, and the chapel which was erected to her memory, over the door of which are written in letters of gold the words 'Sposæ Christi Katharinæ domus.' We visited the house and cell of Catharine, and saw the rough stone on the floor, which they say served her as a pillow, and the little lantern which she carried in her hospital visits during the plague."

The American translator of Father Raymond's "Life of St. Catharine" says :—"When going from Rome to Siena, as one descends the rough declivities of the Radicofani, the lines gradually soften on the horizon, and plantations of olive trees in graceful rows adorn the hill sides. The valleys present a high state of cultivation and broad streamlets murmur beneath shady foliage.

Chateaux of the middle ages, with farm-houses of picturesque architecture, animate the landscape, and as one advances on this road, festooned by luxuriant vines, nature appears milder and more gay. One could fancy one heard the distant strains of a concert, whose chords sound louder as one approaches the city which presents little of the agitation and feverish life of our modern cities. The Italian language is more melodious here than elsewhere, and the population offers types of a beauty distinctly its own."

Sismondi, in his "History of the Italian Republics," mentions the high estimation in which Catherine of Siena was held throughout Italy, during and after her life. In his history also we have a vivid picture of the troubles of Italy during the period in which she lived.

The revival of Greek and Roman literature, the formation of the Italian language, and the creation of modern poetry, the perfecting of jurisprudence, and the rapid progress made in painting and sculpture, architecture and music, are due in a great degree to the men of the fourteenth century; yet that period was far from being a happy one for humanity. Many of the old-fashioned virtues had disappeared, and revolting vices prevailed, especially in the courts and palaces of princes, both lay and ecclesiastical. Base intrigues were the order of the day, and the only recognized means of earthly success. The aristocracy set an example of every crime, and the grossest debauchery reigned in their palaces and castles. Poison and the knife were daily resorted to in the struggle to hold their own against rivals. Troops of assassins were retained in their pay, and a complete protection was granted to brigands in return for the services they rendered their lordly employers. Magistrates were corrupt, and justice sold. Princes derived revenue out of the punishment of criminals. Confessions were extorted by the rack from suspected persons, and criminals were punished with indescribable torture. In politics, frequent treachery destroyed all confidence in treaties and all friendly security among citizens. In war, foreign mercenaries sold themselves to him who paid the highest, and in their marches ruthlessly outraged the innocent inhabitants of the country, and ruined their agriculture. The contempt in which princes and nobles held all law and morality had an influence all the more pervading, because in every city of Italy at that time there reigned a little court, and this little court was for the citizens of each city a school of vice and crime. The several Republics of Italy were at continual war with the great dukes and princes who lived around or in the midst of them, and who, strong in the traditions of their former absolute and despotic sovereignty, looked with an evil eye on the independent spirit of the Republics. This independent spirit manifested itself in constantly renewed struggles to cast off the yoke, first of one tyrant, and then of another; at one time of some aggressive noble, at another of a foreign invader; now of the insolent emissaries of the Pope, claiming with the sword and excommunication the restoration of the revolted temporal estates of the Church, and now of an arrogant oligarchy in their midst, developed from the elected rulers of the people themselves.

No sight could have been more sad, more indecent, it may be said, for a Christian soul to contemplate than the sight which the Christian Church then presented in the persons of its prominent representatives. It was that of a worldly, greedy, grasping power, a power which had lost its influence for good over the conscience of Christendom, and had thrown itself into the fierce conflict of arms and of intrigue with all who disputed its claims to a despotic material sovereignty. The Pope Clement V. had removed the seat of the Papacy to Avignon, in 1305. Six popes after him continued to live in this voluntary exile, far from their duties and their people. They purchased from Joanna, Queen of Naples and Countess of Provence, the sovereignty of Avignon, with vast surrounding estates in that fair and sunny province of southern France. There they established themselves as though they never meant to return. Magnificent palaces and castles were built by them. The College of Cardinals came to be almost entirely composed of Frenchmen. Urban V. and Gregory XI. were French, and strongly attached to their native land. The French king used all his influence to retain the Papal Court in his kingdom, and the prelates were only too ready to yield to this influence, preferring a residence among a people in whom no restless desire of liberty or turbulent spirit of reform disturbed their tranquillity, or interrupted the gay and easy tenour of the Court life of Avignon. This period was compared by Italian writers to the Babylonish captivity. The voluntary exile of the Pope, and his neglect of the interests of his subjects, had a most melancholy influence upon the faith, the morals and the politics of the Church. The corruption of the prelates, the dishonourable and scandalous lives of the young cardinals, and the universal licence of the city were so notorious to all Europe that Avignon received the name of the

Western Babylon.[1] This epithet is found in the bitter invectives of Petrarch, and in the writings of all the most religious men of that time. Avignon gathered to itself the scum of the French and Italian populations, and intriguers and adventurers of all nations flocked thither. "The morals of Avignon," it was said, "are what are called vices in other nations." In the preceding century the Court of Rome had been sufficiently ambitious, avaricious, and dissimulating; but during its establishment at Avignon it became more and more venal and perfidious in its administration, while the Italians marked with disgust its ever-increasing servility to the Court of France.[2] The Sovereign Pontiff gradually lost the affections of the Italian people. He treated Italy as a mere dependency, making over the management of the estates of the Church to agents who became a plague and a curse to the people. These agents were the infamous Cardinal Legates, whose rapacity and cruelty exceeded even those of the ambitious families under whom Italy already had suffered more than she could bear. The conduct of these Legates continually brought the Papacy into worse and worse repute among the Italians. Under the plea of gathering in the revenue of the Church, they plundered the people, and, to enrich themselves, cheated the absent Pontiff of that which he too often exacted with harshness and injustice.

Another grief which pressed heavily on Italy at that time was the presence of the hosts of foreign mercenary troops to which I have already referred. These troops were chiefly composed of English and Bretons, who had

---

[1] Sismondi's "Italian Republics," Vol. vii. [2] *Ibid.*

taken part in the long war between England and France, and who had been driven from their own countries as demoralized military refuse, and unfit to return to the duties of citizenship. There were also Germans, and malcontents of all countries, who travelled over the Alps to sell their services to princes or republics to whom the offer of their alliance was itself a calamity;[1] for, after a victory won by their aid, those who had themselves accepted these dangerous auxiliaries found themselves vanquished in their turn. It was impossible to get rid of these mercenaries; they remained, and lived at the expense of the country; they sometimes retired to the strong castles of the Apennines, whence they periodically emerged, swooping down like birds of prey upon the country populations, pillaging and ravaging and carrying terror wherever they appeared. The fierce English brigand, John Hawkwood, led an immense English and Breton troop into Italy. He sold himself and his followers first to the Pope and afterwards to the Florentine Republic; performing, in the interval, some well-paid services for the Visconti and other fighting princes. He became the chief of that great "school of Italian condottieri" which warred in Italy for two centuries. His troops were accustomed to encamp disbanded and without order; they always fought on foot, carrying great lances such as were used in boar hunting, and advanced on the enemy in closely seried ranks, howling in their uncouth foreign tongues, the harsh sound of which was most terrible to the Italians. Catharine of Siena was several times stopped on her journeys and missions with her companions by the sound

---

[1] " Economie Politique du Moyen Age."

of the approach of these dreaded brigands. This happened on her journey to Florence, where she had been invited to act as a pacificator between that Republic and the Pope; she was obliged to turn out of her path till the danger had passed. One of her most eloquent letters is addressed to John Hawkwood (or Giovanni Augud as the Italian chroniclers write him). Hawkwood was, however, outdone in cruelty by the Papal Legate whom he served at the destruction and massacre of Cesena and Faenza, in 1377. Several of the northern Italian cities had entered into a league against the Pope, and for the defence of their liberties. The Pope sent his Legate, Cardinal Robert of Geneva, with an army to break up this league, if possible. Cardinal Robert drove a hard bargain with Hawkwood for his services in this campaign, and commenced proceedings by endeavouring to detach Bologna from the league. He promised the Bolognese "the pardon of their faults if they would acknowledge the sovereignty of the Church and of the Pope's ministers." The Bolognese replied: "We are ready to suffer all things rather than again to submit ourselves to the rulers whose luxury, insolence, and avarice we have so cruelly experienced." Cardinal Robert, on receiving this reply from the ambassadors of Bologna, sent back word: "Tell them that I shall not leave Bologna till I have washed my hands and my feet in their blood." The Legate's actions were worthy of his threat; he slew, burnt, and plundered. The summer being past, he found himself in need of winter quarters, and obliged the city of Cesena, which had not revolted or joined the league, to receive his troops. His barbarous soldiers, incapable of discipline, began to treat this city as one which they had taken in battle, forcing open the houses, robbing property, and carrying off the daughters of the citizens for outrage and captivity. The inhabitants endured patiently for several weeks, but on the night of February 1, 1377, they made a sudden attack upon the mercenaries, and drove them out of the city. Cardinal Robert, on receiving this news, sent a deceitful message to the people of Cesena, confessing that his soldiers had deserved this punishment, and promising a complete amnesty on condition that they would again open their gates to him. They opened their gates; and the perfidious Cardinal entering, ordered a universal massacre. He sent for Hawkwood, who was at that moment doing the Cardinal's work at Faenza. Hawkwood hesitated for a moment to execute this horrible deed; the Cardinal, persuading, taunting, and bribing, urged him on to the massacre, crying out, "I want blood, blood, blood!" None were spared, neither the aged nor the young; mothers, maidens, and infants at the breast were murdered and flung in heaps in the streets. From morning till night the slaughter continued. The Cardinal stood all day as the presiding genius of the scene, a crucifix held aloft in one hand, and a sword in the other, reiterating, "Kill them, kill them! all, all!" and resting not until the last of the five thousand of the peaceful inhabitants of Cesena was slain. This Cardinal Robert was the man who was afterwards, in 1378, elected Pope as Clement VII., the rival of Urban VI.

It was Catharine the wool-dyer's daughter who first dared to address to the Pope at Avignon letters full of severe truth, setting forth to him the miseries of his Italian subjects, the evils of his non-residence, and the gross cruelty of his unworthy legates ; it was she who prevailed in her endeavour to bring back the Sovereign Pontiff to his country, and to awaken him to a sense of his responsibilities towards his torn and distracted flock.

"Catharine of Siena," says her biographer Raymond, "was to the fourteenth century what St. Bernard was to the twelfth, that is, the light and support of the Church. At the moment when the bark of St. Peter was most strongly agitated by the tempest, God gave it for pilot a poor young girl who was concealing herself in the little shop of a dyer. Catharine travelled to France to lead the Pontiff Gregory XI. away from the delights of his native land ; she brought back the Popes to Rome, the real centre of Christianity. She addressed herself to cardinals, princes, and kings. Her zeal inflamed at the sight of the disorders which prevailed in the Church, she exerted all her activity in order to overcome them ; she negotiated between the nations and the Holy See ; she brought back to God a multitude of souls, and communicated, by her teaching and example, a new vitality to those great religious orders which were the life and pulse of the Church." " When she entered the world (after years spent in prayer and fasting), it was to preach to infuriated mobs, to toil among plague-stricken men, to execute diplomatic negotiations, to harangue the Republic of Florence, to correspond with queens, and to interfere between kings and popes. . . . It is well known how, by the power of her eloquence and the ardour of her piety, she succeeded as a mediator between Florence and her native city, and between Florence and the Pope ; that she travelled to Avignon and induced Gregory XI. to return to Rome, that she narrowly escaped political martyrdom during one of her embassies from Gregory to the Florentine Republic, that she preached a crusade against the Turks, and that she aided by her dying words to keep Pope Urban VI. on the papal throne."[1] We shall see how, like St. Francis, St. Bernard, and Savonarola, Catharine, though a devoted daughter of the Church, became its faithful and fearless monitor, and a prophet to it of warning and rebuke. Appalled by the knowledge which she rapidly attained of the hollowness, hypocrisy, and abominable vices which prevailed among the clergy of all ranks, she shrunk not from open denunciation of their evil deeds; she rebuked the evil-doers, whether princes, cardinals, or the "Holy Father" himself, with the severity of one who has a commission from Heaven, and with the passionate pleading and tenderness of a woman whose soul is filled with Christian love and pity for her kind. The Roman Church had not yet filled up the measure of her sins; the time had not yet come for the grand defection from her ranks of the bold spirits of a Luther and a Calvin. But through all the centuries, from the time when the supreme bishops of Rome ceased to be what they were in the earliest period—saints and martyrs, men of virtue and of humble piety—there never was wanting a succession of prophets, who rose up one by one, to repudiate in the name of Christ and in the face of the world, the corruptions, follies, and crimes com mitted in the name and by the authority of the professed ministers of Christ's religion, the ecclesiastical rulers who had become, in fact, the ministers of injustice and op-

---

[1] "Siena and St. Catharine," by J. Symonds.

pression.   That the spiritual life was not extinct, however, in those corrupt times, and that pure teaching and a Christ-like life were recognized and ardently loved far and wide by the nations, is proved by the ascendency which these prophet-like beings (and none more than Catharine) gained over the affections of the people, by the reverence and awe which they inspired even in the worldly courts of princes, by the fact that even the pride of haughty ecclesiastics bowed before them, by the recognition given to them by the Church herself, and by the loving devotion with which their names and memories continued to be cherished long after their death.

While Italy was thus shaken by the moral and political disorders above described, a terrible scourge visited her, in common with the other nations of Europe. The plague, which appeared in 1348, and again in 1361 and 1374, has been described by Boccaccio and other writers. A succession of extraordinarily rainy seasons was succeeded by famine in 1345 and 1347. The plague followed. Terror seized the inhabitants of every town and village where the first symptoms of the disease appeared ; the contagion spread with unheard-of rapidity; even to converse with one smitten was often fatal, without touching him ; men and women, and even cattle, fell dead in the streets; nature's wild scavengers, the wolf and the vulture, would not come near the tainted dead ; large ditches were prepared, into which the bodies were hurled, so long as anyone could be found to convey them thither. The utmost of human egotism and selfishness were manifested side by side with noble examples of courage and devotion. An impression prevailed that sadness or lowness of spirits predisposed persons

to take the disease, and consequently wild laughter and jest-
ing, gambling and revelling, were heard and seen in the midst
of dying agonies and hurried funeral obsequies ; all business
was neglected, and the population seemed like a vast crowd
awaiting certain death, in very various and strongly con-
trasted attitudes of mind. In Florence three out of every
five persons died, as affirmed by Boccaccio. At Siena, in
the months of May, June, July, and August, 1348, the
plague carried off 30,000 persons. In the later visitations
of this scourge, Catharine appears as the guardian angel of
her own city, and the devoted helper of the stricken and
dying, forsaken often by their nearest relatives. So great
was the terror of the nobles at the first sight of the second
approach of the dreaded scourge, that many of them fled to
the mountains and forests. The famous Bernabos Visconti,
the powerful Duke of Milan, unable to pursue his favourite
occupation of war, the plague having sounded a truce for a
season to the fratricidal shedding of blood, betook himself
to desperate hunting. "In the pursuit of this amusement,
he contrived to perpetrate infinite cruelties, a task, by-
the-bye, to him always familiar. Under pain of death,
he forbade anyone to slay a hare, a wild hog, or any
other game ; and this wicked law he scrupulously carried
out, applying it even to those who within four years previously had either killed or eaten of the game. He
kept 5,000 hunting dogs, which he caused to be dis
tributed among the country people, who had orders to
feed them well, and to bring them once a month to be
reviewed in a certain place. Woe to him whose charge
was found to be lean or out of condition ! Still greater
woe to him who had lost a dog by death ! These were

punished by the confiscation of all their goods, by torture and other penalties. More feared were the dog-keepers of Bernabos than the princes of the earth. At the sight and sound of these and other tyrannies of this inhuman prince everyone trembled, and no one dared to whisper. Two friars ventured one day to expostulate with him, and he immediately had them burnt to death."[1] The excitement of the chase prevailed for a time to quiet his fears, but the reports of a tyranny more irresistible than his own pursued Bernabos. Even while following the wolves of the Apennines with his well-fed hounds in full cry, he would come suddenly upon an untenanted hut, in which, on entering with some imperious demand, he would find the blackened corpse of the owner slain by the plague. Villani and Muratori both speak of the extraordinary terror of Bernabos when he realized that death was at his heels. Sismondi records that "so great was the fright of the Prince Bernabos Visconti that he shut himself into his castle of Marignano; and, determined that no one should come near him, he gave orders to the bell-ringer on his watch-tower to sound the bell the moment he saw anyone enter the territory around the castle. One day Bernabos perceived some gentlemen afar off approaching on the road from Milan, and yet no warning bell had sounded. Indignant, he gave the order to punish the bell-ringer for his negligence by pitching him headlong from his own bell-tower : his servants hastened up the tower to execute the order, and found the bell-ringer, dead of the plague, beside his bell. The fright of Bernabos was intensified by this circumstance; he fled

---

[1] Muratori.

further, to a hunting-tower which he possessed in the middle of wild forests, surrounding himself with a barricade at a mile's distance from the tower, on which barricade he caused to be placed a number of notices, threatening with instant death anyone who dared to cross that barrier. He survived the plague. At the same time, Catharine, full of faith in God, was passing incessantly, night and day, through the streets and hospitals of Siena, and comforting with peaceful words, and kindly, smiling face the terror-stricken and the dying. She also survived the plague. In the one we see the triumph of selfishness, in the other the triumph of faith.

In several of the nations of Europe a strong religious awakening succeeded the devastations of the plague. Multitudes of people humbled themselves before God, seeking to learn wisdom from the chastisement which he had suffered to visit the earth. This penitent desire for reconciliation with God found expression in the undertaking of a vast pilgrimage to Rome, in order to receive there the pardon and blessing which the Pope had offered to all who should undertake this pilgrimage.

In the winter and spring of 1350 a ceaseless stream of pilgrims poured into Italy from all parts of Europe. They bore with unmurmuring patience the rigours of a very severe season, toiling on through ice and snow, piercing blasts, and violent rains, which had destroyed many of the roads. All the inns and other houses on or near the highways being crowded by the first bands of pilgrims which arrived, others—chiefly those from Germany and Hungary —were compelled to camp out at night in large companies on the highways. They lit fires in the open air, and sat closely crowded together, the better to resist the cold. Historians of the time declare that these pious wanderers, conscience-stricken, humble, and fervently desiring salvation, set an example of Christian virtue to all. No disputes or divisions arose among them, nor were they ever heard to murmur at the hardships they endured. The innkeepers of the hostels where they crowded, unable to check any dishonesty or even to receive the payment due from each, owing to their great numbers, gave up the attempt; but never, it was said, was any pilgrim seen to depart without leaving on the table the money which he owed for his food. They sang litanies and hymns, offered up daily prayers on the road, without ostentation, yet with a humble disregard of any scorn or opposition they met with. In general their conduct inspired with awe and reverence the people of the country through which they passed. Several millions of penitents thus made the journey to Rome without any disorders or scandal arising in the midst of the vast multitude.[1]

Such were some of the events of the age and country in which Catharine of Siena lived and laboured.

---

[1] Villani, Vol. i., Chap. lvi.

CHAPTER II.

GIACOMO BENINCASA, the father of Catharine, was a dyer; his occupation was chiefly the preparation of colours employed in dyeing wool; hence his surname of Fullone, or dyer, and hence the name generally given to his and Catharine's abode, "The Fullonica." This house was situated, as I have said, in the humble quarter of the common people, in the Contrada d'Oca. His wife Lapa was simple, strong, and virtuous; Giacomo himself being, according to the testimony of all the contemporary biographers of Catharine, a loyal man, fearing God, and separated from every vice.

There was, without doubt, a decline throughout Italy of the stern virtues and simplicity of life of the previous century; yet in some cities, and pre-eminently in Siena, these stern traditions lingered on for several centuries, and at the time of which I write there were many families of the Italian Republics who maintained the primitive purity of their ancestors, and continued to worship God with the same honesty of conviction. Dante describes the simple life of the twelfth and thirteenth centuries in the words which he places in the mouth of Cacciaguida, his ancestor :—

> "I saw Bellincion Berti walk abroad
> With leather girdle and a clasp of bone ;
> And with no artful colour on her cheeks
> His lady leave the glass.   The sons I saw
> Of Nerli and of Vecchio, well content
> With unrobed jerkin ; and their good dames handling
> The spindle and the flax.   Oh ! happy they ! . . .
> In such composed and simple fellowship,
> Such faithful and such fair equality,
> In such sweet household, Mary at my birth
> Bestowed me."

Villani, the historian of Italy, observes that in the thirteenth and the beginning of the fourteenth century the Italian republicans lived soberly, on coarse viands and at little cost.   " The men and women dressed in coarse cloths ; many wore plain leather, and the Tuscan women were without ornament.   Their manners were simple, and in many customs and courtesies of life they were rude and unpolished; but they were of good faith and loyal both among themselves and to the State, and with their coarse way of living and poverty they did greater and more virtuous deeds than have been done in our times and with greater refinement and wealth."[1]   The virile character of the people of Siena was celebrated by Boccaccio and other contemporaries of Catharine.   Nicholas Tommaseo of Milan, who wrote in 1860 on "The Spirit and the Works of St. Catharine," remarks on the strong and manly character of her mind : "This citizen of an august Republic," he says, " was born in the midst of a turbulent, restless, and warlike people, a people nourished in severe customs, and who, whatever their faults, were in no sense enervated or feeble."   Accord-

---

[1] Villani, Book vi., Chap. lxxi.

ing to Sismondi, the Sienese were esteemed the proudest of all the Italian people. The parents of Catharine manifestly belonged to the generation then passing away ; they were simple, virtuous, and inured to hardship and effort. Although of a humble class in life they won for themselves a certain position among their fellow-citizens. Lapa described the character of her husband to one of the contemporaries of Catharine in the following words : " He was so mild and moderate in his words that he never gave way to anger, although he had many occasions for doing so ; and on seeing any of his household excited or vexed he would calm them by saying, 'Now, now, do not say anything which is not just or kind, and God will give you his blessing. He was greatly injured on one occasion by a fellow-citizen who had robbed him of money and who employed falsehood and calumny in order to ruin his character and the business he carried on. He never would hear his enemy spoken of harshly, and when I, thinking no harm of it, used to express my anger against my husband's detractor, he would say, 'Let him alone, dear, let him alone, and God will bless you. God will show him his error, and will be our defence.' This soon came true, for our enemy acknowledged openly his error." The neighbours of Giacomo also testified to his uprightness and virtue. He was pure and reserved in his speech; consequently his family grew up sensitive to any coarseness or unseemliness in conversation. One of his daughters, Bonaventura, married a young man of Siena who sometimes received in his house foolish and vain companions. Bonaventura became so depressed by the tone of the conversation around her that she fell ill. Her husband inquiring the cause of her illness, she replied, "I have never been accustomed to hear in the house of my father language such as I hear in yours. My education has been widely different, and I assure you that if such conversation continues around me it will be the cause of my death." Her reply inspired her husband with great respect for her and her family. He forbade his guests to speak one word in his house which could displease her. They obeyed, and thus the good government in the family of Giacomo rebuked the licence in the house of his son-in-law.

Giacomo and Lapa had twenty-five children; Catharine was one of two delicate little twins born in 1347. Little Jane, the twin sister of Catharine, died in a few days. "She winged her way to heaven," leaving Catharine on earth to become the mother of many souls. The stories told of our little saint to Raymond, her biographer, by admiring friends and neighbours of the Benincasa family, are full of naïveté and grace, and abound in miraculous incidents which I shall pass over very briefly. Beyond all doubt the child was the darling of her neighbourhood from her earliest infancy, as she was the beloved of her country in her later years.

As soon as she could walk, we are told, she contracted a habit of wandering from home; a habit which developed in her maturer age, and which became the subject of many outward criticisms and of some inward questionings of her own heart. The little vagrant was so beloved, and her childish prattle was "so discreet and so full of grace," that her mother with difficulty kept her at home, and sometimes took alarm when the repeated announcement was made in the large family, that "The baby is lost again." Before she could even speak plainly, we are assured that "the people of the Contrada d'Oca found such consolation and sweetness in her society that she received the name of Euphrosyne, which means joy or satisfaction." "As soon as one conversed with her," says Raymond, "sadness was dispelled from the heart, vexations and troubles were forgotten, and a ravishing peace took possession of the soul." Her smile, of which we hear so often throughout her life, was so bright and sweet that it "took souls captive." She smiled with her eyes as well as her lips, and her friends speak of an "ineffable joy which shone in her eyes." She possessed all her life a frankness of manner which disarmed all prejudice and dispelled reserves and fears: her nature was open and joyous, and her spirit truthful and clear as the day. She loved every living thing. Nature, beasts, birds, and flowers were very dear to her. Every man, woman, and child was to her a friend, a dear fellow-creature to be greeted without reserve, to be comforted, consoled, congratulated, pleaded with or gently rebuked as one beloved of the common Father, and redeemed by the precious blood of Christ.

She began early to have her little visions of celestial glory, and even some premonitions of the career to which she was to be called. The old church of St. Dominic in Siena stands, as I have said, on the summit of a little hill or rising ground separated by a pleasant little valley from the quarter in which Catharine's family resided. This valley so often traversed by her, and this venerable church with its adjacent monastery, were spots familiar and dear to her heart. We shall have to people them in imagination by-and-by with the most intimate friends

of Catharine, the devoted friar preachers of St. Dominic,
and the sisters of the Militia of Jesus Christ, who shared
her active life and accompanied her in many of her missions. The chapel by the side of the church was one of
her favourite resorts for prayer: it was there that she spent
long hours in ecstatic communion with her Lord; and in
the nave and on the steps of the great church she daily encountered the radiant faces of her brethren and sisters in
the faith, and held sweet converse with them. The bell-
tower of the church can be seen from the wool-dyer's house
in the Contrada d'Oca, and its matin and vesper bells sound
clear across the little valley. When Catharine was six years
old, her mother sent her with her little brother Stephen to
take a message to the house of their sister Bonaventura:
their errand being accomplished, the children were about to
return by the valley, when Catharine, looking up to the
golden clouds of evening, saw over the gable end of the
church of the Friar Preachers, a vision of Jesus, very glori-
ously apparelled, and terrible in majesty and beauty. As
she gazed in awe, the Saviour, she said, looked towards her
and smiled lovingly upon her, extending his hand in blessing. While she was lost in the contemplation of this vision,
her little brother continued to descend the hill, imagining
that she was following: turning round, he saw his sister
far off, looking up to heaven; he called to her as loud as he
could call, but she made no answer; at length he ran back
to her and took her by the hand, saying, "Come on, why
are you stopping here?" Catharine appeared to awake
from a deep sleep, and bursting into loud weeping, she
replied, "O Stephen, if you could only see what I see,
you would never have disturbed me thus!" and her eyes

again turned towards heaven, but the vision had vanished, to Catharine's great grief, who turned homewards weeping. From this moment she was observed to become graver and more thoughtful than before.

She had heard many recitals of the lives of the Fathers of the Desert, and about a year after this incident she conceived a strong desire to imitate them. In this she was not singular: it is not uncommon to find children in modern as well as early times, possessed with a romantic idea of pilgrimage, or retirement to the desert. St. Theresa of Spain read with her little brother, when she was a child, the lives of martyrs and hermits. "They determined to be martyrs, they would go to the nearest Moorish kingdom, where as soon as they arrived, their heads would be cut off; and without asking leave, or saying a word to anyone, they started, and had crossed the bridge out of the town, when an uncle encountered them and took them home. The martyrdom project coming to an end, they thought of turning hermits, and built themselves cells in the garden; but here their mechanics failed them; the roofs fell in, and they lost heart."[1] And some of ourselves have known children who, after reading the "Pilgrim's Progress," have hopefully started in search of the land of Beulah and the heavenly City, and after having lost their shoes and been covered with mud in some wayside bog which they would gladly have believed was the veritable Slough of Despond, with the wicket gate and its angel-porter beyond, have returned home, draggled and weary, to the mother's fireside. Little Catharine was so fired

---

[1] "Santa Teresa, a Psychological Study." J. A. Froude.

with the desire to imitate the Fathers of the Desert, that she frequently ran away to short distances from home to hide in some retired spot, where, however, her solitary musings were often rudely or comically broken in upon. One morning, in spite of past disappointments, she set out very early in search of the desert. She believed the ravens would kindly bring her food, yet the little woman was prudent and practical enough to provide herself with a loaf of bread to last over the first day, until she should ascertain more certainly what the conduct of the ravens was to be. Gliding through the gates for the first time in her life, she left the city behind her, and crossed a valley towards a range of little hills beyond. There she saw that the houses were more distant one from another, and thought that she was certainly now approaching the desert. She found a little grotto under a shelving rock, crept in, and with great joy set herself to pray and meditate. She remained there till the evening, when suddenly "God revealed to her that he designed for her another mode of life, and that she must not leave the house of her father." [1] On leaving her grotto, she became anxious on seeing the evening far advanced, and afraid, not of the anger, but on account of the anxiety of her parents. "They will think I am lost, and how sorry they will be!" she said, and the active, swift-footed little girl flew as fast as her feet would carry her, and never paused till she reached her father's house. The gossips said that she was carried by angels, or miraculously transported without once touching the ground, so rapid was her return.

---

[1] Raymond of Capua, "Life of St. Catharine."

Good sense and affection never failed to correct in her any tendency to exaggeration or to egotistical forms of piety.

The desire to be allowed to preach arose very early in her mind. She dreamed that she was changed to a man and received the ordination of St. Dominic, and sighed on awaking to find herself still a girl. She used to collect around her in the little valley an assembly of little girls of her own age, and preach to them with "wonderful eloquence and power." She gained so much the hearts and imaginations of these little girls, that many of them imitated in their degree her manner of life, and continued to be her friends and fellow-workers when they grew up.

At twelve years of age her parents and brothers began to talk of marriage for Catharine. Her father was particularly anxious about her future, and could not be persuaded that anyone of his acquaintance was worthy of such a child, ignorant as he was of the choice she had already made of a union far above all human alliances. Lapa took great pains in dressing and adorning her interesting daughter, caused her to deck her hair with graceful kerchiefs and pins, and "to ornament her neck and arms in a manner calculated to please such as might ask her hand in marriage."

Catharine had other thoughts; her absence of mind and little regard for even such innocent display as her mother's pride in her suggested, perplexed her parents. Lapa called in the aid of Bonaventura, a sister to whom Catharine was much attached. Bonaventura's little manœuvres were for a time successful. Catharine swerved for a brief moment from the straight and difficult path which she had set herself to pursue, but her countenance became sad, her manner nervous, and she often fled suddenly from any company in which she found herself. Her secret determination to devote herself wholly in the unmarried state to the service of God and man was never, however, given up, and the "life angelical" continually attracted her in the midst of the pleasures of earth, in which her heart found no rest. Her habit of prayer, however, had abated, and her spiritual life was in danger of being extinguished. At this time Bonaventura, still young, loving, and beloved, died in giving birth to a child. Catharine's grief was bitter; this blow revealed to her the vanity of all earthly things, and she consecrated herself afresh to a life of prayer and holy service. The desire of her parents that she should marry was now, however, more openly expressed, and a young man of highly honourable character and family was introduced to her as desiring her hand in marriage. She continued a friendly but gentle resistance. This brought upon her a species of domestic persecution which tested her courage and strength of character. Her biographers, in their devout desire to heap honour upon the head of the saint, exaggerated, it seems to me, the unkindness of her parents. Their sternness was, perhaps, even not unwise; for many a young girl in those days, captivated by the thoughts of a life of consecration, would turn a longing eye towards the monastery, and at the first severe trial would waver in her resolution, or having taken the irreparable step, would make the discovery too late that she had mistaken her vocation. There was no intentional cruelty in the conduct of Giacomo and Lapa towards their child; they believed it necessary to test her resolution, and they acted sternly, in accordance with this belief. The storm thus raised and prolonged in their houschold by the divergence and opposition of the wills of those who really loved each other was, however, very painful to both parties. Catharine laboured cheerfully, nevertheless, to fulfil every task imposed on her. She was forbidden to have a room to herself, and was ordered to share one with another member of the family. She chose to share the room of her little brother Stephen, because she could profit by his long hours of absence in the day, and his profound sleep at night, to continue her prayers and vigils. Here she cried daily to her Saviour to direct her path, and to claim her wholly as his own. Her brothers observed her constancy, and said to each other, "we are beaten; Catharine has won." Her father observed her silently, and became daily more convinced that she was not following the fancies of a capricious maiden, but the call of God. He chanced to enter her room one evening when she was absorbed in prayer. When he turned from her door he was covering his face with his hand, as if dazzled; he told Lapa that he had seen a wonderful light resting upon and enveloping the girl; some said that the light he saw rested in the form of a snow-white dove upon her head. Whatever the appearance, it is certain that Giacomo became still more thoughtful and more tenderly respectful towards his daughter from that hour in which he learned how direct and intimate were her relations with heaven.

About this time Catharine had a dream, suggested, no doubt, by the constant and fervent desire of her waking hours to be enrolled in the Dominican Order, and to become a preacher. She dreamed that the good and great St. Dominic approached her, smiling, and said to her,

" Daughter, be of good cheer ; fear no hindrance, for the day is coming in which you shall be clothed with the mantle you so much desire."   She awoke with her heart filled with joy, and on that very day she assembled her father, mother, brothers, and sisters, saying she had a communication to make to them, and thus she addressed the assembled family :—" For a long time you have resolved that I should marry, and my conduct must have convinced you that I cannot entertain such a proposal.   I have never, however, explained myself clearly, because of the respect I feel for you, my parents ; but duty forbids me to be silent any longer : I must now speak candidly to you, and reveal to you a resolution I have made, which is not of yesterday, but which dates from my infancy.   Know, then, that I have made a vow, not in levity, but deliberately, and with full knowledge of what I was doing.   Now that I am of maturer age, and have a better acquaintance with the nature of my own actions, I persist, by the grace of God, in my resolution, and it would be easier to dissolve a rock than to induce me to change my mind.   Give up, therefore, for me, dear friends, all these projects for an earthly union ; it is impossible for me to satisfy you on this point, for I must obey God rather than man.   If you wish me to remain as a servant in your house, I will cheerfully fulfil all your will to the best of my power ; but if you should be so displeased with me as to make you desire me to leave you, know that I shall remain immovable in my resolve. He who has united my soul to his, has all the riches of heaven and earth, and he can provide for and protect me."   At these words all present wept ; sobs and tears prevented for a time any response.   Awed by the firmness and courage of the hitherto silent and gentle girl, the whole family felt that further opposition was impossible. At last the father spoke:—"God preserve us, dearest child, from any longer opposing the resolution which he has inspired; experience proves to us that you have not been actuated by caprice, but by a movement of divine grace. Fulfil without hindrance the vow you have taken; do all that the Holy Spirit commands you; henceforth your time shall be at your own disposal; only *pray for us*, that we may become worthy of him who has called you at so tender an age." Then, turning to his wife and children, he said, " Let no one hereafter contradict my dear child, or seek to turn her from her holy resolution; let her serve her Saviour in the way she desires, and may she seek his favour and pardoning mercy for us; we could never find for her a more beautiful or honourable alliance, for her soul is wedded to her Lord, and it is not a man, but the Lord who dieth not, whom we now receive into our house." After these words some still wept, and especially the poor mother, who loved her daughter in a more earthly fashion, perhaps, than the father did. Catharine humbly thanked her parents, and rejoiced exceedingly.

She was now permitted to arrange for herself the little private room, or cell, which became her sanctuary, and the scene of her marvellous converse with God for so many years, and which is shown in Siena to this day. Here she devoted herself to prayer and to the study of the will of God. For three years she scarcely quitted this cell. She put forth during those years the strength of an athlete in her wrestlings with heaven, determined first to know her Saviour and her own heart, and then to do and to bear in this world whatever he should ordain for her, awaiting the time when he should call her to a still nearer communion with himself. These years were not a time of listless contemplation nor of sentimental piety for the dyer's daughter. They were a stern and energetic preparation for the combats of her future life.

She was very sparing in her diet; she gave but little time to sleep, and her bed was composed of a few planks without any covering; she wore coarse clothing, but "as she cherished cleanliness and exterior neatness as a sign of interior purity," she frequently changed her woollen garments, and allowed no outward marks of asceticism to appear in her person. It was her custom to continue in prayer until the hour of matins, when, at the first sound of the matin bell from the tower of her dearly-beloved church of St. Dominic, she stretched herself on her wooden bed for a brief hour of sleep; she loved to think that an unbroken chain of prayers was ascending to God from the people's quarter of the city, and she would not cease until the brothers and sisters of St. Dominic had begun the matin prayer and hymn of praise. She confided to Raymond, in later life, that this victory over sleep had cost her more than any other, and that she had undergone inexpressible conflicts in triumphing over the natural desire for repose. Such conquests over self and over the infirmities, even over many of the just and natural demands of the body, have never been absent in the lives of those whom, *par excellence*, we call "the saints," those who have left behind them an influence which is of God, and imperishable; an influence which even the most sceptical must confess to have been benign, and charged with blessing for humanity. Catharine's health was delicate, yet she possessed an extraordinary nervous energy, and even a muscular strength which astonished those who saw her exert it in the performance of any generous or helpful act. She suffered all her life from a weakness of the stomach, which made it difficult for her to take any food without pain, succeeded often by violent sickness and vomiting. She was also subject to attacks of weakness and prostration, especially in the spring, which would last several weeks.

Her mother was distressed at the sight of her austerities, and implored her to eat more, as indeed did all her family. The obedient daughter would make the attempt, in order to please her family, but with very poor results; for the sickness became more severe and spasmodic, so that she sometimes fainted away and remained insensible for a long time, through the violence of her sufferings. Lapa would sometimes enter her room in the early morning, and lifting her in her arms, would carry her to her own bed and gently place her there for greater comfort; but her daughter, thanking her kindly, begged the favour of being allowed to return to her planks in her own dear little room; or if she found her mother herself had fallen asleep, she would rise softly, and kneel and pray for that dear anxious mother, and for all her family.

The desire to enter into the third order of St. Dominic continually increased. It may be useful to say a few words here concerning that valiant soldier of Christ, St. Dominic. This active and zealous apostle laboured for very needful reforms in the Church and in the world. In order to work more effectually for these reforms, he brought together a number of laymen, and organized them into a kind of militia.

Those who enrolled themselves swore to sacrifice, if necessary, their earthly goods and their lives ; and their wives engaged themselves also by a vow never to hinder, but to assist as much as possible, their husbands in their work. These associates took the title of Brethren and Sisters of the Militia of Jesus Christ; they wore the black and white habit of St. Dominic. This Militia, after the death of St. Dominic, was placed under the direction of his own Friar Preachers, and assisted that hardworking and truly apostolic body in their labours for the reform of morals and the salvation of souls. The Sisters of the Militia changed their title later into that of the Sisters of Penance of St. Dominic. Catharine had seen and heard many of the wandering Friar Preachers who, in default of a temple made with hands, would gather the people in the fields and by the wayside in the cool of the evening to hear the glad tidings of grace. What life, she thought, could be so blessed as this ? what mission so sacred as this of carrying the lamp of truth from city to city ? Who so happy as these messengers, disencumbered of all worldly ties, and ready for all the martyrdom of life as well as for death ? But she was a woman ! That *she* should ever share so blessed a life, that she should ever be permitted to pour forth in words of fire the burning love of her heart for humanity, seemed for a time an idle dream. Still the desire continued ; still she longed to become a *preacher*, and the first step was that she should be enrolled as a Mantellata ; (such was the name given to the wearers of the cloak or mantle of St. Dominic). We find her mother so far won to accept her child's ideas as to go herself to the Fraternity of St. Dominic to request this favour for her daughter. She received for reply that "it was not the custom to give the mantle to young maidens; that hitherto none but widows of very mature age, or wives consecrated to work with their husbands, had received it; also that the Mantellatas had no cloister or building devoted to them, and that each Sister must be able to rule her life in her own home." On a second application being made by Lapa, the Elders among the Sisters replied, "If she be not too handsome, nor of a beauty too remarkable, we will receive her on your account and hers; but if she be exceedingly pretty, we shall be obliged to refuse, for we are bound to avoid the inconveniences that might spring from the malice of men at the present period." After having conversed with Catharine herself, and observed the maturity of her thoughts, and the strength of her purpose, the Fraternity decided to admit her. Catharine was not beautiful. We gather from the slight mention of her personal appearance, and from the bust and portrait of her executed by contemporary artists, that her face expressed, above all things, candour, sweetness, and vigour. Her countenance was frank and open as the day; she had a habit of looking straight at everyone whom she addressed; her forehead was broad and open, a little too receding for beauty; her hair and eyebrows dark brown; her eyes a clear grey or hazel; her nose was straight and extremely delicate; her chin and jaw strong and rather prominent; her smile is continually mentioned; a loving, gracious smile, which pervaded her whole countenance, lit up her eyes, and often broke into a joyous laugh. Her charm was not that of positive beauty, but of kindness, frankness, and grace. All her movements were full of native grace. "An artist born," as Chavin de Malan says of her, "her attitudes and manner were all unconsciously artistic and beautiful." A true Italian, she used much action in speaking, gesticulated freely, but not excitedly. She spoke rather rapidly and in the sweetest Sienese accent ; she had a particularly graceful and gracious manner towards all who came to visit her, bowing low to greet them, as was the custom in her time, sometimes kneeling when saluting persons whom she deemed especially venerable, and then seating herself by their side for frank and friendly converse. Her manners, with men and women alike, outstripped somewhat the prescribed conventionalities of her times. Young men who would come with some feeling of awe to visit the far-famed saint, and not without fears concerning the interview, were taken by surprise, gladdened and reassured by her frank approach, her two hands held out for greeting, her kind, sisterly smile, and the easy grace with which she invited them to open their hearts. She was, in fact, a true, simple, and self-forgetting woman, a frank and generous friend, the "gracious lady" of Siena, who well deserved all the love and all the confidence which her fellow-citizens first, and afterwards the whole of Italy, lavished upon her. There was nothing affected, nothing artificial about her. With all her refined grace, she yet bore with her to the end the simple and almost blunt manners and habits of the "Daughter of the People." The honest pride in, and affection for her entertained by the Sienese is illustrated in the various titles by which they delighted to speak of her, as well as in many other expressions in regard to her. She is called "the Daughter of the Republic," "the Child of the People," "Our Lady of the Contrada d'Oca," "the Mantellata," "the People's Catharine," "the Beloved Sienese," "the

Painter's Daughter," the " Beata Popolana," which may be translated the "Blessed Plebeian, or Daughter of the People," &c., &c. On receiving the habit of St. Dominic, she did not at once enter upon an active life. Indeed, it appears that it required some holy constraint to draw her out of her cell and to launch her upon the stormy sea of social and political life before her.

And here I must pause to speak of that great secret of Catharine's spiritual life, the constant converse of her soul with God. Her book, entitled "The Dialogue," represents a conversation between a soul and God, mysterious and perhaps meaningless to many, but to those who can understand, full of revelation of the source of her power over human hearts. All through her autobiography (for such her Dialogue and Letters may be called) no expressions occur more frequently than such as these : "The Lord said to me," &c. —" My God told me to act so and so "—"While I was praying, my Saviour showed me the meaning of this, and spoke thus to me." I shall not attempt to explain, nor shall I alter this simple form of speech. It is not for us to limit the possibilities of the communications and revelations which the Eternal may be pleased to make to a soul which continually waits upon him. If you are disposed, reader, to doubt the fact of these communications from God, or to think that Catharine only fancied such and such things, and attributed these fancies to a divine source, then I would give you one word of advice, and one only. Go you and make the attempt to live a life of prayer such as she lived, and then, and not till then, will you be in a position which will give you any shadow of a right, or any power to judge of this soul's dealings with God. But

observe that a brief or fitful effort will not suffice to place
you in this position : you must persevere long in the difficult path of divine research ; you must bring to the task
the sustained self-denial and untiring diligence which some
men bring to the pursuit of discovery in natural science.
Let us imagine a person who had never seen a telescope,
and who was profoundly ignorant of the most elementary
laws which govern the motions of the planets, and suppose
this person to have stepped in between Newton and the
stars, and declared, " Philosopher, I do not believe what
you tell me of the wonderful action of these heavenly
bodies ; I believe you to be deceiving yourself ; I have not
tried any such experiments as you have tried ; and I do
not believe that any such experiments can conduct to any
such results as you speak of, even if any such experiments
can be made. The whole thing is beyond the range and
scope of my own experience, and I cannot conceive how it
can be true. In fact, I deny it." Such a person would be
pronounced unscientific at least ; perhaps he might justly
be called a fool. Not less unscientific is he who, never
having used the means for the discovery of spiritual truth,
and being profoundly ignorant of the most elementary
laws which must be understood and followed in order to
arrive at such truth, declares that he does not believe there
is a God, or does not believe that any communication can
be established between a creature and his Creator, and
attributes to delusion and fancy all that experimental
philosophers in divine things have told us they have
found and seen. Perhaps it might not be unjust to apply
a stronger word than unscientific also to such a one. The
science of which Catharine was a devotee is, let it be

remembered, pre-eminently an experimental science. For many, however, it is needless that I should speak thus; nor will I attempt any explanation or apology for the manner in which our saint constantly speaks of that which the natural eye hath not seen, nor the ear heard, but which God has in all times revealed to them that persistently seek him. Those who have any experience of real prayer know full well that in the pause of the soul before God, after it has uttered its complaint, made known its desires, or sought guidance in perplexity, there comes the clearer vision of duty, and the still small voice of guidance is heard, rectifying the judgment, strengthening the resolve, and consoling the spirit; they know that this influence, external to us, and yet within us, gently and forcibly moves us, deals with us, speaks with us, in fine. Prayer cannot be truly called communion, if the only voice heard be the voice of the pleader. Be still, be silent, then, dear reader, if you are disposed to object. If *you* have not yet heard that voice of God speaking within you, it is because you have not yet pleaded enough with him; it is because you have not yet considered or acted in this matter in a truly scientific manner.

Catharine now learned from our Lord that she "was henceforth to banish from her heart all anxious thoughts concerning herself and her own salvation," so that no distraction should keep her back from the service of the souls of others. Some presentiments, however, of approaching conflict seemed to have urged her at this time to pray especially for the gift of fortitude, and this fortitude was soon to be severely tried. She was to pass through one of those bitter conflicts, the very memory of which is pain to those who have endured them. "The great enemy of man advanced to the dread assault of her soul," as he did with our Lord himself when he was "alone in the wilderness, and tempted of the devil." She was assailed "by the most humiliating temptations, and by exciting phantoms of the imagination which haunted her sleeping and waking. She saw in her dreams impure orgies, wherein men and women seemed to invite her by words and gestures to join with them; she was tormented inwardly; her eyes, her ears, her soul, seemed to her to be defiled." She endured combats too horrible to relate. All the passion of her young southern blood seemed to rise up in a fierce rebellion against her own resolution and the ruggedness of the *viâ crucis*. She combated valiantly, prayed the more earnestly, worked the more assiduously in household work, and augmented her vigils. The enemy refused to retire. She seemed to see persons who came to pity and advise her. "Why, poor little one," they said, "do you thus torture yourself so uselessly? Why all these efforts and self-mortification? You will not be able to continue them; you will destroy yourself, and become guilty of suicide. It is better to renounce these austerities and enjoy the world while you are young; you are naturally strong, and would soon recover health if you live as other people do." To all these suggestions Catharine only opposed prayer. She afterwards gave the advice in general to others in such cases, never to dispute with the enemy, "for he relies," she said, "very much on vanquishing us by the subtilty of his reasonings."

But this deadly trouble passed away, and then there came a period of sadness and bitter conflict which appeals far more pitifully to all our human sympathies.

The woman's heart within her was beating fresh and warm: she was young; her soul was full of music and of poetic imaginations; who more fitted by nature than she to realize the highest and sweetest of human love ? It was the era of romance, the age of the troubadours. She had heard many a fair tale of love; the noblest of earthly lovers seemed to woo her; the vision stood near her, and looked in her eyes; his exquisite human pleadings broke in upon the songs of angels, and extinguished the voice of her heart's Spouse. When she slept, exhausted, she dreamed herself in the midst of a sweet home—*her own;* she seemed to clasp in her arms the little infant which hung upon her breast; and waking, the woman's heart within her was well-nigh broken. Her little room was filled with a strange mingling of heavenly and earthly music. The love-songs of the troubadours interrupted the strains of the Magnificat and the penitential psalms. She had hours of agonizing hesitation of will. Wise and practical coun-sellors seemed to advise her : " Why be so rash as to choose a life in which you cannot persevere ? Why ex-tinguish within you the holy impulses of nature which God has implanted in you ? Many among the saints were married. Think of Sarah and Rachel, and of many of recent years; of your contemporaries; of St. Bridget, Queen of Sweden, wife, mother, and prophet." But the celestial wooer prevailed. The love of loves was again more perfectly manifested to her, the agony was over, and she fell at the feet of Jesus.

Many in our days will disapprove of Catharine's choice ; it will appear to them an error, a sin even, against herself, and perhaps against society ; for what greater boon, some will say, could she have bestowed than descendants who would, no doubt, more or less, have inherited her own nobility and genius? Doubtless Catharine might have married, and given to the world twenty-five children, as her mother Lapa did. No doubt she might have been in this state the recipient and dispenser abundantly of spiritual life to all around her: but she would not have done the work which Catharine of Siena, the subject of this biography, did: her whole soul, her whole time, the whole strength of her affections would not have been reserved to be lavished upon that great family for whom she elected to live—*humanity.*

I do not find that there entered into her thoughts the smallest idea of merit or of reward in renouncing earthly joys and human ties. The most careful search through all her utterances, written or spoken, fails to reveal a single word claiming to herself any merit. Her dying words give the key to the faith or the philosophy which she embraced from her childhood. Barduccio, one of her secretaries, who gathered up her last words, tells us that when she knew she was dying, "she blessed us all, and pronounced these words: 'Yes, Lord, thou callest me, I come to thee; I go to thee, *not on account of my merits,* but solely on account *of thy mercy,* and that mercy I have implored in the name, O Jesus, of thy precious blood.'" The words in italics are emphasized by Barduccio himself, as if to preserve the solemnity with which they were pronounced by Catharine. Nor does she speak of reward, except the reward of bringing blessing to her fellow-creatures. Like St. Paul, she was ready "to be accursed from Christ for her brethren's sake." She was ready to give up all things for the love she bore to her brethren, to humanity. Yet she knew that he who labours to bring his fellow-men to God, will not be required to give up the blessed reward of seeing him face to face to whose feet he has brought this multitude of souls: " For they that are teachers shall shine as the light, and they that have brought many to righteousness, as the stars for ever and ever." Had Catharine's choice been otherwise, she might have been blessed indeed, yet would have missed the peculiar blessing of those of whom Christ spake emphatically, who have " left father and mother, and wife and children, and houses and lands, for my sake, and for the gospel." And what was that peculiar blessing? In her case, at least, it was a greater *power*—power to win, to convert, to suffer, to rule, to command, for the salvation of erring man, and for the glory of God.

For a time peace was granted to the soul of Catharine after this prolonged conflict of many weeks. But " the infernal foe," as the mediæval historians have it, " annoyed at her perseverance and victory," again " changed his weapons," and recommenced his tortures. A still darker period arrived, in which her sufferings were such as almost to deprive her of reason. Diabolical beings seemed to pursue her with screams, inviting her to partake in their abominations; the most cynical suggestions were poured into her mind, and to crown her affliction, her divine helper, who had usually in the worst moments made his sustaining presence felt by her, now seemed to have forsaken her, and she was left with no relief, visible or invisible; her soul was plunged into a profound melancholy, and the strength to continue in prayer seemed about to forsake her. She now summoned all her energy, adjured her own soul, so to speak, to renew and to multiply its efforts in prayer, instead of diminishing them. She cast herself at the feet of God, determined not to murmur, but patiently to await his return and help. Her little room at the Fullonica seemed to be "infested with these impure spirits;" she therefore wisely left it, and remained as long as possible in the church on the hill, where these "infernal obsessions tormented her less." Here she continued for the greater part of three days engaged in constant prayer. The evil spirit seemed still to taunt her, saying, "Poor miserable creature, thou canst never pass thy whole life in this state; we will torment thee to death, unless thou dost obey us." Catharine replied with patience, yet with determination, "Be it so; I have chosen suffering for Christ's sake, and I am willing, if need be, to endure this till death." Immediately on pronouncing this determination, a great light seemed to descend from above, filling the place where she kneeled with heavenly brightness. The devils left her, and One better than the angels came and ministered to her. The Lord Jesus himself drew nigh to her, and conversed with her of her trial and her victory. But she, like St. Anthony, said to him, "Lord, where wast thou when my heart was so tormented?" "I was in the midst of thy heart," he replied. "Ah, Lord," she answered, "thou art everlasting Truth, and I humbly bow before thy word; but how can I believe that thou wert in my heart when it was filled with such detestable thoughts?" The Lord asked her, "Did these thoughts and temptations give thee pleasure or pain?" "An exceeding pain and sadness," she replied; to whom the Lord: "Thou wast in woe and sadness, because I was hidden in the midst of thy heart; my presence it was which rendered those thoughts insupportable to thee ; thou didst strive to repel them, because they filled thee with horror, and because thou didst not succeed, thy spirit was bowed down with sorrow. When the period which I had determined for the duration of the combat had elapsed, I sent forth the beams of my light, and the shades of hell were dispelled, because they cannot resist that light. Because thou hast accepted these trials with thy whole heart, thou art delivered from them for ever ; it is not thy trouble that pleases me, but the *will* that has supported that trouble courageously." Catharine was now absorbed in a joy which could find no expression in words. She had asked the gift of fortitude, and she saw that her request had been granted. "This generous young athlete," says Raymond, "thus combated alone in the arena," and returning victorious, became for the future a fit teacher and guide of men, to whom among all her counsels she gave most frequently this, " Quit yourselves like men ; be strong in the Lord, and in the power of his might."[1] She never again suffered from a renewal of this form of temptation.

It was shortly after the cessation of this conflict that Catharine entered into that yet more intimate covenant with the Saviour of her soul, the recital of which to some of her friends became the occasion of the propagation of the legend immortalized by so many Italian painters of the mystical marriage of St. Catharine. The pictures

---

[1] Tommaseo remarks on the frequency in Catharine's letters to princes and potentates, and men of every degree, of the use of the words " virile " and " virilmente," and of her charges to women as well as to men to act in a manly spirit.

generally represent the Virgin Mary guiding the hand of
the Child Jesus to place on the finger of Catharine a ring,
which was to be a sign of her divine espousals. Fra
Bartolommeo, himself a Dominican, was the first to put
the idea on canvas. One of the most beautiful and often
repeated works of Correggio is the " Marriage of St. Catharine." One of these is in the Studj Gallery at Naples.
Other repetitions are at St. Petersburg, in the gallery of
the Capitol at Rome, and in other places. Catharine's own
account of this dream or vision which she had is very
simple. She saw her Saviour approach, and place on her
finger a ring, on which blazed a diamond of unearthly
purity and beauty. He had said to her, " I, thy Creator
and Redeemer, espouse thee in faith and love. Preserve
this token in purity, until we celebrate in the presence of
the Father, the eternal nuptials of the Lamb. Daughter,
now acquit thyself courageously ; perform with a dauntless
spirit the works which my providence will assign to thee ;
thou shalt triumph over all enemies." She had been long and
intensely dwelling upon the words spoken by our Lord to
his disciples, " With desire have I desired to eat this Passover with you ; " and she had realized in all its extent and
meaning what she had given up in order to be more entirely
the servant of God and of humanity. That her heavenly
Guide should have at this moment granted her such strong
consolation and such a perfect sense of mutual recognition
and union between her spirit and his, was consistent with the
infinite loving-kindness and fidelity with which he treats
the souls which give up all for the kingdom of heaven's
sake.

About this time Catharine taught herself to read, for

she had had hitherto no knowledge whatever of letters.
She desired to be able to study for herself the Scriptures,
especially the Psalms and Gospels, as well as the lives and
writings of the fathers, confessors, and martyrs. She
learned with such rapidity that her friends declared that
the angel Gabriel himself had come down to her cell with a
spelling-book to teach her, for nothing but a miracle, they
thought, could account for her sudden accession of learning.
It was not till many years later that she learned to
write; and yet some Italian writers rank this woman with
Petrarch and Boccaccio, as one of those who "formed the
·Italian language, such as it was in the fourteenth century."
The dignity and beauty of her language have even led
writers to compare her style, not unfavourably, with that
of Dante. She wrote several poems of some merit; but
her books, in which her own "philosophy" is set forth,
her letters, many of which are preserved to us, and her
written prayers, afford the chief justification for the high
opinion formed of her powers as an author by her contemporaries and by later historians.

Up to this period she had never been under the direction
of any spiritual pastor or guide. Raymond says: "He
whom she loved gave her neither an angel nor a man to
be her director, but appeared to her himself in her little
cell, and taught her all that was most needful for her to
know. 'Be assured, father,' she said to me one day,
'that nothing that I have learned concerning God and our
salvation was taught me by man; it was my Master, our
Lord Jesus Christ, who revealed it to me by his inspirations.'" This Raymond of Capua, so often quoted,
did not make her acquaintance until the period of the

plague of 1373 in Siena, when Catharine was twenty-six years of age. Raymond was, indeed, one of the spiritual sons of Catharine, having been a mere formal functionary of the Church up to the time of his acquaintance with her. He afterwards became her intimate friend and fellow-labourer, and finally her biographer; but more of this hereafter.

With this part of Catharine's history terminates her silent and retired life. We shall now see how she was gradually drawn among the busy haunts of men, how she was claimed as a guide to consciences, and called to public action as a counsellor and diplomatist.

CHAPTER III.

THE Sienese manifested from the earliest period of their
history the proud spirit of independence which characterized them throughout. Tacitus tells how they drove out
the senator Manlius Patruitus, and how the Roman Government was obliged by a solemn decree to teach them a lesson
of humility.[1] When the tide of the Gothic invasion had
swept over Italy, the Northern conquerors set their affections more especially on fair Tuscany, and sought to establish
themselves in her plains and mountains, always preferring
the country to the cities. Siena, gathering herself together,
so to speak, with all her force, succeeded in preserving herself from the foreign influence, and maintained throughout
the dark ages her own municipal administration. Her
inhabitants continued to live by industry, manufactures,
and the arts. From the eighth to the tenth century was
the period of the lowest state of political and spiritual servi-
tude for Italy. Siena, with other powerful cities, received,
however, during that period, the training of misfortune, and

---

[1] "Additumque senatus consultum, quo Senesium plebes modes-
tiæ admoneretur."—TACITUS, *Hist.*, Lib. iv., Tom. iii.

emerging from it, strove for and won many rights and franchises. She declared herself independent, and became the first city of Tuscany. She maintained for a long time this place of honour, although she had an illustrious rival in the republic of Florence, which afterwards eclipsed her. A long series of conflicts between the Florentines and the Sienese succeeded the first great rupture between the two republics in 1082.

The internal administration of the republic of Siena was as follows : The city was divided into three portions, called the Tierce of the City, the Tierce of Camollia, and the Tierce of St. Martin. Each Tierce had its own banner, and its auxiliaries in the country around. The poet Tondi sang of the valour of the citizens of Siena, ranged under their three banners. There then came a subdivision of the inhabitants, which was according to the arts or trades. There were the Great Arts and the Inferior Arts. The seven great arts comprised jurists and notaries, merchants in foreign tissues, bankers or exchangers, clothiers, physicians, chemists, and merchants in silk and in furs. The inferior arts were those of retail clothiers, butchers, saddlers, shoemakers, and masons. Each division of the Great Arts had its council, a chief magistrate or consul for the administration of justice in that division, and its gonfalonier, or standard-bearer, around whom it rallied in times of battle. There was no paid or permanent army, but every citizen bore arms in time of war. Commerce, which was the source of the wealth of the Italian republics of the Middle Ages, was also in a great measure the source of their independence. The rich *bourgeoisie* supplied the cavalry for war ; no " cavaliere " was admitted into the army till he had passed a severe novitiate in military exercises, supplemented by pilgrimages, fasts, and trials of moral and physical strength. "He then," says Brantôme, "spent the night in vigil and prayer; in the morning he was clothed in a white tunic, emblematic of the purity of life which he was expected henceforth to maintain." The infantry, drawn from the representatives of the Inferior Arts, also passed through a novitiate which tested their valour and skill. In the centre of the republican army was the famous Carroccio, a car upon four wheels, drawn by four pairs of oxen covered to the feet in rich cloths. A horn or "antenna" rose from the centre of the car to a great height, upon which floated the standard of the republic, with its device of a golden lion, not rampant, but marching forward;[1] a fitting device, "for these intrepid artisans were never known to flee." Lower down, about the middle of the antenna, a Christ upon the Cross, with outspread arms, seemed to bless the army. A kind of platform in the front of the car was reserved for the most valiant soldiers, told off for its defence; behind was another platform for the trumpeters and musicians. An act of religious consecration and worship was celebrated upon the car before it left the city, and white-robed priests accompanied it to the battle-field. As the Carroccio of Siena, drawn by the large mild-eyed oxen of Tuscany, wound its way through the gates and down the sloping olive-clothed hills from the city, crowds followed its course with straining eyes, from the walls and ramparts and house-tops. The loss of the Carroccio was to the republic like

---

1 "Non rampante, ma caminante."—TOMMASI, *Historia di Siena.*

the loss of the Ark of the Lord to the Hebrews—the greatest public calamity; and all that each city possessed of most valorous, the nerve and flower of the army, was chosen to act as the guard of the sacred car; the fiercest of the conflict was waged around it; and its presence often decided the fate of the battle. It was looked upon with superstitious reverence, and by a law of the republic a lamp was caused to burn night and day before the car which bore the destinies of the people. The Carroccio had a great influence upon military art in Italy. It was necessary to make the city infantry redoubtable, in order to resist the feudal cavalry, to give them firmness, equilibrium, weight, and self-reliance. Their evolutions must be measured and deliberate, even their retreat slow and well-ordered; all must needs be harmonized with the strong and steady march of the oxen of the Apennines.

In 1260 a great battle was fought between the rival republics of Florence and Siena. During the fiercest hour of the action, near the Castle of Montaperti, "an unusual alarm and disorder appeared in the Florentine ranks; suddenly many soldiers dropped their arms and stood still, each under the delusion that he was betrayed by his comrade."[1] Jacopo del Nacca, the brave gonfalonier of Florence, rallied his followers and held aloft his standard, until his own treacherous countryman Bocca degli Abbati cut off his right hand, and he and his colours fell together.

It was a great victory for the Sienese, who returned triumphant to their city with troops of prisoners; the captive soldiers gathered round the women who had

---

[1] Villani, Lib. vi.

carried out bread to the army, imploring their protection; the bells rang and the people rejoiced; young girls presented bread and wine to the wearied soldiers; and the victorious army marched to the great cathedral to give thanks to God in solemn anthems. In that cathedral there may be seen to this day the antenna of the Florentine Carroccio, firmly riveted to one of the pillars, a memento of the military greatness of an extinct republic.[1] When the dust and the passion of the battle had subsided, the results were reckoned up. Florence had lost 10,000 men; the river Arbia had rolled its waves, reddened with blood, over heaps of slain; and "the flowers on its banks remained faded all that year;" there were 15,000 captives; the Florentine Carroccio had been taken; and the "beautiful city sitting upon her hills, wept, disconsolate." It was the memory of this defeat which Dante, some years later, in the bitterness of his exile from his beloved Florence, recalled to his countrymen, in his great poem, where the Tuscan Camiccione asks the poet, with tears, if he desires to wound him by reviving the memory of that terrible day :—

> "Piangendo mi sgridò; perchè mi peste ?
> Se tu non vieni a crescer la vendetta
> Di Mont 'Aperti, perchè mi molesti ?"—*Inferno*, xxxii.

At the close of the twelfth century Siena exchanged its modest municipal government for the dignity of a consulate. In less than eighty years this form of government expired; the rivalries of the Guelphs and Ghibellines hastened its ruin; and towards the end of the thirteenth century the last consul, Ugurgieri, was driven forth from

---

[1] Chavin de Malan.

the city gates with execration, and the clerk of the city exchequer paid ten florins to the artisans who provided the ropes and grappling-irons by which they pulled down and demolished his house.   The chiefs of the popular party now took the management of affairs into their own hands, and in order, if possible, to shut out the nobles henceforth from all share in the government, they established a cunningly-devised system of elections which would insure the future members of the government being exclusively of the plebeian class.   The government was composed of nine persons, three from each of the Tierces of the city.   This government, or signory, was called the "Mount of the Nine." The elections were so managed that the sovereign authority became in effect the monopoly of fewer than a hundred citizens ; this was a violation of the ancient charter of the city.   The Nine soon became a kind of "Oligarchy of the Inferior Arts."   They became odious to the nobility who were excluded from all share in the administration, and finally lost the confidence of the mass of the people themselves, who resented the outrage upon the constitution of the republic.   The three principal Guelph republics of Tuscany, *i.e.*, Florence, Siena, and Perugia, ought, by an understood agreement which had been formed, to have made common cause in defence of their liberties ; but the Nine failed in their allegiance to their allies.   The widely-feared and ill-famed family of the Visconti, Dukes of Milan, already possessors of almost the whole of Lombardy, dreamed of a day when they should bear rule over the whole of Italy ; they were the enemies of the peace of the country and the scourge of its inhabitants for nearly a century. The Nine of Siena were discovered to have made some secret overtures to this ambitious family, actuated by selfish political motives, and in fear of the increasing disaffection of the people of Siena. This increased the anger of the Sienese, and especially of the division of the Inferior Arts, upon which more especially the Nine had brought dishonour by their acts. This state of things lasted till the year 1355, when Charles IV., Emperor of Germany, entered Siena on his way through Italy to be crowned King of Rome. The terrible internal wars and troubles of Italy had drawn upon her the ambitious regard of the German sovereigns. "The yellow-haired German never crossed the Alps except with the view of conquest; he thought it would be an easy thing to leap into the empty saddle of the wild horse of the Apennines, to master its fury, and render it obedient to his rule."[1] Charles IV. was an intriguing and greedy prince, possessing little courage; all his negotiations with the Italians were deceitful; he had no intention of embracing their quarrels; he made fictitious alliances with all the Northern Italian republics, and while treating in a friendly manner with the enemies of the Visconti, he was receiving the ambassadors of the great Duke of Milan and drawing up conditions of alliance with him also. He believed he should thus remove every obstacle to his triumphal march to Rome, to be crowned king of the imperial city, this title having being conferred on him by Pope Innocent VI., with a promise of making it a reality. The Sienese, who cared little about the personal designs or prospects of

---

Dante apostrophizes Italy as "The riderless horse of the Apennines," and asks, " What does it avail thee that Justinian adjusted thy bridle if thy saddle is empty ?"

Charles, took advantage of his passing through Siena in order to enable them to cast off the hated yoke of the Nine, which they had endured for seventy years. The moment he entered the city he was greeted by cries of " Welcome the Emperor ! Down with the Nine !" Charles was greatly alarmed ; he came seeking allies who would strengthen him, not a people with a grievance who would seek his help. He looked about him eagerly to try and discover, without delay, which was likely to prove the stronger party in this divided State, in order that he might give his royal countenance to that, independently of the justice of the question contended. His sympathies were with those actually in power ; but, on the other side he saw the chiefs of the nobility of Siena, who had thrown in their lot with the people to rid themselves of the oligarchy of the Inferior Arts. Among these there were the Tolomei, the Malavolti, the Piccolomini, the Sarracini, and the Salimbeni. The last were a powerful race, " as hard as oak," an immense tribe, and proud of their fecundity. He saw rich merchants and the mass of the humbler people also ranked against the government. This party was evidently the one on whose side he should declare himself. Charles made no effort, therefore, to check the popular revolution, and by the third day the sedition had assumed a very serious character. All business ceased ; ateliers were closed ; the streets were barricaded ; the Nine, shut up in the palace of the Signory, sent to the Emperor to implore his aid. The Emperor came, rode his horse into the palace, and commanded the Nine to give up to him the seals of office ; he bade them release him from a promise he had made before his arrival to maintain their authority, asked for the charters he had given them, and burnt them before their eyes. The people forced the prisons, freed the prisoners, entered the church in which were kept the banners of the Nine, and dragged them through the mud of the streets. The cry was heard on all sides, "Down with the tyrants! let them die the death!" The houses of the ruling faction were burnt to the ground, their persons insulted, and several of them murdered.[1]

The humble industries of the Contrada d'Oca suffered at this time with all other industrial and commercial interests. The workshop of Giacomo was closed. Catharine's two eldest brothers, Benincasa and Bartolommeo, were old enough to join in the popular revolt, and they, with the other apprentices of Giacomo, had left their wool-dyeing for the crowded streets. Catharine was then eight years old, of an age to understand her just and gentle father's comments on the events passing before them; none more than he resented the violation by the Nine of the constitutional rights of the people, but in him indignation was always tempered with mercy. Catharine, in her visits to the church of the Friar Preachers, saw the aisles silent and deserted; the benches, wooden chairs, and every available portion of the church furniture had been removed for building barricades in the narrow streets. All that she saw and heard contributed to encourage in the young girl the strong republican love of liberty, and to confirm her in the conviction that human life is no holiday pastime, but a prolonged struggle between opposing elements, for nations as well as for the individual.

---

[1] Muratori, Vol. xv., p. 148.

When the first excitement of the revolution had been partly subdued, the Emperor, acting on the counsels of some of the popular citizens and nobles, appointed thirty commissioners to make inquiry with a view to the reform of the government, and continued on his way towards Rome. On his return he found Siena still in a state of revolution. The people had excluded to perpetuity the order of the Nine from all participation in the government. They had elevated in their place twelve magistrates, chosen from the *bourgeoisie.* The Emperor did not favour the change, seeing that it promised no advantage to himself. He proposed to give to the Republic an arbitrator, or chief, to act as a moderator between the different parties, and succeeded in persuading the people to accept, in this capacity, his natural brother, the Bishop of Prague and Patriarch of Aquileia, who was then in his suite. The instinct of liberty, so strong in this people, led them to suspect and revolt against this arrangement almost as soon as it was completed. It was an unpleasant sight to them to see the blonde face of the German Patriarch at the windows of the Pallazzo Pubblico; and they sent him to live in a private house. A sense of general uneasiness prevailed, and the Patriarch could not move or speak without giving offence. On the 14th of May, 1355, some incident occurred which excited the anger of the people ; the hot sun of the approaching summer stimulating the passions already so turbulent. They fixed iron chains across every street to stop the cavalry which guarded the Patriarch, and forced him in person to recall the lately-appointed and superseded Twelve to the Pallazzo. Charles was then at Pisa; he confessed himself in fear and terror of these obstinate republicans, and wrote from Pisa that the Patriarch must be sent to him, safe and sound, and that without delay.[1] "The Patriarch placed his resignation in the hands of the people, gave back to the republican officers all the neighbouring castles which he had garrisoned, and decamped, to the great relief of the Sienese, who re-established the Twelve, and returned to their merchandise and workshops."

Thirteen years later, in 1368, a fresh revolution took place. The Twelve had, in this interval, become as tyrannical and hateful to the people as the Nine had been; but they were still more detested by the ancient nobility. The two great families of the Tolomei and the Salimbeni, living in their fortified châteaux in the neighbourhood of Siena, called together all their vassals, and marching to the city, demanded the possession of the Pallazzo Pubblico and the reins of government. The Twelve retired in terror, without a conflict; the nobles, masters of the Republic, proclaimed the restoration of the Consulate of the twelfth century. Ten consuls were chosen by them from among themselves, and three from the number of the proscribed Nine. The people could not, however, accept their own exclusion from all share in the government, and revolted; both parties had recourse again to the Emperor Charles. Charles, promising his protection to all, caused to be installed at Siena, as his imperial vicar, Malatesta Unghero, with a guard of eight hundred German soldiers; the nobles vigorously opposed this step; they defended their rights to a supreme part in the government, and resorting again to arms, they fought

---

[1] Muratori.

during one long day in the streets, and not until they had been beaten from gate to gate of the city, did they retire to their country castles. The popular party, now in the ascendant, set themselves the task of constituting a new form of government, and establishing a just distribution of political rights among the different orders of the State. Not desiring to obliterate their past, they recognized the existence of the Nine, and that of the Twelve, by the election, from their ranks, of a certain number of members of the new administration. They created, however, a new and more numerous order, largely recruited from the popular party, and this order received the name of the Reformers. The Twelve, still smarting under their recent deprivation of power, began, however, at once a series of intrigues with the view of recovering the supreme authority. They eagerly entertained the secret propositions of the Emperor Charles, who had formed a plan to sell Siena, and several other Tuscan cities, to the Pope. Charles needed money above all things; he had left his crown of gold in pawn with the Florentines for one thousand six hundred florins, and was anxious to redeem it. The city of Siena, which he was plotting to betray, had already lent him a large sum of money. Seeing that he could count on the alliance of the party of the Twelve, and of the numerous tribe of the Salimbeni, who had deserted the side of the nobles and joined the Twelve, he marched towards Siena, and haughtily demanded that the great Castle of Talamone, and four other strong fortresses surrounding Siena, should be delivered up to him. These fortresses, and especially that of Talamone, were the necessary defences of the Sienese against attacks from without. The government of the Reformers rejected the demand. Diplomacy having failed, Charles resorted to force. In January, 1369, the party of the Twelve and the Salimbeni had offered a direct insult to three members of the new government, and endeavoured to drive them out of the Pallazzo Pubblico; at the same moment the Emperor, armed from head to foot, marched with his German troops to the aid of his representative, Malatesta Unghero; the Cardinal Guy de Montfort, who had come to collect the spoils of treason, rode by Charles's side. The Reformers stood firm; they sounded the tocsin, and the "Captain of the People," Mattenio Menzano, made a dashing attack upon the German army. The enraged people joined in the fray; Malatesta and his troop were driven back. The Emperor, who had advanced as far as the Croce del Travaglio, was impetuously attacked by the artisan militia; his Germans took to flight after some hard fighting, and he himself took refuge in the palace of the Tolomei; for seven hours he defended himself there, until the slain of both parties choked up the entrances and the streets near the palace. He was finally forced from this retreat into the stronger castle of the Salimbeni. Towards evening a complete victory was proclaimed for the Republic. The honour of this victory belongs to the illustrious plebeian Menzano, the captain, or tribune, of the people. Menzano was a man justly esteemed, even by his foes. Malavolti, the chronicler of Siena, and a noble, remarks, with aristocratic insolence, " This man, Menzano, although a plebeian, was a man of a great soul, and very valiant." Menzano entreated the Emperor to quit the city, and "in order to render this entreaty more efficacious, he published, with sound of trumpet, a declaration forbidding anyone to furnish Charles or his soldiers with food." Neri di Donato, a contemporary plebeian historian, gives the following account of the humiliation of Charles: "The Emperor was alone in the Salimbeni Palace, a prey to the most abject fear. The eyes of the whole people were turned upon him; he wept, he sobbed, he apologized, he embraced everyone who came near him, protesting that he had been betrayed by Malatesta, by the Salimbeni, by the Twelve. . . . At the same time he was treating, as well as he could, with the government and the people alike, offering freely his forgiveness, and many more favours than anyone asked of him. Trembling from head to foot, and half dead with hunger, he seemed to have lost his head; he wished to get away, but could not, having neither horses nor money. Menzano then restored to Charles a portion of what he had lost. Scarcely had this relief been accorded him when Charles regained a degree of his old assurance, and demanded, in consideration of the affronts he had endured and the favours he had granted, a sum of twenty thousand florins, payable in four years. The Sienese consented, and flung him the first year's contribution on the spot, on condition that he would leave the city that moment, which he did."

The Sienese had fought nobly for their liberties, and against imperial treachery; it was long, however, before the agitation subsided, and the citizens could return to their industrial occupations. Such was the great revolution which confirmed the freedom of the Republic in the days of Catharine of Siena, and during which she was more than once summoned by her fellow-citizens to act as a pacificator.

These revolutions which had their heroic side, had also their bad side. They tended to estrange from each other the different classes of citizens. The " Popolo Minuto," or class of the Inferior Arts, were the first to suffer : political strife invaded the workshops and created suspicion between the working people and the manufacturers. The workmen in the manufactories of woollen stuffs revolted against their employers ; they demanded a greater share in public affairs, and formed themselves into a band or trades-union, which was foremost in acts of violence during this revolution. A long conflict between the Great Arts and the Inferior Arts ensued, the last act of the drama being the execution of the Captain of the people and the Gonfalonier of the city in 1371. Commerce was almost ruined, and a great number of families emigrated, carrying their industries to other cities : amongst others, the family of Catharine went to establish their art in Florence ; her three brothers, Benincasa, Bartolommeo, and Stephen, appear to have settled in Florence on the death of their father, which occurred during these times of commercial depression. The widowed Lapa, with Catharine, and some others of the family, remained in the old house at Siena ; Catharine's niece, the eldest daughter of Benincasa, although still very young, was esteemed sufficiently skilful and prudent to take the management of a Fullonica, or wool-dyer's establishment, in Siena. Possibly she carried on a portion of the business in her grandfather's premises, when her father migrated to Florence ; or she may have opened an establishment of her own. Many of Catharine's letters during this period are addressed to her three brothers in Florence, from her own little room in Siena.

Another unfavourable result of these popular revolutions was the gradual extinction of the nobility of the Apennines, which was a valuable element in Tuscan life. That nobility served to curb the excesses of the democracy of the cities; (this is acknowledged by Tommasi and other democratic historians); they offered an asylum to all citizens banished for their opinions, they encouraged the cultivation of the soil, and endowed the Republic with a flourishing agriculture.[1] Many of these noble families were of a character worthy of their high descent; some of them lived in great simplicity and virtue, having profited by the lessons of adversity learned in their exile. Dante has immortalized the chivalrous Salvani, who came down one day from his mountain home, and appeared in the great square of Siena, where, forcibly repressing his native pride, he kneeled down, and continued kneeling until by his humble attitude he had moved the proud people to release from political imprisonment a blood relation of his own. The people, touched by his prayers, threw down before him, piece by piece, the ten thousand florins of gold required for the prisoner's ransom. Dante, with his own proud soul bitterly wounded by unjust exile, has well described the repressed scorn and the mortal "trembling in the veins" of the proud gentleman forced to beg for so touching and so honourable a cause.[2]

The chief biographer of Catharine records concerning her, that apparently about the year 1364 or 1365, "the Lord engaged her little by little to mix herself up with her brethren and sisters in this earthly exile." The first charge given to her by her divine guide in regard to her

---

[1] Chavin de Malan.　　　　[2] Purgatorio, xi.

entrance into active life, would not seem to us a very formidable one: "Go, quickly, my daughter," the divine monitor said, "it is the hour of the family repast; join thy parents and thy family; remain with them, and I will be with thee." But Catharine had lived so long in solitude, that to her mind such a step appeared as a very grave one, as an exchange of a life of perpetual prayer for one of dangerous and worldly interests and occupations. The family was very numerous; and several of her father's apprentices lodged in the house. There was much busy life at the Fullonica, much coming and going, and constant intercourse with workmen, traders, and manufacturers of Siena and other cities. Catharine burst into tears on hearing this injunction of her Lord. "Wherein have I offended thee, my God?" she cried, "that thou dost send me from thee? What should I do at table? It is not by bread alone that man lives: are not the words that proceed out of thy mouth far better to impart vigour and energy to the soul of a pilgrim? Thou knowest better than I that I fled from the society of men that I might find thee, my Lord and my God; and must I now mingle anew in worldly affairs, to fall again into my former worldliness and stupidity, and perhaps offend against thee?" Then the Lord answered her. The answer, she told her confessor in reply to his questioning, "was not given in these very words; but these," she said, "are the things which he made me to understand as the expression of his will concerning me." The words, (given as translated from the "Acta Sanctorum" of the Bollandists), were as follows: "Be calm, my child; thou must accomplish all justice, that my grace may become fruitful in thee and in others. I desire not that thou shouldst be separated from me; on the contrary, I desire that thou shouldst become more closely united to me by charity towards thy fellow creatures. Thou knowest that love has two commandments, to love me and to love thy neighbour. I desire that thou shouldst walk, not on one, but on two feet, and fly to heaven on two wings. Call to mind that from thy infancy I have encouraged thee by my spirit in zeal for the salvation of souls. This zeal increased in thy heart so much, that thou didst wish to disguise thyself as a man, to enter into the order of preachers, and go forth into foreign countries, so that thou mightest become useful to souls. Why then dost thou wonder and grieve if I now lead thee to that which thou hast desired from thy childhood?" Then Catharine answered: "Lord, not my will, but thine be done; for I am only darkness and thou art all light. But I beseech thee, O Lord, if I presume not too much, how shall that be done which thou hast said, and how can I, who am so miserable and so fragile, be useful to my fellow creatures? for my sex is an obstacle, as thou, Lord, knowest, through many causes, as well because it is contemptible in men's eyes, as because propriety forbids me any freedom of converse with the other sex." To whom the Lord, as the angel Gabriel to Mary: "The word impossible belongeth not to God: am not I he who created the human race, who formed both man and woman? I pour out the favour of my spirit on whom I will. With me there is neither male nor female, neither plebeian nor noble, but all are equal before me; and I can do all things equally well; it is as easy for me to create an angel as the lowest insect, the whole host of heaven as one worm. It is written concerning me that I have done whatsoever I will; and nothing that is intelligible can be impossible to me. Why, therefore, dost thou ponder concerning how this thing is to be done? Dost thou think that I cannot accomplish what I have resolved upon? But, inasmuch as I know that thou hast spoken thus, not because of faithlessness, but through humility, I will answer thee. I desire thee then to know that at the present time the pride of man has become so great—especially in those who esteem themselves to be learned and wise—that my justice can no longer bear with them, and is about to visit them with a just chastisement. But, because I love mercy, and because my pity is ever over all my works, I will first send to them a salutary and useful confusion, that they may acknowledge their error and humble themselves; even as I did with the Jews and Gentiles when I sent them simple persons filled by me with divine wisdom. Yes, I will send to them *women*, unlearned, and by nature fragile, but filled by my grace with courage and power, for the confusion of their frowardness. If they acknowledge their error and humble themselves, I will cause my pity and mercy to increase towards them, that is, towards those who shall receive with reverence my messengers, and obey my teaching conveyed to them by these frail but chosen vessels. But if they contemn this rebuke designed for their healing, I will visit them with so many humiliations that they will become a by-word to the whole world; for herein is the most just and most frequent punishment of the proud, that whereas they, carried away by the wind of their pride, seek to exalt themselves above themselves, they are cast down, and fall even below themselves. Wherefore, my daughter, do thou make haste to obey me, without further hesitation, for I have a mission for thee to fulfil, and it is my will that thou appear before the public. Wheresoever thou mayest go in the future, I will be with thee; I will never leave thee, but will visit thee, and direct all thy actions." Catharine, prostrating herself at the feet of her Redeemer, replied, "Behold the hand-maiden of the Lord; be it unto me even as thou wilt." She then immediately quitted her cell, and joined her family as God had commanded her.

After an apprenticeship in active duty in her father's house, where she was the ever-ready and joyous servant of all, she began to visit and relieve the poor of Siena. There was at that time no public or organized charity; neither was there in Siena any considerable destitute class; yet there, as everywhere and at all times, there were individuals and families reduced to sore distress by sickness, the chances of war, or other misfortune. Catharine, it is said, "had the gift of discernment, giving only to those whom she knew had a real need, and in such cases she did not wait to be asked to give." There were some poor families in her neighbourhood reduced to great poverty, who would never solicit alms. She used to rise early every morning, and leaving her father's door at the first sound of the great bell of the Pallazzo Pubblico, (for it was forbidden to the people of Siena to leave their houses before this signal was given), she would carry to the dwellings of these poor people what would serve them for the day's necessities, and lifting her gift through the opening in the upper part of the door, which, in summer, the poorer people used generally to leave open for coolness, she would pray for God's blessing on the house, and glide quickly away in the cool shadows of the early morning, leaving the sleeping inmates ignorant of who their daily benefactor might be. What she had to bestow being exhausted, she sought her father, and asked him if she might deduct, according to her conscience, the portion of the poor from the ample means which he had realized by his industry. Giacomo cheerfully consented, because he saw clearly that his daughter " was walking in the way of perfection ; " he announced to his assembled family the permission he had granted. " Let no one," he said, " prevent my beloved child from bestowing our goods on the poor. I grant her full liberty ; indeed, she may, if she likes, dispense all that is in the house." Catharine made use almost too literally of the generous permission of her father, so much so, that "all the inmates of the house, her father excepted, complained of her donations, and locked up what they had that she might not distribute it to the poor."

I have spoken of the favour and affection with which Catharine was regarded by her fellow-citizens ; but this favour was the reward of her long perseverance in well-doing, and of her own sweet, unfailing charity, extended, during many years, to her enemies as well as friends. The goodwill of society is easily and quickly won by those who maintain an amiable and harmless mediocrity in virtue ; but those who are inspired and enabled to rise above the ordinary standard of excellence, or who step beyond the conventional limits of what is commonly esteemed becoming and consistent, run the risk of incurring more or less, for a time at least, the displeasure of society. Their sternness of virtue seems to rebuke the lower attainments of others; and it is more frequently among the pious and the good that their critics and

detractors are to be found than among the ignorant and
erring multitude. In the history of the Thebiad it is related that a young man in secular clothing presented himself
at the gate of a great monastery under the direction of St.
Pacomius.   He was invited to enter the community, but the
extraordinary austerity of his life, and his exalted spiritu-
ality, so frightened the other monks, who were at that time
also men of austere lives, that they revolted against the
superior, and came in a body one day to tell him that unless he immediately dismissed this monk they would one and
all leave the monastery that very day. In like manner a
kind of revolt broke out for a time among the Dominicans
of Siena and the friends and neighbours of Catharine, on
account of the singularity of her life of painful self-denial.
"Everyone murmured against her," says Raymond; "some
spoke against her fasting, and said, 'I warrant you she
feeds herself well enough in secret;' others said that all
the saints had taught by their word and example that we
should never be singular in our way of living; others said
that all excess, even excess in self-denial, is vicious, and
that such as fear God should avoid it; some declared that
they respected her intentions, but believed her to be the
victim of dangerous illusions; others, again, more coarse
and vulgar, calumniated her publicly, and declared continually that she was actuated by mere vanity, which
prompted her to wish for notice." . . .   "She scarcely
could at this time attend any public exercise of piety
without drawing on herself the censures of those who
ought to have been her defenders."[1] . . .   "It was
especially odious to those religious professors in whom

---

[1] Raymond, Part ii., Chap. iv.

self-love was not wholly conquered, that one so young
should surpass all others by the severity of her morals and
the fervour of her prayers. If they allowed her to go to
Communion, they demanded that she should finish her
prayers immediately, and leave the church."[1] It very often
happened that Catharine "fell into an ecstasy" while engaged in prayer. She became absorbed in the contemplation of heavenly things, and lost to all sense of the world
around her. When in this rapt state of contemplation, her
soul would seem to leave her body, and she sometimes
became for a time quite insensible to all that was passing
around her. On one such occasion Raymond found her in
the church "ravished out of her senses," and heard her
saying, in an undertone in Latin, "Vidi arcana Dei" (I
have seen the secrets of God). She continued to repeat
these words some time after, when she had returned to her
house. Raymond asked her, "Why do you repeat these
words ? Can you not speak to us of some of the glorious
things you have seen ?" She replied that it was impossible :
"The distance is so vast between what my spirit contemplated when God caught up my soul to himself, and what I
could describe to you in human language, that I should feel
I was falsifying what I saw in speaking of it ; all I can say
is that I saw ineffable things." Like St. Paul, she was
caught up to the seventh heaven, and "saw things which it
is unlawful for a man to utter." On one of these occasions
she was observed by some of her detractors, rudely carried
out of the church, and brutally flung down upon the church
steps in a state of insensibility, these persons protesting
against her "illusions," and pretending to believe that

---

[1] Raymond, Part ii., Chap. iv.

harsh measures might prove a salutary cure for them. Raymond came to the spot, and found two or three of her female friends bending over her under the burning rays of the noonday sun, weeping, chafing her hands, and waiting for her return to consciousness. Catharine herself never spoke of this or any ill-treatment she received. During this time she also suffered much in health, especially from severe headache, and a continual and sometimes violent pain in her side, accompanied by extreme thirst.

Catharine was the first young girl who had ever been enrolled as a sister of St. Dominic. She was not much more than sixteen when she first appeared on her errands of mercy in the garb of a Mantellata. From the age of eighteen to twenty she became constantly engaged more and more in many and varied active labours and offices of charity. The courage and originality of mind required in her time to set aside the maxims of traditional propriety were beyond what we can at this day easily imagine. Among the Greeks and Romans in ancient times, the highest praise that could be bestowed on a woman was that "she was never seen out of her own house," and the Christian tradition had been so far in accordance with the heathen one : the Apostle had commanded that the young women should be " keepers at home." Monastic ideas and customs in the middle ages had strengthened this tradition in prescribing but one alternative for the young maiden, marriage or the cloister. Yet despite the minute directions of the Apostle Paul, wise and prudent, no doubt, for the state of the society in which he lived, the germs of all true freedom which dwelt in the doctrine and teaching of Christ slowly became fruitful in this direction, and to those who waited upon God, as Catharine did, for direct personal guidance, the path before them gradually widened into greater freedom, and the sphere of responsibility and duty presented itself more largely, and was judged by them more courageously and directly, apart from conventional traditions.

It is not to be wondered at, however, that even in republican and liberty-loving Siena the conduct of the youthful Mantellata should have been severely judged; there can be no doubt that the discipline this severe judgment involved for Catharine led her more fully to know herself and her motives, while it fortified her character. She had already begun to act, in stormy scenes, the part of a peace-maker. During the revolution of 1368, the artisans, as we have seen, were often at variance with their employers; Catharine on several occasions sought to reconcile the contending parties and to persuade each to make concessions; she was also frequently entreated by the wives of banished nobles to visit them in their châteaux near Siena, to advise in difficulty and console in adversity. Full of loving kindness and simplicity of purpose, she obeyed all such calls without hesitation. One of her contemporaries records that he "had seen her address a multitude of two thousand persons in the streets," beseeching them for the love of Jesus to be at peace with each other, and to search each one his own heart to discover there any lurking egotism, and give up any selfish demand which could only be gratified at the expense of his neighbour. "Those who could not hear her voice were moved even to tears by the beaming charity and sweetness of her countenance while she spoke and pleaded."

The first intimation Catharine received that evil reports were circulated against her was from the mouth of a poor beggar woman called Tecca, whom she nursed when deserted by everyone else. Tecca was a leper, and had been condemned, as was the custom, to be carried outside the walls of the city to a kind of pest-house. Catharine heard of it and the tears filled her eyes; she exclaimed, "This dear one also was redeemed by my Saviour. He loves her; she shall not be cast forth thus." She had her placed in a hospital where she herself waited on her till she died. This poor ignorant woman, however, ill-requited her benefactress. Catharine was a few minutes late one morning in arriving at the hospital. Tecca lost her temper and taunted her, saying, "Good morning, my lady, queen of the Contrada d'Oca; you love to stay all day in the church of the Dominican friars, don't you! it is there you waste your time, my fine lady; you are never tired of those *dear friars!*" A sudden blush covered Catharine's face, for she heard in the poor woman's words an echo of what was falling from many idle or spiteful tongues; but she kept silence and continued to minister to the leper to the last. Much more serious were the reproaches of Andrea, one of the Sisters of St. Dominic, who also was tenderly nursed by Catharine when dying of a frightful cancer. The disease was so repelling that no one could be found to wait on Andrea. As soon as Catharine knew this, "she comprehended that God had reserved for *her* this poor forsaken one, and hastened to comfort her." According to Raymond, "the devil blinded this afflicted woman, and so far succeeded in filling her with malice against Catharine that she publicly calumniated her;" she was, however, only the exponent of the injurious opinion which had been gaining strength in many minds against the young Mantellata.

These slanders gained ground so much that the elder and more experienced of the Sisters of St. Dominic formed themselves into a kind of committee of inquiry to examine into the matter. Some of the sisters addressed to Catharine during the inquiry very cruel and cutting remarks; at last the chief among them requested her to reply and say how it was that she had suffered herself to be seduced. Catharine replied patiently and gently, "I assure you, ladies and dear sisters, that by the grace of Jesus Christ, I am innocent. I am, indeed I am, a virgin." She appears to have taken this trial less to heart than many others which assailed her; yet she was observed to dwell more alone at this time in her secret chamber, and to be constantly in prayer. Her friend Alessia, who always maintained her part, overheard her in prayer, pleading thus with her Lord: "Thou knowest, O my Saviour, the efforts of the 'father of lies' to hold me back from what thy love urges me to undertake; help me, then, O my Lord and my God, for thou knowest I am innocent; and suffer not the evil one to prevail against me." Having poured out her soul to God, "her Saviour appeared to her, holding two crowns, one of gold and another of thorns, and bidding her choose which she would. She took the crown of thorns and pressed it on her own head. After this time she was filled with a greater joy than ever, and her countenance was always radiant and covered with smiles, so that all men wondered at her secret joy, seeing how many pains and trials she had."

Palmerina, a distinguished lady of Siena, had publicly consecrated all her great wealth to God, and joined the sisterhood of St. Dominic. She had a noble nature, but a strange jealousy of Catharine entered her mind, and, yielding to it more and more, she became like one possessed. So great was her hatred of Catharine that she could not hear her name mentioned without becoming violent, and took every occasion of speaking against her. The fact became notorious, and Catharine frequently heard men speak of it. It filled her with grief; she shut herself up in her room, and had recourse, as always, to prayer. "Lord God," she said, "wilt thou suffer that I should be the occasion of loss to a soul which thou hast created so nobly? Is *this* the good that thou hast promised to effect by me? No doubt my sins have been the cause of it, but I will continue to claim thy mercy for my sister, till thou savest the soul of that beloved one from sin and death." Her prayers were heard. Palmerina sent for her, and with a changed heart and an abundance of generous tears, asked her forgiveness. Moreover, she would not rest until she had proclaimed publicly her error, and the blamelessness of Catharine. Catharine had been impressed by seeing this generous soul under so dark a cloud, so distorted and disfigured, so to speak, by malign influences; and she prayed earnestly that God would grant to her the special favour of being able in future, under all circumstances, to see spiritually the beauty of every human soul, and to discern the truth through all exterior appearances. "Thus she, giving thanks to God, humbly prayed with her whole heart that he would grant her the favour that she might always see the beauty of the soul of everyone who conversed with her, in order that she might thus be the more fired to procure their salvation."[1] She added, when recounting these things to Raymond, " O Father, could you but see the beauty of a rational soul, you would sacrifice your life a hundred times, were it necessary, for its salvation." From this time she showed a wonderful discernment, and was able to see the truth concerning those who came to her, through all outward disguise or appearances.

The fault-finding of neighbours, however, did not cease, and her confessor, who was at that time Father Thomas della Fonte, a reverend and good man, was so far influenced by all he heard around him as to think it his duty to take Catharine severely to task, and to ask her to moderate her fasts and her prayers, and to live a little more like other people. This seems to have been a great addition to her trials. Though she had "learned all that she knew from God alone," and was accustomed to take refuge at all times in prayer, yet she was too dutiful and right-minded not to feel troubled by the rebukes of her friend and confessor. A long controversy with him ended, however, by his admitting that she was right; he said to her, " Henceforth act accordingly to the inspirations of the Holy Ghost; for I perceive that God will accomplish great things in you." Father Raymond, whose narrative is usually dry and tedious, and who seems rarely to be carried away by undue enthusiasm, sums up his account of these conflicts between Catharine and her critics with the following burst of eloquence and honest emotion :[1] " They who surrounded her measured not her

---

1 " Acta Sanctorum," Bollandists.

words and deeds by God's rule, but by their own. They, dwelling in the valley, presumed to judge of the tops of the mountains; they ignored principles, yet discoursed prudently about results ; they disturbed themselves unreasonably, and blamed the rays of that radiant star; they desired to direct her whose lessons they themselves could not even understand."

I will not dwell on the accounts given by her biographers of the long internal conflict of that humble courageous soul, on the wondrous visions granted to her, and her ever-deepening experience of the power of God and of the love of Christ, which passeth knowledge. Catharine's own Dialogue and letters must be read by those who desire to become further acquainted with her inner life, her doctrine, and the secret of her sustained communion with God. About this time, when emerging from the period of trial arising from the narrow criticisms of those who did not yet know the secret of her power, nor understand the awful simplicity of the one sustaining motive of her life, she was admitted into a fresh spiritual baptism ; peace, strength, and confidence were renewed and increased ; she saw, heard, and conversed with her Lord; the path she ought to tread was revealed, plain and straight before her, and she had only to obey that beloved voice which spoke to her heart. "One day when she was praying in her little room, the Lord appeared to her and said to her, 'Learn, my daughter, that henceforth thy life shall be filled with such wonders that ignorant and sensual men will refuse to believe them ; many even of those who are attached to thee will doubt thee; thy heart shall become so ardent for the salvation of men that thou shalt forget thy sex and all its fears ;

thou shalt no more avoid, as formerly, the conversation of men, but thou shalt cheerfully endure every kind of fatigue to save their souls ; thy conduct will scandalize many ; but be not afraid ; I will be ever with thee, and deliver thee from the deceitful tongue and from them that speak falsely ; follow, therefore, courageously my inspiration, for I will draw, by thy aid, many souls from destruction, and guide them to my kingdom in heaven.'" And again, at a time when Catharine had been so ill as to believe herself to be dying, being absorbed in deep contemplation, Christ said to her : " Return, my daughter, to life ; for the salvation of many souls demands it. Thou shalt no longer live as thou hast done ; thou must leave the retirement of thy chamber, and continually pass through the city, in order to save souls. I will be with thee continually ; in thy going out and in thy coming in I will lead thee. I will entrust to thee the honour of my holy name, and thou shalt speak of me to the lowly and the great, to the multitude, to seculars, priests, and monks. I will impart to thee speech and wis-dom, which none can resist ; thou shalt stand before kings and rulers and pontiffs for my name's sake ; for thus, and by this means, will I bring low the arrogance of the mighty ! "[1]

Catharine answered : " Thou art my God ; I am but thy poor handmaid ; may thy will ever be accomplished in me ; but remember me, my Lord, and ever incline unto my aid, according to the greatness of thy mercy."

---

1 " Acta Sanctorum."

CHAPTER IV.

ONE of the greatest of the evils which prevailed in
the age in which Catharine lived was the spirit of strife
and discord which reigned everywhere, not only in the
country at large, but between rival families and factions
in every commune and every province. The history of
the Italian republics is one long record of personal jealousies, family feuds, and civil wars. It is evident from
Catharine's letters that she did not shrink from strife and
conflict in any case where the establishment of true peace
involved a struggle between opposing principles; yet she
saw in the actual strife around her only elements which
were hostile to all true progress towards that advent of
Christ on earth for which she laboured. She continually
urged the necessity of war with evil, and in many forcible
passages in her letters, she reminded the restless and ambitious spirits with whom she pleaded that it was impossible they should rightly govern others until they had
learned to govern themselves; she declared that their
rivalries, animosities, and lust of power were a sign of
weakness and not of strength; while she prophesied to
them that those among them who were then striving to
be the greatest would eventually take the lowest position.

Her words were very remarkably fulfilled in many instances. She continually laboured to inspire her own chosen friends with a cheerful and holy calm in the midst of the political agitations continually renewed around them. She wrote to Monna Mitarella, the wife of the Senator Mugliano, whose life was in danger during one of the Sienese revolutions: "It seems to me you have both been in great fear, but that you have placed your hope in God and in the power of prayer. I entreat you in the name of Jesus to continue firm in this sweet and steadfast peace. My sister, fear nothing that men can do; fear God only." To the proud and unhappy wife of Duke Bernabos Visconti she wrote beseeching her to exercise a spirit of trust and humility, so that the cruel and stormy spirits of those among whom she dwelt might recognize the power in her of that peace which is founded on the Rock of Ages. She was often called to mediate between hostile families; she visited regularly the prisons of the city, comforted and sometimes procured the release of political prisoners, and in her walks through the city she would track the steps of the poor outcast woman, ask to be allowed to enter her dwelling with her, and, embracing her tenderly and frankly, would sit down by her side and plead with her concerning the beauty of that soul which was in peril of eternal death. One of her letters, addressed to "a woman of the city who was a sinner," reveals more than any other, perhaps, the gift which she had asked, and which had been granted to her, of seeing the loveliness of human nature even in its utmost degradation. "I weep, my child, and am full of sorrow because thou, created in the image of God, and redeemed by the precious blood of Christ, regardest not thy own dignity. Return, I entreat thee, as a daughter and a servant redeemed, to the wounded side of the Son of God."[1] The families of the Tolomei and the Malavolti have been mentioned in the record of the political troubles of Siena. Over both of these families Catharine exercised a great influence. The eldest son of the family Tolomei, a licentious young man, "whose hand, though so young, had been twice imbrued in the blood of his neighbour," became, under her influence, a sincere convert, and persevered in virtue till his death. His two beautiful and worldly sisters gave up all the frivolities they had delighted in, and became active coadjutors of Catharine in the "Militia of Jesus Christ." The younger brothers followed in the steps of their elder brother and sisters, and their gentle mother, Rabes, whose prayers had been unceasing for the salvation of her children, called for Catharine and blest her, in great joy pronouncing the words: "Now lettest thou thy servant depart in peace, for mine eyes have seen thy salvation." The house of the Malavolti fell under the blight of its own haughty and licentious character. Several of Catharine's letters, addressed to Agnesa, the widow of Orso Malavolti, reveal the melancholy story of that lady's trials. Her son, Antonio, was beheaded in 1372 for a shameful outrage on a young girl, in which foul deed he was abetted by his cousin, Deo di Veri Malavolti. The widow Agnesa never again quitted her solitary home, but she sought for and cherished

---

[1] "Pero figliuola mia io piango e dogliomi che tu, creata alla imagine di Dio, ricomperata del pretioso sangue suo, non raguardi la tua dignità. Tu, come figliuola e serva ricomperata di sangue, entra allora nelle piaghe del figliuolo di Dio.—*Lettera a una meretrice,* Lett. 373.

the poor girl who had been the victim of her son's licentiousness. Catharine writes to the widowed lady: " I think God is calling you to a great perfection in thus severing you from earthly ties. I understand that you have called to you this child. It pleases me much that God should have thus chosen you, and drawn her out of so much trouble." Another of the family, young Francis Malavolti, "a youth of noble birth," says Raymond, "but of contemptible manners," was taken by one of his father's friends to visit Catharine. He frequently came to talk with her, " enjoyed her salutary lessons, but would return to his former habits, especially to gambling, of which he was passionately fond." Catharine prayed earnestly for his salvation, but he gave her much trouble, and tested severely her patience and hopefulness. She wrote to him : " You come to see me, and then, like an untamed bird, you fly back to your vices ; fly as often as you please, but the time will come when God will enable me to throw a noose round your neck which will prevent your ever escaping again." After many warnings to the irresolute youth, she concludes : " Come back, come back, my dearest son ! I may well call thee dear, so much hast thou cost me in tears, and prayers, and bitter grief." Catharine died before her prayer was answered ; but after her death Francis gave up his evil habits ; great domestic trials subdued his heart, and he became steadfast in the service of God. Andrea di Nandino, a rich citizen, "a gambler, and addicted to every vice," was induced by the earnest entreaties of his wife and children to listen to the words of Catharine, but for a very long time he continued hard and unmoved. Then Catharine, seeing she could not prevail with him, addressed herself to God alone. She continued for a whole night to plead for this soul. "Remember, Lord," she said, "that thou didst promise to aid me in saving souls. I have no other joy in life than that of seeing them return to thee. Didst thou not, O loving Jesus, bear this man's sins with ours? O restore to me my brother, and draw him out of his hardened state." Andrea was soon after smitten with remorse for his sins, and became "a new creature in Christ Jesus."

Catharine was spending some hours one day in the house of her dearest friend and fellow-worker, Alessia, who was also a Mantellata. Alessia, happening to look out of the window, saw, at a distance, a great crowd approaching, and in the midst a cart, in which were chained two notorious brigands, who were being taken from prison to the place of execution. They were condemned to have their flesh torn with hot pincers, and then to be beheaded. The first part of the sentence was actually being executed in the sight of the multitude, whose shouts mingled with the agonized cries of the tortured men. Hearing Alessia's cry of horror, Catharine went to the window and looked out. She turned away, and fell on her knees, the tears streaming down her cheeks, and thus, as Alessia records, she cried to the Lord : "Ah, Lord, who art so full of pity, abandon not in their hour of agony these poor creatures of thine, redeemed by thy precious blood. The thief who was crucified by thy side was visited by thy grace and confessed thee publicly, and to him thou didst say, 'This day shalt thou be with me in paradise.' In that word thou didst give hope to all who might resemble him. Thou didst not abandon Peter when he denied thee; thou didst not despise Mary the sinner, nor Matthew the publican, nor the Canaanite, but didst invite them to thee. I entreat thee by all thy mercies, Lord, hasten to relieve these souls." Catharine obtained leave to accompany the criminals as far as the city gates; she prayed and wept continually. When the cart containing the criminals halted at the city gate, "a ray of divine light penetrated the hearts of the two unhappy men;" they expressed an earnest desire to make full confession, and when the man of God came to them, they wept and expressed heartfelt sorrow for their crimes; they accused themselves and prayed aloud to the Redeemer that he would wash away their sins and receive their souls; they then marched onward to death with countenances full of frankness and joy. They spoke gently to their executioners, and gave thanks to God; their torturers themselves were deeply affected, and dropped their horrid instruments, not daring to continue their cruelties.

There dwelt in Siena a painter of great genius called Vanni. As was so common among his countrymen, he harboured a secret hatred against certain persons whom he deemed dangerous rivals or enemies, and he had more than once satisfied his vengeance by striking in the dark. Several assassinations had been perpetrated at his instigation; he was wily and hypocritical in his treatment of those who tried to mediate between him and the objects of his hatred. Catharine heard of him often, and desired earnestly to arrest him in his evil course, and to save those who might become his victims; but he carefully avoided her. A venerable man, Friar William of England, living in Siena, and whose portrait Vanni seems to have painted, pressed him much to see Catharine; he at last consented sullenly, refusing to pledge himself to follow any advice she might give him. "I myself," says Raymond, "was at the Fullonica, waiting for Catharine, who was occupied somewhere in the city in the salvation of souls, when Vanni arrived. I went to meet him with a glad heart, told him of her absence, and pressed him to wait a little; and, to beguile the time, I introduced him into her little room. After ten minutes or so, Vanni grew weary, and said listlessly, 'I promised Friar William I would call on this lady, but she is absent, and my work makes it impossible for me to stay longer; be so kind as to excuse me to her.' I was much distressed at Catharine's absence, and in order to detain him I began to speak of reconciliation with one's enemies; but he interrupted me, saying, 'See, now, you are a priest and a religious man, and this good lady has a great reputation for sanctity; I must not deceive you, and therefore I tell you frankly that I do not mean to do anything of the kind which you advise me; it is useless to preach to me on this subject; you will gain nothing by it. It is already a great concession on my part to have spoken to you with so much freedom of what I conceal from others; but you will obtain no more; so do not torment me further on the subject.' At that moment Catharine arrived, and her appearance was evidently as disagreeable to Vanni as it was welcome to me. As soon as she perceived us seated in her room she smiled, and received this man of the world with great grace and kindness. She seated herself, and inquired the motive of his visit. Vanni repeated what he had just said to me, declaring that he would make no concession. She represented to him with much force and sweetness how much he was his own enemy, but he hardened his heart against her arguments.

She then retired in order to pray alone, and I conversed with Vanni so as to gain time. Not many minutes had expired before he looked up and said to me, 'For politeness sake I will not refuse her entirely. I have four great enmities; I will give up the one which it will give you the most satisfaction for me to give up.' He then rose to go away, but before he had reached the door he suddenly exclaimed, 'My God! what a consolation my heart feels through this one word of peace which I have uttered;' and he added, 'O my Lord and my God! what power is it which retains and triumphs over me ? Yes, I am vanquished—I confess it. I cannot draw my breath.' The heart which had been so long bound in the iron bonds of hatred and sullen revengefulness was stirred to its depths, and struggling to free itself from that cruel bondage, it already experienced the sense of approaching freedom and peace. Catharine again approached him. He fell on his knees sobbing, and said, 'Dear lady, behold me ready to do whatever you desire me relative to peace and all else. I see now that Satan held me in chains. I resign myself to your guidance: in pity, direct my soul.' Catharine regarded him with a joyous smile, and gave thanks to God. 'Dear brother,' she said, 'I spoke to *you*, and you refused to listen; then I turned to God, and he has not rejected my petition.'" Vanni went straightway and was . reconciled with all his enemies. "For many years after this," (continues Raymond), "I was Vanni's confessor, and am witness that he made constant progress in virtue, and that he bore with resignation some sore trials which befel him through the hostility of others."

Catharine's labours were so much increased that the Pope, Gregory XI., to whom a report had been conveyed of her good influence, granted to her, by a special bull, three companions, invested with the powers reserved to bishops, to accompany her in all her missions, to hear confessions, and to aid her in her work. One of these was the good and honest Raymond, so often quoted, an indefatigable labourer, a simple-hearted Christian, and an excellent man of business. Every evening after her day's work was over, Catharine, says Raymond, went up the hill, rejoicing, to the old Dominican church, and laid at the feet of her Lord and Saviour the spiritual conquests of the day; and there she would remain till the sun had set, and the stars lighted the sky, absorbed in the contemplation of the love and power of Christ, and pouring out her soul in prayer for the fuller accomplishment of the great promise of the Redeemer, the descent of the Holy Spirit on all flesh. "Breathe on these slain and they shall live," she cried; and when, in answer to her prayers, there was "a shaking" among the multitude for whom she prayed, she asked again that this multitude might "stand upon their feet, an exceeding great army;" and the divine breath was felt, and many that were spiritually in their graves came forth. "I have seen," says Raymond, "thousands of men and women hastening to her from the tops of the mountains and from all the country round Siena, as if summoned by a mysterious trumpet: frequently she was obliged to speak to a great number of people at once; sometimes her words did not reach them, but her very look and presence made them desire to renounce their sins and become sharers in the deep peace and joy which shone in her dear face."

" We worked all day," Raymond says, " we heard the confessions of men and women, soiled with every variety of crime. We sometimes remained fasting until the evening (having no time to eat) and yet we were not able to receive all who came. I acknowledge, to my shame, that the multitude was often so great that I was fatigued and depressed; but as for Catharine, she never interrupted her prayers and efforts, but rejoiced continually in conquering souls for her Master, while she simply recommended her friends, (Alessia and the other Mantellatas,) to take care of *us* and our material wants, while we held the nets which she knew so well how to fill. The sight of her consoled us greatly, and made us forget our fatigues."

Some years after the revolution of 1368, which inaugurated the government of the Reformers, the Sienese republicans, wearied and impoverished by internal strife, too easily allowed themselves to fall under the rude domination of certain proud and ambitious plebeians, who sought out, by means of a system of espionage, all whom they suspected of disloyalty to their persons and government, and made use of their administrative powers to secure their condemnation. Agnolo d'Andrea was condemned to death for not having invited these tyrants to a fête which he gave in the environs of the city. Catharine was present at his execution, to impart strength and consolation to the victim; returning to her cell, she was aroused by the rushing movement of a crowd, in pursuit of the Senator Mugliano, whose conduct during the execution had offended the majesty of the plebeian leaders and whose life was now threatened. She went boldly forth to calm, if possible, the multitude, and followed the senator to his hiding-place to strengthen his faith and rally his courage.   The letters to the wife of this Senator Mugliano have already been alluded to.

A young knight of Perugia, named Nicola Tuldo, was accused at this time of having spoken against the government, and of having incited his friends at Siena to revolt against their haughty and oppressive rule ; he was declared guilty of high treason and condemned to die.   Indignant, or rather enraged at this unjust and cruel sentence, the poor young man paced up and down his prison like a caged lion, driven to desperation.   He was too proud to humble himself and ask pardon ; his turbulent and passionate soul had carried him far away from the early instructions in virtue which he had received, and now, proud, wayward, and sullen, he was left without a ray of hope or Christian consolation.   During his stay at Siena he had often heard the name of Catharine.   "Perhaps," he said to himself, "this poor girl might save me ; they tell wonderful things of her conquests of faith and charity ; she would pity me, I am sure she would, and if I must die, I so young, if I must leave this life so full of brilliant hope for the future, if I must leave my beloved mother and family at Perugia—Perugia ! O my country." . . . His jailer, who overheard his broken utterances, sent a messenger to the Fullonica to ask if Catharine would come.   The rest of the story is told by Catharine herself, in a letter to Raymond, then absent from Siena.   (It is one of the very few letters in which she mentions her own acts.)   "I went to visit him whom you know ;   he was very much comforted and consoled ; he saw Friar Thomas, and confessed, full of humility. He besought me by the love of God to promise that I would be with him at the hour of execution ; I promised, and I have kept my promise. In the morning, before the bell of the Campanile had sounded, I was with him in the prison ; he was greatly comforted by my arrival. I went with him to the holy communion, which till then he had never received. He was perfectly submissive to the will of God, and the only cloud which now rested on his soul was the fear that he might not be strong at the last moment. But the Saviour in his infinite mercy so fortified him, and so inspired him with the désire of his presence, that he continued to repeat without ceasing, ' Lord, be near me ; Lord, do not leave me ; if thou wilt be near me, all will be well with me, and I shall be content ;' and as he prayed thus he leaned his head upon my breast. I felt a great desire to shed my blood, with him, for my beloved Saviour. Longing for this joy, and perceiving that he still had some fear, I said, ' Courage, my brother beloved, we are soon going to your heavenly marriage feast ; you are going there bathed in the precious blood of the Son of God, and with the dear name of Jesus on your lips—O pronounce that name without ceasing—and I am going to meet you at the place of execution.' At these words, (think of it, dear father,) every vestige of fear seemed to leave him, and a great light visited his heart: he who had before raged and rebelled, now called the place of justice a holy place ; he seemed filled with exultation, and asked, ' How comes such grace to be shown to *me ?* and will *you,* joy of my soul, indeed await me at that holy place ! I will go there then with a strong and joyous step, and you will there speak to me sweet and blessed words of the love of God ? Observe, father, how changed he now was, to call the place of execution a holy place. I went then, to the place of execution, early, and continued without ceasing to pray. Before the arrival of the melancholy cortège, I kneeled down and placed my neck on the scaffold, wishing for that martyrdom for myself; but the axe did not respond to my wishes! I prayed earnestly that at the supreme moment light and peace might be abundantly shed into the heart of Nicola; and resting on the promise, 'If ye abide in me, ye shall ask *what ye will*, and it shall be done,' I asked further that the favour might be granted to me of seeing in a vision his soul ascend to God. My heart was so full, and so powerful was the impression granted to me that this promise would be fulfilled to me, that in the midst of that vast crowd of people I saw no one, and heard nothing but the promise. Then Nicola arrived, walking like a gentle lamb, and laughed for joy when he saw me: he turned to me, and asked me to make on his breast the sign of the cross; I did so, saying in low voice: 'Go, gentle brother, to your eternal marriage; soon you will have entered into the life which knows no ending.' He kneeled down calmly, and I, kneeling by his side, placed his neck on the scaffold, and whispered to him of the Immaculate Lamb. His lips murmured but two words, 'Jesus' and 'Catharine.'[1] As he spoke these words, the axe fell, and I caught his head in my hands. I closed my eyes, and said, 'Lord, *I will;* thou hast promised me what I will;' and as clear as the daylight I saw the Son of God receive into his bosom this dear soul; full of love and mercy, he received him who

---

[1] "La bocca sua non diceva se non Jesù e Catarina," Letter 97.

had so meekly accepted the death of a criminal, received him not for his own works, but for love's sake alone. . . . A deep peace fell upon my soul. So dear was that blood to me that I could not bear that they should ever wash it off my dress, which was all sprinkled with it. I envied him, because he had gone on before ; he left us, full of joy and love, like a bride, who having reached the bridegroom's door, turns and bows her head in thanks and farewell to the companions who have accompanied her to the threshold, and enters the home of her beloved."[1]

Catharine dwelt in her native city till she was about twenty-five years of age, at which time she undertook the first of her important missions to other cities ; during this period, however, she accomplished several evangelizing journeys in the country around Siena, and more than once visited Monte Pulciano, not far distant from the Lake Thrasymene, to visit the sisters of the monastery of St. Agnes of Monte Pulciano, where two of her nieces, the daughters of her sister Lysa, had been received. To one of these, Eugenia, a girl of a gay and easy temperament, Catharine wrote many letters. Reproving her on one occasion for frivolous conversations of which she had heard a rumour, Catharine says : " Take care ; if I hear of it again I shall run to you and administer so severe a dis cipline that you will never forget it ! Be always self-possessed and calm. . . . If a stranger asks to see you, and your superior wishes you to respond, go and see him, in the name of obedience, but waste no time, and show yourself as savage as a porcupine !"

---

1 Some passages of this beautiful letter have been omitted, as disconnected with the recital.

In 1372 good Giacomo, Catharine's father, died. While the family all wept around his bed, Catharine alone remained calm and even joyful, for she realized the fulness of peace into which her beloved father had entered. She kissed him, and said, "Blessed be the Lord God for this entrance into eternal life. How happy should I be were I where thou art now, my father!"

Then Lapa fell ill, and drew near to death. She was a true and simple-hearted Christian, but she dearly loved life, and revolted against the thought of dying. She besought her daughter to obtain for her the favour of a longer life. Catharine, seeing her mother so far from resigned to the will of God, and too much devoted to the things of earth, retired to her room, and prayed earnestly that her beloved mother might live and become more prepared for the kingdom of God.   The physicians had already pronounced Lapa's malady to be past cure ; but she recovered, and lived till her ninetieth year. Long before she died she wished and prayed for death, and often said that God had " riveted her soul to her body." " How many," she said, " of my children and grand-children have I followed to the grave ! it is I alone who cannot die."

In 1374 the plague broke out in Siena. Multitudes fell dead in the churches and in the streets, as spoiled fruit falls from the trees.[1] The harvests stood unreaped, and all business was arrested. The hoarse cries of the gravediggers (*beccamorti*) resounded through the streets—"Bring out your dead !" The doors of the houses opened, and

---

1 " Morti cadevano a terra a guisa che i pomi fracidi.'—Tommasi, *History of Siena*, Book x.

"corpses were seen carried out by other corpses;" sometimes the priests, and those who carried the dead, sat down for a moment of repose, and never rose again. In some streets no voice responded to the cry of the *beccamorti;* the terrible smell of putrefaction alone signified the presence of death. The strongest minds were subdued by melancholy or fear; the tribunals were empty; the laws were no longer enforced; at each assembling of the Signory there were fresh vacant places, and no one any longer dared to ask the cause of absence. Many of the rich and the powerful quitted the city and isolated themselves in their country châteaux. The conduct of Catharine and her friends the Mantellatas in this emergency was sublime; they devoted themselves to the poorest of the stricken population, entering without fear the most infected quarters; they sang hymns of joy while wrapping the poor discoloured corpses in their winding-sheets; many of the sisters fell, chilled by the icy hand of death, in the midst of their holy work; " but their companions, knowing well that they had entered into the presence of Jesus, pressed the last kiss on their foreheads, and hastened back with increased zeal to their labour of love."[1] It was during this time of severe trial that some of the firmest of Catharine's life-long friendships were begun, or more closely cemented.

It may be well here to gather into a group the principal friends, fellow-workers, and disciples of Catharine, so that we may realize a little the varied and pleasant character of that "mystic family," as it was sometimes called, which went forth with her on the great highway of the world, bringing

---

1 Chavin de Malan, Chap. xi.

hope and blessing to their fellow-men, and leaving foot-prints worthy to be traced by those who came after.

The good Raymond of Capua must be first mentioned; he tells us himself of his introduction to Catharine. "In 1373 I was summoned to Siena, where I exercised the function of lector in the convent of my order, that of the Dominicans. I was serving God in a cold and formal manner, when the plague broke out in Siena, where it raged with greater violence than in any other city. Terror reigned everywhere. Zeal for souls, which is the essence of the spirit of St. Dominic, urged me to labour for the salvation of my neighbours. I necessarily went very often to the Hospital of la Misericordia. The director of that hospital at that time was Father Matthew of Cenni, an attached friend of Catharine. Every morning, on my way to the city, I inquired at the Misericordia whether any more of the inmates there had been attacked with the plague. One day on entering, I saw some of the brothers carrying Father Matthew like a corpse from the chapel to his room; his face was livid, and his strength was so far gone that he could not answer me when I spoke to him. 'Last night,' the brother said, 'about eleven o'clock, while ministering to a dying person, he perceived himself stricken, and fell at once into extreme weakness.' I helped to lay him on his bed; . . . . he spoke afterwards, and said that he felt as if his head was separating into four parts. I sent for Dr. Senso, his physician; Dr. Senso declared to me that my friend had the plague, and that every symptom announced the approach of death. 'I fear,' he said, 'that the House of Mercy (Misericordia) is about to be deprived of its good director.' I asked if medical art could not save him; 'We shall see,' replied Dr. Senso, 'but I have only a very faint hope; his blood is too much poisoned.' I withdrew, praying God to save the life of this good man. Catharine, however, had heard of the illness of Father Matthew, whom she loved sincerely, and she lost no time in repairing to him. The moment she entered the room, she cried, with a cheerful voice, 'Get up, Father Matthew, get up! This is not a time to be lying idly in bed.' Father Matthew roused himself, sat up on his bed, and finally stood on his feet. Catharine retired; at the moment she was leaving the house, I entered it, and ignorant of what had happened, and believing my friend to be still at the point of death, my grief urged me to say, 'Will you allow a person so dear to us, and so useful to others, to die?' She appeared annoyed at my words, and replied: 'In what terms do you address me? Am I like God, to deliver a man from death?' But I, beside myself with sorrow, pleaded, 'Speak in that way to others if you will, but not to me; for I know your secrets: and *I know that you obtain from God whatsoever you ask in faith.*' Then Catharine bowed her head, and smiled just a little; after a few moments she lifted up her head and looked full in my face, her countenance radiant with joy, and said: 'Well, let us take courage; he will not die this time;' and she passed on. At these words I banished all fear, for I understood that she had obtained some favour from heaven. I went straight to my sick friend, whom I found sitting on the side of his bed. 'Do you know,' he cried, 'what she has done for me?' He then stood up and joyfully narrated what I have here written. To make the matter more sure, the table was laid, and Father Matthew

H

seated himself at it with us; they served him with vegetables and other light food, and he, who an hour before could not open his mouth, ate with us, chatting and laughing gaily. Great was our joy and admiration; we all thanked and praised God. Nicolas d'Andrea, of the Friar Preachers, was there, besides students, priests, and more than twenty other persons, who all saw and heard what I have narrated."

Catharine's prayers brought health to many sick persons. She believed in the promise, " The prayer of faith shall save the sick;" and doubted not its fulfilment in answer to earnest prayer, in every case in which that fulfilment was for the good of the sufferer and for the glory of God. The other methods she employed, besides the all-powerful one of prayer, were to persuade the patient to make a full confession of sin, then to speak peace to his conscience, through faith in Jesus Christ, and to inspire him with a joyous courage and resolution. Physicians well know how closely connected is bodily health with mental conditions; but most will question the power even of the highest faith to arrest the progress of a poison actually working in the blood. Into such questions it is not my present intention to enter; my part is to present a simple narrative, concerning which those who read may draw their own conclusions. After our Lord Jesus Christ had ascended to heaven, the first apostles received, together with many other spiritual gifts, showered down on the day of Pentecost, such gifts of healing, that the sick were brought by their friends and laid in the streets of Jerusalem, that perchance the shadow only of Peter passing by might overshadow them and restore them to health and life. No historian of the Church has yet ventured to assign an exact date to the cessation of the so-called miraculous gifts of healing; perhaps when we see all things more clearly, we shall know that these gifts only ceased in proportion to the decay of the faith which claimed and exercised them; and we may be able again by the prayer of faith to heal the sick and cast out evil spirits.

Father Raymond then recounts how, having fallen ill himself through his excessive exertions in the plague-stricken city, he crawled to Catharine's house, where not being able longer to stand up, he fell prostrate, and lay half-conscious till she returned from her labours; how she, placing both her pure hands on his forehead, remained absorbed in prayer for an hour and a half, how he fell into a peaceful slumber, and how on awaking in perfect health, she said to him, "Go now, and labour for the salvation of souls, and render thanks to the Lord who has saved you from this great danger." Raymond appears to have been indebted to his great powers of work, his good sense, exceeding uprightness and truth, rather than to any remarkable talents or genius, for the position and influence he gradually attained in the Church : an honest, faithful, sensible and laborious man, he proved to be the most useful if not the most inspired of Catharine's helpers. He had a habit of questioning all he heard from her concerning her revelations, and of frequently reporting to her the opinions and criticisms of the world on her actions. "People all wonder that you do so and so," he said to her, or, "Many are offended with you for such and such a thing; might you not modify your austerities, and adapt your habits a little more to what the world understands?" &c., &c. "One day," he says, "I rebuked her privately for not preventing some persons from bending the knee when they approached her; when she answered me, 'God is my witness, Father, that I observe very little, sometimes not at all, the actions of those who surround me, for I am thinking only of their souls.'" He confesses that he questioned her severely concerning what God had revealed to her of the path she ought to pursue, "for I had found many deluded people," he says, "especially among females, whose heads are easily turned; and the remarks made by people around me troubled me." Catharine accepted frankly all his warnings and advice, and he, satisfied of her sincerity, soon became far more her disciple than her teacher or censor. This he asserts of himself with characteristic honesty. In her relations with Raymond, the gentle gaiety and sense of humour which Catharine possessed, appear more, perhaps, than in other relations. She would rally him on account of his too great solemnity and gravity on occasions which did not especially call for such conditions of mind. He records her great delight in talking of the things of God; when she could find a willing listener, she would speak much, and rather rapidly, on these topics. "While she was actively employed, or spoke of heavenly things," says he, "she seemed to be redolent with the vigour of youth, and when she ceased, she became languid and without energy. Often she spoke to me of the profound mysteries of God, and as I did not possess her sublime elevation of soul, I would fall asleep. But she, absorbed in God, would not perceive it, and continued talking; and when she discovered me asleep, she would arouse me in a louder voice, and gaily rebuke me for thus allowing her to converse with the walls."

Father Thomas della Fonte was one of the earliest friends of Catharine's youth, and supplied to Raymond the record of her life which preceded her acquaintance with the latter.

Three miles from Siena stood the ancient monastery of Lecceto, where dwelt many good monks who were Catharine's friends. William of England, already mentioned, was one of these; his soul was penetrated with grief on account of the corruptions of the Church, concerning which he often held counsel with Catharine during her evening visits to the convent, when they sat under the shade of the trees. Many of her letters are addressed to him, whom on account of his learning and the honours he had obtained at Oxford and other universities, she called her bachelor (*bacceliere*). Brother Anthony of Nice was another of her friends of Lecceto, as were also John Tantucci, a doctor of theology of the University of Cambridge; Felice da Massa, who accompanied her to Avignon; and Girolamo, bursar of Lecceto, a man of an ardent and daring temper, whom she calls "the sublime madman of the Cross."

In a secluded hermitage in Vallombrosa there dwelt a learned Florentine who had retired from the life of the city to devote himself to the study of the Scriptures, and to writing. He was familiarly known as "John of the Cell." He was advanced in years when he made the journey to Siena in order to converse with Catharine, of whom he had heard. He became her firm friend and ever ready servant. He preserved to his death, and in spite of a life of seclusion, a sociable and merry temper; his manners were courteous, and his conversation witty and pleasant. The Florentines styled him the new Socrates,

on account of his wisdom and independence of character.[1]
Many stories were told of his absence of mind ; when engrossed in solving some deep mental problem he would
stand with uncovered head for hours in the woods or on
the highway, regardless of the burning sun or falling dew.
Catharine selected old John of the Cell to carry many of
her most important despatches to Rome and elsewhere.
There being no postal communication in those days,
Catharine was often exercised in mind concerning her
many letter-carriers.   John of the Cell was old, but
energetic, and his shrewdness, wit, experience, and reputation for learning made him a fit and trusty messenger
in negotiations with the Pope and other princes.

Andrew Vanni, the painter, has been already mentioned.
In 1378 he was elected "Captain of the people" in Siena.
Catharine wrote him a long letter, on his election.   Chavin
de Malan styles this letter "a noble Christian lesson in
political economy."   She adjures him to be guided by a
spirit of justice in all his public life, to allow no narrow or
contradictory motives to mingle with the great principles
of justice and love of the people : " the only means to
preserve peace in thyself, in the city, in the world, is constantly to guard and maintain holy *justice.*   It is through
the violation of justice that so many great evils have come
upon us ; and it is because I so earnestly desire to see
justice reign in thee and our dear city, that I write thee
these lines.   In order to be a just ruler, justice must first
reign in thy own conscience ; otherwise thou canst never
establish it in the State."

---

[1] " Festivus Sermo, et senectus oppido jucunda, ut alterum
Socratem diceres."   Bollandus, "Acta Sanct."

We shall have to speak presently of the brothers
Buonconti of Pisa. Many other friends of Catharine
are known only by name; they shared her labours, and
those who survived her strove to immortalize her teaching.
Among these were Gabriel Piccolomini, Francesco Landi,
Pietro Ventura, Cenne d'Jacomo, Neri Ugurgieri, Nicolo
Ugolino, the poet Anastagio di Monte Altino, Masaccio
the painter, and many others.

It is not easy to make a selection for special notice
among the brave women who worked with her, Mantellatas
and others, so numerous and so devoted were they. The
Florentine lady, Giovanna Pazzi, was one of the most intelli-
gent and spiritual of her friends, and a laborious worker for
God. Giovanna di Capo we find with her also in Florence
during the revolution there, of which we shall have to speak.

The laughing Cecca (*ridente*) is constantly mentioned by
Catharine—a bright, merry soul, called sometimes also
by her friends the "mad" or the "mischievous Cecca."
Her sallies of wit often enlivened the journeys and labours
of the sisters.[1]

Catharine Ghetti, and Angelina Vanni, sister of the
artist, may be mentioned; also the noble and venerable
Lady Bianchina Salimbeni, widow of John Salimbeni, the
head of the proud aristocratic family prominent in the
Sienese revolutions already noticed.

Catharine, a lover of all children, conceived a great affection for a dear little child called Laurencia, the daughter
of a famous jurist at Siena. This child, when about eight
years of age, became lunatic, or, as it was then expressed,

---

[1] Letters 114, 116, &c.

possessed of the devil. Her parents had exhausted every means within their reach for her recovery. They took her to the church of St. Dominic and made use there of every relic and charm connected with the saints believed to exercise a special healing power over possessed persons; but in vain. Their friends then earnestly advised them to take the child to Catharine. They accordingly sought Catharine in her own house. Catharine, for the first time, I think, in her life, felt fear. It is not permitted to us to fathom this trouble of her soul, or the secret of her fear, for she kept silence respecting it. She only replied to the messengers who came to announce the approach of the little possessed one, "Alas! alas! What are they doing? I myself am daily tormented with the devil, and do they imagine I can deliver others?" As the parents of Laurencia entered her door, Catharine fled and hid herself so effectually in the attic that she could not be found, and the poor parents departed, leading away their struggling, shrieking little girl. Catharine stopped her ears, but the sound had entered her soul, and she wept bitterly; she, however, sternly forbade anyone to speak to her of this child, or to mention the subject of demoniacal possession. What hidden anguish may have lain at the bottom of this apparent cowardice we know not; but even in this she became "more than conqueror" through his strength who loved her. Father Thomas della Fonte, full of pity for little Laurencia and her parents, resorted to the following stratagem: He brought the child to Catharine's room when she was out, and left her there, saying to the servant, "Tell Catharine when she returns that I command her to let this child remain near her all night." When Catharine returned, she perceived in a moment, by the furious countenance and wild cries of Laurencia, that this was the child she had refused to see. She saw there was no escape, and kneeled down, forcing the child to kneel and pray with her. This was no easy task, and the struggle continued all night till the morning, Catharine exerting all the force of her will to subdue the child, and wrestling in prayer against the evil one, till great drops of perspiration fell from her face, and her strength was almost exhausted. Early in the morning Alessia came in, and saw the end of the struggle, little Laurencia lying in a quiet sleep on Catharine's bed, and Catharine, with uplifted hands, silently praying still. Catharine kept the child for many days, never leaving her, instructing, soothing, and teaching her to pray. One day, however, having been at the house of Alessia, she found the evening so far advanced that she proposed to remain there for the night. While quietly conversing with her friend, she suddenly paused, arose, and said, "Haste, put on your cloak and come with me; the infernal wolf has again got hold of the innocent little lamb we had saved." Alessia objected that it was not proper for women to go out so late at night, alone, to which Catharine only replied, "Make haste and come with me." They found the child wildly excited and agonized with terror. Catharine clasped her in her arms, and with an indignant voice exclaimed, "Thou wicked serpent, thou dost think to recover thy dominion! but I have faith in Jesus, my Saviour." She then kneeled down and prayed, Alessia also praying with her. The child became calm, and some days later was restored to her grateful parents. She lived for sixteen years after, Catharine's devoted friend, perfectly sane and peaceful.[1]

The people of Siena complained of a prolonged visit which Catharine paid to the Lady Bianchina Salimbeni, at her home, the Castel Rocca, near Siena. "She stays too long," they said; "it is not right that a daughter of the people should remain so long in the house of a Salimbeni; what can a plebeian have to do with that family?" Catharine heard of the popular jealousy on her account, and sent to say, "I am coming, but not before I have accomplished what I have to do here." A fierce feud had arisen between two families in the neighbourhood of La Rocca, and she undertook to mediate and avert the shedding of blood. While absent on this work, Lady Bianchina caused a poor lunatic woman who lived near to come to the castle; she knew Catharine's repugnance to the subject of possession, and feared to ask her directly to deal with this woman, but placed her in the entrance of the castle. When Catharine returned, she perceived the poor demoniac, and turned pale, saying pleadingly to Lady Bianchina, "May God forgive you, lady, for what you have done! Do you know that I myself am often tormented, and how can you expose me to risk by leading before me a possessed person?" Catharine, obliged to go out again to finish her work as a peace-maker, said sternly to the possessed, "See here! Place your head in this spot exactly, and do not move one inch till I return." The possessed obeyed, though with piercing cries and sobs. When Catharine returned, she found the patient in the same position, though filling

---

[1] Raymond, Lib. ii., Cap. viii.

the house with her groans and shrieks. Catharine had just seen peace concluded between the rival families, and returned, wearied and exhausted, to this scene of violence of another kind. She appeared angry, and exclaimed, "Get up, you wretch! Hold your peace, and depart for ever from this poor creature, so dear to Jesus the Son of God." At these words, "Jesus the Son of God," the possessed woman fell fainting on the floor, and was carried to a bed. In a few minutes she seemed like one awakened out of a deep sleep, and calmly asked, "Where am I? How did I come here? Who are these kind friends?" "She was never troubled again," says Raymond, who took care to see her occasionally for many years after. The Lady Bianchina kissed her angelic plebeian guest, with her own hands folded the beloved, well-patched little dominican cloak around her, and bade her return to Siena, to satisfy those who murmured.

Of all her women friends, she whom Catharine most dearly loved was Alessia. Alessia was very early left a widow, and from the time that she became a Mantellata she was Catharine's inseparable companion. She was a woman of strong good sense, true humility, and ready powers of adaptation. It is to her that we are indebted for much of Catharine's inner history, for she was sometimes even the sharer of her private devotions. It may be asked, how it can be known that Catharine used such and such words and arguments in prayer as are recorded? The explanation is in the fact that Catharine herself kept a record of some of the wonderful answers which were granted to her prayers, and of her own pleadings with God; while, at the request of her most intimate friends, she dictated from memory a record of much of her soul's experience, including the directions and revelations she received from her Lord. Much of this is developed in her book, the "Dialogue." Alessia was, moreover, a witness of the travail of Catharine's soul in several of those great emergencies when she sought the immediate interposition of the divine hand.

Such were Catharine's friends and companions; but those of whom I am about to speak were, in a more special sense, her own spiritual children. When the question of her canonization first came to be discussed at Rome, several of those who had been most intimately acquainted with her were requested to write down their recollections of her. These documents, sought for in vain by the followers of Bollandus for insertion in the "Acta Sanctorum," were afterwards found in manuscript at the Grande Chartreuse, and published by Dom Martene. There is so much freshness and reality in these personal notices that I shall here give very briefly the substance of portions of them, reserving other portions for the later dates to which they refer. The first is that of Friar Thomas of Siena. He was very young, he tells us, when he first made the acquaintance of Catharine, her father, mother, and whole family; he entered the order of the Preaching Friars about the same time that she became a Mantellata. "She dwelt near the church of the Preaching Friars, and spent the greater part of every night in prayer; when she heard the matin-bell she rested; she constantly exhorted the brothers of St. Dominic to give themselves to the Lord; and concerning some who had fallen, she would say to us, 'O let us mourn and pray for them—yea, let us mourn over these dead ones.' She was exceedingly fond of flowers, and delighted in weaving them into crowns, wreaths, and garlands, which she gave to her friends to remind them of the love of the Creator. She often gave me a bouquet. She was never idle. When not engaged in prayer or active ministrations, she dictated letters to her secretaries. Among those whom she called to the faith and service of Jesus, were these, known to me :—Gabriel Piccolomini, Neri of Landoccio, Christopher Ghanni, who translated her 'Dialogue' into Latin, and collected her letters after her death ; Stephen Maconi, and Francis Malavolti. I was present at the execution of Nicola Tuldo ; Catharine was by his side, and caught his head in her hands. Tuldo's eyes were fixed on heaven with so firm a gaze that his eyelids remained motionless ; the spectators wept, thinking they saw in this young man before them a martyr rather than a political criminal, and his funeral presented the aspect of a solemn religious festival. Catharine was always affable, kind, and gladsome, even in the midst of the greatest sufferings : trials seemed welcome to her. Once a man of God came from Florence to examine personally what had been told him of her. She was then, on account of severe illness, extended on the planks which served her as a bed. To test her humility he began to administer to her the most harsh and humiliating reproofs. She bowed her head and listened submissively, to the end, without changing countenance, and assured him that she felt very grateful for what he had said. Her visitor exclaimed, after he had left her, 'She is pure gold without alloy.' She generally dictated her letters and book while walking up and down her room, sometimes kneeling down to pray for more light. She taught herself to write after she was grown up. Soon afterwards she wrote to Stephen, ' You must know, dear son, that this is the first letter I ever wrote with my own hand;' and to Raymond, ' I wrote this letter myself, for God has given me facility in writing, that when I come from prayer I may unburden my heart.' She valued much her dominican cloak, because in it she had been solemnly consecrated to the service of Christ. ' I will never part with this dear mantle,' she said ; and whenever the precious cloak became worn or had a rent in it, she mended and patched it with the greatest care ; the many pieces in it were all inserted by her own hand. I took that cloak myself, after her death, from Siena to Venice, where it is preserved in the Dominican church there. Barduccio, of Florence, who was one of her secretaries, was particularly dear to the blessed one ; he was with her when she died, in Rome, and afterwards returned to Siena, sick, where he died, still very young, with a smile on his face."

Friar Bartholomew, of Siena, was a pupil of Thomas della Fonte, who often took him with him to visit Catharine at the Fullonica. He afterwards accompanied her on her missions to Pisa, Lucca, Genoa, Avignon, Florence, and Rome. *He* also says of her, that "she was very fond of lilies, roses, violets, and all flowers, and used to make them up into superb wreaths and bouquets. Her companions were young maidens like herself, wearing the mantle of St. Dominic. I often saw them sitting weaving flowers and singing together. When I began visiting her in the house, she was young, and always wore a smiling countenance ; I also was young ; but I never experienced any trouble in her presence. On the contrary, the more I conversed with her, the more I became in love with all the stern virtues. I knew many young laymen and monks who used to visit her, and they all experienced impressions similar to mine ; the sight of her, and all her conversations, breathed angelic purity. Her eloquence was wonderful, and great multitudes of men and women flocked to hear her preach. Ignorant people asked, 'Whence comes so much knowledge, seeing she has never been to school ?' Some thought the Friar Preachers had taught her, but, on the contrary, it was she who taught them. Frequently she dictated to two or three secretaries at once, and that without any hesitation or confusion. She told me of the command she had received from the Lord, after she had remained so long in prayer that her soul was separated from her body, and she was caught up to his presence. God then said to her, 'I have appointed thee, my daughter, to a new manner of life. Thou shalt travel ; thou shalt go from city to city as I will indicate to thee ; thou shalt live with the multitude, and speak in public : I will send some to thee, and I will send thee to others, according to my good pleasure. Be thou ever ready to do my will.'[1]

"I never saw the least shade of melancholy in her countenance, which was always cheerful, and even merry. When the pain in her side tortured her cruelly, and hindered her from rising, her friends pitied her, and said,

---

1 Deposition of Bartolommei di Dominici di Siena, given Oct., 1412, received and written out by Adama (Notary) with all requisite formalities, sent to the Bishop of Venice, and deposited afterwards in the library of the Grande Chartreuse at Grenoble. The words are exactly translated, as given by Bartolommei from Catharine's own mouth. This deposition was also copied by Tomaseo Petra, Secretary to the Pope.

'Mother, how you are suffering!' She would smile and say, 'I feel a gentle trouble in my side;' and she would add, 'I think I know how my Lord suffered when one of his hands was already nailed, and they drew the other arm with such violence that his ribs were disjointed.' Whenever she spoke of the martyrs, her face would flush and her eyes gleam, and she would spread out her white robe, and smilingly say, 'O, how lovely it would be if it were all stained with blood for the love of Jesus!' Till the last years of her life our Lord granted me the grace of being united to her by the bonds of a pure and holy affection."

It is from Friar Bartholomew that we have the account of the influence of Catharine with a venerable nobleman of Siena, called Francis, but whose family name he conceals. This gentleman was more than eighty years of age, when Alessia, who had married his son, and who now in her widowed state lived in the house of her father-in-law, besought Catharine to see and converse with him. To facilitate this, she begged Catharine to become her guest for some weeks in winter, in order that in the long evenings she might have opportunities of conversing with him. Catharine found the old nobleman very hard and worldly, as he had been indeed all his life; at first he mocked, and turned to laughter her efforts with him; but at last, he " yielded to the fire of her discourse," and said : " I am determined to confess and to pray; but I must tell you that I bear a deadly hatred against a certain prior, and intend if I can to kill him." Catharine said " such affecting things to him concerning this prior," that at last he exclaimed : " I will do whatever you order me; speak, then; I obey." Catharine, kneeling before him, then said, "For the love of our Lord and Saviour Jesus Christ, I beseech you, dear father, to forgive this prior, and to go and be reconciled to him." He promised, and before sunrise on the morrow he took a splendid falcon of which he was very fond, and bent his steps, alone, to the church at which the prior officiated. The prior, seeing his enemy enter, immediately fled; but the old man sent a canon after him to assure him that he had come to bring him good news, and not to injure him. The prior, on hearing that Francis was alone and unarmed, surrounded himself with many friends, and then permitted his visitor to be introduced. Francis, with his falcon on his wrist, bowed low, and said, "The grace of God has touched my heart, and I am come to offer to be reconciled with you; and in proof of my sincerity, I beg your acceptance of this falcon, which is my great pet." The prior, in astonishment, accepted peace, and Francis, returning to Catharine, said, "I have obeyed your orders; now what else shall I do?" Catharine begged him to see and converse with one of the most fervent of the Fathers of St. Dominic, who refrained from imposing any penance upon him, for "he was very aged, and in great indigence, although he was noble." The only penance which Catharine prescribed was that he should pray very earnestly; and he who had scarcely ever in his life entered a church, now rose early every day, and walked in silence to the cathedral, where he passed prolonged hours at the foot of the cross. This child-like and teachable old disciple continued ever faithful; and full of love and charity to all men, in a few years he slept peacefully in God.

The same witness also records the story of the conversion of Lazarini. Lazarini was a learned man, and professor of philosophy at Siena; his lectures were brilliant, and attracted crowds of pupils. He was one of the severest critics of the life of Catharine, and openly attacked her character. He resolved to pay her a visit, thinking to find material for further condemnation. He repaired to her house one day, at the hour of vespers. "He asked me to go with him," says Bartholomew, "and I consented, believing he would repent of his motive. We entered her room; Lazarini sat down on a chest, and Catharine on the floor at his feet; I remained standing. After some moments of silence, Father Lazarini began: 'I have heard many persons speak of your sanctity, and I have been anxious to visit you, hoping to hear something edifying and consoling to my soul!' Catharine, who understood him perfectly, promptly replied: 'And as for me, I am rejoiced at your arrival, for I desire an opportunity of profiting by that learning with which you daily delight your numerous disciples.' She paused, showing no disposition to impart anything. This interchange of empty compliments continued for some time, and as the night was coming on, Father Lazarini said: 'I see it is late; I must go; I will return at a more suitable hour.' As he arose, Catharine sincerely commended herself to his prayers, and he, as a matter of form, asked her also to pray for him, which she cheerfully promised to do. He went away, thinking that Catharine might be a good person, but that she was far from deserving her great reputation." Early the following morning, when he arose to study the subject he was to explain to his pupils that day, he felt a great oppression at his heart, and involuntarily began to weep. When they called him at the hour of the class, he could not speak to his pupils. Returning to his room, he became indignant with himself: "What ails me?" he said; "this is too absurd! Is my mother dead? or has my brother fallen in battle?" The day passed, and the second morning came, and yet the sadness continued; he then began to desire to converse with Catharine again. The sun was scarcely risen when he again knocked at the door of her room, in a very different frame of mind from that in which he first visited her. Catharine, who had never ceased to pray for him, and who knew what her Lord had done, opened the door gladly. They had a long interview, at the end of which Professor Lazarini conjured her to direct him in the way of salvation. Overcome by his instant entreaties, she at last said: "The way of salvation for *you* is to despise the world, its vanities and its smiles, and to become humble, poor, and destitute, like our Lord Jesus, and like the blessed St. Francis." Lazarini saw that she had read his heart; for he had loved the world' and its favours and pleasures. He went home, distributed his money and costly furniture, and even his books, reserving only such as were necessary to aid him in his lectures, and became truly poor, and a follower of our Redeemer. From this time his pupils increased in numbers; for to his learning and eloquence there was now added a kindliness and humility which won for him the affection as well as the admiration of those who heard him.

Stephen Maconi, a young nobleman of Siena, also wrote down his personal recollections of Catharine, at the time when her canonization was proposed. He says: "I must confess that, though a citizen of Siena, neither

I nor my family became acquainted with Catharine and her relatives previous to the year 1376. At that time I was engrossed with the business and pleasures of life, and had no idea whatever of becoming acquainted with her. Our family were then at open war with a family more powerful than our own, and it seemed impossible ever to come to any agreement, notwithstanding the repeated efforts of honourable citizens to act as mediators. Catharine had then a great reputation in Tuscany, especially as a reconciler of hostile persons and tribes. I was told that she could certainly obtain peace for us, if I asked her. I paid her a visit, and she received me, not as I had expected, with the bashful timidity of a young maiden, but with the tenderness of a sister towards a brother who had been absent on a long journey. I was perfectly astonished, and listened eagerly to her when she engaged me to repent and live like a good Christian. I said to myself, 'digitus Dei est hic.' When I explained the object of my visit, she said without hesitation, 'Go, my son, trust in the Lord; I will do all in my power to bring about a reconciliation.'"

The enemies of the Maconi were the Tolomei and the Rinaldini. Catharine fixed a day for the reconciliation, in the church of St. Christopher; but the pride of these two families would not yield, and they failed to keep the appointment. When Catharine was informed of it, she said, "They will not listen to me; but whether they will or no, they will be obliged to listen to God." She went to the church, where she expected to find Stephen, his father, and his other relatives. There she kneeled down before the altar, and offered up instant prayer to Heaven. While she was praying, those who had refused to be reconciled entered the church, unknown to each other. "God had brought them there." They paused at the sight of Catharine kneeling in prayer, unconscious of their presence. While standing silently for some minutes, it seemed to all the members of those rival families that the Spirit of God, the Spirit of peace and goodwill, descended upon them; they were vanquished, and ready to give up all their animosities. They charged Catharine with the arrangement of the conditions of peace, and became perfectly reconciled.

Stephen was one of the members of a confraternity which held its meetings for religious exercises in a subterranean room of a church at Siena. On one of these occasions he suffered himself to be drawn into a conspiracy against the government, planned in this room. Catharine discovered it, and said to him, " O Stephen, my son, what evil are you plotting in your heart ? Is it thus that you change the house of God into a workshop for treason ? What a stupid project ? and for this you risk the loss both of your soul and body." Stephen repented of his design, and perceived that there were many things of which he must purge himself in order to become worthy of Catharine's friendship. Stephen continues : " I now visited her often, and by the influence of her words and example, I felt within me a blessed change. She one day asked me to write some letters for her at her dictation. I accepted with joy, and as I continued to record her thoughts and advice in this way, my heart became inflamed with the love of God, and filled with contempt for the things of this world. I was also so filled with shame for my past life, that I could not bear to think of it. This change, of course, appeared outwardly, and nearly all the city was in astonishment. A little while after, Catharine said to me when we were alone, 'You will presently see, Stephen, that the dearest wish of your heart will be accomplished.' Her words amazed me, for I was not conscious that I now wished for anything at all in this world, and I said, 'What is that dearest wish?' She replied, 'Look into your own heart, and see.' I said, 'My very dear mother, I do not find there any greater desire than that of ever remaining near you.' She answered at once, 'It shall be fulfilled.' For myself, I could not understand how that could be, without violating the rules of propriety, for I thought of the great difference there was in our rank and outward circumstances; but He to whom nothing is impossible, willed that she should be sent to Avignon, and then, notwithstanding my great unworthiness, I was chosen to travel in her company. I quitted with joy my father, my mother, my brothers and sisters, and all my kindred, so happy was I to serve her.[1] It will be seen that for several years I had very intimate relations with Catharine, because I wrote her letters. She also consulted me about her thoughts and movements, and dictated to me a portion of her book. She loved me with the tenderness of a mother, and indeed far more than I deserved; consequently several of her disciples conceived a strong sentiment of jealousy. I studied with the greatest care her life and actions, and I declare, on my soul and conscience, and before God and the Church militant, that I have

---

[1] Letter of Stephen Maconi to Fra d'Antonio, of the Convent of SS. John and Paul in Venice, and afterwards found in the library of the Grande Chartreuse.

been intimately acquainted with several great servants of God, but have never seen anyone of so exalted a virtue. I never heard a frivolous word from her lips. She suffered constantly from ill-health and pain, but never did a shadow of trouble overcast her face ; never did she utter a word which might indicate anger or impatience ; and this last is assuredly a mark of high perfection."[1]

I shall return later to the narrative of Stephen. It remains only to notice briefly a venerable disciple of Catharine, whom she called " My Lord Nicholas dei Sarracini," an old soldier who had achieved glorious exploits on the battle-field, and whose pious wife continually urged him to confession and a godly life. He remained long indifferent to all her pleadings. One morning, however, he said to her, " I saw in a dream last night that lady of whom you so constantly speak to me, Catharine of the Contrada d'Oca ; let us go and speak with her." Catharine, from her knowledge of the human heart, spoke to the old knight in such a manner that he affirmed " she told me all things whatsoever I did ;" he learned to pray, and became a humble believer. In about a year from this time he died in great peace. This concludes the notice of the principal friends and fellow-workers of Catharine.

---

[1] Letter of Stephen Maconi to Fra d'Antonio.

CHAPTER V.

THE plague had subsided in Siena. The report of Catharine's devoted labours among the stricken people having reached Pisa, many of the inhabitants of that city expressed a strong desire to see her. They therefore sent a deputation to Siena to entreat her to pay them a visit, promising, in order the more to attract her, that her presence would be profitable to many erring souls. Catharine, suspecting her own instinctive love of journeying and adventure, hesitated for some time; but after taking counsel with her divine guide, and talking the matter over with Raymond, she set out, accompanied by several fathers of St. Dominic, including Raymond himself, by her mother, Lapa, and by three or four of the most devoted of the Mantellatas. She was hospitably received at the house of the brothers Buonconti, merchants. It was a beautiful evening in the month of June, 1375, when this faithful little band of pacific conquerors entered Pisa and crossed the well-known Piazza, where those four striking monuments, the Baptistery, the Cathedral, the Leaning Tower, and the Campo Santo, at that time almost modern, had been irregularly scattered by the hand of genius.[1] Catharine paused to gaze for

---

[1] Chavin de Malan.

the first time, on these great masterpieces, and over the plain beyond, sweeping towards the mountains which rise between Pisa and Lucca. At Lucca, she and her companions had tarried several days; she was there a sufficient time to add a group of disciples in that city to the "mystic family," now greatly increasing in numbers and strength. Gerard Buonconti, at Pisa, came forth with a goodly company to meet Catharine and her friends, and conduct them to the apartments prepared for them. In this company there were many of the Mantellatas of Pisa; there was the archbishop, Francis Moricotto di Vico; Peter Gambiacorti, the signore, or chief of the government of the republic of Pisa, leading by the hand his little daughter Tora, who afterwards became the Mother Clara of happy memory in the annals of the Church; Bartolomeo Serafini of the Carthusians, and others. There were Dominicans, solitaries from the hills, artizans, merchants, and good men and women of every condition. This Peter Gambiacorti is worthy of a special notice. The Pisans had maintained a long contest against the tyrannical rule of Giovanni Agnello, the late head of the government, who, at the instigation of the Emperor Charles IV., had usurped the unconstitutional title of Doge. The father and uncles of Gambiacorti had been prominent in this resistance, and, by a most unjust sentence, had been condemned and beheaded; he and his family were banished, and his estates were confiscated. The popular party however prevailed, and after some years its chiefs reversed the sentence of exile against the family, and Peter was recalled. He and his children, after a long time of absence, spent in great poverty, re-entered Pisa on foot, carrying olive branches in their hands. The streets re-echoed with shouts of congratulation, and the bells of the Leaning Tower rang out joyfully. Peter, his wife, and his children, boys and girls of various ages, proceeded to the cathedral, where he offered, at the foot of the great altar, solemn thanks to God, "in the name of all exiles," and took an oath to "live as a good citizen among his equals, and to forget and forgive all past injuries." But the men of the new régime did not all share Gambiacorti's magnanimous sentiments, and the smouldering revenge burst forth that very day in acts of violence against the persons and property of the colleagues of Agnello. They set fire to the house of the deposed Doge ; a high wind blew, and carried the fire so rapidly that there was danger of the whole city being burnt down. The first act of Peter Gambiacorti, after his vow made before the altar, was to hasten to the defence of his former enemies ; he fought all day against the fire, drove back the incendiaries, and calmed the excited people. Standing in the midst of the smoke and flames, he cried to the people, "*I have pardoned with all my heart*—I, whose father and friends perished unjustly on the scaffold ! By what right do *you* refuse to pardon ?"[1]

It is not surprising that such a man should have become one of Catharine's friends and correspondents, or that she should have found the chief of the republic the most eager recipient among her Pisans, of all that she could impart concerning God and eternal things.

Catharine had a commodious room assigned to her in

---

[1] Bernard Marangoni, "Chronicles of Pisa." Quoted by Sismondi, Vol. vii., Chap. xlviii.

tho house of the brothers Buonconti, and here she spent many hours every day in writing letters on the affairs of the Church and the Republics. Neri de Landoccio, a young knight of Siena, of whom mention has already been made, was her first secretary : he was with her at Pisa, and to him and to Raymond she dictated her correspondence. For social and spiritual converse with friends, the little chapel of St. Christina was reserved. It adjoined the house of the Buonconti, and here the Mantellatas and others assembled in the evenings for pleasant intercourse and sacred music.

The thought of a crusade had early taken possession of Catharine's mind. During this visit to Pisa the idea attained greater prominence in her thoughts, and she began at once to communicate to others her zeal in this direction. The ambassador of the Queen of Cyprus was at this moment in Pisa, on his way to the papal court at Avignon, to convey to Gregory XI. the earnest entreaty of the queen that he would call upon all the Christian powers to unite in a crusade against the Turks and Saracens. This queen's territory had been invaded by the Turks, and she had witnessed the sufferings of the Christians at the hands of the infidels, her own life had been in peril, and she had been obliged to place her little son under the protection of Raimond Beranger, the grand master of the Knights Templars at Rhodes. The Cyprian ambassador, drawn by a secret sympathy, paid a visit to Catharine as soon as she arrived in Pisa, and conferred with her at great length concerning the project of a crusade. Catharine wrote to a friend in Siena, "To-day the ambassador of the Queen of Cyprus paid me a visit; he is on his way to the holy father to solicit his help for

the Christian lands under the infidels." This idea of the
crusades we know had taken hold of many great minds
before Catharine's time. The motives for such an enterprise are not sufficiently clear to us in our day to enable
us fully to comprehend the strength of the pure religious
fervour which filled the souls of those holy men who
preached the necessity of the undertaking as a pledge
of fidelity to Christ ; but in Catharine's case it is easy to
gather from her letters and conversations, that although
loyalty to her Lord was the leading principle in this, as in
all her thoughts and acts, she regarded the undertaking
also from the point of view of a politician. She saw her
country filled with, and ravaged by troops of foreign
mercenary soldiers—Germans, Bretons, English, and Hun-
garians. She saw the Visconti and other ambitious nobles
continually at war with their own countrymen, and Christian blood shed every day by Christian hands. She longed
to see a practical means of diverting into a legitimate channel
the furious passions and restless fighting zeal of these lawless
troops, and of her own countrymen who made use of them.
It would be, she conceived, a double benefit to society, to
rid Christendom of the presence of these brigands, and to
change this rude military ardour itself into a chivalrous zeal
for a holy cause. Duguesclin had purged France of the
demoralizing presence of military adventurers, and she
dreamed of the possibility of doing the same for Italy.
Her task was, however, a more difficult one than his,
owing to the violent opposition of interests in her own
land ; and, as we shall see, her design was thwarted by
the revolt, now so near, of almost the whole of Italy
against the Pope, and by the great schism which followed.

Raymond says, in reply to some of her detractors, who asserted that Catharine had prophesied that a crusade would take place, and that her prophecy had proved false : " I acknowledge that Catharine always desired a crusade, and that she diligently laboured to bring it about ; it was one of the motives of her journey to Avignon ; she wished to engage the Pope Gregory in a holy war. I am witness of this, because when she conversed with the Sovereign Pontiff I acted as interpreter. Gregory XI. spoke Provençal, and Catharine could only speak in the dialect of Tuscany. Gregory therefore addressed her in Latin, which I interpreted. He said to her, ' Peace must first of all be established among Christians, and after that we may organize a crusade.' Catharine replied, ' There is no better means, father, of attaining to peace among Christians than the undertaking of a crusade ; all the turbulent soldiers, whose presence now promotes division among us, will gladly go forth on such an adventure ; few will refuse to serve God in the profession they love. The fire in Italy will thus be extinguished for want of the fuel which feeds it. You will accomplish several good objects at once ; you will obtain peace for Christians, and save many criminals by removing them from the scene and occasion of their criminal acts ; besides which many infidels may be converted and saved.' " Raymond adds, however, " I never heard Catharine indicate in any manner whatsoever that a crusade would take place ; on the contrary, she was always very reserved on the subject, resigning the whole to divine Providence, while expressing a hope that God would look in mercy on the people, and thus save many believers and unbelievers."

Catharine now set herself, with all her characteristic energy, to the propagation of this idea. She wrote several letters full of fire and persuasion to the celebrated Joanna, Queen of Naples ("bella e turpida regina"). She acquaints her with the good news that the Pope had already sent a bull to the Provincial of the Friar Preachers, to the General of the Minor Friars, and to another friend of her own, recommending them to preach a crusade through all Italy. "I therefore pray you, and would constrain you, madam," she writes, "in the name of Christ crucified, to animate your soul and prepare yourself by a humble attitude before God, to aid this work. If *you* will take up the cross, many will follow you. Awake, my sister, and act courageously! It is no time to sleep : time itself sleeps not ; it flies like the wind."

But Joanna, in the midst of intrigues, and absorbed by the ambitions and pleasures of life, had no heart for any such enthusiastic project. She made many beautiful promises, which Catharine for some time hopefully confided in, but which proved empty and vain. Hungary was continually threatened by Turkish invasion ; Catharine wrote, therefore, in the same sense to the Queen of Hungary ; she also wrote to Bernabos Visconti, stirring up in him his ambition of glory. She then turned to the most famous of the Condottieri and brigand chiefs. She had long grieved over the lawlessness and cruelty of the Englishman, Hawkwood, and she eagerly entertained the idea of engaging him in the holy war, for his own good and that of her country. To Hawkwood she wrote very earnestly : "Retire, I beseech you, a little into yourself, my brother, and contemplate the dangers and punishment to which you are exposing your soul in the service of the devil. My soul earnestly desires your salvation; I desire to see you change your manner of life and become the servant and soldier of Christ. . . Fight no more with Christians: it is a cruel thing that we, who are Christians and members of one body, should thus tear and devour one another. I beseech you to prepare yourself by humility and virtue for the time which is coming, in which you may give your life for Christ; and thus you will show yourself a true and valiant knight. Brother Raymond will carry to you this letter: give credence to what he says, for he is a true and faithful servant of God. . . Remember, brother, how short is your time on earth."

Having despatched Raymond with the letter to Hawkwood she wrote to other warlike captains; among whom were Alviano, and the Count d'Agnolo. The former had a great respect for Catharine, and the purity of his life was such that other soldiers sometimes rallied him as being secretly a member of the mystic family. She selected old John of the Cell to convey the letter which she wrote to Agnolo, a man who required to be very discreetly dealt with. Her ardent appeals produced for a time a great movement in the minds of men. The military chiefs began to dream of rich harvests of glory and of spoil on the plains of Asia. Preparations began to be made for departure. Women shared the general enthusiasm, and formed a company which they called "the servants of the pilgrims," to march to the Holy Land. Their enthusiasm was sometimes more sincere than wise, so much so, that Friar John of Vallombrosa was obliged in his sermons to moderate their indiscreet zeal.[1]

---

[1] Letter of Friar John to Catharine, Vol. iii., p. 220, Edition Gigli.

Catharine was beginning to hope for the realization of her cherished dream, when the first shocks were felt of the great Tuscan revolt against the Church, in which a large portion of Italy was soon to be implicated. She soon became sorrowfully convinced that the discords among Christian States would, for a long time probably, prevent the realization of a crusade. She saw that those souls must first be reconquered who were being lost to the kingdom of Christ, and that the Church itself must first be purified. Raymond says : " At the moment when the cities and lands which belonged to the see of Rome began to revolt against the Sovereign Pontiff, we were at Pisa. The news of the defection of Perugia reached Pisa ; distressed to observe among Christians so little fear of God, or love of his Church . . . I went to see Catharine, together with Friar Pierre di Villetri ; my heart was drenched in grief, and my countenance announced to her the melancholy event which had occurred. At first she mingled her sorrow with ours, for the loss of souls and the scandals of the Church ; but very soon, perceiving that we were too much cast down, she cheerfully chided us, saying : 'Do not weep before the time ; there will be far greater cause for tears by-and-by ; what you now see is but milk and honey to what will follow.' I asked her, in grief and alarm : ' Can we see anything worse than what we now see, unless it be the renunciation altogether of the faith of Christ ?' She replied, ' You now see the laity in rebellion, but in a little while you will see the clergy much more culpable than they ; as soon as the Pope shall manifest an intention of reforming the morals of the clergy, they will revolt, and present the spectacle of a grievous scandal to the whole world.

There will be a great schism; Christendom will be divided, and the robe without scam will be rent in two; arm yourselves, therefore, with patience.' When Urban VI. succeeded to the papal throne (continues Raymond), and the Church was rent with the great schism, I beheld the verification of all that Catharine had predicted. . . Some years afterwards, when we were at Rome, I begged her to tell me what she believed would happen in the Church after these miseries. She replied: 'After many tribulations and trials, God will purify the Church by means unknown to man; he will awaken many souls out of sleep; and the reform of the Church and of her ministers will be so beautiful that the prospect of it fills my soul with joy. . . . Give thanks to God for the great peace which he will give to his people after the tempest is past.'"

Catharine had come to Pisa, exhausted by her efforts during the plague, and in the hope that a rest and change of scene would restore her failing powers. Since the month of January in that year, she had suffered from great bodily weakness; a reaction, affecting her spirits as well as her body, had succeeded the superhuman efforts she had made during the year of the plague. And now we are to follow her through a period of suffering of a nature seldom experienced except by persons of fine and nervous constitutions, possessing great strength of affection and spiritual aspiration. She had not found the repose she hoped for; her labours of correspondence in connection with the desired crusade, had been exhausting; and her faith was now severely tried by the gloomy signs of the approaching political tempest, into the midst of which she knew that she must be drawn, inasmuch as the honour

of God and the salvation of erring souls were involved
in the approaching rupture.   The families of her gentle
hosts, the Buonconti, were full of solicitude for her; she
was now obliged to moderate her active labours, and to
rest on her bed for many hours daily in silence and darkness, on account of the severe headaches from which she
suffered.   On one occasion the pain was so violent that
Gerard Buonconti, who had entered her room to ask after
her health, observed the contracted nerves of her forehead, the throbbing of her temples, and her poor, thin
hands tightly clenched in agony ; his eyes filled with tears;
turning over in his mind various schemes for her relief,
he thought that it might be of use to bathe her temples
with a generous wine.   Having in his house only the thin
wine of the year, he sent to a friendly merchant who had
dealings with all the vineyards of France and Spain, to beg
some of his oldest wine.   " Willingly would I give you of
my best," replied the merchant, "but my cask is exhausted;
come and see for yourself if you will."   The two honest
men went together to the cellar on their errand of kindness, and on tapping the cask supposed to be empty, the
old wine flowed abundantly, and its quality was pronounced
to be supremely excellent.   The possessor of it was stupefied
with astonishment, and all his servants continued to protest
that for three months past the cask had been dry.   "It is
a miracle !" they cried ; "the virtue of the saint has
accomplished this !" and straightway a report flew through
the city that Catharine had miraculously multiplied the
wine of her hosts, without even rising from her bed to
pronounce the word.

Some days after, Catharine, convalescent, was going

through the streets with Lapa to pay a visit to an apostolic nuncio just arrived from the papal court, when her presence was announced by some workmen who recognized her. A great crowd of people gathered around her ; the excitement caused by the sight of a few scores in one street, soon drew together hundreds from all parts of the city, so much so that " the workshops were all forsaken, the faces of the inhabitants crowded the doors and windows of the houses, and all business ceased for a moment in the universal desire to see this wondrous person, the dyer's daughter of Siena. 'Go to ?' they said ; 'let us see who this woman is who drinks no wine, and yet can miraculously fill the casks !'"[1] "Catharine," continues Raymond, "was exceedingly grieved by this noise and excitement concerning her. She was forced to pause ; weak and trembling, she leaned on her mother's arm, and lifting her eyes to heaven, she frankly complained to her Saviour : 'Lord, why dost thou suffer me to be covered with confusion in this way before all the people ? Did I ever ask wine from thee ? Thou knowest that, by an inspiration of thy grace, I have all my life abstained from wine, and now wine is suffered to be the cause of my being made ridiculous. I beseech thee to put this matter right, that all this foolish excitement may cease !'" Very shortly (the story continues), the wonderful wine came to an end, and the last which was drawn was so unpalatable that those who would have drunk it dashed it from their lips. The sudden brief outburst of popular favour was followed by as sudden a reaction, and people murmured,

---

[1] "Qualis ist hæc quæ vinum non bibens, vas vacuum miraculoso vino potuit adimplere."—Raymond, Cap. 16.

criticized, and doubted. Catharine's friends came to her the same evening, with serious faces, to tell her that the people were actually beginning to say things seriously derogatory to her dignity. Catharine answered only with a merry laugh. How much of honesty of purpose, and of shrewdness in her estimate of the worth of popular opinion is expressed in her conduct of that morning, and in the laugh with which she replied to her regretful friends in the evening! Her illness increased, in spite of all the kind efforts of friends, and her own fortitude in combating her physical weakness. She fainted repeatedly, and on one occasion she continued in a state of insensibility during the whole day. The deathly pallor of her face, and her rigid immovability made her anxious friends believe that she was actually dead, and she herself spoke afterwards of her soul having really quitted the body that day, of glorious things which she had seen in the city of God whither celestial beings had conducted her, and of long and blessed converse with her Lord. Her mother, her hosts, the Friar Preachers and Mantellatas, her companions, all continued kneeling in her room till the evening, with tears entreating God to restore her to life. Towards the hour of vespers the sisters observed the beating of her heart, and two silent tears stealing from beneath the closed eyelids. With deep sighs of relief, they all gave thanks to God; but Catharine, awaking from her long trance, wept bitterly. Her chastened soul was not yet made entirely willing to return to the pains and toils of earth, from the ineffable foretaste granted to her of the joys of heaven. A sad presentiment, moreover, seemed to haunt her of approaching calamities for her countrymen. But she had not yet traversed the whole length of the valley full of the shadows of death. She began now to speak more than ever of the sufferings of Jesus Christ; the thought of his passion was never absent from her mind; and she whispered continually in her prayers the deep desire to be made more and more a partaker of his sufferings; her soul thirsted with a deeper thirst than ever for the living God, and for perfect oneness with Christ; at times she seemed plunged in sorrow, yet she embraced and clung to the sorrow; words failed her when she endeavoured to speak of her soul's travail at that time. "We cannot follow her," her friends said; "we must leave her alone with her Lord; there is a mystery in his dealings with her which we do not fathom." And we, at this day, will do wisely to echo those words, and not attempt to explain her sorrow or her ecstasy, the intensity of the outgoing of her soul towards God, or his deep and secret revelations of himself to her. We leave her alone with her Lord.

What follows shall be told in the words of her friends, the witnesses of her sorrows and her joys. Catharine remained silent for many hours every day at the foot of the cross, her frail body exercised with severe pain, while her soul unweariedly pressed on to a closer union with Christ, and participation in the sufferings of Calvary. One day she was alone in the little chapel of St. Christina. "The hour of the consummation had arrived." She remained longer than usual, entranced: her senses seemed to be dead. A few of her intimate friends entered and remained in a remote corner of the church; they saw her prostrate, her forehead on the earth, like one dead: after a long and motionless silence, she slowly raised herself and kneeled;

then she stretched forth her arms until her figure assumed the form of a cross; her countenance was "all on fire;" she seemed absorbed, possessed by some high, unearthly passion; her eyes were fixed, as if ravished by something which others saw not; she remained thus, perfectly motionless, for some minutes, and then suddenly fell like one who had received a death-blow. She was carried to her bed in the house of the Buonconti. When she began to return to herself, Raymond was by her side, and she whispered to him in a low voice: "Father, I bear in my body the marks of the Lord Jesus." Later in the day she spoke further on the subject, "I saw my Lord," she said, "extended on the cross, and from each of his five wounds there streamed forth towards me a ray of heavenly light. My love for him, and the desire of my soul to throw itself out of the body towards him, were so strong, that they raised me from the ground on which I was prostrated, and supported me while I gazed upon him. The five bright rays streaming towards me, pierced my hands and my feet and my side with an acute pain, and I fell as if dead. I besought the Lord that his blessed wounds might not appear visibly in my body; hence none but myself knows my secret pain." Catharine knew that the stigmata believed to have been borne by the great St. Francis of Assisi had won for him a superstitious worship which that great saint himself repudiated, and which, had it been bestowed on herself, she would have dreaded and fled from. Some fear of this kind, some awe which she never expressed, seems to have inspired the immediate and earnest request that she might not bear visibly the sacred marks, at the same time that she so ardently

desired to be made even outwardly like unto him whom
her soul loved, and to realize the most intimate union possible in this life. Such was the incident which gave rise to
the belief held after her death that her experience exactly
coincided with that of St. Francis, or with that at least
which was attributed to him; for there is no spoken or
written word of Francis of Assisi on record in which he
himself claims the honour of having received the stigmata.[1]
Catharine remained for some days after this in a state of
profound weakness, and tortured with pain. She afterwards told a friend that the anguish which she experienced
in the realization of the sufferings of Christ, was greatest
at the moment when she was pleading for the salvation of
some persons whom she dearly loved. "Promise me that
thou wilt save them!" she cried, and stretching forth
her right hand to Jesus, she again implored in agony:
"Promise me, dearest Lord, that thou wilt save them.
O give me a token that thou wilt." Then her Lord
seemed to clasp her outstretched hand in his, and to
give her the promise; when he withdrew, and her hand
dropped, "she felt a piercing pain as though a nail had
been driven through the palm."

Her health having become gradually somewhat restored,
Catharine resumed her active habits. From that time
forward her face beamed with a still more wonderful peace
and joy, at the same time that her whole frame bore the
traces of severe conflict. An atmosphere of heaven seemed
to surround her; she was like one who possessed a secret

---

[1] Beccafumi and other painters have represented the stigmatiza-
tion of St. Catharine in the Church of St. Christina.

which all men desired to know, but which can be imparted
by God alone, in direct communication with the soul of man.
The multitudes who were attracted to her "took notice of
her that she had been with Jesus;" and with that half-
unconscious thirst which lingers in every human soul,
urging it to cry, "who will show us any good?" many
besought her to tell them what she had in secret learned
of God.

During her stay at Pisa she encountered enemies as well
as friends, and there seems to have been a great conflict of
opinion in regard to her. Many simple folk among the
Pisans, not knowing how to express sufficiently their love
and admiration for her, knelt down, on meeting her in the
street, and kissed her hand. She was sharply rebuked for
allowing this. The austerity of her life and the fervency of
her prayers became the object of criticism here, as at Siena.
While some praised her, others maintained that she was
solely actuated by feminine vanity, and some even that she
was instigated by an evil spirit. The learned men of the
University thought it worth while to dispute with each other
as to whether she courted praise, or whether she only enjoyed it when it came to her, and on this account took
great delight in appearing before the public. Some said,
" What folly it is in people to run from all sides to see her!
She is only a woman; she ought to remain in her house if
she desires to serve God." Two or three of these determined, if possible, to put an end to the scandal, as they
termed it, of the public admiration for her. A celebrated
physician among them, called John Gutalebracia, resolved
to confound her by propounding difficult questions on the
Scriptures. He invited a renowned jurist, Master Peter

Albizi, a man of mature age and great prudence, to accompany him, and they proceeded to the villa Buonconti. The doctor opened the conversation in the following manner: " Master Peter Albizi and I have heard, madam, of your virtues and your learning, and we are come in the hope of receiving from you some spiritual instruction. We are anxious to know how you understand that passage in which it is said, God spoke in order to create the world. Has God a mouth and a tongue ? " He addressed to her several other questions of the same kind, and with assumed respect awaited her reply. Catharine answered, " I am astonished that you, who are teachers of others, as you inform me, should present yourselves before a poor woman whose ignorance it would be much more proper that you should enlighten. But, as you wish me to reply, I will do so as God will enable me. What benefit will it be to you or to me to know how God spoke in order to create the world ? God is a Spirit, and what is necessary for both you and me to know is, that our Lord Jesus Christ, the Son of God, assumed our nature, and suffered and died for our salvation. Yes ; the essential for me is to believe this, and to think upon it, in order that my heart may be filled with love towards him who so loved me. This is the true science." She continued to speak with so much fervour that Master Peter was unable to restrain his tears ; suddenly, taking his bonnet of crimson velvet from his head, he dropped on his knees and asked her forgiveness for having come with the sole intention of perplexing or tempting her. Catharine, giving him her hand, conjured him to rise. She seated him beside her, and they held a long and animated conversation on spiritual subjects.

Before he left, he begged her to do him the favour of presenting his little new-born baby at the baptismal font. She cheerfully undertook to do so; and from that hour he who had been bitterly prejudiced against her, became one of her warmest friends. Another gentleman, who enjoyed a great reputation for piety, wrote her a letter full of excellent arguments, reproving her for allowing any honour to be shown to her. He recalled to her the example of our Lord and of the saints; exhorted her to go home and live in retirement, reminding her that the true servants of God loved solitude above all things, and that only hypocrites sought renown. Fra Bartholomew of Siena, who was one of Catharine's companions at Pisa, says: "This letter was forwarded under cover to Father Raymond, who communicated its contents to me. We were very indignant, and intended not to show the letter to Catharine, but to answer the writer ourselves, and to reproach him with his impertinence and ignorance of spiritual things. While we were whispering together on the subject, Catharine perceived us, and inquired whether anything was troubling us. As soon as we told her, she claimed the letter, and when we hesitated to give it to her, she said, 'If you refuse it to me, I insist at least that you read to me what concerns me in it.' Raymond then read to her part of the letter, and she rebuked us gently for feeling angry. 'You ought,' she said, 'to join with me in thanking the author of that letter; he gives me very valuable advice. Do you not see that he fears that I may wander from the path of humility, and is anxious to save me from that snare? Now, I must have that letter, and return thanks to the writer of it.' She did so, in fact, at once, and in a most admirable manner. As Father Raymond, however, would not accept her view of the matter, and continued to protest that he would write himself, she gave him a very severe look, and reproached him for discovering evil where only good was intended."

"It often happened," says Raymond, "that persons unknown to us, of honourable and respectable appearance, but in reality addicted to vice, would present themselves before Catharine. Having a marvellous insight into character, she would refuse to look at them or answer them when they addressed us ; and if they insisted, she would say : 'First, let us purify ourselves from our faults, and escape from the bondage of Satan, and then we will converse about God.' By this means she soon disencumbered us of the presence of many whom we afterwards discovered to be incorrigible profligates."

Gerard Buonconti one day brought to her a young man of twenty years of age, whose system was shattered by the long continuance of a quotidian fever from which he was then suffering. He had consulted many physicians in vain he was so weak as scarcely to be able to stand to salute her. Filled with pity for him, and seeking an interview alone with him, she laid her hand on his shoulder, and gently whispered to him concerning the weight which she saw to be pressing on his soul. He was a stranger to prayer, to true faith, and to peace. She charged him at once to pour forth his heart in confession of all his past sins and negligence. He met her advice with truthfulness and simplicity, and conferred for some time after with good Friar Thomas della Fonte, to whom Catharine had commended him. He began at once to feel his soul lightened and his body strengthened. She then said to him, "Go, my son, in the peace of Jesus Christ, who will hear thy prayer. This fever will no more torment thee." Not many days after, he returned in restored health, to render thanks to her and to God ; his countenance was full of happiness and joy, and he walked with a firm, elastic step. Raymond saw him some few years later on a journey through Pisa, and affirmed that he had become so robust that he could not have known him, had he not explained who he was. He continued to be a faithful follower of Christ. Raymond says, moreover, "I was witness of this work of healing, and can say, like St. John, 'he who hath seen beareth witness.' There were also others who witnessed it ; Catharine's host, and Lapa, Friar Thomas, Friar Bartholo-mew, and all the devout women of Siena who had come to Pisa with Catharine."

Catharine, like most of the Sienese, possessed a great love and cultivated taste for music. She sometimes went in the evening to hear the organ in the church of St. Stephen at Pisa. where "the breeze gently waved the Turkish banners sus-pended from the vaulted roofs, trophies of the valour of the ancient Christian knights," no doubt suggesting thoughts of the new crusade for which she hoped. On leaving this church one evening she was met by a messenger, who conveyed to her an urgent invitation from the community of the Car-thusians established in Gorgon Island, to pay them a visit. This little island is situated nearly half-way between the Pisan shore and the most northerly cliffs of Corsica, and about thirty miles from Leghorn. Dom Bartolommeo of Ravenna was then prior of the Carthusian monastery in that island. He and his monks had been more than once obliged to defend themselves against bands of Saracens, who landed and overran the fields which they had cultivated, and attacked the convent in the hope of plunder. A few years after the date of Catharine's visit, the Saracens drove out the last of the poor religious, having murdered many of their companions, and took possession of the island. Dom Bartolommeo had often urged Catharine to spend a few days in his island, that his brethren might profit by her instructions. "He entreated me," says Raymond, "to second his request. Catharine consented, and we made the voyage thither, to the number of about twenty persons. We arrived a little after sunset; the prior met us, and conducted Catharine and her companions to the house where they were to lodge, about a mile from the monastery. The following morning he assembled all his monks outside the convent, and entreated Catharine to address a few words to them." It must have been an unusual spectacle, that of a great community of monks assembled thus, within no consecrated walls, but under the blue skies, seated on the ground, in the shade of the olive trees, or standing erect, and intent on all that passed; the dyer's daughter of Siena, in all the stern simplicity of her character, cheerful and frank in aspect and demeanour, silently waiting till stillness had fallen upon the wondering and obedient crowd; her friends, Alessia, Cecca, Lysa, and others, in their white gowns and dominican cloaks, grouped around her; Raymond, Dom Bartolommeo, and her youthful secretary and knight, Neri di Landoccio, conferring together as to the most suitable arrangements for this singular audience, so that the speaker might be distinctly heard, and the hearers freed from all distraction.

One can imagine how grateful in this hot July or August weather must have been the sea breezes from the blue Mediterranean, so near that the splash of its waves upon the shining pebbles of its tideless shore could be distinctly heard ; and how pleasant the soft shade, the silence and the calm, after the busy life and heat of the city. When Catharine was requested, as Raymond says, to " favour them with some words of edification," she at first declined, " excusing herself on the grounds of her incapacity and her sex ; saying that it was more meet that she should listen to God's servants than that she should speak in their presence." Yielding at last to the earnest invitation of Father Bartolommeo, and the murmured entreaties which ran through the crowd of expectant monks, she began to speak, " saying what the Holy Spirit inspired her to say in reference to the many illusions and temptations to which solitaries are liable, and concerning the means of triumphing over them." Contemplating, as she spoke, the assembly before her, she distinguished many a young face which told a pathetic tale of disappointment, or of conflict, or of yearning hope ; her maternal heart was moved to its depths, and overcoming the constraint which she had felt at first, she pleaded with them as a tender mother with beloved sons, or as a loving sister with brethren. Her clear voice was distinctly heard amidst the breathless silence which was maintained ; and there was, says Raymond, " so much method and ability in her discourse that I was filled with amazement, as indeed were all her audience." Another of her companions described her eloquence, on this and on other occasions, as resembling a flowing river : " She did not, like some orators, carefully seek and select illustrations or flowers of oratory, but her speech was like an impetuous torrent, which in its onward flow drags into itself, and whirls along with it all the flowers growing near, and profusely scattered upon its banks." When she had ceased, and the gentle murmur of the wondering and grateful assembly had taken the place of the hushed stillness filled only by her tender voice, the prior turned to Raymond and whispered: "Dear brother Raymond, I am the confessor of all these brethren and disciples, and know the hearts of each; and I assure you that if this saintly lady had herself heard all their confessions, she could not have spoken in a more just and suitable manner; she perceived all their wants, and did not utter a word which was not useful to them. It is evident that she speaks by the inspiration of God." The following evening Catharine and her company embarked again for Pisa; at midnight the wind lowered to a dead calm, and the pilot of their little vessel became very anxious. "We are in a dangerous channel," says Raymond; "if the wind from the north, which usually follows such a calm, had risen upon us, we should have been thrown upon some rocky islands, or drifted into the open sea. I spoke to Catharine of our danger. She answered in her accustomed tone, 'Why do you give way to distraction? There is no cause for fear.' I remained silent, for I was reassured by her calmness; but soon the wind veered in the direction dreaded by the pilot, and I drew her attention to it. 'Let him change the helm, in the name of God,' she said, 'and sail in the direction of the wind which heaven shall send him, and not against it.' The pilot obeyed, and our vessel turned its back on the shore whither we were destined. We were all troubled in mind, but *she* continued in prayer, with her hands clasped and her head bent forward ; and we had not advanced far before the favourable wind that had forsaken us, blew afresh, and we sailed quickly towards the shore of Italy. We arrived at the desired port at the hour of matins, singing the Te Deum as we touched the shore."

In the autumn Catharine and her friends returned to Siena; as the winter approached, some increase of bodily strength was granted to her, and in the silence of her little room at the Fullonica she sought wisdom, insight, and force for the greater labours to which she was yet to be called.

The condition of Italy became more and more calamitous. We have already seen how the Republic of Siena had been distracted by the rivalries of its different political factions. The whole of Lombardy was ravaged by "those wild beasts"[1] the Visconti. The kingdom of Naples, under the influence of the disorderly court of Queen Joanna, became a prey to rival parties, to unruly passions, and to wars of revenge. The state of Rome, abandoned by its popes, was still worse. In the midst of its desolation there yet remained, however, a remnant of its ancient spirit, which for a time enabled it to reassert its liberties under Rienzi, "the last of the tribunes," whose revolution was the most prominent event of the fourteenth century in Rome. Catharine of Siena was the faithful ally of Rienzi in the earlier part of his career. Neither the efforts of Rienzi, however, nor the warnings of Catharine were sufficient to avert the impending cala-

---

[1] Villani, L. ix., Ch. 103.

mities of Italy and of the Church. The Tribune fell a victim to his own weakness in embracing the luxurious manner of life against which he had at first protested, and lost the confidence of the people who had proclaimed him the liberator of Italy. The prophetic spirit of Catharine foresaw the great approaching defection; but she looked beyond that, to a time when Christendom, purified by still greater afflictions than those which befell it during her own life, would return to its primitive simplicity and " acknowledge the Saviour who had redeemed it by his own blood."

Bernabos Visconti, Duke of Milan, continued to incite the whole of the north of Italy to rebellion against the Pope, while Gregory ceased not to send his fighting legates one after the other with their large armies of mercenary Bretons, English, and Germans, to out-manœuvre the movements of Bernabos. He publicly excommunicated him and his captains. Bernabos, requiring time for the recruiting of his forces, resorted to dissimulation in order to obtain it. He sent Andria Doria of Genoa as his ambassador to Avignon to convey to the Pope his submission, and implore his pardon. Gregory, who was pacific and timid by nature, readily granted it. Bernabos, however, in the meanwhile had made his preparations for a treacherous attack first upon Genoa and the Doria family, of whose services he was availing himself ; and, secondly, upon the pontifical allied army. The revulsion in the mind of Gregory, on learning this, was very great, and he swore to undertake a war of extermination against the Visconti. More than ten Italian cities submitted to the furious attack of his legates ; for indeed the people were not sorry to be thus forcibly relieved from the Milanese tyranny. An unexpected revolution, however, occurred, which checked the success of the papal army and changed the course of events. The powerful republic of Florence, hitherto so loyal to the Church, now rose up with great vehemence against its authority.

It is not necessary to give in all their details the causes of this revolt; it is enough to say that it was more than justified by the oppressive government of the pontifical legates. The long course of crimes, treasons, and cruelties of which these legates had been guilty against the Florentine subjects of the Pope was crowned by an act which proved to be more than their patience could endure. During a season of great scarcity, when the harvests of Tuscany barely sufficed for the nourishment of the starving citizens, the legates sent their own soldiers into the fields to reap the corn; this they shipped off in their galleys from the ports of Leghorn and Genoa to be conveyed to other ports, where they received good prices for the cargoes. At the same time they forbade the importation to Tuscany of the corn of the Campagna. These measures, executed with a high hand and under pretence of "teaching a salutary lesson of humility to the Florentines," excited that people to fury; and in the streets of this hitherto loyal and orthodox city were now to be seen crowds of rebels crying, "Down with the government of the priests! Viva la Liberta!" They burnt the convents, forced the prisons, and published a plébiscite abolishing for ever the horrible institution of the Inquisition. They suppressed the canonical tribunals, and abandoned the clergy to popular vengeance as the enemies of the public good. The news of this revolution filled the heart of Catharine with dismay. She had already laboured assiduously, by her letters to Pope Gregory, to the Signory of Florence, and to the Visconti, to restore peace, by bringing each to the recognition of the true principles which should govern the State and the Church. She had entreated the Pope no longer to leave the conduct of his affairs in the hands of the worldly and rapacious legates, and had counselled the Florentines to endeavour to come to an understanding with the sovereign pontiff by means of an embassy to Avignon, rather than by resorting to arms. Secretly in her heart she had determined not to rest until the Pope should resume his responsibilities in Italy; this aim she never lost sight of, and never ceased to commend it to God in prayer until she saw its accomplishment.

Gregory trembled when he heard of the revolt of his faithful Florentines, and began to be even in fear of his own furious legates, who had exceeded so far the powers entrusted to them. He wrote as follows to the magistrates of Florence: "As for ourselves, we take God and man to witness that it is not through our will or fault that these wrongs of which you complain have been perpetrated. Dear children, we warn you, we beseech you, we implore you to put away this tumult of your spirits, and to return to God. Consider the horrible misfortunes which will result from this revolution. Make restitution for the crimes you have committed against the Church, and we shall grant to you abundantly our apostolic benediction." This letter had no effect in allaying the approaching storm, though the most moderate of the republican leaders employed their utmost efforts to prevent the outrages committed by the enraged and hunger-stricken people. The refuse of the population living on the banks of the Arno, fell with violence upon a Chartreuse convent in Florence, dragged out the prior, who had assisted the legates in their great corn robberies, and tortured him to death in the most horrible manner. They roasted him alive by the river side, tearing off his flesh with pincers, and throwing it to the dogs. The laughter and mockery of the people were mingled with the howling of the dogs as they quarrelled over their horrible repast. The spirit of revolt spread like a conflagration. The red flag bearing the word "Libertas" in letters of silver was carried to Viterbo, Orvieto, Spoleto, Todi, and many other cities. Perugia drove out from her midst her cardinal and all the priests. The whole country re-echoed with the cry of "Down with the Church." The brigand chief Hawkwood, hearing in this cry the promise of great gains for his mercenaries, forsook the banner of the Church, which he had degraded, and went over to the service of the rebels, who offered him high pay. The soul of Gregory was desolated with the news of this widespread revolt, for he perfectly understood that this hatred against the Church was bound up with deep sentiments of patriotism and the love of freedom, and that it could not be denounced as an unmixed evil. He had recourse to ecclesiastical weapons. He excommunicated the Florentines and all their adherents, as contumacious rebels. The city was placed under an interdict; he ordered all the churches to be closed, and prohibited the administration of the Sacraments. All commercial treaties with the Florentines were declared null, and the nations were warned to have no dealings with them. It was forbidden, under pain of excommunication, to furnish the

city with corn, wine, or wood. The seizure of their merchandise was declared to be legitimate ; the right to make
testaments and to inherit property was forbidden them.
They were declared the slaves and the offscouring of the
world.[1] The Florentines met these ecclesiastical fulmina-
tions at first with derision and scorn. Gradually, however,
they saw their great merchants emigrating and establishing
themselves in London, Canterbury, Norwich, &c. They
found the merchants of other cities unwilling to deal with
them ; their vessels and their agents were shunned ; their
commerce was almost destroyed. The more sober of the
revolutionists resolved to attempt a reconciliation with the
Pope. Two ambassadors were selected, one of whom was
the generous "captain of the people," Barbadori. They set
out for Avignon. Gregory granted them a public audience
in the great hall of the Consistory. The ambassadors prostrated themselves before him, and kissed the apostolic feet.
Barbadori then stood upright; and in a voice tremulous with
emotion, he addressed the Pontiff in his beautiful Tuscan
tongue, which was not understood by Gregory, except
through the medium of an interpreter. " Most holy father,"
he said, " we beseech you, listen to us as an equitable judge,
and not as one of a party. If you had sent to the Italian
cities good legates or prefects, who, instead of exercising
an accursed tyranny, would have caused your power to
be reverenced, you would never have had anything with
which to reproach us, and we should never have had to
plead our own defence. Your legates ought to have
remembered that they were not dealing with barbarians

---

[1] Bull of Gregory XI. Raynaldus, "Eccles. Annals."

or Turks, but with Christians and free republicans. Their tyranny has passed all bounds; they are guilty of all crimes. Beasts without reason even know how to distinguish good from bad management: they submit to the one and resist the other. Men are not worse than beasts if they revolt against misrule." He then describes the conduct of the legates, and the reaping of the cornfields of Tuscany by the papal troops, and recounts the long history of the fidelity of Florence to the Church. He concludes thus: "If your legates, holy father, have acted with your authority, which we cannot believe, we come to complain to you frankly of the injustice of the Roman Church. If, on the contrary, they have acted without your sanction, it was they who deserved to be punished, and not the people of Florence. If you do not condemn them, and if you suffer your anger to fall only on those who have resisted their wickedness, we must appeal to the supreme judgment of God and to the verdict of public opinion." The speech of Barbadori produced a great sensation in the assembled consistory. The Pope, who had resolved, at the advice of his cardinals, not to speak one word himself to the ambassadors, was so moved, that he spoke nevertheless, under a certain impulse of pity and generosity, promising henceforward to deal equitably with the Florentines, and by means of carefully appointed officers in place of the cardinal legates. For several days after this interview, consistories continued to be held, in which the most violent opposition of opinion prevailed. The Italian cardinals were in favour of pacific measures towards their countrymen. The French cardinals, who were in a large majority, and who were unable to form any conception of the moral force and passionate love of liberty of the Italian people, cried out for inexorable and violent measures. The ambassadors were again admitted on the fourth day to receive the pontifical decision. Excommunication and interdiction, with all their terrible results, were to be maintained, and war was again declared. The two ambassadors stood silent and apparently stupefied, for several minutes. Barbadori seemed to be oppressed with a deep sadness; but at last he broke silence. Looking around him, and seeing none but enemies, he advanced towards the great crucifix at the end of the consistorial hall, and in a voice of solemn entreaty and defiance, pronounced these words: "Great God! we, deputies from the Florentine people, appeal to thee and to thy justice from the unjust sentence of thy vicar. O thou, who canst never err, and whose anger is ever tempered with mercy, thou who willest that the peoples of the earth shall be free and not enslaved; thou who abhorrest the tyrant, be thou this day the help and the shield of the Florentine people, who in thy name will strive for their rights and their liberties."[1] The ambassadors then left the room, and returned to Florence with their sorrowful tidings.

The hatred of the people against the ecclesiastical government now became still greater than before. They spoke even of abandoning the Christian faith, and establishing another creed and another worship. Vast preparations were made at Avignon for the renewal of the war. Cardinal Robert, Count of Geneva, took the command of 10,000 men, composed chiefly of Germans

---

[1] St. Antoninus, "History of the Pontificate," Tit. xxii

and Bretons. The advance of Cardinal Robert upon the revolted republics, and the horrible massacre of Cesena, executed under his orders, have been already alluded to. From the smaller cities he advanced towards Florence. The people and signory of Florence, in dread of his approach, once more took counsel together on the possibility of again making overtures of peace.

Catharine, as we have seen, had been living at the Fullonica, after her mission to Lucca, Pisa, and Gorgona already described. She had been in correspondence during the winter with the magistrates and other citizens of all the revolted cities. On New Year's Day of 1376 she was attacked with a low fever, which lasted to the end of April. Father Raymond, who had been on some religious mission to Florence, returned from that city to Siena at the beginning of May. He lost no time in visiting his friend, whom he found stretched on her little bed, and suffering extremely. He sat down and recounted to her all the details of that terrible revolution in Florence which has just been described, and of the unsuccessful embassy to Avignon. Catharine listened in silence, and for several hours was plunged in deep sorrow. Her prayers offered up for so many years seemed not to have been heard. The peace of Christendom and the reform of the Church, which she so ardently desired, appeared to be farther off than ever. Great darkness and depression took possession of her soul during those sad hours. Raymond reports a few words of bitter anguish which escaped her during the day, not addressed to him nor to any man, but apparently the expression of a great inward conflict. Towards evening she arose, though scarcely able to stand upright; then for an hour she remained prostrated at the foot of a crucifix in her room, in an agony of prayer. "She arose from that attitude," says Chavin de Malan, "with the fortunes of Christendom in her hand; her voice was now to be heard above all the discordant voices of the world; and she was about to trace with a firm, unfaltering hand the path in which men ought to walk." The same evening, before she slept, she wrote a letter to Gregory XI. The purport of this letter, which is of great length and full of eloquent pleadings, was to convince Gregory that it was his duty to return without delay to Italy. She pointed out to him, with the indignation of a true patriot, how the interests of her country were made of no account in comparison with the satisfaction of the avarice, and lust of power and of pleasure, of its delegated rulers. She described to him how his bishopric of Rome was misgoverned, and how infidelity or indifference had taken possession of men's minds. She says, "I wish (*io voglio*) that you should be a true and faithful pastor, one who would be willing, had he a hundred thousand lives, to sacrifice them all for the honour of God and the love of humanity." "Do all that is in your power," she continues, "and having done so, you will be exonerated before God and man. . . . Do not imagine that you can reduce your subjects to submission by the sword. You will never succeed with them unless you use weapons of benignity and grace. . . . The spirit of strife and the absence of virtue, these are two things which are causing the Church to lose ground more and more. If you wish to recover what you have lost, your only means of doing so is to retrace your steps, and to reconquer your lost dominions by the encouragement of virtue and by peace.

Pardon, beloved father, my presumptuous boldness. I crave your benediction." Nicolo Tommaseo says : " Catharine saw it necessary to strike at the root of the evil, which was the immorality of the clergy and the odious government of the papal legates." De Malan says : " The letters which Catharine wrote at this time to Gregory initiate us into a new kind of diplomacy, very unlike that generally resorted to." These wonderful despatches of the dyer's daughter were carried to the Pope by a poor monk of La Chartreuse. About a week later she sent him other letters by the hand of Neri de Landoccio the young Sienese nobleman who had now been for three years her secretary. Again and again she wrote to Gregory, pleading with him boldly and frankly, at times as a child with a father, at others as a wise and stern monitor. " Consider," she says, " these two evils before you ; on the one hand your temporal possessions, of which you are being deprived, and on the other, the souls which are being lost to you. Which evil is the worst ? Open the eyes of your intelligence, and look steadily at this matter. You will then see, holy father, that of the two evils the latter is by far the worst, and that it is more needful for you to win back souls than to reconquer your earthly possessions. . . . You now place your confidence in your soldiers, those devourers of human flesh ; and your good desires for the reform of the Church are hindered. Place your hope rather in Christ crucified, and in the good government of the Church by virtuous pastors ; let it please your Holiness to seek out true and humble servants of God as pastors in the Church, men who desire nothing but the glory of God and the salvation of souls. Alas ! what corruption and confusion we now see. Those who should be models of virtue and simplicity, those who ought to be stewards of the wealth of the Church for the good of the poor and of erring souls, are a thousand times more entangled in the luxury and vanities of the world than the laity; for, indeed, many of the laity put the pastors to shame by their pure and holy lives. It seems, indeed, that eternal justice is now permitting to be done by force that which is not done for love's sake. It seems that God permits the Church to be robbed of her power and wealth in order to teach her that he wills her to return to her primitive state of poverty and humility, and of regard for spiritual rather than temporal things; for ever since she has sought temporal possessions, things have gone from bad to worse. It seems just, indeed, that he should permit her such great tribulations. Open your eyes, father, and see what these people are who are called apostles of the flock, and how they devour the poor; how their souls are filled with greed and hatred; and how they have made their bodies vessels of every kind of abomination." She pleads with gentle charity for the rebels: "We are in sympathy with you, holy father, and I know that it is thought by all that your revolted subjects have done ill, and are without excuse. Nevertheless, on account of their great sufferings under bad pastors and rulers, and the unjust and iniquitous dealings of the latter, it has seemed to them that they could not act otherwise. They have been infected by the conduct of some of the great captains, who, as you know, are devils incarnate; and they have also acted under the influence of fear. Mercy, my father! I ask mercy for them. Pity the ignorance of your children; give them some salutary discipline, if it pleases you; but oh! grant us peace. . . . Come back to your distracted flock and your country, to the place of your predecessor, the Apostle Peter. Do not delay —do not fear; for God will be with you. . . . I should be very blamable if I wrote thus to you with the idea of teaching you a lesson. I am constrained only by love of the truth, and the strong desire which I have to see you, gentle and beloved father, in peace and quietude, for I see that at present you cannot have an hour of either."

The Pope had hitherto commanded sixty episcopal cities in Italy, and one thousand five hundred fortified places. These cities were, for the most part, now included in the league of rebellion against him, and his dominion was now "reduced to a few meagre strips of land." Catharine having despatched her letters to the Pope, set herself to write earnest appeals to the governments of all the republics with whom she had any personal influence. She prevailed with Lucca and Pisa to maintain their allegiance to the Pontiff; and she put forth all her strength of persuasion to restrain the Ghibelline leaders of Florence from further violence. Some of the gravest of the Florentine citizens, with Nicolas Soderini at their head, supported by the ruined and despondent merchants, determined to wait upon the Eight, or Council of War, to beseech them to make terms of peace with the Pope. For, it must be observed that the former government of Florence had been superseded by eight rulers elected by the people, and designated the "Eight of War" ("Otto della Guerra"). These men were chosen for their resolute and warlike dispositions, and promptitude in action. They were members of the

Ghibelline, or popular party. Nicolas Soderini was a man of illustrious family, in politics on the side of the Ghibellines. He had been chosen as Gonfalonier of Justice in 1371, and was held in high esteem by the republic, on account of his impartiality and moderation in all political contests, and his tried patriotism. The Council of War, overawed by this weighty deputation, consented to take measures for a reconciliation with Gregory. The sincerity of their desire for peace was, however, from the first, doubted by Soderini. They owed their high position to the emergency of the actual revolt, and the prospect of continued war. The establishment of peace would be the conclusion of their term of power; they had experienced the fascinations of office, and, yielding to the dictates of selfish ambition, they soon became, as we shall see, very half-hearted seconders of those who desired to see an end of this disastrous strife. Soderini had heard much of Catharine, and believing that her influence with the Pope would be greater than that of any of the counsellors of Florence or princes of Tuscany, advised that she should be invited to act as mediator. The Council of War consequently commissioned Soderini to go to Siena and negotiate this matter with Catharine. Catharine at once left the Fullonica and proceeded to Florence. She saw that the efforts of man had failed, and she thought she read in the appeal to herself, a confession on the part of the Florentines that their hopes must now be placed in God and in those whose strength is derived from God. The magistrates and chief citizens of Florence came out of the city to meet her, and conduct her to the house of Soderini, whose guest she was to be.

It was the middle of the month of May when Catharine entered Florence.[1] She had been there two years previously, to attend a chapter of the Preaching Friars and a high festival of the Brothers and Sisters of St. Dominic. She could not have failed to contrast the circumstances of the two visits. When she first saw Florence, nature was smiling and gay, such as those can imagine it who have seen that beautiful city in spring; the bells were ringing, and the busy people working in the open air, were singing and laughing while at work. All was activity and hopeful life. But *now* there rested such a blight upon the city as we can only picture by endeavouring to understand the vast and terrible influence of certain great religious ideas or superstitions of the time. The curse which had been pronounced acted like the destroying breath of some pestilential vapour, blighting the social life of the people, drying up the sources of their activities, and isolating them from the brotherhood of the world, as outlaws and criminals. The fields still bore traces of the war; the city was in deep mourning, and its excommunicated people loitered sad and inactive, on the banks of the Arno. That river, at other times so alive with the commerce and traffic of all nations, now flowed sullenly beneath its untenanted vessels, whose sails drooped idly. The splendid merchandise which formerly was seen passing to and fro, was

---

[1] In an old manuscript at Siena, cited by G. P. Burlamacchi in his notes upon Catharine's letters, there occur these words—almost the only notice we have of her previous visit to Florence :—"There came to Florence in May, 1374, during the chapter of the Friar Preachers, . . . one dressed in the habit of St. Dominic, whom they called Catharine, daughter of Giacomo of Siena."

seen no more ; the storehouses and ateliers were closed, and
on all sides resounded complaints, weeping, recriminations,
curses, and cries of revolt. The celebration of the mass and
all religious services had been interdicted, and the churches
were forsaken. It is not to be wondered at that all eyes
should have been directed to that poorly-dressed and fragile
woman as she entered the city, the mediator elected by the
Eight of War, on whom all their hopes seemed now to
depend ; and that curiosity should have prompted crowds
of people to watch the gateway of Soderini's palace, in
order to see her as she passed out and in on her diplomatic
errands to the various political leaders.

Catharine spent fifteen days in Florence, making herself
completely mistress of the whole case in which she was
called to take so prominent a part. Her days were spent
in consultation with the chiefs of the different parties in
the republic, in endeavouring to calm the agitation which
prevailed, and to promote a common agreement upon some
patriotic and energetic action, which she urged them to
adopt, apart from all political jealousies among themselves.
At the end of this time all parties agreed to request her,
as a favour, to undertake for them a mission of pacification
to the papal court at Avignon, promising that chosen
ambassadors should follow her in a few weeks. Catharine accepted the responsibility. She sent her faithful
Raymond on in advance to speak with the Pontiff, and
prepare him for her arrival. The Florentine republic
saw no further than the one important object they had
at heart, the removal of the papal ban, and the restoration
of their blighted commerce and civil life ; but Catharine
had larger ends in view. She cherished in her heart the

hope of accomplishing three great objects : the restoration of peace between the Pope and his revolted subjects, his own return to Italy, and the organization of a crusade. Although weak and suffering in health, she set out, in the first week of June, upon this momentous embassy.[1] Few details of this journey are preserved. Travelling then was slow and difficult, and several weeks were oc-cupied in traversing the route to Avignon. That the journey was performed by land appears from the Bull of Pius II. for the canonization of Catharine, in which appear the words, "to reconcile the Florentines and the Church, she did not hesitate to cross the Apennines and the Alps in order to reach Gregory, our predecessor."

We can only imagine what the toils and what the pleasures of that journey may have been, along the beautiful Riviera, passing beyond the maritime Alps and the Esterels, by Frejus and Toulon to Marseilles, and thence, through the flat and desolate portions of the department of the Bouches du Rhone, entering the sunny and verdant land of Provence. Catharine, impatient to reach her destination, lost no time on the way; but Stephen informs us that sometimes when they came in sight of a mass of lovely mountain flowers, her face would flush with pleasure, and she would call upon her fellow-travellers to admire their colours; and that "on descrying an anthill she said, 'those little creatures came from the sacred thought of God; and he used as much care in forming the flowers and insects as in creating

---

[1] "Laborem non recusavit, et fiduciam gerens in Domino operis exequendi iter assumpsit debilis corpore."—S. Antoninus.

the holy angels.'" A large company travelled with her; among them, Stephen Maconi, who had come with her to Florence; Neri, her secretary; Felix da Marta; a certain Brother Guido; Neri dei Pagliaresi; Nicolo di Mino Cicerchi, and John Tantucci, the theological doctor of Cambridge, a man of science, who at first had been a severe critic of Catharine's actions, "strongly suspecting any virtue which did not lie in the line of his own experience and attainments," but who became later her earnest friend and coadjutor. She was joined by the generous brothers Buonconti, from Pisa, who arranged for the accommodation of the travellers on the many nights they were obliged to rest on the journey; and, finally, three of her Mantellatas accompanied her.

CHAPTER VI.

THE last long, hot day of journeying was over, and the evening dews were falling, when Catharine and her friends entered Avignon, on the 18th of June, 1376. Pope Gregory had given orders that she should be well received, and he placed at her disposal, for the accommodation of herself and her friends, the palace of an absent cardinal, with the chapel attached to it. After two days allowed for repose, Catharine was summoned to the presence of Gregory. The papal palace stood on the summit of the rock of the Domes, commanding a magnificent view of the Rhone and the surrounding country. Each succeeding Pope of the " Captivity " had added something to its splendour. By the side of this French Vatican stood the ancient basilica of Notre-dame-des-Doms, on one side of which were the cloisters of Charlemagne and on the other the houses of the canons—gothic buildings with massive buttresses. The great hall of the Consistory and the hall of public audiences had been lavishly decorated with paintings and sculpture by Clement VI. The galleries of the palace, the broad marble staircases, the colonnades, the exquisite gardens, with their fountains and rare flowers, the suites of luxurious apartments softly cushioned, and perfumed with the most delicious odours, have all been described by annalists of the Papacy, and praised in the quaint songs of the troubadours. It was to such a scene of almost oriental luxury and magnificence that the poor daughter of the wool-dyer of Siena was introduced. After she had ascended the winding road leading up the rock of the Domes, she was conducted to the hall of the Consistory, where the Pope and the cardinals were assembled in solemn state. Gregory was majestically seated on a magnificent chair, the cardinals, robed in purple, forming a circle round him. The royal grandeur of the supreme pontiff must have presented a striking contrast to the simplicity and poverty of Catharine, attired in her white serge gown and her carefully-patched Dominican cloak. Antoninus, in his chronicles of Florence, says that there reigned in her the authority of one who comes direct from the presence of God, charged with a message from him to men. She evinced no timidity or embarrassment in the presence of the princes and potentates of earth, for she realized the presence of one greater than they, the King of kings, whom she served. Gregory regarded for a moment with silent astonishment this poor and self-possessed ambassador from the proud Florentine republic, but he saw in her also the generous woman who had written to him with so much affectionate candour, giving him such wise and severe advice as none of his princely counsellors would or could have offered to him. He felt her power even before she had spoken. It was evident to those who observed the interview that her ascendency over the mind of Gregory was complete from the first moment.[1] She addressed the pontiff in the dialect of Tuscany, Raymond acting as interpreter, and Gregory replied in Latin. After a prolonged conversation, during which Catharine exposed in a brief and masterly manner the circumstances of the Florentine rebellion, and the present condition of mind of the citizens, Gregory said: "I commit the treaty of peace wholly to your decision. This is a proof to you that I truly desire peace. I wish the negotiation to rest entirely in your hands; and I entrust to you the honour of the Church."

Raymond says that he and the others present at that interview can affirm before God and man that the holy father committed the treaty of peace and interests of the Church into the hands of the Mantellata. Gregory then retired, and the cardinals also, the latter to consult together concerning the effect upon their own personal interests which the spiritual authority of this strange visitor might possibly have.

The Eight of War of Florence had made an engagement with Catharine to the effect that as soon as she should have won the Pope to terms of peace they would send several of their weightiest citizens as ambassadors to sign the articles of the treaty. But the time passed on, and no ambassadors arrived. Morning after morning and evening after evening Catharine sent out her scouts, Neri and her faithful Stephen, to look for their coming; but in vain. Sick at heart, she endeavoured, but with little success, to beat back the suspicions which haunted her,

---

[1] "Veramente assai efficace e pronto fu l'imperio di Catarina sopra l'animo del papa."—CAPECELATRO, *Storia di S. Catarina e del Papato del suo Tempo.*

of treachery on the part of the Florentine leaders to the
cause which they had committed to her. The fidelity of
Soderini, however, she refused to doubt. "Thou, mine
own familiar friend, whom I trusted," she said to herself,
"thou assuredly hast not joined hands with traitors." The
bitterness of the internal conflict induced by this suspense,
which lasted several weeks, may be seen in her letters addressed at that time to friends in Florence. Immediately
after her first interview with Gregory she had written, in
all the joy of her heart, to inform the Eight of War of the
happy result of that interview, beseeching them to send
their ambassadors without delay to sign the terms of peace ;
but she had received no reply ; and meanwhile rumours
had reached Avignon of a fresh outrage against the Church
perpetrated by the Eight of War, in the form of an oppressive tax levied upon the clergy of Florence, which occasioned the ruin of the humbler priests. She wrote to the
Eight of War : "I have much reason to complain of you,
inasmuch as I hear you have put a very heavy tax on the
clergy. If this be true, it is a great wrong, on two accounts ; first, because you have no right to do such a thing,
and cannot do it with a good conscience before God ; and,
secondly, because by this step you will destroy the hopes
of the peace which the holy father is ready to conclude.
He will now only feel a greater indignation than ever
against you. One of the cardinals, who really desires
peace, said to me : ' It seems to me that the Florentines are
not sincere in desiring peace ; for if they were, they would
avoid at this moment all that is irritating to the Holy See.'
And I think he is right. You do me personally a great
wrong, and put me to shame before the world, seeing that I

am maintaining one mode of speech while you maintain another. I cannot tell you how great was my joy when, after a long interview, the holy father said to me, in conclusion, that, if matters at Florence were indeed as I had told him, he was, on his part, disposed to do all that you wished ; but you are aware that he will not give a public and definite answer until the arrival of your ambassadors. I am astonished that these have not yet joined us. As soon as they come I shall see them, and I shall again see the holy father, and I will then write to you without delay of the results arrived at. But do not go and root up all the good seed which has been sown, with your taxes, and your evil reports, and your delays. For the love of Christ, consider your own best interests ! " She wrote, moreover, to many of the most influential citizens, urging them to use their influence with the Eight. It became more and more apparent, however, that the Eight of War, while talking of peace, secretly desired to prolong the breach. Gregory said one day to Catharine : " Believe me," my daughter, " they are playing the part of hypocrites. The ambassadors will not come, or if they do, they will come without ample powers to treat for peace." And so it proved to be. It was not until nearly two years after this that Catharine saw the end of her labours attained. Meanwhile she began to perceive that this delay, which was so severe a trial for herself, and so great a risk for the peace she ardently desired, was providentially overruled to serve an end yet more important than the immediate conclusion of peace between Florence and the Pope. The long weeks of her enforced residence at Avignon gave her the opportunity of becoming more intimately acquainted with

Gregory, of sounding his feelings concerning his speedy return to Rome, and of maintaining that long and difficult conflict with his irresolution and with the opposition of the cardinals, which, as we shall see, had to be encountered before the great exodus could be accomplished. She laboured night and day towards this end. Among her published prayers there is one, designated "a prayer made at Avignon," in which she dedicates herself afresh to the service of God, and pours forth her heart in sorrowful pleadings for her country and for all mankind. She prays also for Gregory : " I implore thy boundless mercy, Lord, for thy bride, the Church, and I beseech thee to enlighten thy vicar on earth, that he may know thy will, and love and obey it. Give him, my God, a new heart ; increase thy grace in him ; make him strong to bear the standard of the holy cross, and dispose him to carry to the infidels the treasures of thy mercy, which we have received through the passion of the spotless Lamb. Change the hearts of the people who desire war, and give us peace, that we perish not."

The ambassadors arrived at last. Catharine's heart beat high with hope, but only for a moment ; she perceived at the first glance that these were the ambassadors only of the Eight of War, and not of the republic of Florence. The Pope had given her full powers to treat on behalf of the Church, and the Eight of War had engaged to support her efforts, and ratify such terms as she should approve. She hastened, therefore, to meet them, and, with a smiling face, congratulated them on their arrival. They received her coldly. Cavaliere Strozzi, speaking for all, said : " We have come to confer with the holy father ; we have received no power whatever to treat with you ;" and they turned

their backs on her. Catharine retired to her secret chamber in the absent cardinal's palace. The weakness of her
womanhood triumphed for a moment over the courage of
that robust and heroic spirit, and she wept bitterly. But
she resorted, as was her wont, to earnest prayer, and arose
from her knees strengthened to prolong the struggle. The
letter which she wrote that evening to Buonaccorso di Lapo,
a powerful citizen of Florence, is full of sadness: "I have
not been able to confer with your ambassadors, as you
promised me. You are using strange methods to obtain
peace : this affair will never be rightly managed except by
true servants of God, freed from self-love and ambition.
I have done, and will do all I can, even to death." The
negotiations between the ambassadors and the Pope had no
result, except to postpone the conclusion of peace, and the
former returned to Florence.

Catharine continued to have frequent audiences with
Gregory, and with true womanly tact she availed herself
of these in order to awaken his conscience to a sense of his
responsibility to his Italian subjects and of the necessity of
his return to Rome.

Gregory was a weak and irresolute man. The morality
of his life has never been impugned. He was naturally
inclined to good, and, although surrounded on all sides
by an atmosphere of moral turpitude, he maintained a
blameless life ; but he was no hero; he had but little of
that in him which Catharine so much admired in the
noblest of her countrymen, the *virility*, the power of self-
sacrifice and endurance, of which she so frequently makes
mention in her letters. He was born in France, and had
never been in Italy ; he loved his native land, though

not exactly as a patriot loves his country ; he enjoyed his beautiful residence at Avignon, and yielded to the enervating influences of the luxury and magnificence which surrounded him. The scandalous life of some of the cardinals and other prelates gave him pain, but he avoided as much as possible the knowledge and mention of it. It was not in him to rebuke or restrain the excesses of his Court, although he never by his acts or words encouraged or made light of the prevailing laxity of morals ; he led a life of ease and enjoyment, forming at times good resolutions, and capable even of enthusiasm when a noble example was for a moment presented to him.

In order to reach the apartments of Gregory, Catharine had to pass, with Raymond, through a suite of state rooms, unparalleled, it was said, in the whole world for magnificence. From the windows they looked out upon a wide expanse of undulating country, watered by the Rhone and the Durance, studded with lordly castles and bounded by the mountains of Beaucaire, and by the hills of Vauclause and the distant Alps. Masterpieces of art arrested the eye at every step. There were rare manuscripts and gorgeously illuminated missals, lying open upon tables of inlaid marbles, or on desks of carved oak and ebony. Gregory took pleasure in showing his treasures to his Italian visitors. One day Catharine remained for a long time apparently engrossed in the study of one of these volumes. Gregory had been standing, alone and silent by her side ; at last he said, " It is here that I find repose for my soul, in study, and in the contemplation of nature." She raised her head, looked as it were into his soul, and, in a tone of inspiration, said to him, " In the name of God, and for the fulfilment of duty, you will close the gates of this magnificent palace, you will turn your back on this beautiful country, and set out for Rome, where you will be amidst ruins, tumults, and malaria fever."[1] Gregory's soul was just sufficiently highly tuned to accept this call and to prepare himself for martyrdom ; although he did so with many sighs.

But the moment that it became known that a serious impression had been made on the Pope in regard to this question, an organized and determined opposition commenced. Of the twenty-seven cardinals present at Avignon, three were Italian, one was Spanish, and twenty-three were French. The French cardinals abhorred the idea of banishment from their native land, and still more of the correction of their immoral lives which such a step, they instinctively felt, would render at least expedient. All the associations of Avignon were dear to them, and Italy seemed full of vague horrors. Even the Italian cardinals showed little loyalty towards their country, and increased the alarm of the others by their report of the tumultuous and revengeful character of their countrymen. A rumour was set afloat, carefully kept alive, and often repeated in the presence of Gregory, that a secret plot had been formed at Rome, in connection with the revolted cities of the League, to bring the Pope to Ostia and there to have him poisoned. Gregory's health was feeble, and but for the good Dr. Francis (Francesco), the Italian physician of the Court, he would have been made

---

[1] A *résumé* of the conversations of Catharine and Gregory was found among the papers of Raymond in the archives of the Dominicans at Siena. Others of their conversations, and some of her prayers, were also written down by Petra, the Pope's stenographer, the same who took down the depositions of Friars Thomas and Bartholomew.

to believe that the climate of Rome was certain death to every Frenchman. The personal hatred of Catharine felt by some of the cardinals is easily understood; for she made herself obnoxious to them, not only by her design to put an end to the "Babylonish captivity" of the papacy, but by her acute discernment of character, and her fidelity in rebuking vice. By Gregory's desire she addressed the assembled cardinals and prelates, several times, in the great hall of the Consistory; and curiosity attracted them to hear her, where better motives were wanting. All her companions seem to have been impressed by the almost awful authority with which she spoke on these occasions. Her soul was filled with a holy wrath against the abominations and vices which prevailed at Avignon, and with which the very air seemed to be impregnated; she had read the bitter and fiery remonstrances which St. Bridget, the Queen of Sweden, had addressed some ten years previously to Gregory, on the scandalous life of the clergy and the shameful example set by them. It appears that neither of these Christian ladies had any heart to speak softly or to prophesy smooth things, when they saw men given up to the cruelty of lust, and the weak and the poor entrapped and ruined to minister to their shameful pleasure; for the Queen of Sweden, as well as Catharine, used great plainness of speech. The former wrote: "Listen, Pope Gregory XI., to what the Lord God says to thee: He asks of thee why thou dost rebel against him, why thou dost neglect the poor, and give indecently of the spoils of earth to thy rich ones; for thy worldly Court is the ruin of the celestial Court, the Church. All who come within the influence of thy Court fall into the gehenna of perdition; and in these days, houses of ill-fame are more honoured than my holy Church." [1]

Catharine was requested one day by Gregory to speak to the Consistory on the subject of the Church. Looking round upon that magnificent Court, and on the faces of those men, which were far from bearing the impress of pure and saintly lives, she asked why she found in the Pontifical Court, in which all the virtues ought to flourish, nothing but the contagion of the most disgraceful vices. The Court remained silent, and Catharine waited for a reply. Gregory then asked how she had come to the knowledge of what went on in his Court, seeing she had been so short a time in Avignon, and lived so much apart. He then, amidst murmured approvals, attempted to soften the stern judgment which she had expressed. Catharine had been maintaining a humble posture before the Pope; but she "left that position," says Raymond, "and assumed an air of authority which astonished everyone." Standing erect, she raised her thin white hand to heaven, and said: "I declare, in the name of Almighty God, that I perceived more distinctly the horrors of the sins which are committed in this Court, while I was yet in my little room at Siena than even those do who are in the midst of these vices." "The Pope remained silent," says Raymond; "I could not overcome my surprise, and shall never forget the tone of authority with which Catharine spoke to that great audience." Even after this, Catharine, says Stephen, "frequently delivered most eloquent discourses as well as highly

---

[1] "Quia jam nunc magis veneratur lupanar quam sancta mater Ecclesia."—*Letters of St. Bridget.*

practical ones in the presence of Gregory and the cardinals, and there reigned so great an authority and so wonderful a grace in her lips that all declared, 'Never man spake like this woman ;' and many said, 'It is not a woman that speaks, but the Holy Spirit himself.'"

But there were in the Papal Court more subtle and dangerous antagonists than the prelates, who opposed the scheme of the return to Italy. These antagonists were the great ladies of the Court, the elegant leaders of fashion. "The most brilliant and beautiful of the women of Provence, attracted to the Court of Avignon, had established since the reign of Clement V. a real influence there—an influence, unfortunately, too often dangerous or criminal." Courtiers and ecclesiastics, seeking places and benefices, knew that their only chance of success lay in the personal favour of Madame Miramonde de Mauléon, or Cécile des Baux, or Enémonde de Bourbon, niece of Innocent VI., or Briande d'Agout, whose wit was as captivating as her beauty, or Lauretta di Sada, or Estéphanette de Romanin, Provençal poets and singers as well as graceful leaders at Court.[1] To one or other of these it was necessary to pay assiduous court in order to succeed in that world of pleasure and ambition. This "voluptuous academy" had been all in a flutter since the arrival of Catharine. At first the ladies left her unnoticed, or merely regarded her with languidly critical or insolent glances as she passed through the sumptuous corridors to the papal audience chamber. "She is very

---

[1] "Ces deux dames qui romansoyent promptement en toute sorte de rithme provensalle, les œuvres desquelles rendent ample témoignage de leur doctrine."—*Vies des plus Célèbres Poëtes Provençaux,* JEAN DE NOSTRADAMUS.

peculiar;" "she has no beauty to speak of;" "how odd is her dialect;" "it would be amusing to hear her conversations with the holy father." These and similar remarks expressed the slight estimation in which she was held by the Court ladies, who entirely failed to comprehend her character, motives, and mission. But the cardinals and others began to speak of Catharine as of one whose words carried weight. The brother of the King of France, the chivalrous Duke of Anjou, had come from Paris, at the instigation of the French King, to dissuade Gregory from leaving his native land, and to express the unwillingness of the French Government and Court to allow him to transfer the Papal Government to Rome. Gregory's reply to the duke was, "I beseech you, cousin, to speak with Catharine of Siena." The result of the conference of the duke with Catharine was that he became one of her most ardent disciples, that he accepted her view of the duty of the Pontiff to return to Italy, and that his soul became enflamed with the desire, inspired by her, of becoming the leader of the crusaders to the Holy Land. The good and gentle wife of the Duke of Anjou was out of health, and suffering greatly The moral atmosphere of Avignon did not please her, and her husband took her to his beautiful residence at Villeneuve, the Versailles of Avignon. The duchess had become enamoured of Catharine's character even before she had seen her, and she now earnestly entreated that she would pay her a visit at Villeneuve. Catharine gladly accepted the invitation, and remained many days there, enjoying the lovely country around, wandering in the woods or by the river, and spending many hours by the couch of her invalid friend. This honourable pair, the duke and duchess, became, in all sincerity, the humble followers of Christ. France had been exhausted by the long war with England, which as yet was not concluded. The Duke of Anjou now earnestly invited Catharine to go with him to Paris to see the King, Charles V., in order to persuade him to put an end to the war. Catharine respectfully but firmly declined. She did not recognize it to be a duty to undertake such a journey, and she had no desire to be further familiarized with the life of courts. These facts reached the ears of the ladies of Avignon, and created much excitement among them. This singular woman was beginning to exercise an influence more powerful than their own, though of a very different nature. "What could it mean? what shall our part be?" they asked among themselves. Obviously, they must set themselves to oppose the mad design of abolishing Avignon; for to withdraw the Sovereign Pontiff was to bring to an end the splendid world over which they reigned. This would not be a task of great difficulty; so much power and influence, so much skill and art would be brought to bear upon it. With the exquisite tact and management which belong to high-born ladies, they therefore set themselves to combat the influence of the *Popolana* of Siena, acting, however, in a manner wholly different from that of the prelates and ecclesiastical courtiers. They took Catharine under their protection, and patronized her with the sweetest aristocratic grace. They made religion the fashion; in place of balls and tournaments they instituted afternoon parties for pious conversation, edifying recitals, and penitential music. The Pope's sister, the affable and graceful Countess of Valentinois, was the leader of this organized assault upon the stern simplicity and moral fortitude of the Mantellata. She besought Catharine to pay her a visit in her own apartments in order that she might confer with her on those beautiful truths of which she had spoken in the hall of the Consistory; and at the close of their first interview she whispered in her ear, with that soft tone of voice which she believed the "mystics" assumed, "Ah! how happy should I be if I could assist at some of your exercises of piety. At what hours do you pray in the chapel?" Catharine had attended one of the liturgical festivals in the great basilica of the rock of the Domes, which perplexed her spirit and confused her senses, accustomed to the comparative simplicity of the offices of her own church of St. Dominic of Siena, and to the silence and poverty of her room at the Fullonica. The whole Court attended these high festivals. The Pope presided, robed in a cope of magnificent tissue of cloth of gold, of English manufacture; a silver mitre on his head, from which hung pendants of crimson silk; his feet, in green velvet slippers, resting upon a cushion also of green velvet, veined with gold; his hands in gloves of cloth of silver, embroidered with gold and pearls, and with the words Jesu and Marie worked upon the back in very fine emeralds. He was seated upon a Byzantine throne of white marble, under a daïs of crimson velvet. His deacon and sub-deacon stood by his side in robes of scarlet cloth covered with gold needlework; the cardinals were ranged in two lines, with their white mitres and scarlet copes, embroidered, as was also that of the Pope, with *fleurs de lis*, peacocks, and griffins, in gold and precious stones. The floor of the church was spread with rich Flemish carpets representing stories from the Bible, and from the roof hung great candelabra of gold and silver. The altar was draped with fine linen, embroidered with gold and emeralds. The light of the lamps was reflected from thousands of jewels, the perfumes of the most exquisite incense ascended from a hundred vases of massive silver, the harmonies of the choral liturgies rose and fell, and the whole formed an influence intoxicating to the senses and ravishing to the souls of those who believed such sacrifice to be really acceptable to God. Catharine preferred the more modest worship of the chapel attached to the residence allotted to her; and thither the Court ladies followed her for a short time, having gracefully bribed Stephen to inform them privately of the hours when Catharine might be found there absorbed in prayer. The gentle rustling of their silk robes did not disturb her collected spirit; but it was hoped that on rising to leave the chapel, she might be touched by the sight of the kneeling forms in remote corners of the sanctuary, bowed in beautiful penitence before the sculptured saints. Honest Father Raymond confesses himself that he was deceived by these delicate arts; he was "moved by such unexpected signs of grace;" he even expressed admiration of the beautiful costumes, the elegant sweeping trains, and graceful curtsies of the *grandes dames;* he also thought it well to expostulate with Catharine on her want of gratitude. "In truth, it is not good in you, dear mother, to be indifferent to such courtesy; all the great ladies make profound reverences to you when they meet you, and you turn away your head; when they approach you with amiable words about religion you reply roughly, 'we must first get out of the pit of hell and out of the grasp of the devil, and then we will speak of God;' and straightway you fly from their presence. I find it difficult to forgive you, above all, for the manner in which you received that beautiful lady the other day, who wished to entertain you at her house; you scarcely even looked at her. Is it well to treat your fellow-creatures thus?" Raymond, disposed, in his kindliness of heart, to think well of all, understood more imperfectly than Catharine the private character of many of those of whom he spoke. Her answer was almost rude : "Father, if you could know, as I do, the vileness which proceeds out of the beautiful mouths of these proud mistresses of the cardinals, you would vomit forth the remembrance of it."[1] The eyes of the indulgent confessor were rudely opened, however, by several proofs of petty malice on the part of the disappointed intriguers. Elys de Beaufort-Turenne, the vain and pretty niece of the Pope, seeing her uncle in profound meditation after an interview with Catharine, and suspecting that his thoughts were bent upon the return to Italy, conceived a desire to settle the question in a fashion of her own. She followed Catharine to the church, and, feigning a deep devotion, she prostrated herself by her side, and pierced her foot with a small stiletto; either she had not the courage to strike a more vital part, or her intention was limited to the infliction of pain. Catharine limped from the church in great agony, leaving the traces of the bleeding foot on the pavement, and continued lame for some time, although

---

1 "Quædam mulier quæ erat cujusdam magni prælati ecclesiæ concubina quum loqueretur cum ea . . . Si sensissetis fœtorem quem ego ex illa sentiebam dum loqueretur mihi, evomuissetis quidquid habuissetis in ventre."—S. Antoninus, *Chronicon.*

at the moment that the wound was inflicted she took no notice of it, but remained immovable in prayer.

Catharine continued, at the request of Gregory, to hold conferences in the hall of the Consistory. The study of the Scriptures had passed out of use at Avignon; but Catharine's discourses were invariably founded upon some portion of the holy Word. "Her insight and clearness of interpretation astonished the learned doctors," and in her ardent love of the truths of which she spoke, she would become almost unconscious of the presence of persons of authority in the Church, and her countenance would glow with joyful emotion, so that they looked upon her face "as it had been the face of an angel." Three prelates of very high rank, who had been absent from Avignon when Catharine arrived, came to Gregory and asked, " Holy Father, is this Catharine of Siena really as saintly as is pretended?" Gregory replied, "Truly I believe she is a saint." "If it please your Holiness, we will go and pay her a visit," they added " I think," answered the Pope, " you will be extremely edified." The following account of the interview is given by Stephen, in his letter written by request to be produced at the canonization of Catharine, and afterwards placed, with the other testimonies, in the *Amplissima Collectio* of Dom Martene. " Now coming to our house towards nine o'clock, the prelates knocked at ou r door. It was in summer. I ran to open to them. ' Give Catharine notice,' they said, ' that we wish to speak to her.' Immediately the Blessed came down, with Friar John (of Cambridge) and several other friends. The prelates bade her be seated. She sat down beside them on the terrace. Then they began speaking to her in a haughty tone and with biting words, endeavouring to irritate or wound her. 'We come from our lord the Pope,' they said, 'and we wish to know whether the Florentines did actually send you to him as is pretended. If they did send you, it proves that they have not a man among them of sufficient ability to treat of such important business with so great a potentate. If they did not send you, we are amazed that an insignificant little woman such as you should presume to converse with his Holiness on so high an affair.'[1] Catharine, always calm, answered them humbly, but in a manner which clearly excited their surprise. After she had fully satisfied them on this point they proposed to her some very difficult and subtle questions, especially on the subject of her own intimate converse with heaven, asking her to explain the meaning of the apostle's words when he declares that Satan transforms himself into an angel of light, and desiring to know how she could prove that her own revelations were not delusions of the demon. The conference lasted till late in the night, and I was witness of it. Catharine spoke with marvellous prudence and wisdom. Friar John Tantucci, who was a doctor of theology of Cambridge, often desired to reply for Catharine; but, in spite of his learning, the prelates were so skilful that they contrived to beat him in argument, and at last said to him, 'You should be ashamed to argue so in our presence; let *her* reply; she satisfies us better than you do.' One of the prelates was an archbishop of the Minor Friars, a hard

---

1 "Si vero non te miserunt, valde miramur, cum tu sis vilis fe mella, quia præsumis de tanta materia loqui cum domino nostro Papa."—Dom Martene.

man, who disputed with a pharisaical pride; he would not accept in good faith what Catharine said, and wrested her words. The two others finally turned upon him, and said: 'Why question her any longer? She has answered all these things more clearly than any doctor among us could have done.' Then the dispute came to be between these two and the archbishop. At last they withdrew, and reported to the Pope that they had never found so humble and enlightened a soul. But Gregory, when he learned the next morning how the prelates had treated Catharine, was extremely pained and mortified, and sent an apology to her, assuring her that the prelates had acted entirely on their own initiative, and that he had not given them any kind of commission to do what they had done, and recommending her to refuse to see them if they should come again. In the evening, Master Francis, the Pope's physician, said to me, 'Do you know who those prelates are?' 'No,' I replied. 'Well,' said he, 'know, that if the learning of these three were put in one scale of the balance, and that of the whole Roman Church in the other, the acquirements of these three would outweigh the others; and if they had not found Catharine so solid in knowledge and wisdom it would have been the worse for her.'"

Catharine was yet to be further tried by the irresolution of Gregory. The Cardinals revolted openly against the scheme of the return to Italy. They cited as a precedent the conduct of Clement IV., who never undertook any important matter without taking the votes of the whole college of cardinals, and declared that Gregory was not justified in acting independently. They threatened vaguely a schism in the Church and a revolution at

Court. Catharine daily contested all their arguments with Gregory. "They tell you of the example of Clement IV.," she said; "but they say nothing of Urban V., who, when he became convinced that a certain course of action was right, never consulted anyone." Tried to the utmost by the weakness and vacillation of the Pontiff, whom, however, on account of his gentleness, she sincerely loved, as a mother loves a faltering and tempted son, she withdrew for a season from his presence, and was no longer seen in the vatican of the rock of the Domes. She entered into the secret presence of her Saviour, and her soul passed once more through that baptism of strong desire, of tears, and of passionate intercession, by the strength of which she ever achieved her wonderful conquests in the kingdom of grace, and over the souls of men with whom persuasion and argument had failed. In those solitary hours her gaze was fixed far beyond the present, and her heart embraced all the sorrows of earth, while, like the prophets of old, she prayed that the great deliverance might be hastened, and cried to him who is the Desire of all nations, "Even so, Lord Jesus, come quickly!"

Tormented with conflicting emotions, Gregory, who had noticed with pain her absence from the Court, again sent for her. She went to him at once. In a perturbed manner he asked of her "her opinion concerning his return to Rome," as though that opinion had never been expressed. Catharine maintained silence for a time, allowing Gregory to become more and more urgent in demanding her verdict on the subject. At last she humbly excused herself, saying that it did not become a poor ignorant woman like her to give advice to the

Sovereign Pontiff, who had around him so many able counsellors. Gregory moved uneasily in his chair, perplexed
as to her meaning, and beginning to tremble lest his best
adviser, his guardian angel,—disgusted with his pusillani-
mity,—should have forsaken him. He said, after a considerable pause, "Catharine, I do not ask you to give me
advice ; I ask you to declare to me the *will of God.*" Still
she continued her reserve : she had already declared to
him the will of God, and he had still hesitated to obey.
She understood when to speak, and when to keep silence :
she knew that to multiply words, even in the holiest cause,
is often to weaken the spiritual force which impels the soul
of man in the direction of that cause. At last Gregory
said : "I command you, in the name of obedience, to tell
me what is the will of God in this matter." She bowed her
head, and replied : "Who knows more perfectly the will
of God than your holiness, who has pledged himself by a
secret vow ?" At these words Gregory started, and remained silent with astonishment ; for he believed that no
one but himself knew that he had taken a vow when under
the influence of the letters of the Queen of Sweden, to return
to Rome. From that moment his mind was made up. He
now took Catharine fully into his confidence, and, with a
softened heart, entreated her advice on all the details of
the great undertaking. She counselled him to resort to a
" pious stratagem ; " to cease to speak of the great question
in the presence of the cardinals and Court, but to entrust
the needful preparations confidentially to the Duke of
Anjou, and other discreet and trusty servants. She advised that, having acted so as to allow the opposition to
subside, and having made all ready, he should suddenly

announce, in the most public and decided manner, his determination to start for Italy, and that he should take care that the briefest possible time should intervene between this announcement and his departure. Gregory accepted the advice and acted upon it.

Catharine had now accomplished her social mission, and with a deep sense of relief she prepared to return to her beloved home in Siena. But Gregory, who had now learned to doubt the force of his own resolutions, prayed her not to depart a single day before he himself set out for Italy. She therefore consented to remain. The interval was employed by her chiefly in correspondence concerning the crusade. She wrote several letters to Bernabos Visconti, hoping to turn the ill-applied energies of that fierce warrior in a direction in which they would at least cease to be a curse and a terror to his countrymen. She wrote again to the true-hearted Queen of Hungary, whose country was continually invaded by hordes of Turks. She also wrote to the King of France, pleading hard for peace with England, and representing to him the sufferings caused by war, to the aged, to women, and to children. She had some correspondence also of a more private nature. The mother of her friend and secretary, Stephen Maconi, had written to reproach him with the length of his absence from home. Catharine wrote in reply: "Take courage, dear lady; be patient, and do not distress yourself because I have kept him too long; I have watched over him well; for affection has made of us two but one, and all your interests are mine. I wish to do for him and for you all that I can, even to death. You, his mother, have borne him once; and I— I travail again in birth, every day, not for him only, but for you and all your family, offering to God without ceasing, and with tears and anguish, my strong desire for your salvation."

Lapa also complained of her beloved daughter's prolonged absence, and Catharine replied to her in a long letter, which appears to have been sent from Genoa on the return home from Avignon; in common with many others, it bears no date, and only an approximate date can be assigned to it : " If I have remained long, my beloved mother, it has been by the will of God, and not by my own, or by the will of man ; if anyone tells you to the contrary, he is mistaken ; for I tell you the truth.   I must follow the path which God indicates to me by his providence ; and you, my dear, sweet mother—you ought to be content, and not unwilling to suffer something for the honour of God . . . . Remember how you used to act when it was a question of our temporal interests, when your sons often took long journeys and were absent for a length of time on business, and in order to make money ; and now, when it is a question of the things which concern our eternal life, you pine so much, and tell me you will die if I do not soon come home; this is because you love the mortal part of me more than the immortal part."

The hour of the departure was at hand.   All was ready. The Pope's announcement of his determination had been made ; he had continued firm, in spite of the cry of dismay and grief which arose from the splendid circles which adorned that "earthly paradise," as the courtiers were pleased to call Avignon.   The severest trial which Gregory experienced was the opposition of his father, an aged man, who, when he heard of the determination formed by his son, waited for him at the door of his bedroom, and when he appeared, threw himself at his feet and clung to his knees, uttering a shriek which echoed through the whole palace. " Can it be," he cried, " that I shall never see again my own flesh and blood? How couldst thou deceive, not only thy country but thy own father. Thou art going to encounter unheard-of dangers! Thou shall not leave this palace, except over the body of thy father, slain with grief." But Gregory rose for a moment to the height of heroism : he gently raised his father and replied, solemnly, " God hath spoken : he will enable me to overcome all dangers and trials."

Catharine had negotiated, at the suggestion of Gregory, for the preparation of three galleys at Marseilles, without communicating the fact to anyone. On the 13th of September, 1376, the gates of the papal palace at Avignon were opened long before sunrise, and an unwonted excitement was seen to prevail; for on that day Gregory was to set out to restore the glory of the papacy to Rome. The people of Avignon stood in crowds around, mute and displeased. The Pope's favourite horse on which he rode forth, reared at the gate of the palace, and backed, to the risk of the rider's life. Three times it repeated this capricious performance ; and finally the pontifical grooms forced it back, with many curses, to its stall, and brought out another horse for his Holiness to ride. This was regarded as an extremely evil omen, but Gregory maintained his presence of mind and resolution. The details of this remarkable journey, this " Odyssey of the fourteenth century," have been preserved to us in the rhythmical account written by Peter Amély, a romantic Provençal singer, who held the post of chaplain to the Pope, and accompanied him on his journey. This account is quoted by De Malan in his " Life of St. Catharine." The poem is affected and prolix ; but a translation of portions of it will enable us to realize, better than the description given by any other chronicler, the temper of mind in which the exiles quitted France.

"On Tuesday, the 13th of September, Gregory XI. left the palace, with the cardinals, mounted on white horses sumptuously caparisoned. Chariots followed, loaded with treasure ; then came the chaplains and domestic servants of the Pope, and the carriages of the cardinals and of the suite. Armed knights, with equerries, soldiers, and valets, headed and followed up the rear of the *cortége* which traversed the sorrowing city. We reached Orgon, an arid and stony district, where vegetation is scanty. We spent the first night in this uncomfortable abode. . . . On Wednesday we arrived, shortly before sunset, at the royal city of Aix. There everything pleased the eye : the beauty of the country around, the splendour of the palaces, and the hilarity of the citizens, who came out in crowds to meet the Prince of the Apostles. The aged bishop of Aix, accompanied by his numerous clergy, came in procession to receive the Sovereign Pontiff, whom they conducted through the streets, which were carpeted with bright-coloured silk fabrics, and thickly strewed with flowers. On Friday, after crossing a chain of rugged hills, we halted a few hours at Trets, where a sumptuous repast was prepared for us. We continued our course, and spent the night at Saint-Maximin. . . . On Saturday we arrived, by a rough and rocky road, at Auriol, a little town picturesquely situated in a fertile country of corn and vines. Towards evening, as we pursued our way, an immense and rejoicing crowd which met us, carrying torches and banners, and accompanied by music and singing, announced that we were approaching Marseilles. Alas! we began already to be tormented by the cruel heat of the south, which was made more suffocating by the pressure of the multitudes of people. . . . The next morning the north wind, however, was blowing freshly, and the gentle Pontiff came forth from the matin service in the abbey of St. Victor, and entered the magnificent galley which was waiting for him. Ah! how was my heart torn at the thought of bidding adieu to my native land! Sighs and lamentations resounded on every side; all were sobbing; the Pontiff himself wept. The wind was favourable then; but what happened afterwards I must record."

This account of the voyage, narrated by the sentimental poet of Provence, enables us to realize the slowness and difficulty of travelling in those times, compared with the rapid transit possible in our own days, from country to country, and even from one hemisphere to another. The summer had been fine, but the autumn was peculiarly unfavourable for the expedition, and the faint hearts of the unwilling exiles almost failed before the voyage was half completed. A succession of storms, accompanied with thunder and lightning, and lowering skies, tried their spirits to the utmost, and delayed their passage. It seems hardly credible that this journey from Marseilles to Rome should have extended over three months, owing to the severe storms, frequent pauses, and prolonged delays while waiting for the vexed sea to become calm. "We set sail," continues Peter Amély, "amidst the lamentations of the Marseillais. At Saint-Nazaire we stopped and landed to dine, and embarked again. Towards evening the sky darkened, the wind howled, and a horrible tempest arose, which forced us to land again upon a desolate part of the coast, where there was not a single habitation. A pelting rain, thunder and lightning, and furious winds made us believe that death was at hand for us. We all huddled together, trembling and in consternation. But in a few hours the storm passed over, and a strong wind carried us rapidly into the harbour of Toulon. We encountered a second tempest, worse than the first, off the coast of Frejus. Even the mariners turned pale, and the passengers moaned, calling upon St. Cyriac. We ran rapidly, however, with the wind, past the Isle of St. Marguerite, and in the evening arrived in safety at Antibes, where we joyfully landed. On Thursday, October the 9th, the storm continued. We passed by Nice, and entered the sunny port of Villafranca with indescribable joy. We had suffered the utmost horrors of sea-sickness, and now fell like famished men upon the excellent viands prepared for us, and afterwards slept peacefully. On Friday we again set sail, although the sea was tempestuous. We had reached the point of Monaco, when the pilot declared that it would be dangerous to proceed, and we were compelled to put back to Villafranca. Before we regained that port the stern of the galley was broken, and the sails torn to pieces. The pontifical valets discharged all of the most valuable articles into the small boats. All was in confusion : one could hear nothing but the roaring of the waves, heartrending cries, and angry vociferations. Who can describe what we endured ? But the next day the sea was more calm. ' O lily of pontiffs ! ' we said, ' behold how the sun shines forth! All nature seems again to smile, and thy servants salute thee in the delicious city of Savona.'"

Catherine had parted from Gregory at Avignon, to pursue a route of her own, with her companions, to Toulon. Her journey was much more expeditious than that of the Pontiff: it was unimpeded by regrets, murmurings, or hesitations. She set out with a cheerful heart, and full of hope. Gregory had given her a hundred florins for the expense of the journey, to which the Duke of Anjou had added a hundred francs,—not a mean present in those days, even from a duke. She remained for two days at Toulon. She and her companions arrived there towards evening, when she immediately retired to her room to pray, as was her unvarying custom at the evening hour. "We had been careful," says Raymond, "to say nothing of her arrival in the town; but the very stones seemed to proclaim it." They had not been there an hour, when a numerous multitude of women gathered round the door of the inn, asking where the saint was who had come from the pontifical court. The hostler having confessed that she was there, it became impossible to keep back the crowd; for now men also came in great numbers, pressing round the circle of women, and desiring to see Catharine, if but for one moment. For from the secret heart of the poor, hungry multitudes arises again and again the protest that it is not by bread alone that man lives. The mass of men will strangely and strongly at times incline towards one whom they believe has dwelt in a peculiar manner in the presence of God, and who can impart some knowledge of that hidden well of living water for which humanity thirsts, even when apparently satisfied with the turgid fountains of the world's pleasures and interests. The foremost among the women pressed into the vestibule of the inn ; but Catharine remained concealed in her chamber. One of the women, who was very retiring and careworn in appearance, carried in her arms her sick baby, a pitiful object, but *her* treasure. She besought the friends of Catharine that she would take the infant in her arms and cure it; "for," she said, "she has power with God, and can heal diseases : she can restore to me my baby which is dying." The message was taken to Catharine, but she declined to undertake this, or to appear; for she dreaded the publicity of the occasion. But the entreaties and sobs of the poor mother, whose petitions were seconded by the other women, were too much for her compassionate heart : she came out of her chamber, and said, "Where is the little one ?" The mother pressed forward, and Catharine, full of pity, took the baby in her arms, and, pressing it to her breast, she prayed earnestly and with tears to him who said, "Suffer the little children to come unto me." From that moment the child revived, and the whole city was witness of its rapid return to health, and of the joy of the poor mother. The Bishop of Toulon, hearing of this event, sent for Raymond, and earnestly requested him to obtain for him an interview with Catharine.

Catharine arrived at Genoa, and there waited several days for Gregory. The papal galleys must needs stop at Genoa for water and repairs ; and she knew instinctively that the Pope would require to imbibe, when there, a fresh stock of courage and resolution. As the days passed on, and the vessels from Marseilles did not appear, fears began to visit her tried soul. She knew Gregory's weakness, and the sullen, unwilling spirit of many of the companions of his exile from France. The elements, too, had seemed to oppose themselves to the return to Rome; and she pictured to herself in imagination all that Gregory might have had to suffer, from the voyage and from the complainings of those around him, and dreaded lest the trial might be greater than his faltering courage could endure. In the collection made of Catharine's prayers, is one entitled, " A Prayer offered up at Genoa, when waiting for the Arrival of Gregory XI.," in which she beseeches that God will pardon all the weaknesses of the Pontiff; that he will deliver him from the timid counsels of those who would hold him back from the performance of duty, and inspire him with a true love for souls, and readiness to suffer all things for the welfare of the Church. It was thus that she waited, praying without ceasing for the consummation of that for which she had laboured, and which she believed to be in accordance with the will of God.

CHAPTER VII.

CATHARINE and her friends remained more than a month at
Genoa, at the house of an honourable lady named Orietta
Scott.   Stephen says, in his deposition : " We were nearly
all sick while there.   Neri di Landoccio fell ill the first.
He suffered dreadful pain ; he could neither lie in bed nor
stand up, but would crawl about on his hands and knees all
night when other people rested, and thus increased his pains.
When Catharine heard of it she was filled with compassion,
and ordered Father Raymond to call in the best medical
aid.   He promptly brought two skilful physicians, who prescribed for Neri, but he became no better."   Raymond says :
" We were all at dinner when the news came to us that
Neri was rather worse than better.   Stephen ceased to eat ;
he looked very sad, and, leaving the table, went straight
to Catharine's room.   He threw himself at her feet, and
with tears adjured her not to suffer his dear friend, who
had undertaken this journey for God and for her, to die far
from his family, and be buried in a strange city.   Catharine was deeply affected ; she said : ' If God wills, Stephen,
that your friend should thus early reap the reward of his
labours, you ought not to be afflicted, but rather to rejoice.'
But Stephen insisted : ' O dearest, kindest mother, hear
my request.   You *can* do it if you will ; you can obtain this

favour from God.' Catharine replied, with a look full of pity, 'I only exhorted you to conform to God's will. To-morrow, when I go to receive the Communion, remind me of your request, and I will pray to the Lord for Neri; and meanwhile do you pray without ceasing for his recovery.' Stephen did not fail to throw himself in her path as she went to the church, and said: 'Mother, I entreat you not to deceive my expectations.' Catharine remained an unusually long time in the church, in prayer. When she returned, she smiled on Stephen, who was waiting for her, and said, 'Be of good cheer, my son; you have obtained the favour you have sought.' Stephen, not quite able to believe for joy, eagerly asked, 'Will Neri get well ?' 'Undoubtedly he will,' Catharine replied. Stephen hastened to the bedside of his friend. He found the physicians there, who said, 'Although we had given up all hope, his symptoms have changed within the last hour, and we can now entertain hope of his recovery.'" In a few days Neri was quite well. But Stephen, worn out by his fatigues in nursing the patients, and by his anxiety about his beloved friend, was attacked by a violent fever. "As everyone loved him," says Raymond, "we resorted to him to try and console him, and all nursed him by turns." Stephen himself gave the following account of it: "Catharine came, with her companions, to pay me a visit, and asked me what I was suffering. I, quite delighted at her sweet presence, answered gaily, 'They *say* I am ill; but I do not know what it is.' She placed her hand on my forehead; and shaking her head and smiling, she said, 'Do you hear how this child answers me ?—They *say* that I am ill, but I do not know of what;—and he is in a violent fever !'

then she added, addressing me : ' But, Stephen, I do not allow you to be ill; you must get up and wait upon the others as before.' She then conversed with us about God, as usual, and as she was speaking I began to feel quite well. I interrupted her to tell them so, and they were all in astonishment, and very glad. I arose from my bed the same day, and I have enjoyed perfect health since that time."

We left speaking of the papal expedition at the moment of its arrival at Savona. After many delays the galleys bearing the exiles from Avignon entered the port of Genoa on the 13th of October. Catharine welcomed Gregory joyfully, but quickly perceived by his countenance that the conflict had been renewed between his better nature and his fears, the latter seconded by the influence of the cardinals. During the delay of ten days in Genoa, to which he was compelled by the continuance of foul weather and the violence of recurring storms, his courage was much tried, for alarming reports continued to arrive every day from Florence and the other revolted cities. Gregory had believed that the news of his return would have stirred up a strong reaction in his favour ; but the aggravated conduct of the cardinal-legates, who feared that their power would come to an end with the Pontiff's return, had further estranged the suffering people of Tuscany, and the signs of disloyalty and rebellion were thus increased rather than diminished. The astute courtiers who accompanied Gregory took advantage of these reports to unsettle the mind of the Pontiff; and but for the extraordinary determination and ardour of Catharine, there can be little doubt that they would have succeeded in inducing him to turn back. They dreaded her influence, and therefore, as soon

as possible after landing, they prevailed upon the Pope to
call a consistory, and in that consistory, Gregory had
actually confirmed the decision almost unanimously voted
by the cardinals, to return to Avignon.[1] The courtiers,
believing their triumph secure, began to boast of it openly,
as of a victory as beautiful as unexpected, when "the
resolute Mantellata interposed and audaciously confronted
in her own person alone, this torrent which threatened to
swallow up the great design for which she had toiled."
Gregory, surrounded by selfish and adverse counsellors,
vexed by reports of rebellion, sullenly received by the
Italian people, and deprived of all reliable human aid,
again sought to fortify himself by the counsels of Catharine. Catharine never came into his presence unasked,
nor did she volunteer advice; but she knew what had
passed, and remained in her own chamber, where, as ever,
praying to her Father in secret, she was again rewarded
openly by that Father who seeth in secret. Knowing
the jealousy of her influence felt by the cardinals
and courtiers, and that a violent opposition would probably now arise to any proposed conference with her,
Gregory paid a visit to her house in the night.[2] When
all the city slept, he knocked at her door, and entered,
unaccompanied, and wrapped in his cloak, to ask of her
this time not only wise counsels, but power, through
her prayers, to obey those counsels. The Lady Orietta
Scott, a faithful friend and disciple of Catharine, was
present at this interview, as were Father Raymond and

---

[1] Capecelatro, *Storia di S. Catarina da Siena*, Lib. v., p. 213.
[2] Tommaso Caffarini, *Supplemento ad Legend.*

others.   Catharine was true to her mission.   She insisted that at all costs, the Papacy must be re-established in Rome, and adjured Gregory to believe that the greater the perils and difficulties which he might even now have to encounter, the more ought he to feel himself called upon to be strong and to accept these things from the hand of God, as a discipline intended to elevate his own soul, and purge away all taint of weakness and egotism induced by the long residence amidst the luxury of the Western Babylon.   When the Pontiff took leave of her she remained sleepless, on her knees, pleading with Heaven until the morning.

Undaunted by the angry sea and howling winds, and apparently now calmly indifferent to the displeasure and murmurings of the courtiers, Gregory embarked at Genoa on the 29th of October, and set sail for Rome.

The poet, Pierre Amély, continues : " We set sail again on our perilous voyage.   After a short pause at Porto-Venere, where we had a most miserable dinner, we arrived the same evening at Leghorn, where the people received us amicably.   Here we passed the night.   O lion of the tribe of Judah ?   O pearl of pontiffs ! be of good courage, and appear before this ferocious and indomitable Tuscan people.   Show them the power of the keys !   Rebuke their audacity, and confound their pride. . . .

" Behold us at Porto-Pisano on the 6th of November. Is there no fear that we may fall victims to these most cruel Italians, who breathe only hate and fury ?   The ambassadors of Pisa and Lucca come down to the shore with magnificent presents ; but take care, O gentle Pontiff ! suffer not thyself to be seduced by their flattering words.   If they had not abjured their ancient faith, would they not have come to thy aid against the rebellious Florentines ? . . .

"Now we set sail from Piombino on the 16th of November, before the sun has risen. The evening falls upon us, calm and fair, as we reach the port of Hercules, where, after an excellent dinner, we retire to pleasant sleep. . . . But an unfriendly and violent wind blows on the morrow. . . . We are driven upon the isle of Elba. The prince of pastors seeks some rural oratory in which to offer up his prayers to Heaven; and here, behold, we find ourselves in a thick forest of olives. The storm prevents us fixing our tents. The Archbishop of Narbonne, the chief chamberlain of the Pontiff, and the Bishop of Charpentras, our great referee in difficulty, are desolated because they can find no shelter for the successor of St. Peter. O cruel sea, thou sparest none ! the holiest and the most powerful thou engulfest in the same wave with the most miserable Already, before we reached Genoa, hadst thou absorbed our most valuable property, and drowned our companion the Bishop of Luni ;[1] and now the Cardinal Lagery suffers most cruelly through thy furious agitations, and is obliged to be carried on shore on the shoulders of a country clown ! Gradually the tempest becomes so horrible that several of our galleys are capsized, and much of our wealth is engulfed. . . . On the 21st of November the Cardinal of Jugie, worn out by exposure and sickness, renders his soul to God. May the august Trinity reward him with the joys of Paradise for the favours he lavished upon his humble

---

"A cagion del mare grosso, si affogò, il vescovo di Luni, e si ruppero molti legni."—MURATORI, *Annali d'Italia*, Vol. xii., p. 593.

little servant, the poet Peter Amély, whom he admitted every day to dine at his table !

"At last the weather permits us to start for Porto-Ferraio, and we steer our course back to Piombino, where the people burst into acclamations of joy on seeing the gentle Pontiff safe and sound ; but their congratulations are sterile, for they bring us no presents. The next day we arrive at Orbitello, where the furious sea pitilessly rends the coast. The landing is perilous and difficult. The apostolic sub-deacon, who carries the crucifix before the pearl of pontiffs, is obliged to swim to shore. And what a bleak shore ! There my poor companions, nurtured until now in every delicacy, are obliged, alas ! to dine on pork, or on fricassée of those obscene frogs which deafen our ears with their croaking. We are deprived of wheaten bread, of good wine, and of cream ; moreover we are devoured by malaria. We are forced to leave our sick at Orbitello, and hurry out of this accursed land ; otherwise we should all be dead. The Pontiff humbly walks down to his galley, leaning on his stick ; for he also suffers. He is preceded by torch-bearers, to lighten the darkened atmosphere. We toil on through the stormy waves, and at last the high towers of the city of Corneto appear in sight. . . . Its streets are wide and handsome. In spite of its former disloyalty, which the jewel of pontiffs freely forgives, its inhabitants receive us with extraordinary enthusiasm. . . .

"On Tuesday, the 13th of January, 1377, we left Corneto, after a sojourn of five weeks. In the evening, the lily of the Papacy entered his galley, and passed the night there, after making tender enquiries concerning the health of each one of us. The physicians and astrologers of Avignon, who prophesied a fatal termination to our voyage, had apparently misread the constellations; for we sailed all night upon a tranquil sea, by the light of a brilliant moon, and wafted by a gentle breeze from the north. The morning of the following day we reached the mouth of the Tiber, and entered Ostia, a city with splendid ramparts, but sad and deserted. In the evening several venerable men, deputed by the Romans, arrived to offer assurances of their fidelity. The joy of these Envoys, on seeing the Pontiff, was such that the words died upon their lips. The people of Ostia, lighting torches, danced and clapped their hands in the streets, in a frenzy of delight. The following Friday the Pontiff rose in the night to celebrate Mass, and after long continuance in prayer, he took a few moments of sleep, and then arose and himself sounded the trumpet to awake us all. We were then rowed up the Tiber by powerful oarsmen. We sang praises to God as we went; but the Pontiff, who had shown signs of failing health, was suffering great pain during this transit, and our hearts were saddened by the sight of his pallid countenance." The fantastical Provençal poet concludes his account with the arrival of the Pope at St. Peter's. The return of Gregory to Rome has been described by several of the annalists of the Church; it forms also the subject of a fresco in one of the stanze of the Vatican, painted by Vasari, and sometimes attributed to Raphael.

The entrance into Rome was joyful and magnificent. According to the custom of the times, some hundreds of comedians (*istrioni*) attired in white, preceded the *cortége*. There were companies of dancers also, who performed graceful evolutions and solemn dances, to the sound of stately music. The whole population came forth to meet the Pontiff; the senators and councillors of Rome advancing at the head of the expectant crowd. The people, dressed in holyday attire, as if for a high festival, rent the air with cries of "Viva il Pontefice! Viva Gregorio!" Joy and sympathy were written on every face. The excitement increased as the procession advanced towards St. Peter's. The people knew not how sufficiently to express their gladness and the glow of their affection towards the Pontiff as he passed. They stretched forth their arms towards him; they kneeled and kissed the earth which he had trodden; men and women wept for joy, and little children wept also through sympathy, though ignorant of the cause for which they wept. The roofs of the houses were covered with spectators, and every window was filled with eager and joyous faces. The streets were laid with crimson carpets and silken stuffs contributed by the richer citizens. Winter flowers were profusely scattered on the Pontiff's path, and rained down upon him from the windows and housetops. The air was filled with the sounds of triumphal music, of songs and anthems of praise; and the ringing of the bells from all the churches and campaniles mingled with the joyful acclamations of the people.

But in this triumphal procession into the imperial city on this glad day, there was one figure wanting—that of her who had inspired the undertaking now consummated. Catharine had never failed to be by Gregory's side in times of trouble or wavering purpose; but at this moment of triumph and congratulation she was absent. Alone, in her humble little room at Siena, she was silently gathering her forces for the future. She knew that a difficult task awaited Gregory, after the first joyous moments of his reception in Rome. Public triumphs are brief; but evils which have struck deep roots in a nation can only be eradicated by long and patient effort.

This outburst of popular rejoicing was the expression of a long-cherished hope. The Roman people had suffered much during the desertion, for seventy years, of their supreme bishops. They had cherished the memory of their past greatness, in the midst of their misfortunes; and they now dreamed of a return to their ancient glory. The population had enormously diminished; languor and depression had entered into all the business and social life of the people. There was little nobility of character or example among them, and much corruption of morals. Many of the ancient monuments were destroyed. The basilicas and churches were in ruins, and the services of religion were neglected.

Petrarch, in one of his letters to the Popes of Avignon, thus personifies Rome abandoned by the Pontiffs: "I saw waiting at the gate of thy palace, O Pontiff of Avignon, a venerable matron whom I seemed to recognize; and yet I did not dare to pronounce her name. Her countenance was sorrowful; her garments were poor and neglected; yet there shone in her an ineffable majesty; most noble were her features and bearing, and her speech was that of one long accustomed to rule imperially. The greatness of her soul beamed through the thick veil of sadness which enveloped her. I asked at last her name, and she murmured it forth. It reached me through the void, in the midst of sobs; it was Roma!"[1]

---

[1] Petrarch's "Epistles," *Ad Bened. Pontif.*

Gregory looked upon the desolated city with fear and anxiety, for he saw how great were the hopes which had been awakened by his return, and how difficult the task before him. His was not the spirit to grapple with so serious an enterprise; moreover, the mortal disease which caused his death fourteen months later, already had its hand upon him; and physical suffering and languor were added to his natural indolence of disposition. Catharine now urged him, with all her might, to set about the reforms which she saw to be the only salvation for the Church. She warned him especially concerning the election of new cardinals and the promotion of ecclesiastics of different ranks. "I write to you, father, in the name and in the power of Christ crucified. In his name I adjure you to see that the ministers you appoint be men of virtue and faith; that they preach repentance in that name, and that they be men who have first purified themselves." It is thus that she pleaded in her letters to Gregory after his return to Rome. "Alas! father," she writes, "do you not see that so far from being men of virtue, these priests and monks run greedily after all the delights of this world; that they seek riches and place and honours, with open and indecent avidity; that they who ought to be wholesome plants planted in the garden of the Lord, are but fœtid weeds, full of impurity, giving forth poisonous odours. Do thou, father, as an instrument in God's hand, put away all timidity and all spirit of negligence, and with solicitude do all that thou canst; thus shalt thou be the true minister of God; thus shalt thou fulfil the will of God, and the desire of his servants who are dying for grief in seeing such offences against our

Creator, and such trampling under foot of the blood of the Son of God. Forgive my presumption, holy father; my sorrow pleads my excuse. Be ready to give thy life for Christ crucified. Determine to uproot vice, and to plant virtue." In another letter, taking a severer tone, she tells the Pontiff that it were better to give up the keys of St. Peter than that the Church should be ruled by one who hesitates to extirpate vice. "God demands that justice shall be executed on those who devour and destroy the holy Church. Since he hath given you authority over the Church, and you have accepted that authority, you are bound to make use of your power; and if you make not use of it, it would be better—more for the honour of God and the health of your own soul—that you should abdicate the authority which you have accepted."

Political troubles continued, however, to distract the mind of Gregory from the moral and spiritual reforms to which Catharine ceaselessly urged him, and to which he might otherwise have sincerely directed such force as he possessed. Rebellious Florence continued to be the chief thorn in his side. Raymond's narrative continues: "When the Vicar of Christ was, through Catharine's influence, re-established at Rome, we all went back to Italy. Catharine then sent me to Rome, to lay before the holy father several projects for reforming the Church, which would have been very useful had they been carried out. During my sojourn in Rome, I was commanded by my Order to accept the charge of prior of a Roman convent; and thus it became impossible for me to return to Siena. Before leaving Tuscany, I had had an interview with Nicholas Soderini, (the citizen of Florence, before mentioned, who had continued true to Catharine and her principles). We had spoken of the affairs of the republic, and in particular of the ill-will of the Eight of War, who while pretending to desire peace, continually fomented rebellion. Soderini said, 'I assure you that the people of Florence and all the honest citizens desire peace ; but some obstinate spirits that govern us are a hindrance.' I asked if there was no remedy to be found for this, and he replied, 'Yes ; if some respectable citizen, taking deeply to heart the cause of God, could come to an understanding with some of the leaders of the Guelph party, and obtain the deposition from office of one or two of the worst of those who at present govern us, I think the public good might be secured.'

"I had been occupied several months in fulfilling my charge as prior and in preaching the word of God, when one Sunday morning an Envoy of the Pope came to inform me that his Holiness desired my presence at dinner. I obeyed, and after the repast the holy father said to me : 'I am told that if Catharine of Siena were to go to Florence, peace would be concluded.' I replied, 'Not only Catharine, but we all, holy father, are ready to serve you, and to suffer martyrdom if need be.' The holy father then said to me, 'I do not desire that *you*, Raymond, should go to Florence, because they would maltreat you ; but I wish that she should go, because she is a woman ; for, because she is a woman, and because of the great veneration they have for her character, they will take care not to harm her, and will listen to her advice. Consider what powers it is suitable to grant her, and present them to-morrow morning for my signature, that this business be not delayed.' I obeyed, and forwarded the bull of Gregory to Catharine, who promptly set out for Florence."

On this, her third visit to Florence, Catharine was destined to witness stormy scenes and to suffer much, through the difficulty of the attainment of the peace between the Florentines and the Church for which she had already so long laboured, and through the internal discords of the republic itself, for which she was to some extent unjustly held to be accountable. She, immediately on her arrival, obtained interviews with some of the leaders of the Guelph party, concerning the obstructive temper of the Eight of War, who had now become obnoxious to most of the good citizens of Florence by their evident ambition to establish themselves as permanent rulers of the State, at the expense of the true interests of the republic. "They deserved not to be called rulers, but *destroyers* of the commonwealth," says Antoninus, the Archbishop of Florence, already quoted, who wrote the chronicles of Florence from 1313 to 1459. The same chronicler says that Catharine counselled the deprivation of office of two or three citizens who were the main hindrance to the restoration of peace and good order; that the Guelph leaders called upon the *Priors of the City* (in whom was vested the power to elect the Council of War, and consequently to depose any member of it), to admonish the Eight of War. The admonition, and all arguments in favour of peace, were haughtily rejected, and the Priors proceeded to depose one of the Eight. They soon after proceeded to deprive of office two or three other citizens. "From this a double fire blazed forth; on the one side from the party of those deposed, and on the other from the Guelph party, who now, abandoning the principles of strict justice, proceeded to degrade from office certain citizens against whom they had some private grudge, and to take vengeance on the Ghibelline party and the Eight of War, who had for so long a time been in the ascendant, and had formerly banished many of the Guelphs." It soon became evident to Catharine that what had been begun with an honest purpose, and for the good of the commonwealth, was being turned to a base and evil end through the jealousies and desire of revenge existing in the rival factions in the State. She mourned over this, and denounced it openly. "She condemned especially," says Antoninus, "the hunting out of office and banishing of so many and such useful persons, and she protested against the wickedness of turning a judicial action, undertaken in order to obtain peace, into an intestine war to gratify their private hatred." She warned the Florentine leaders that if they continued to seek their own private interests thus, in place of the good of the commonwealth, and in doing so to commit such crimes as they now hesitated not to commit, "a time of such woe for Florence would shortly arrive as neither they nor their ancestors had ever yet experienced." Machiavelli records the history of that prolonged and fierce revolution in Florence, which caused Catharine's words to be remembered as prophetic.

The conflict between the Guelphs and Ghibellines became more fierce and more complicated every day. But in the midst of it the peace with the Church was finally concluded, and the ban removed from the city and its commerce. Of this I shall speak presently. The Guelph party was represented by the powerful families of the Albizzi and the Strozzi; that of the Ghibellines by the

Eight of War, the families of the Ricci and the Alberti, and by Salvestro dei Medici, the ancestor of the great Lorenzo dei Medici and of Pope Leo X. Salvestro was a man of very low origin, who had, by his skill in commerce, attained to great wealth and enormous credit. He was now elected gonfalonier of the city, and for a time guided his party successfully in its opposition to the Guelphs. The number and character of the citizens deprived of office and exiled, at the instigation of the Guelph nobles, were such as to excite displeasure even among the most moderate citizens, who refrained from taking part with either faction. The Ghibellines demanded the re-election and return of these deposed citizens. The demand was at first partially and hesitatingly granted. This was not enough to satisfy the long-cherished animosity of the Ghibellines, and the Guelphs felt instinctively that further and larger demands would follow, the denial of which would be the signal for civil war.

Everyone knew that the feud was not at an end; that the vanquished Guelphs would not submit to their defeat, nor the vanquishers be satisfied with their victory. The more cautious of the citizens made preparations for a revolution which they believed to be inevitable; they fortified their houses, and transported the more valuable of their effects into the churches and monasteries; the workshops remained closed, and the whole aspect of the city was one of mutual distrust and defiance. The people of Florence, like those of Siena, were divided into political corporations according to their arts or trades; the two great divisions being those of the Great Arts and the Inferior Arts. On this occasion the division of the

Great Arts favoured the Guelphs, and that of the Inferior Arts the Ghibellines, thus causing a most complete and serious antagonism of the elements of industrial and civil life, in preparation for the approaching revolutionary encounter. But, besides this antagonism there existed another, namely, between the lowest class of the citizens, who had no political existence, and the class to which they sold their services as labourers—the higher artisans and merchants belonging to the divisions of the Great and Inferior Arts. This lowest class of workpeople was very numerous, and had greatly increased during the last ten years. They worked for all the trades and arts, but had no voice in the State. The art or manufacture of wool, which had attained to the first importance in Florence, had in its service the greatest number of these workmen, *i.e.*, the wool-carders and weavers, who came to be distinguished as the fiercest and most discontented spirits of the time. These wool-carders and weavers had some just ground of complaint. Not only had they no political existence, but they seldom were able to obtain justice from the legal tribunal of the woollen manufacturers, when any complaint was brought to that tribunal either by employers or employed. Most naturally was this the case, for the members of that tribunal were drawn solely from the class of the employers, and those who had a representation in the State. "There were at Florence," says Sismondi, "men whom unceasing mechanical labour, extreme poverty, and entire dependence had deprived of the capacity for harbouring liberal sentiments; who were unable to deliberate except with a kind of intoxication of mind, nor to act except with a rude fury. These men received the name of the *Ciompi*, a corruption of

a name which had descended from the times of the tyrannical Duke of Athens." The Ciompi were chiefly recruited
from among the poor wool-carders. These men had been
watching their opportunity to seize upon those civil rights
which had not yet been granted to their pacific demand.
They were uneducated, and, for the most part, ignoble and
wretched. Led on by a wool-carder called Ronco, they
began deliberately to prepare for the work of pillage and
robbery. Salvestro dei Medici had the boldness to invite
these *sans-culottes* to his aid, believing them to be an
element which would serve the purposes of his party. He
afterwards experienced the truth of Machiavelli's words:
"There is no man bold enough to stir up a revolutionary
movement in a city who can, at his will, either curb the
movement at the point at which he desires to arrest it, or
guide it towards the object at which he aims."[1]

In a short time the whole city was under arms. The
Eight of War had an advantage in having the control of
the weapons at the service of the State. The mob armed
itself with every kind of rude implement which could be
used for the destruction of life or property. Arrests on
each side took place daily. Many attempts were made
by the Guelphs to admit through the city gates numbers
of armed peasants who waited outside and in the country
round, and who would have ranged themselves under the
leaders of that party. Quiet was partially restored for a
few days by the firm attitude of Louis Guicciardini, who
now held the office of Gonfalonier of Justice. He assembled the leaders of the Ciompi, with the Signory and the

---

[1] Machiavelli, *Storia Fior.*

Syndics of the Arts, in the Grand Piazza, and thus
addressed them: "The more we grant you, the more do
you increase your demands. You asked us to deprive the
captains of parties of their authority; we did so. You
wished that we should burn their counting-houses and
offices; we consented. You demanded that the exiles and
those deprived of office should be recalled and reinstated;
we permitted it. At your entreaty we have pardoned
those who have pillaged houses and robbed the churches;
to satisfy you we have sent several citizens into exile
who were obnoxious to you; to favour your party we
have restrained by ordinance the powers of the nobles.
Will your demands have no limit? You must see that we
bear much better our defeat than you your victory. Will
you, by your discords, bring this city, during peace, into
a slavery to which no external power, during war, has ever
been able to reduce her? For, know, that your victories
over your fellow-citizens will never produce anything
but slavery, and that the property of which you have
robbed us, and will rob us, will never yield anything
except poverty. Wherefore we command you, and, (if
the honour of this republic obliges us to use the word),
we implore you, to calm your spirits and to be content
with what we have done; or if it be needful that we grant
you yet something more, demand it in a manner becoming
to good citizens, and not by tumult and the show of armed
force." The syndics were much moved by this frank
address, and thanked the gonfalonier, promising him to
labour for the re-establishment of peace in the city. The
signory also at once prepared to make reforms and restore
order. But the wild spirits called up from the depths of

society by Salvestro dei Medici and other demagogues were not to be so easily conjured into peace.

The Ciompi foresaw, or imagined, punishments being prepared for *them* in particular, on account of all the crimes of which they had been guilty during the tumult, and exhorted each other to save their own lives by yet more audacious acts; "a great peril can only be escaped by a perilous path," they said. The insurgents consequently assembled the same evening in great numbers before the prison of San Piero Maggiore and demanded the release of the prisoners—their friends and fellow-workmen. They burnt to the ground the house of Guicciardini, the Gonfalonier of Justice, and seized the gonfalon, or standard of justice, which had been suspended from his windows. This revered standard, regarded by the Florentines with almost religious awe, was now carried by the mob to every place where they vented their fury. They marched from house to house, pillaging and burning, and often dedicating to ruin whole families on a word of accusation pronounced by a single enemy.

Catharine had had a house assigned to her when she came to Florence; it was near to San Giorgio, and belonged to the family of Canigiani, who were her friends and allies. Barduccio, who became one of her secretaries, was a member of this family; and it was during this visit to Florence that she first made his acquaintance. Here she remained, steadfast to her purpose, and endeavouring daily, and not without result, to influence the more sober of the citizens to act in such a way as to secure some good results when the present tribulations should have passed over. Stephen Maconi had preceded her to Florence, and had put in practice his native talent for oratory. "His facile and eloquent speeches had persuaded many citizens to remain in quietness" and wait their opportunity to avail themselves of a better spirit among the people.[1] But the torrent of revengeful feeling and popular disaffection was not yet to be driven back. News was brought to Catharine that the house of her friend Nicholas Soderini had been burnt to the ground and his family driven outside the gates. Not an hour had elapsed before the mob gathered round the house of the Canigiani. The account of what followed is given alike by Raymond, the Bollandists, Archbishop Antoninus, and Ammirato. The Eight of War had not forgotten how Catharine, by her conduct in the embassy to Avignon, and by her letters, had exposed the insincerity of their professions. They knew her to be the friend of Soderini, and that she had approved the deposition from office of one of their number. It was enough for them to give the slightest hint on these matters to the ruthless bands of insurgents ; the cry was quickly echoed that Catharine was an enemy to the public good and to the democratic party. The mob ran to the house of the Canigiani, and set fire to it. Catharine and her friends escaped, and accepted the offered hospitality of one kindly disposed citizen after another. But one house after another of those with whom she took refuge was attacked and pillaged and then set on fire, so that finally no one dared to receive her and her followers. The leaders of the insurgents pointed her

---

[1] Frigerio, *Vita di S. Catarina.*

out to the mob wherever she went, and she could not safely be seen in the streets. Cries were heard of "Where is that accursed woman ? Bring her out and burn her alive ! Cut her in pieces !" The citizens, who no longer dared to shelter her, begged her to depart from the city. "Catharine lost nothing of her ordinary tranquillity," says Raymond. "Confident of her own innocence, she rejoiced to suffer for the sake of the cause she had at heart." She encouraged her companions with more than her usual sweetness and cheerfulness of manner. Chased from every retreat, she retired into a deserted garden which she found, and there kneeling down, she poured out her soul in prayer before God. While she was thus engaged, there approached a band of the wool-carders of the quarter of San Giovanni. They were armed with halberds, swords, and clubs, and were crying out, "Where is the wicked woman ? Where is Catharine ?" Catharine heard, and joyfully came forward, ready for martyrdom. She went up to the leader of the furies, who was in advance of the rest, and was shouting the loudest, "Where is Catharine ?" He was brandishing a sword in his naked arms. She kneeled down before him and said, quietly and fearlessly, "I am Catharine. Do whatever God permits you to do to me; but in his name I forbid you to come near or to touch any one of these who are with me." At these words, the man who had threatened her seemed to lose his strength and dropped the point of his sword to the ground. "He seemed unable to bear her gaze. He ordered her to go away, to leave his presence."[1] But she, full of confi-

---

[1] "Expellebat eam a se, dicens, recede a me."—BOLLANDUS, *Acta Sanct.*

dence, replied, "I am very well here. Where would you have me to go? I am ready to die for Jesus Christ and for his people; that, indeed, is the end of all my desires. If you are charged to kill me, act fearlessly; here I am in your hands; and be assured that no harm will come to you from any of my friends." The man turned his face aside, that he might no longer meet her looks, and eventually slunk away, taking his followers with him. Catharine's disciples and friends gathered round her to congratulate her on her escape from so great a peril; but she, remaining on her knees, wept. Many feelings combined to wring from her those tears. She had not been accounted worthy, she thought, to suffer death for Christ's sake; she was filled also with pity for the poor creatures who had just departed, so possessed with the spirit of discord and hate. She regarded them as victims of an evil power, and remembered that by ignorance and suffering and the absence of all spiritual light they had been drawn into committing such acts of violence and revengefulness; and she prayed, " Father, forgive them, for they know not what they do." Her friends now seriously advised her to return to Siena; but she steadfastly refused to do so, saying, " God has commanded me not to quit the territory of the republic of Florence until the peace with the Church is concluded." They dared not longer oppose her; and two brave citizens, a tailor and his wife, concealed her for several days in their house. Some time after, however, Catharine consented to retire with her disciples to the monastery of Vallombrosa, near Florence. They went there on foot, and arrived in the evening at this cool and shadowy retreat among the hills, whence they returned a few weeks later to Florence.

It will now be necessary to go back to the month of March of that year, in order to trace the events connected with the Papacy. The efforts of Catharine to obtain the long-desired peace between Florence and the Church had begun to bear fruit in the midst of the internal troubles of the republic. She prevailed upon Gregory to moderate his demands, and gradually influenced a few of the leading citizens of Florence in favour of holding a congress to agree upon the conditions of peace. The King of France also wrote to Gregory, advising a meeting for arbitration. Bernabos Visconti, to the surprise of all, now also declared himself in favour of such a settlement. The reason for this became afterwards apparent. Bernabos had prevailed upon Gregory to agree that, in return for his mediation, he should receive a large portion of the eight hundred thousand florins which Gregory hoped to receive from the League of revolted cities, as restitution for the wrong done by them to the Church. It appears from the correspondence of Catharine that Bernabos had, on one occasion during her public career, deemed it worth his while to send ambassadors to treat with her. When, and for what purpose, this deputation was sent to Catharine it is not easy to ascertain; but it appears probable that it occurred at the time when the arbitration was proposed, and when the Duke of Milan appeared before the surprised world in his new character of a promoter of peace. His real motive, as we have seen, was avarice. He may very probably, however, have desired to establish relations with Catharine in order to be able the better to act for a time this part before the world. Her letters do not throw any light on his intentions. She merely replied with searching appeals to his conscience, and warnings to him to repent and live as a Christian. This was not at all what Bernabos asked or wanted of her, and the correspondence ceased.

The presence of the Pope in Italy tended greatly to facilitate the peace. He had already withdrawn many of the legates from the positions they had held as agents in governing; he had remitted the taxes imposed by them; his return to Italy was itself a guarantee of his desire for a good understanding with the republics; and he had already begun to win back in some degree the estranged affections of his subjects. Sarzana, in Liguria, was the place chosen for the meeting of the congress. The Pope sent there his plenipotentiary, the Cardinal de la Grange, Bishop of Amiens. Four ambassadors were sent from Florence and two from Naples, from the court of Queen Joanna. The Venetians and Genoese were also represented by chosen ambassadors, while the Duke of Milan was supposed to represent the interests of Lombardy. Difficulties arose concerning the enormous tribute demanded by the ambassadors of the Church. The arbitrators had almost reached a settlement of the question by arranging a partition of the burden among the various revolted cities, which would, it was hoped, be accepted by all, when the news reached the assembled congress of the death of Gregory. This event deferred the ratification of the peace for four months, during which period occurred the events of the Florentine revolution already described. In the course of the same period the great schism took place which divided Christendom, and which stands on the page of history as a scandal presented before the whole world by the Church which professed itself one and indivisible, governed by an infallible chief.

Raynaldus, in his "Ecclesiastical Annals," gives the character of Gregory XI.: "He was of an affectionate and domestic nature; he loved his own people and family; he yielded, indeed, too much to their wishes, especially in the matter of promotions. He was blameless in his private life, and pitiful and generous to the poor. Immediately on his return to Italy he remitted all the duties and taxes upon the carriage of corn, hay, wine, &c., which the legates had imposed on the people of Italy; and by a solemn decree he forbade the imposition in future of any such taxes on his subjects. He possessed a cultivated mind, and was a lover of learning and learned men. The anxieties and cares which he encountered on his return to Rome contributed, with the progress of an internal disease from which he had long suffered, to bring about his death at the age of sixty-seven."[1] He died at midnight on the 27th of March, 1378.

The death of Gregory, and the Schism which succeeded, sounded a truce for a season to all civil wars in Italy, and effected a great change in the public feeling throughout the nation towards the Church. The hatred which the Italians had felt towards the French who had seized on all the dignities and powers of the Church, had led them on to fight against the Church itself. After the death of Gregory, the same hatred urged the Italians to rally round his successor, an Italian. The pontiffs and prelates of Avignon had conspired against the liberties

---

[1] Raynaldus, *Annales Eccles.*, V. xvi., p. 555.

of Italy; their policy had been grasping and perfidious. They had filled the peninsula with their fierce mercenary bands of Bretons; they had bribed to submission the Queen of Naples and had secured the protection of the King of France. All this power was destroyed by the great Schism of the West. The Court of Rome was deprived henceforward of the support of the Ultramontanes. Its wealth, already dissipated in civil war, and now divided between two rival pontiffs, was no longer sufficient for the subsidizing of troops, nor for the keeping up of any luxurious state. The Italian Pontiff was at the mercy of the republics which his predecessors had endeavoured to crush. Happily for him, the animosity of these republics had vanished, together with the danger which they had incurred from the power and avarice of the Ultramontanes.[1]

On the 7th of April, the cardinals entered into conclave for the election of the new Pope. Eleven of the cardinals were French, one Spanish, and four Italian. A short residence in Italy had deepened the aversion of the French cardinals towards that country, and they only awaited the election of a new Pope in order, as they hoped, to re-conduct the Pontifical Court to Avignon. This was well known in Rome, and now produced great excitement. The people flocked round the Vatican on the day on which the doors were to be locked upon the cardinals in conclave. They essayed by clamour to obtain some influence over the deliberations. "We want a Roman," they cried, "a Roman, or at least an Italian." A great part of the crowd even rushed into the Vatican and clamoured at the doors

---

[1] Sismondi, "History of the Italian Republics," Vol. vii., Chap. l.

of the chamber where the cardinals were assembled. "These accursed Romans," says the French biographer of Gregory, "were armed, and refused to go out." After some hours of uproar, the Bishop of Marseilles prevailed upon the greater number of them to retire; forty or fifty, however, refused to do so, and continued to run about in all the corners of the building, under the pretence of seeing whether there were any armed men concealed, any points of egress, or means of communication with the outer world. This pretended search lasted an enormous time, while the multitudes outside continued to shout, "A Roman!—we must have a Roman!" The uneasiness of the cardinals increased the more on seeing the approach of a deputation from the Gonfaloniers and Municipal Council of Rome. They received the deputation in the little chapel of the Vatican. The chief Gonfalonier represented to the Sacred College how grievously the whole of Christendom had suffered by the absence of the Popes from Italy. The churches and buildings at Rome had fallen into ruin; there were several cardinals who had never in the whole course of their lives visited the churches whose titles they bore, and who had allowed them to be deserted, although they continued to be to themselves a source of income. The ecclesiastical States had been left a prey to venal, insolent, and arbitrary vicarious rulers; a universal revolt had been the consequence of this mode of government, so different from the just and careful administration of the early Church. It was by a most happy providence, they added, that the good Pope Gregory had come back to die in Rome, so that the Sacred College was forced to assemble in the ecclesiastical capital for the election of his successor. Hence it was most desirable that the wishes of the Romans, and of the Italians in general, should be considered on the momentous choice about to be made. The deputation retired to allow the cardinals to deliberate. They were presently again introduced, and Cardinal Corsini, Bishop of Florence, whose heart was nevertheless wholly with the Italians, replied in the name of the Sacred College, that he was astonished at the attempt made to influence a decision concerning which neither fear nor favour, nor the clamours of the people ought to have anything to do; and that the Holy Spirit alone by his inspiration would determine the choice. The deputation retired very ill-satisfied, and the people renewed their noise, and the cry, "Give us a Roman!" Despite of the firmness shown by the Bishop of Florence the popular clamour did influence the Sacred College. The people remembered that for three centuries the right of electing the Pope had belonged to them, and the cardinals very well knew that it would be a risk to ignore the past and to set aside entirely the wishes of the Romans. The French cardinals were divided into two parties concerning the election. Both parties desired a French Pope, but personal rivalries prevented them from agreeing as to whom they would elect. Seeing that they ran a risk, by their division, of giving a dangerous advantage to the Italians, the French cardinals at last agreed upon the Cardinal Archbishop of Bari. This cardinal was a Neapolitan by birth, and a subject of Queen Joanna, who had always favoured the French supremacy in Italy and the residence of the papacy at Avignon. He had also lived for several years at Avignon, whence it was hoped that his sympathies might have become already more enlisted on their side than on that of the Italians; as an Italian, he would satisfy the Italians; moreover, he had the reputation of being a sternly religious as well as a learned man. The hour came for collecting the suffrages. The cardinals being all seated, the Bishop of Florence, who was the senior cardinal, pronounced with a loud voice the name of the Cardinal of St. Peter's as the future Pope. The Cardinal of Limoges, the next in order, then arose and said : "The Cardinal of St. Peter's is unsuitable, because, being a Roman, it will appear as though the Sacred College had yielded to the clamours of the Romans; besides which, he is old and infirm. The Bishop of Florence is not eligible, because he comes from a city in revolt against the Church; Cardinal Orsini is a Roman, and is, besides, much too young. Thus the three Italians who might be considered eligible are rejected ; and, therefore, I propose the Cardinal Archbishop of Bari." All, with the exception of the Cardinal of Florence and the young Cardinal Orsini, who himself hoped to have been elected, voted for the Cardinal of Bari ; and he was canonically elected. The College, however, feared to announce to the people the fact that they had not elected a Roman ; all the more, because as a curious ancient custom allowed, the people claimed the right of pillaging the palace of the newly-elected Pope and carrying away his goods. The tumult of the impatient people continued to increase in and around the Vatican, while the Cardinals sat nervously on their chairs, each one afraid to propose the proclamation of the result of the election. Cardinal Orsini at last ran to a window, and beckoning to the people to be silent, he declared to them that the new Pope was elected. They clamorously demanded the name, and Orsini, in the midst of confusion replied, " Go to St. Peter's, and you will learn." The words St. Peter's, repeated by the crowd, gave rise to the belief that the Cardinal of St. Peter's was elected. The people were mad with joy, and the house of the old cardinal was stripped from top to bottom. Meanwhile the cardinals remained in the Vatican. The people returning from the sack of the house of the Cardinal of St. Peter's and finding the doors of the Vatican still closed, forced them and rushed in to do homage, they said, to the new Pope. The fear of the cardinals increased on seeing that the people were still in error as to who was the new Pope, and they dreaded to enlighten them. They were seized, in fact, with a panic, and endeavoured to escape, some by the great doors which the people had forced, and others through the chaplain's private rooms. The populace forced an entrance into the small chapel where the venerable and unambitious Tebaldeschi, Cardinal of St. Peter's, was sitting, quietly meditating on the passing events. They prostrated themselves before him as Pope, and asked his benediction. It was in vain that the aged cardinal replied, " I have not been elected ; I am not, and I do not wish to be Pope." His feeble voice was lost amidst the surrounding tumult, and those who heard the last words thought he was only modestly declaring that he had not desired election. The more the mistake gained ground, the more troubled and anxious became the cardinals. The greater part of them left the city that evening, and sought refuge in their country-houses, taking care only to spread the news as they quitted the gates that Cardinal Bari was the elected Pope. Bari, not less troubled than the rest, had concealed himself in a secret room in the Vatican, while the mob feasted upon the remains of the provisions which had been provided for the Conclave. The agitation calmed down a little; and the next morning the Bishop of Florence announced the facts concerning the election to the Gonfaloniers of the city assembled at the Capitol, and besought the Roman people to accept the new Pope. The people were not slow in reconciling themselves to the decision, and Cardinal Bari was publicly elected Pope, under the title of Urban VI. Urban pronounced his initiatory oration; the bells rang, and Te Deums were sung.

Urban was thus, manifestly, duly and legitimately elected; and although clamour had accompanied the process of election, yet the result was afterwards confirmed by all the cardinals, deliberately, and in the midst of calm and of popular contentment. But the character of Urban was, unfortunately, in some respects, ill suited for the emergencies of the times in which he was elevated to the papacy. He was altogether unlike his predecessor, Gregory XI. He was firm, stern, and uncompromising, indifferent to the luxuries, refinements, and even comforts of this life. He was determined to reform the Church; but his manner of advising and promoting reforms was rude and repelling, and sometimes unjust. His temper was his bane. He was proud, insolent, overbearing, and passionate. His manner continually offended and estranged those around him, even when his actions were praiseworthy and his intentions good. His dark olive complexion, quick glancing black eyes, and lean, nervous hands indicated the bilious and restless temperament referred to by papal biographers. "He was a man of great probity and virtue," says Muratori, "but wanting in humility. Instead of winning the affection of the cardinals and prelates, and thus labouring for the reform of the Church, he showed openly his detestation of their dissolute lives, their cupidity and luxury and simony. He besieged the palaces of some of them, and rudely introduced many novelties and reforms, very necessary in themselves, but so imposed as to show a contempt for the liberty of the persons on whom he imposed them." He quickly excited against himself, as well as against his reforms, the anger of the French cardinals, who "saw not only their libertinism but their liberty threatened."[1] Doubtless his proud and haughty manner was a hindrance to the success of his proposed reforms; yet it cannot be believed that the utmost of courtesy and gentleness would have availed to reconcile the French cardinals to a moral and self-denying life, or to avert the revolt which Catharine had long before foretold, when she said to Raymond, "As soon as the Pope shall attempt to reform the morals of the Church, you will see that the conduct of the clergy will be worse than that of the laity; they will rebel against the Holy See," &c. The gluttony of the high ecclesiastics had often been the object of the satirical attacks of Petrarch, and the cardinals could merrily quote at their feasts the classic denunciations of the poet; but Urban excited something more than mirth and laughter when he ordered that no more than a single dish was ever to be seen upon the table of any prelate of whatever rank, and when he

---

[1] Muratori, Vol. xii., p. 606.

himself set the example, holding to his own rule, even on occasions of the greatest hospitality. He endeavoured, in the same abrupt manner, to put a stop to simony; and he threatened with excommunication all prelates who should accept of any presents. He announced his intention never to leave Rome, and commanded the cardinals to make preparations for spending both their summers and winters there. The Gonfaloniers of Rome having formally petitioned him, on his election, according to custom, to create some new cardinals, he replied, in the presence of the Ultramontane cardinals: "I will not only make a *few* promotions, but I will make so many that henceforward the Italian cardinals shall always outnumber the foreigners in the Sacred College." Cardinal Robert of Geneva (the promoter of the massacre of Cesena) turned pale with anger and left the hall.[1] In the consistories Urban was far from being conciliatory. He interrupted the cardinals when they were speaking. "You have said enough," he would say to one. "Hold your tongue; you do not know what you are talking about," to another. He so far forgot himself as to call the high-spirited young Cardinal Orsini a fool;[2] and he accused the Cardinal de St. Marcel, in full consistory, of embezzling the money of the Church. "*You lie* like a true Calabrese," replied that fiery Frenchman, who resented the insult to himself as a gentleman and a prelate. Such amenities failed to promote harmony in the carrying out of the reforms.

---

[1] Tommaso di Acerno, "De Creatione Urbani VI."
[2] "Item cardinali de Ursinis dixit quod erat unus sotus."— TOMMASO DI ACERNO.

The French cardinals, alarmed at the threatened reforms, and disgusted with Urban, retired to the pleasant shades of Anagni, where they had made great preparations for spending the summer. It was the end of June, and the great heat had already begun to shake the nerves and aggravate the irritable tempers of many of the prelates. Urban quickly sent to recall some of the cardinals, who ought, he averred, to be by his side, to conduct the business of the Church. They declined to come. The bitterness on each side was increased by the refusal of Urban to pay back to Gaetano, Count of Fondi, a debt of 20,000 florins which he had lent to Gregory XI., and which Urban protested had been borrowed by Gregory for his private expenses, and not for the Church. Gaetano repaired to Anagni, to nurse his wrath by conferring with the cardinals, whom he further stirred up against Urban. The governor of the Castle of St. Angelo, in Rome, now refused any longer to obey the orders of Urban. It was evident that a revolt was imminent. Cardinal Robert of Geneva, who continued to retain some fierce Breton troops in his pay, marched them to Anagni, to be at the service of the cardinals. The Romans essayed to stop their crossing of the bridge of Salario, and were defeated by them with the loss of five hundred men. The cardinals, inflated by this triumph, hilariously informed Urban that they would never return to him, either in Rome or anywhere else, and patronizingly advised him to take to himself a coadjutor in the government who might instruct him in better modes of carrying out impossible reforms. When Urban angrily reproached them with their profligacy and with the misery they caused to the poor, (for he appears to have had a real sympathy with the humbler classes of the people), they replied, with the usual hypocritical cant, that " vices of the kind alluded to with such painful and unseemly plainness of speech by the Pontiff, had existed from the beginning of the world, and must always exist ;" that Moses, the great lawgiver, had wisely provided for and legislated for these evils, thus recognizing them as a perpetual necessity of human society ; that all men, and still more all women, were frail ; that it was utopian to pretend that immorality could be rooted out; that Christianity itself had never done anything towards purifying society of the evil indicated by the Pontiff; and that " those men and women who were generally considered to be saints would be seen to be, in fact, no better than others, could the secrets of their lives be known."

Catharine had made the acquaintance of Urban at Avignon, and had had several conversations with him during the journey to Marseilles. She understood already sufficiently the character of the man, and that his domineering will and the harshness of his manner might prove injurious to his influence, while his honesty, uprightness, and zeal would be powerful agencies in the carrying out of the reforms of the Church. Her letters to him, consequently, abound in gentle warnings, and earnest advice to "temper zeal with charity," to accept all contradiction and opposition with " tranquillity of heart," and to gather around him, above all, wise and Christian counsellors to aid him in his great work. At the same time she continued to denounce incessantly and with ever-increasing indignation the horrible immorality existing among the clergy, and to point out, as the only hope for humanity, a searching and a " scorching" repentance, a thorough reformation, and a return to the pure and simple preaching of Christ crucified, and to primitive simplicity of life and manners. Her letters, indeed, voluminous and lengthy as they are, presented to us in their collected form, give the impression not unfrequently of wearisome repetition, so constantly are the same thoughts and counsels reiterated, so consistently does the writer "know nothing among her fellow-men save Jesus Christ and him crucified," and so great is her fidelity and fearless persistency in reproving the wickedness of her times. In one of her letters she describes with a touch of scornful irony the appearance, in those days, of the "ministers of Christ," or those who ought to have been so. They presented the appearance of gay knights, with their plumed bonnets, their military boots and spurs, their jewelled swords, their silken sashes embroidered with gold, and their carefully curled hair, looking like worldly "gallants" rather than pastors of Christ's poor and forsaken flock. She declares that the knowledge of their impurities causes her soul to faint within her, and she longs for Christ to appear again and drive out with his inexorable scourge the profaners of his sanctuary.

Precisely at this time there lived in far-off England a stern monk who, in order to rebuke the luxury of the clergy in his own land, had adopted a life of extreme poverty, and who, lean and fasting, and dressed in a coarse garment, was going barefooted on his missions, preaching repentance, and carrying terror to the consciences of wicked professors and false teachers. He laid the wooden cross he carried over the backs of the vicious priests, fulminating terrible curses upon their cupidity, impurity, and pride, and beating them till they cried out for mercy. This monk was John Wycliffe, Catharine's contemporary. In their opposition to practical ungodliness, the spirit of the fiery reformer animated both.

The French cardinals, during their residence at Anagni, laboured to detach the four Italian cardinals from their allegiance to Urban. They entirely failed with Tebaldeschi, the old cardinal of St. Peter's ; but with the three others they so far succeeded as to obtain from them a declaration of neutrality. Tebaldeschi, alone remaining in Rome with Urban, died in the first week of August, declaring with his last breath that Urban had been duly elected. Urban was thus deprived of his last support in the Sacred College. The French cardinals, assured of the alliance of the King of France and the Queen of Naples, proclaimed unanimously, on the 9th of August, 1378, that the Holy See was vacant. They declared that Urban had been illegally elected under the intimidation of a mutinous populace, and they pronounced his election null. When this intelligence reached Urban, he at once elected twenty-nine new cardinals. The Frenchmen, hearing this, in the bitterness of their wrath and jealousy, called a consistory at Fondi, retired in conclave, and proceeded to the election of a new Pope. Their choice fell on Robert of Geneva, the instigator of the massacre of Cesena, whom they elevated to the papal throne on the 20th of September, with the title of Clement VII. Two days previously, *i.e.*, on the 18th of September, Catharine addressed a long letter to Urban, in which she urged him to accept with humility "all fatigues, calumnies, contempt, injuries, insults, injustices, and the loss of temporal good, and to seek the honour of God alone in the salvation of souls." Thus alone, and by the practice of Christ's precepts, she tells him, can the victory be gained by the true over the false leaders of the Church. "You know, father, that without enormous suffering and labour it will be impossible to attain to that for which we long, the reform of the Church by good, honest, and holy men. In bearing magnanimously the blows which will be brought to bear on you by those who wield the sword of schism, you will receive light, the light of truth; and the truth will save us, in the midst of the clouds and darkness of falsehood and schism. O my father! gird upon you the armour of God. Take the sword of truth; now is the time to draw it from its sheath, and to use it first against yourself, in banishing evil from your own soul, and then against the ministers of the Church. I say against yourself, father, because no one in this life is without sin, and reform must begin first in ourselves. Love of virtue must first flourish in ourselves before we can plant it in our neighbour. Make war against vice; and if you find you cannot change the hearts of men, (which God alone, making use of human agents, can do), at least, holy father, reject and drive far from you those whose lives are guilty and impure. Do not, at least, tolerate any longer acts of debauchery; I do not say immoral dispositions, because you cannot command men's wills, but you *can* forbid their acts. No more simony, no more excess of pleasures and luxury, no more gambling, no more buying and selling of that which belongs to the poor, no more merchandise of the holy things, and of the blood of Christ, no more priests and canons who, while they ought to be mirrors of virtue, are barterers and cheats, spreading all around them the contagion of their own lechery and impurity." She mourns for the Church and for the souls which are lost: "I am as one who has not where to lay her head; for wherever I turn I see the *inferno* of many iniquities, and the poison of egotism; and above all in' our city of Rome, which ought to be a holy place, we see a den of thieves; and all through the fault of these wicked pastors, who have never reproved sin, either in words or by their own lives. . . . Self-love will make men rise up against you, father; they will not endure your reproofs. Kindle in your breast, nevertheless, the fire of holy justice, and be fearless, for you have need of courage and a manly heart. 'If God be with us, who can be against us?' Rejoice, then, and be glad, for one day your joy will be full. After all these toils the true repose will come—the reformation of the Church. Though you should see yourself deserted by all, do not slacken your pace in this rugged path, but run all the more perseveringly, fortified by faith, guided by the light of truth, and upheld by constant prayer, and the companionship of the servants of God. . . . Seek out good men. Besides the Divine aid you need the aid of God's servants, who will counsel you with faith and sincerity, and without passion or self-seeking. It seems to me you are greatly in need, father, of such counsellors. I would fain no longer write, but speak with you; I would be on the field of battle by your side, bearing every trial, and combating till death for the truth, for the honour of the Lord, and for the reform of the Church. Pardon me if I have spoken too boldly. I crave your blessing."

It will be necessary to return for a moment to the

events of three months previously. Catharine had retired for a short time to Vallombrosa, near Florence. Towards the end of June she sent Friars Bartolommeo and John Tantucci to Rome with a letter to Urban, beseeching him to sign the treaty of peace with Florence which had been agreed upon at Sarzana. She entreated him not to give too much heed to the reports which might have reached him of the revolution in Florence, for which the mass of the people, she said, were not so much to blame as some furious and selfish spirits who had incited them to violence. Urban responded at once to her appeal, and that of the chief magistrates of Florence. He sent two legates from Rome, who pronounced solemnly the removal of the ban of excommunication from the republic; the churches were opened again, and new life and hope seemed at once to be communicated to the people of Florence, despite the still dark and troubled state of internal politics. Some weeks later the ratification of the treaty of peace, with a letter from the Pope, was received and read publicly before the assembled people in the great Piazza. Catharine's joy was unbounded. She wrote a letter to the magistrates of Siena, to be read to all her friends in that city, in which she called upon them to praise God, who had heard the prayers of his people. She had returned to Florence from Vallombrosa, and had strengthened by her presence and counsels her friends the Soderini family, the Canigiani, and others. The head of the family of the Canigiani had been deprived in the revolution of all the offices he had held; his house had been burned and his property confiscated. Young Barduccio Canigiani, who had fled from the burning house with his father and mother, became

from this time the constant companion and the secretary of
Catharine till her death. He returned with her to Siena
towards the end of July. She spent a part of the autumn
of 1378 in composing her book, the "Dialogue," much of
which Barduccio transcribed for her.

The revolution of the *Ciompi* was not finally subdued
until the end of August. The demands of the revolutionaries had continued to become more and more immoderate
and their conduct more tyrannical. Great numbers of the
citizens, of both the Guelph and the Ghibelline party,
retired from the scene of strife to the country, or to other
cities ; the priors of the Great and Inferior Arts followed this
example and went into voluntary exile, with the exception
of Acciamoli and Nero, two of the most courageous of those
who had laboured to restrain the popular frenzy. These
two met one day alone, in the Palazzo Pubblico, and realized
that they were the only remaining magistrates in the city.
They listened for a moment to the roar and tramp of the
multitude without, glanced round at the vacant offices
and deserted corridors, and then decided to place the keys
of the palace in the hands of the people, and take their
departure. The doors of the palace were now thrown
wide open, and the mob rushed in,—the triumphant mob
which had now got rid of all government and all laws,
and had seen the last of its magistrates depart. The evening before, this mob had elevated one of their own number, a wool-carder, to the office of Gonfalonier of Justice.
His name was Michael Lando. At this moment Michael
Lando appeared, uncombed and unwashed, his clothes
hanging in rags, and his feet and legs bare from the
knees. He rushed up the great stairs of the palace,

followed by the people; when he reached the audience chamber he turned and faced the multitude, and shouted, "This palace is yours, O sovereign people; this city is yours!—what is now your sovereign will?" The people with one voice replied that Lando must continue to be Gonfalonier of Justice, and establish a reformed government. Michael Lando was master of the people; he might at this moment have instituted an absolute government and made himself tyrant of Florence. His rule would have been as absolute as that of the Duke of Athens. But happily for the republic, Michael was a patriot: he sincerely loved liberty and his country. He set himself at once to re-establish order, and took stern means to make the laws respected and obeyed. He recalled and re-assembled the Syndics of the Arts, and proceeded to make new elections from the middle classes of the people. The new government was formed on the same principles as the former; but the men who composed it were for the most part new, and on the whole well chosen. The malcontents and disorderly mob were astonished; and, disappointed of their hoped-for plunder and license, they came in a threatening manner to the palace to complain. Michael told them plainly that their manner proved in itself that their demands were contrary to the laws; he commanded them at once to lay down their arms; for he would yield nothing to force. By his firmness during several weeks of conflict, he quelled the revolutionaries, and quietness was to some degree restored. Nicolas Soderini and other citizens were permitted to return. The Eight of War were the only members of the former government who had remained during this time in Florence. They had made

use of the people for their own ends, and were now determined to share with them the fruits of victory. They
opposed Lando in his schemes for reform, and proclaimed
one of their own number head of the government. But
Lando sent for them and informed them that the people
had won the right to govern themselves, and that the
counsels of the Eight were now no longer needed. He then
ordered them to leave the palace. " Thus those who had
let loose the passions of the populace in the hope of using
them in their own interests, were the first to be duped and
destroyed by their own guilty policy." [1]

---

[1] Machiavelli, Lib. iii., p. 240.

CHAPTER VIII.

CATHARINE was now thirty-one years of age. The drama of her life began to draw to its close. The evening of her days—if the term can be justly made use of in her case—was not peaceful. It passed in the midst of tumult: of storms overhead, and conflict within. She was not permitted to see her cherished hopes for the reformation of the Church in any but the feeblest manner fulfilled. Yet her faith did not fail. Like many others who have given themselves to God, with desire to be made his instruments in the working out of his merciful designs, she was led, step by step, into a larger sphere of aim and hope and action, than in the beginning of her career she had dreamed of. Like many other reformers, she at first hoped for a more quick return for her labours; but as the years went on, she learned, as they have learned, that God had greater designs in view than any which came within their human calculations; that her place in the great work was that of a pioneer; that after she had laboured, others would enter into the reward of her labours; and that, although the fields were already white to the harvest, the time of reaping was not yet. She learned to look, without loss of faith, even upon the deepening of the surrounding darkness, the prelude to the coming dawn. She acknowledged the necessity and the justice of great tribulations to be endured before peace could rest upon Zion.   She foresaw a further letting loose of the powers of hell before the arm of the Lord should be fully revealed for their destruction.   For " to the Lord one day is as a thousand years, and a thousand years as one day.   Therefore impatience was subdued, while hope remained in greater strength than before.   Though the shadows darkened on her earthly path, and the clouds gathered over her head as she advanced to her eternal rest, she continued firm in the faith that the time would come when the knowledge of the Lord should fill the whole earth. Her spiritual vision was fortified, and the horizon of her hopes extended.   Her writings, towards the close of her life, reveal the increasing yearning of her soul over her fellow men.   She dwelt upon the Lord's command to his disciples to " Go into all the world, and teach all nations," and to " preach the Gospel to every creature."   Hers was not a soul which could contentedly contemplate a " world lying in wickedness," a desert land unreclaimed for God, outside the boundaries of a privileged church or nation. No amount of wickedness appalled her into the belief that any sinners must be left to perish as outcasts from God and hope.   In her last exhortations to her friends she bade them hope for all ; " for there is no man on earth," she said, " however wicked, who may not repent and live."   But in order to win the dark and erring multitudes to the fold, the Church, which possessed the saving knowledge, the Church, which had been commissioned to evangelize the world, must first be purged, reformed, and revived ; and she held fast the belief that the day of purification would come for the Church, the spouse of Christ, "the antechamber of the kingdom of glory, the image of the celestial," as says St. Ambrose. She did not shrink from the scourging and mutilation which she foresaw to be in store for it. "God will absolutely purge his Church," she wrote to Urban, "whether you do your utmost or not to accomplish that reform for the promotion of which you are elevated to a position of so great dignity. He will not spare. He will cut away without fail all the rotten wood of this tree, and will plant it again in a manner of his own." There can be little doubt that, had she lived two centuries later, in the midst of the convulsion which rent Christendom, she would have stood firm on the side of evangelic truth, and joined her protest to that of the Reformers. We cannot doubt that she, who so feared and abhorred the temporal domination and worldly magnificence of the Church, would have hailed the time when the pride of ecclesiastical Rome should be laid low; and above all, that she would have rejoiced to see the word of God, unchained and free, taking wings, and flying to the ends of the earth, the priceless possession of the nations, bringing to each in their own tongue the glad tidings of salvation.

But Catharine never raised a protest, it may be said, against false doctrine. Her efforts were directed solely to moral reformation, her attacks being mainly aimed at the vices, worldliness, and ungodliness of the clergy. The same may be asserted concerning the earlier part of the career of almost all the great reformers of the succeeding centuries. Savonarola, Wycliffe, Huss, and Luther, each and all attacked in the first instance the immoral and irreligious life of the clergy, and denounced the practical abuses and corruptions of the Church.

Like St. John the Baptist, they at first preached, " prepare
ye the way of the Lord, make his paths straight ; " like him,
they called upon all men to repent and put away their sins,
in expectation of the salvation of the Lord which was at
hand.   Thus did Catharine.   She, like her countryman
Savonarola, clung firmly to the life which still remained
buried amidst corruption, in the heart of the ancient tree,
while she feared not to see the whole mass of the " rotten
wood " cut away.   It was only by degrees that the later
reformers were each led on to a wider view and a deeper insight, and were taught to perceive wherein the doctrine as
well as practice of the Church of Rome was based on error.
But Catharine's life was short ; her brief career was crowded
with active ministrations.   There was not room in it for
much that she might have achieved, spoken, and written, had
her life been prolonged ; nor perhaps was there pause
enough in her life to have made it possible for her to enter
upon the grave and laborious task of doctrinal controversy
and reform.   Her own example and teaching indicated,
however, a great simplicity of belief in her own case.   It
would be difficult to give a distinct answer to the question
as to what were her views or opinions on points of doctrine rejected by the reformed churches ; for in her works
there is found little or no allusion to many of these
points.   Probably if herself questioned as to her belief,
she would have replied, as a daughter of the Church, that
she held all that was taught by the Church.   Yet many
of these doctrines taught by the Roman Church appear
to have dropped out of her soul and life, so to speak ; or
rather, it may be said, the one pre-eminent truth which
she loved, above all other, so filled her soul that it over-

shadowed and eclipsed all other teachings. Her writings and discourses are permeated from first to last with that simple evangelic truth, that Jesus Christ the Son of God took upon himself our nature, and died and rose again for our redemption ; that by apprehending and loving this truth, by believing in and by loving him who thus loved us, we are saved, and by love are made conformable to him. "This," as she said to the Pisan, Albizi, "this is enough for you and me. This is the true science." In the matter of the dogmas concerning prayers for the dead, the invocation of saints, the "real presence," &c., it is difficult, nay, indeed, impossible, exactly to formulate her views, seeing that she rarely expressed herself in a positive manner on these subjects. Her written prayers are all, with one exception, addressed to the Father in Heaven, to Jesus Christ, and to the Eternal Spirit who helpeth our infirmities. The one exception is the prayer written on the feast of the Annunciation. In the first sentences of this she apostrophizes the Virgin Mary, enumerating her virtues, and setting these forth before her own soul as worthy of imitation. This apostrophe breaks off, however, suddenly into an address to God. "I contemplate, O Eternal! this supreme act of thine (the Incarnation), and perceive how thou hast regarded the dignity and glory of human nature. Love urged thee to create man. Love urged thee to redeem him. . . . Thy power and thy love have done all." . . .

Catharine, then, was not a reformer in the sense of being an opponent of erroneous doctrine, or a promulgator of a purer creed. The lessons to be derived from the study of her life do not lie in the direction thus indicated. It is something else which we learn from her. It is, more-

over, a useful and a holy lesson. She may have seen
more or less dimly the truth concerning the dogmas
above mentioned; but one truth she certainly saw
clearly; and she held with all her heart and soul and
strength to that truth. She shrank from no toil nor pain
nor sacrifice in order that she might find and win Christ,
and be found in him, and that thus she might bring
blessing to man. Her philosophy was based upon a deep
humility, and a conviction of the weakness and sinfulness
of man. Yet she perceived and realized withal,—that
which many who talk loudly of progress and the perfecti-
bility of the human race do not see,—the beauty and worth
of every human soul, even in the midst of its utmost
ignorance or bondage to sin. She loved, she prayed, she
endured. She fought a good fight; and she fell, in the
heat of the battle, vanquished, and yet a conqueror.

During the few months of comparative repose which
Catharine had enjoyed at Siena, after her return from
Florence, she completed her work, "The Dialogue," and
wrote many letters to Italian politicians and ecclesiastics,
in order to fortify them in their attachment to the cause of
Urban VI. She corresponded also unremittingly with
Urban concerning the reform of the Church.

Raymond's narrative continues: "The Sovereign Pontiff
Urban VI., who had become personally acquainted with
Catharine at Avignon, commanded me (in October, 1378)
to write to her, and beseech her to come to Rome, for he
desired her presence and support in the midst of the
troubles which surrounded him. I wrote to Catharine, who
replied to me thus: 'Father, several persons of Siena, and
many sisters of my order, think that I travel too much.

They are greatly scandalized by it, and say that a religious ought not to be ever on the wing. I do not think that these reproaches ought to trouble me, for I have never travelled except by the will of God, or that of the Sovereign Pontiff, and for the salvation of souls; but in order to avoid giving any cause of offence to my neighbours, I had resolved not to leave my home again. Nevertheless, if the holy father desires that I should go to Rome, his will, and not mine, must be done. In this case, will you be so good as to intimate to me his will in a written document, signed by himself, so that those who are offended at my travelling about, may know that I do not undertake this journey of my own initiative.' I communicated this reply to the Sovereign Pontiff, who gave me an order for Catharine to repair to Rome."

Catharine prepared for her departure without delay. More than forty persons accompanied her. The number would have been much greater had she not opposed the wishes of many in this respect. Great nobles of Siena besought her to suffer them to go with her on this, which seemed to them destined to be a momentous journey, to the capital of Christendom. Some few of these nobles did accompany her, on foot, and in the garb of poverty. Her mother, Alessia, Lysa, and Giovanna di Capo, were among the women of the group. Catharine invited these pilgrims to form an agreement to live in great simplicity and poverty while in Rome, putting their trust in divine providence. This she did, in order the more effectually to rebuke the luxury of the times. Catharine turned as she left her native city, and gazed long upon its loved walls and towers, the grassy slopes falling from its ramparts, and the winding roads and paths so familiar to her from childhood.   Offering up a prayer for the peace of her fellow-citizens, she turned her face towards Rome.   She never saw Siena again, for she died in Rome one year and four months from that time.   Perhaps she had some dim presentiment of the moral and spiritual martyrdom throug h which she was shortly to pass ; but her road was still upward and onward.   Like St. Paul, who thirteen centuries before had entered Rome, also to suffer and to die there, she " pressed forward toward the mark of the prize of her high calling in Christ Jesus."   Her thoughts seemed to dwell much at that time on the career and martyrdom of the great Apostle of the Gentiles.   In a prayer written soon after reaching Rome these words occur : " Eternal Father, thou didst send thy apostles as lights into the world. We are in greater need than ever before of such light ; raise up among us, we beseech thee, another Paul, to re-buke and revive us, and bring us light."   She constantly spoke of the martyrs.   In writing from Rome to Stephen, who had not accompanied her, she says : " The blood of the holy martyrs who so willingly gave their lives for him who is the Life, witnesses against our coldness, and cries to you and others to arise to the help of the holy Church ; " and again, " I walk in paths bedewed with the blood of the martyrs."   She and her companions reached Rome on the 28th October, 1378, shortly after the election of the anti-Pope Clement VII.   They took up their abode in a house in the street of Santa Chiara. Here Catharine established a simple rule of life for her numerous family, in order that the residence in Rome might prove useful to themselves and others. They had neither gold nor silver; but God provided for their few and simple wants. They had all things in common, following the example of the primitive Christians. She arranged that the women should each in turn charge themselves for one week with the task of providing for the necessities of the household, while the rest devoted themselves to work and to prayer. Alessia was placed in charge over all.

A few days after her arrival in Rome, Catharine received a message from Pope Urban, desiring that she would come to the Consistory, and speak before the assembled cardinals on the subject of the Church, and in particular on the Schism and the present troubles. She obeyed. "She spoke learnedly and at some length, exhorting all to constancy and firmness." She thus concluded: "God,—most reverend father,—is eternal wisdom and strength, and we, if we desire to be invincible, must put our confidence in him. What harm can come to him who, in Christ, is clothed with the vesture of divine fortitude? Whom do the blows of your enemies injure? Themselves only. Their arrows return upon their own breasts. Arise, then; be of good courage, father. Arise, and be of good courage, ye also, pastors, who surround the chief pastor. Enter into this conflict without fear. If God is with you, who can be against you? Unite yourselves with Christ, and fight, like men, for him. . . . . Yes, fight; but let your only weapons be repentance and prayer, virtue and love." When she had ceased speaking, Urban appeared full of wonder. He gave a brief *résumé* of her address, and then turned to the cardinals and said:

"How deeply blamable are we, brethren, when we give way to hesitation and fear. This poor humble woman confounds us. I call her poor and humble, not in contempt, but in allusion to the weakness of her sex.[1] It would be natural that she should be timid, even though *we* were of good heart; and see, whereas we are fearful, she is tranquil and fearless, and encourages us with her noble words. Does she not put us all to shame?" Then after a pause he added, with ardour and a radiant countenance, "What should Christ's Vicar fear, though the whole world were against him? Christ the Omnipotent is stronger than the world. He can never forsake his Church."

The Schismatics did wisely to choose Robert of Geneva as their leader. He was "the man of the Schism." He was related to several of the most powerful princely families in Europe. He was young, enterprising, and ambitious. He had not completed his thirty-sixth year when he was elected as Clement VII. He was, nevertheless, an experienced soldier, and well versed in all the intrigues of courts and factions. The wholesale massacre of the inhabitants of Cesena illustrated his indomitable will in the performance of whatever he had resolved upon. He feared not God, neither regarded man. He said openly, "Assuredly, I would not serve God if I did not find it profitable."[2] He was tall of stature, powerfully built, and very handsome; his manners were graceful

---

[1] "Questa donnicciuola ci confonde; donnicciuola dico, non per dispregio, ma per espressione della naturale fragilità muliebre."— RAYMOND, *Vita di S. Catarina,* Italian Version.

[2] "Certe non servirem Deo, si non faceret mihi bonum."— RINALDI, ii , 30.

and courtly, his appearance in public was commanding, and his dress always magnificent. He was lavish in expenditure, and by the profuseness of his gifts and bribes, he won many to his side. He was eloquent and self-possessed, and unscrupulous in the use of every art by which men win popularity.

Germany, Bohemia, Hungary, England, and almost the whole of Italy held to Urban; France, Spain, and Savoy were on the side of Clement. The English clergy gave as their reason for adhering to Urban that "a report had reached England that Clement was a man of blood." Queen Joanna of Naples had at first sent ambassadors to Urban to congratulate him on his election. She had replied to the earnest letters which Catharine had written to her from Siena, "the words of a saint will certainly not be lost upon me." But, under the influence of personal and political motives, she soon after declared herself openly on the side of Clement. The Clementines also had a footing in Rome itself. The strong castle of St. Angelo, which dominated the approaches to the Vatican, was commanded by a French ally of Clement, the Captain Rostagno. "There now began to be witnessed," says Muratori, "a series of monstrous scandals in the Church. Urban excommunicated Clement and his cardinals, while Clement, on his part, excommunicated Urban and his followers. The same benefices were bestowed on different persons by the rival popes, and each appointed his own bishop to every see which became vacant. Hence arose numberless private and public conflicts, strifes, and murders. The nobles espoused the side of one or the other as it best served their own interests. . . . Many of the adherents of Urban were arrested, executed, or banished by the Clementines, and similar injustices and outrages were perpetrated on the other side." Clement, however, possessed great resources, and was able to buy many adherents to his side, and to collect a large army of Bretons and Gascons; while Urban, among the ruins of Rome, found himself impoverished on all sides. He was obliged to make great sacrifices to procure the necessary resources for defence. He himself lived almost in poverty. He could not inhabit the Vatican, owing to its proximity to the castle of St. Angelo. He counselled the cardinals to give up every superfluity, in order to be able to contribute to the defence of the Church. On the advice of Catharine, he appointed a commission to negotiate the sale of a part of the domains of the Church; and the gold and silver chalices, crosses, and candelabra of the churches were changed into money.[1] "The Church," said Catharine, "has no need of perfumes, of incense, or of precious stones and gold. She needs courage and faith." In the same spirit she wrote to Urban concerning the reform of the Church (for she addressed several letters to him while in Rome, where he also was) : " I desire not that you should pause to direct your attention to the subject of vestments, and considerations of more or less importance of this nature; but that you should at once seek men who will act uprightly, and not with falseness or reserves; men who are above being seduced by flatteries or gold, and who will oppose vice and encourage virtue."

Catharine judged that the most necessary thing to be done for the healing of this hateful division was to win

---

1 Rinaldi, Anno 1380, N, 17.

France and Naples to the cause of Urban ; for without the support of these kingdoms the Schism could not continue. She constantly expressed her conviction to Urban that it was not Clement and his cardinals to whom attention should be directed, but rather to France and Naples. The vicinity of the kingdom of Naples to Rome would constantly endanger the peace and security of the Church, through the infection of the spirit of rebellion ; whereas the alliance of that kingdom would be the greatest support to the Pope. Catharine, therefore, applied all her energies to convince the conscience and win the heart of Joanna of Naples, and of Charles V. of France. Her correspondence with the former had created in her heart a strong desire to see that unhappy woman face to face. Not only did she desire to gain her as an adherent to Urban, but far more, it seems, did she wish to win that poor soul to Christ. Her letters to Joanna are numerous and long, and full of the most passionate and tender pleadings and warnings which one woman could address to another on matters vital to her present and eternal interests. Joanna was then more than fifty years of age; she still possessed great beauty and personal ascendency.[1] Her life had been an unhappy one. She had been crowned queen at the age of nineteen ; she had had four husbands ; but she had no child to succeed her. Her first husband was the young Andrea, brother of Ludwig, King of Hungary. The horrible tragedy of his death, occurring a short time after the marriage, created a great

---

[1] An old chronicle of Bologna says that Queen Joanna was a woman of great spirit and adventure, and that she could leap upon the back of a horse when it was in full gallop, and command it perfectly.

sensation in Europe.   The Court had gone for the summer to Aversa.   At midnight, September 18th, 1345, two messengers entered in haste the bedchamber of the queen and the prince, on the pretext that a revolution had broken out in Naples, which required the immediate return of Andrea.   The young prince arose in haste and followed the messengers, who strangled him in a gallery of the castle, and then threw his body from a window into the garden. It was supposed at first by those who found the corpse that he had accidentally fallen from the window, while wandering through the castle in the dark.   But the indifference of the queen, who remained alone in her chamber till the morning, and the known fact of an intrigue and suspicion of a secret alliance she had already formed with Prince Louis of Taranto, whom she afterwards married, were sufficient to convince most persons that she had connived at, if not instigated, the horrible deed.   The Neapolitans received her coldly ; Ludwig, King of Hungary, denounced her openly ; and her whole future life was a continual but unavailing attempt at flight from the pursuit of this haunting shadow, the dark deed of her youth.   Like our Mary Queen of Scots, she had, among historians, on one side ardent defenders and admirers, and on she other, severe judges and bitter enemies.   Her third husband was the Infanta of Spain, who separated himself from her, and her fourth was Otho, Duke of Brunswick, who survived her.   It was during her unpopularity in consequence of the suspicions attaching to her in connection with Andrea's death, that she fled to Provence, where, finding herself in great need of resources, she sold her large domains in that country to the Popes of Avignon.   Joanna appears not to have been unmoved by the ardent appeals of Catharine. Her heart was ill at ease, and there had been no peace for her in life since the tragedy of her youth. Catharine wrote to her again and again, dictating her letters on her knees, with strong crying and supplication to God for her unhappy sister. These letters spoke of pardon and perfect cleansing, of infinite love and holy peace. They were found, at the time of the collection of Catharine's letters, carefully sealed, and with evidence of having been much read. We are, however, left in the dark as to whether Queen Joanna ever opened her heart to the truths of which Catharine wrote, or whether she retained any memory of her words of love and hope, to console her in her own last dark hours. She died two years after Catharine's death. Charles Durazzo, cousin of the murdered Andrea, and nephew of Ludwig, King of Hungary, was the next heir to the kingdom of Naples ; but Joanna, afraid and jealous of the influence of that family, nominated as her successor, Louis, Duke of Anjou, of the royal family of France. Charles Durazzo, on receiving intelligence of this, set out from Hungary with a numerous army, and marched to Naples to defend his right of succession. After many manœuvres on both sides, a collision took place, in which Charles defeated the troops of the queen, and took her prisoner. She was imprisoned in the castle of San Felice, where she lingered many months. A few weeks before her death she sent to her friends and defenders the message, " think no more of me, except to make preparation for my funeral, and to pray for my soul." Charles Durazzo, hearing of the approach by sea of the Duke of Anjou with an army to release the queen, deemed it expedient to place that unhappy lady beyond all possibility of recovering her crown, and sent an assassin to the castle, who strangled Queen Joanna with a silken sash, thus causing her to die the death of Andrea.

But to return: Catharine had directed all her energies to win and confirm, in the first place, all the Italian powers who were wavering in their allegiance to Urban. Her reputation for saintliness and for singleness of purpose, and the love which the Italians generally bore for her, gave her great power in persuasion with her own countrymen. By her efforts mainly, the fidelity of Siena, Florence, Perugia, Bologna, and Venice was assured. The ambassadors, sent from these and other cities to congratulate Urban on his election, had not, for the most part, taken home a good report of their reception, or of the courtesy of the Pontiff. "How is it that the Pope makes so many enemies ?" it was asked. "It is not what he does," one ambassador replied, "but his manner of doing it, which gives offence." Malavolti, the father of the chronicler of Siena, was one of the ambassadors appointed by that city to congratulate Urban. The chronicler says that the stiffness and asperity which the Pontiff showed to his father and the other Sienese ambassadors "were intolerable, the more so because Urban was not of high birth, and had been elevated to the Papacy beyond his utmost hopes, and in spite of his sour and difficult temper." All the gracious kindness and unconquerable energy of Catharine, consequently only availed to ward off during the brief period of her own life the consequences of Urban's unchristian and unchastened temper. After her death he was continually at cross-purposes with those around him, and by his rude disposition contrived to estrange even his sincerest partisans. Yet his judgment of the state of the Church and the world in his day, was courageous and truthful. He was also stern with himself, if he was so with others; and his desire for the reformation of morals was strong and sincere.

Catharine, Princess of Sweden, daughter of the St. Bridget, the widowed Queen of Sweden, already mentioned, happened to be residing in Rome at this time. She bore a high reputation for wisdom and piety, and was beatified in the year 1398 by Boniface IX. Urban had perceived the strong yearning of heart which Catharine of Siena had to bring Queen Joanna to repentance and faith in Christ, as well as to win the support of the kingdom of Naples for himself. He conceived therefore the design of sending her, together with Catharine of Sweden, to the Court of Naples, on a mission both public and personal. Raymond says: "Our Catharine did not shrink from the charge it was intended to impose on her, and offered to go without delay; but the Princess of Sweden did not like to undertake the voyage, and refused in my very presence the mission that was proposed to her." "Our Catharine" paid a visit to the Swedish princess, in her humble retreat in the little monastery of the Clarissas in Rome. The first part of their interview was of a diplomatic nature. Catharine of Siena, full of zeal and courage, did not imagine that a woman of the race of the stern North could hesitate to obey the wish of the Pontiff, and become an ambassador to a Court with which she was already acquainted. But the Swedish princess hesitated, and after a short discussion of the proposed embassy, she began to speak of the experience which her longer life had given her (she was fifteen years older than Catharine), and of her knowledge of men. She recounted how she had been twice to Naples, to gather up there remembrances of her sainted mother; she spoke of the worldliness of the Neapolitan Court, and endeavoured to impress upon Catharine how fruitless such an embassy as that proposed by Urban was likely to be. The Swedish princess had had the reputation of extraordinary beauty, and she still retained much of the freshness of youth, with a most attractive grace of person and manner. She entertained Catharine with the story of her life, to which the Sienese, always ready and hoping for instruction from the lips of a fellow-Christian, listened attentively. "My royal mother, St. Bridget," the princess began, "was, as you know, left a widow, and went on a pilgrimage to Rome. I felt, from my earliest years, a great desire springing up in me to follow her manner of life, and to rejoin her at the tombs of the Apostles. Many obstacles, however, presented themselves. The greatest of all was the ardent love of Prince Edgar, to whom I had been affianced. For his sake I remained at home for some time; but seeing my heart set upon another kind of life, Prince Edgar at last consented to give me up, and to let me go to Rome. In March, 1350, he himself accompanied me to the vessel, and confided me to the care of the venerable Maréchal Gustave Thunasson. In August we arrived in Rome. For eight days I sought my mother in vain. Every day I went to St. Peter's, hoping to find her among the crowd of pilgrims. How great was my joy at last, when I felt her tender arms around me, and her kiss on my cheek! She had returned from Bologna, where she had been engaged in the reform of monasteries. . . . You can form no idea," continued the princess, "of the terrible state of Rome at that time. The licentiousness and brutality of manners were so great that my mother was obliged to hide me ; and we could not even visit the sanctuary and temples without being attended by an imposing escort. I was then twenty years of age. All the great lords of Rome desired my hand in marriage. I did not know how to escape them. In vain I assured them that I had vowed to live a virgin ; this did not satisfy them. Some, blinded by passion, even endeavoured to carry me off by violence, having failed to win me by promises and flatteries.[1] One day I accompanied some pious women to the tomb of St. Sebastian in the Catacombs. A young noble who had aspired to my hand, had concealed himself with his followers among the vines near the entrance, with the intention of carrying me off when we reappeared. But just at the moment when we were about to appear, a stag darted out of the thicket near them ; they followed it a little way, and meanwhile we had passed, and were safely entering the city.[2] My mother had had a presentiment of the danger and the deliverance I had met with, and when I returned to the house she met me with the words, 'Blessed be the stag which has saved my

---

[1] " Unde multi magnates cupiebant eam matrimonialiter sibi copulari. Ipsi vero cæco amore capti, quod promissionibus et blanditiis non poterant, minis et violentiis extorquere moliuntur."— *Life of Catharine of Sweden, at the end of the Revelations of St. Bridget*, printed in Rome, 1556, cap. viii.

[2] Catholic art always represents St. Catharine of Sweden with a stag by her side.

child from the beast of prey ! '" The princess then proceeded to tell Catharine of adventures she had gone through on a journey to Assisi to visit the Portiuncula of St. Francis; there they fell among brigands, and she recounted the means taken by her mother to save her, her beautiful daughter, from the brutality of these licentious men ; again, how, on returning to Rome, and being of a more mature age, she was permitted to nurse the sick in the hospitals; and how she founded, near her mother's house, a hospital especially devoted to pilgrims from Sweden and the north of Europe; how, when her mother died, she bore her corpse to the sepulchre of her ancestors at Wastena ; and how she afterwards visited Naples, there to gather up all the recollections of her mother's missions and teaching which the Neapolitans had cherished. Finally, after enlarging on the disorders and dangers she had found in Naples, and on its present unhappy condition, she concluded by declaring, " Ah no ! I can never return to Naples. God ever protected me while there ; but, though I do not doubt his power, I dare not tempt his merciful providence. Our journey there would be useless for them, and dangerous, perhaps even fatal, for us."

The Swedish princess ceased, and Catharine of Siena, who had all along been silent, continued to be so. She was sitting on the ground, and two large tears rolled down her face and fell upon her hands. What were the thoughts of our Catharine at that moment ? The story does not tell us. But as we contemplate these two, the stern and simple Sienese full of thoughts of noble and useful enterprise, and the beautiful high-born lady pleasantly prattling of the romance of her own past life, the wondrous beauty of her youth, and her many suitors, we are constrained to acknowledge that there are in the Roman Calendars saints of widely different degrees of self-forgetfulness and magnanimity.

After some minutes of silence, Father Raymond, who was present, said to the Swedish princess: "Venerable sister, we have all confidence in your experience, and I will take care to report to the Sovereign Pontiff what I have now heard." And they separated. Raymond continues the narrative: "I acknowledge that, through imperfection of judgment and want of faith, I myself did not approve the project of the Sovereign Pontiff. I thought that the reputation of women consecrated to God is so precious, that we ought to beware of tarnishing it by the least appearance of evil, or breath of suspicion. The Queen of Naples might, I thought, follow the counsels of certain agents of Satan by whom she was surrounded, and cause these two good women to be insulted, or forbid them an entrance into Naples. I went therefore the same afternoon to Pope Urban, in one of the halls of the Palace of the Lateran, and laid before him my views on the subject. The Sovereign Pontiff looked disconcerted; he remained a long time in reflection, with his head leaning upon his hands. At last he looked up, and said: 'Your opinion deserves weight. It is more prudent for them not to go.' Although the evening was far advanced I went to Catharine to communicate to her the decision of the Pontiff." Catharine was at that time suffering from great exhaustion, and had cast herself on her face across her couch, when Raymond entered to report his interview with Urban. He detailed to her the conversation, anticipating a sense of relief for her in being acquitted from so serious an obligation. But he had not yet fully comprehended the character of his friend. She rose from her bed and stood up. Tears were in her eyes, and she said to him, with resolution, almost with fierceness of voice and manner: "If Agnes, Margaret, and a multitude of other holy women had indulged in such fancies, and reasoned in this fashion, they never would have won the crown of martyrdom! Think you not that we have a Spouse who is stronger than men, who can save us from the hands of the wicked, and preserve our honour in the midst of a whole throng of debauches? All these objections of which you have spoken are foolish and vain. They spring from a miserable want of faith, and not from genuine prudence." Raymond found no words with which to reply, and remained humbly silent and rebuked. He says, "I blushed inwardly because I was still so far from her lofty standard; and in my heart I admired and wondered at her constancy and faith. But as the Sovereign Pontiff had decided that she should not go, I did not dare to re-open the subject."

Being thus thwarted in her earnest desire to speak face to face with Queen Joanna, who was at this moment, in the opinion of all, the greatest supporter of the Schism and hindrance to the peace of the Church in Italy, Catharine determined to send to her an ambassador chosen by herself, with further despatches, which this ambassador should beg to be allowed to read to Joanna. She selected Neri di Landoccio, a man of engaging presence and accustomed to deal with men, who was now experienced in working for his beloved leader, and had entered deeply into all her feelings and wishes on this subject. Neri proceeded upon his mission. Though the earnest messages he carried from Catharine, and his own persuasions failed to alter the course which Joanna had entered upon, his presence in Naples contributed to retain the majority of the people in their allegiance to Urban. Of this, more hereafter. Catharine wrote at the same time to several honourable ladies of the Court of Naples whom she hoped might have some influence with Joanna. All these despatches are found in the collection of her letters.

Urban now conferred with Catharine concerning the best means to be taken to avert the calamity of a public declaration on the part of the King of France in favour of Clement, and shortly decided to send Father Raymond as his nuncio to the French Court. "It appeared advantageous to the Sovereign Pontiff," continues Raymond, "to send me into France, because he had been informed that it would be possible to detach the King of France, Charles V., from the Schism. The moment I became aware of this project, I went to take counsel with Catharine. Notwithstanding the regret that my absence would occasion her, she advised me to obey the wishes of the Pontiff without delay. 'Hold it for certain, father,' she said, 'that he is the truly-elected Vicar of Christ; I desire that you should endure every risk and fatigue to sustain him, as you would for the Catholic faith itself.' I had never entertained any doubt on this subject myself, but this saying of Catharine so encouraged me to combat the Schism, that I consecrated myself from that moment to the work; and I continually recalled it to my mind, in order to fortify myself in the midst of my difficulties and trials. Some days previous to my departure she called me to her, to converse with me concerning the consolations and revelations she had received from God; she allowed no other persons to be present or to join at that time in our conversation. After an hour of converse, she then said to me, 'Now go whither God calls you. I think that in this life we shall never again discourse together as we have just now done.' Her prediction was accomplished. I departed, and she remained. Before my return she had gone to her heavenly home, and I had no more the blessing of listening to her lessons of holiness." Catharine accompanied her friend to Ostia, where he was to embark; and there, where St. Augustine received the parting words of his mother, Monica, Raymond spoke his last adieu to her to whom he owed, under God, his own spiritual life. "It was for this reason, probably," continues Raymond, "that thinking she should see me no more on earth, she accompanied me to the place where I was to embark, wishing to bid me a last farewell. When we were about to set sail, she kneeled down on the shore, and after praying, made over us the sacred sign of the cross. Tears filled her eyes, and she gazed after us in silence; but her countenance seemed to say: 'Go, my son, in safety, and in the name and under the protection of that blessed sign; but in this life thou shalt never again see her who blesses thee.'" Catharine remained long kneeling on the shore, her eyes fixed on the vessel till it became a mere speck on the horizon, the vessel which contained, she said, that "rarest treasure with which God has gifted our earth, the heart of an apostle."

Catharine, as we have seen, had continually urged Urban to seek out and to surround himself with good men, and wise and honest counsellors. He appears to have fully recognized the need he had of such men, in order to give effect to his designs for the reform of the Church. Catharine seems to have had great faith in what might be accomplished by the united action of true men of God, and spoke to Urban of the advantage it would be to call to Rome without delay all the best men of the Church throughout Italy. This idea appears to have existed in her mind apart from her partisanship for Urban. She had hoped to find in him the fearless reformer which the times called for. He had very imperfectly answered to these hopes; but he was a sincere lover of good and virtuous men, and in nothing did he more readily respond to Catharine's counsels than in respect to this matter. He joyfully assented to her proposition to form an association or community of men pre-eminent for purity of life, strength of faith, and tried virtue. This community would, it was hoped, act as a leaven, permeating gradually the whole of the Church, while by its united force in active effort it would stem and turn back the tide of immorality till now unchecked. On the 13th December Urban granted to Catharine a Brief empowering her to invite to Rome, in his name, whomsoever she desired or considered it useful to ask. She wrote without delay to the friends she had won in the course of her labours throughout Italy, whom she believed would be most able and willing to come to the rescue of the divided Church in its time of need. She met, it would appear, with an unexpected amount of difficulty in the case of some whose help and presence she most desired—those recluses whose saintly character, learning, and maturity of judgment would, she believed, have rendered them a strong support to the Pontiff in his efforts for reform. Some of these replied that they did not feel it right to leave the solitude in which God had placed them, that they feared the influence of the moral atmosphere of Rome on their own souls, and that they believed they could best serve the Church by their prayers offered up in silence and solitude. Friar William of England and Friar Anthony of Nice were among the recalcitrants. It will be remembered that these two Friars inhabited the pleasant convent of Lecceto, a few miles from Siena. Catharine had often had pleasant and useful intercourse with them, while sitting in the shade of the woods which surrounded the convent, and Friar William more especially had there testified to her his sorrow for the troubles of Italy, and formed with her many projects for the purification of the Church and the reformation of morals. Two days after receiving the pontifical Brief, she addressed to Friars William and Anthony the following letter: "My dear sons in Jesus Christ, I, Catharine, the servant of his servants, write to you with the desire of seeing you forgetting yourselves, seeking your only rest and peace in Jesus crucified, and hungering for the honour of God, for the salvation of souls, and the reformation of the holy Church. We see the Church at this day in such necessity, that, to succour her, it is necessary to quit our solitudes and give ourselves up to her service. For if we wish sincerely to do any good, we must not pause and say, 'I shall not find *peace* in doing this or that.' God has given us a good Pastor (Urban VI.), who loves the servants of God, and gathers them around him. He is applying himself to combat vice and encourage virtue. He is not influenced by the fear of human judgment, and is acting as a just and courageous man. We ought to hasten to his aid, and thus prove that we have really at heart the reformation of the Church. If you have this desire, brothers, you will obey the will of God and of his Vicar; you will bid farewell to your solitude, and hasten to the field of battle. I entreat you, then, for the love of Jesus, to respond promptly and without hesitation to the request of the holy father. Do not be afraid of leaving your retreat. If you want woods, there are woods and retreats here also. Courage, then, dearly-loved sons; do not sleep. It is time that we should awake out of sleep. I will say no more. I commend you to the holy benediction of God.—Rome, December 15, 1378."

Friars William and Anthony appear to have had some little difference between themselves, arising out of the contemplation of the proposed journey to Rome. Catharine writes to William : " We ought not—if we do indeed love our neighbour, and care for men's souls—to think too much of our own spiritual consolations. We should give ear to the complaints and wishes of our neighbour, and especially be compassionate towards those who are bound with us in the same bonds of charity. If you fail to do this, you are greatly in fault. Yes, I wish that you should pity the troubles, and have regard to the wishes of our brother Anthony. I desire that you should not refuse to hear him, and I wish also and demand that *he* should listen to *you*. I conjure you, for Christ's sake and for mine, act thus, for thus you will maintain true charity. If you fail to do so, you will sow seeds of discord. I conclude, beseeching you to be as branches closely united with the true Vine, and transformed into the image of Christ crucified."

She wrote to three friars of Spoleto—Friars Andrea,

Paolo, and Lando, who willingly and with ardour obeyed the injunction of the Pontiff, and came to Rome. Another of her letters, conveying the same invitation, was addressed to Dom Bartolommeo dei Serafini, the prior of the monastery of Gorgon Island, to whose monks she had preached. He, and Father Matthew of the Misericordia of Siena, whom she had cured of his sickness, and many other good men, also responded to the invitation. She wrote to John of the Cell, who lost no time in leaving the delightful shades of Vallombrosa to hasten to Rome. The following is a portion of the letter she addressed to him: "Shall we be found asleep at the moment when our enemies are at the gate? No! A great need is calling us, a great want is urging us, and love ought to wake us up. Have greater misfortunes ever befallen the Church than those which we see to-day? We ought to hasten to the support of the holy father, who is surrounded with so many troubles; the more so as he invites with humility and kindness the help of the servants of God. He wishes to have such always about him. Reply, then, promptly to the Sovereign Pontiff, Urban VI. I conjure you by the love of Jesus to fulfil without hesitation the will of God in this matter. You will now prove by the course you elect whether you truly love God and desire the reformation of the Church, or whether you are chiefly devoted to your own consolations. I am convinced that if your self-love has been thoroughly consumed in the furnace of charity, you will not hesitate to abandon your cell; you will be content to inhabit the cell of self-knowledge, and be ready to give your life, if need be, for the truth. This is the moment for the servants of God to proclaim boldly the truth, and to suffer for it."

She also wrote to her old friend, who, at the time of her first acquaintance with him, was inhabiting a cave in a rock near Siena, and living the life of a hermit. He was never called by any other name than that of " the Saint." " He had led," says Raymond, " during more than thirty years a solitary life. He found, in his old age, the precious pearl of the gospel, in becoming acquainted with Catharine. For her, he quitted his peaceful cell and his accustomed manner of living, in order to labour, not for his own soul only, but *for the good of others.* He affirmed that he thus found greater peace of mind and more profit to his soul than he had ever enjoyed in his solitude. Above all, he made great progress in patience. He suffered much from a disease of the heart, and Catharine taught him to support his continual anguish, not only with resignation, but with joy. He related to me several circumstances which transpired during my absence from Rome, and a short time after her death he went also to join her in the celestial mansions."

The two friars of Lecceto having continued to express a great unwillingness to leave their retreat, she wrote to Anthony as follows : " My very dear son in Jesus Christ, I, Catharine, the servant of his servants, write to you in the strong desire to see you fully established upon that living rock, the holy Jesus, in such wise that the building which you raise may not be shaken by winds and storms. . . . This is a sifting time, one which shows us who are the true servants of God, and who are the self-seekers who love God only because of the consolation brought to their own souls. Such persons look around them and pronounce where spiritual comfort and consolation are to be found, and where they are not to be found ; they seem to imagine that God is in this place, and not in that. It is not as they imagine ; for I perceive that, to the true servant of God, all places and all times are acceptable. When the time comes for him to leave his spiritual enjoyments, and undertake labour and fatigues for God, the true servant does not hesitate ; when the time comes for him to bid farewell to his solitude, he does it, like the glorious St. Anthony, who of a truth dearly loved solitude, but who left it in order to fortify his fellow Christians. Many other saints have done the same. The rule of the true saints has always been to come forward in times of necessity and misfortune ; but not in times of prosperity, for they fly such times. There is certainly no occasion to fly *now*, in the fear that too much prosperity would cause our hearts to be carried away with vain-glory and pride ; no one can find anything wherein to glory just-now except sufferings. It seems to me that we are wanting in light when we allow ourselves to be blinded to duty by the love of spiritual consolations : our motives may be good, but the eternal God alone can give us true and perfect light. It seems, by the letter which Friar William has sent me, that neither he nor you are minded to come to Rome. I do not wish to reply to his letter, but I mourn from my heart over his simplicity, for he seeks little either the honour of God or the good of his neighbour. If through humility and the fear of losing peace of soul, he really fears to come, he ought to testify that humility by asking the Sovereign Pontiff to excuse him, and to allow him to remain in his solitude . . . . It appears, according to what he writes to me, that two servants of God among you have had a revelation made to them, by which they are taught that the Vicar of Christ and the person who counselled him on this matter, (she alludes here to herself) have followed a human and not a divine impulse, and that it is the devil and not God who is trying to draw these servants of Christ away from their settled peace and consolation. It is asserted that if you come here you will lose the habit of devotion, and that you could no longer give yourselves up to prayer. You must be very slightly established in devotion if a change of residence would cause you to lose the habit of prayer. It seems that God takes account of places then, and he is only to be found in woods and solitudes, even in times of public necessity! Go to! we began by declaring that we desired the reformation of the Church, and that foul weeds should be rooted out, and sweet flowers (which are the servants of God) should be planted in her: and now we pretend that to call these servants out of their peaceful solitudes in order that they ·may save the bark of St. Peter from shipwreck, is an error inspired by the devil. It would be well that each man should speak for himself alone, and not for other servants of God. Friar Andrea of Lucca and Friar Paolo have not acted in this fashion. These great servants of God are aged and in weak health ; yet they have not made that an excuse for seeking repose, but started at once for Rome, in spite of the fatigue and difficulties of the journey. They obeyed, and have arrived, and although they would wish exceedingly to return to their cells, they do not attempt to shake off this obligation, but have willingly given up all the consolations of solitude. They have come, not to command, but to be made perfect through suffering, in the midst of troubles, tears, watchings, and continual prayers. This is the right course. Let us say no more about it ! May God in his mercy purify us, and give us light, that we may not walk among shadows. I conjure you, the Bachelor, and the others to pray for me, that I may be guided in the path of humility. Dwell ever in the remembrance of God."

I have given these letters at length because of the interest which attaches to the views expressed in them by Catharine of the monastic life, a life held by her, in common with all mediæval Christians, to be a holy life, if subordinated to the highest uses, but, as it appeared to her, a life to be abandoned, at the call of God, for an active and still holier life.

The writer of the above letter we see to be the same who in her childhood made a brief trial of the life of the Fathers of the Desert, and was drawn away from it by the strong voice of affection within her, and the consciousness that there were those outside who thought of her, and needed her, and who would mourn her absence. She was grieved when she found that some of her friends did not fly to meet the call of duty and affection as quickly as she had done, when, after the day spent in the cave, she sped over the hills and through the city gates of Siena, to rejoin her parents, and brothers, and sisters. The following passage from the "Dialogue,"[1] on the subject of prayer is dictated in the same spirit as the rebuke to the friars of Lecceto: "Perfect prayer, then, consists not in the multitude of words, but in the strength of the desire which raises the soul towards God. . . . Every Christian ought to contribute towards the salvation of souls, according as he is inspired by a holy desire. Everything which is said and done for the salvation of men

---

[1] Dialogue, lxvi, p. 168.

is a continual prayer, but a prayer which does not exempt us from the use of mental and vocal prayer at certain times. All that is done for the love of God and of our neighbour, all, it may be added, which is done for ourselves also, with a just and right aim, may be called prayer, for those never cease to pray who never cease to do good. Love for our fellow-creatures is a constant prayer; but this very love will always incite us to actual prayer at stated seasons, and for prescribed times, and even far beyond those prescribed times, if the salvation of a soul, or any emergency in which we find ourselves demands it."

. There are Christians enough assuredly, in our own days, to whom such arguments as Catharine used to the friars might be very suitably addressed; Christians in whose hearts lies a deep, though it may be an unconscious and un-confessed selfishness. Their ears are dull to the daily cry of the needy and the oppressed, they do not hear the earnest call to join with God's advanced guard in the battle against vice and oppression and diabolic cruelty. The sacred seclu-sion of their homes is so sweet. They love so much their own secure and safe " retreat." And well it is they do so. Our secure and virtuous homes are the strength of the nation. It is well too that they should cherish their religi-ous privileges, and seek to maintain spiritual peace and con-solation in the uninterrupted enjoyment of those privileges. Yet a time will come when the possessors of these priceless treasures will have to give an account of their stewardship of such wealth. For an exceeding bitter cry is arising from creatures standing outside our doors, God's redeemed ones also, who have neither home nor hope on earth. Their cry rebukes our ease and our enjoyment, and our greediness of our religious privileges. It seems at times prophetic of woe to those who dare to answer it with pious sophistries.

Friar Anthony was not long in arriving in Rome. It is not clear whether Friar William ever did so. He died in the same year as Catharine, about fifteen months after this time. He was not idle, however, in the service of the Church. Baluze says that at Catharine's suggestion he wrote several letters to his countrymen the King of England and the Archbishop of Canterbury to secure their allegiance to Urban VI., and in this he was not unsuccessful.[1]

Among the most eloquent of Catharine's letters is one which she wrote at this time to Ludwig, King of Hungary. He was a faithful adherent of the Roman Pontiff, and had been invested with the title of "Gonfalonier of the Church." Her letter to him is full of powerful pleading, her aim being to prove the validity of Urban's election, and to urge the King of Hungary to recognize the need of a reformation in the Church, and to give his support to those who were promoting that reformation. She wrote also to Charles Durazzo and other princes, in the same manner and with the same ends in view.

We must follow Father Raymond a little way in his northern mission. He had scarcely left Rome before the Clementines made preparations to embarrass his movements and prevent the success of his embassy. They could not afford to allow the words of so ardent a disciple of Catharine and upholder of Urban to reach the ears of the King of France. Charles V. was now wavering as to the side he should espouse, and the arguments of Raymond

---

[1] Baluze, " Vitæ Pap. Avenion," T. i., Col. 1085.

might deprive the schismatics of the support of France, without which they could not have continued to assert their existence. They promptly took steps, therefore, to prevent the nuncio from landing at Marseilles. Raymond continues the narrative of what took place after his parting from Catharine. "Although the sea was infested by pirates, we arrived happily at Pisa, and had an equally prosperous voyage to Genoa, notwithstanding the numerous galleys of schismatics pursuing their way to Avignon. We journeyed by land from Genoa, and got as far as Ventimiglia. Here a monk of my Order, who was a native of that place, sent me a letter, in which he said, 'Beware of passing Ventimiglia, for treachery is prepared for you, from which, if you fall into the snare, no human aid can save you.' On this warning, having taken counsel with the companion whom the Sovereign Pontiff had appointed me, I returned to Genoa. Here I remained, by the order of the Pope, preaching a crusade against the schismatics." A second time, however, Raymond essayed to cross the frontier into France, and appears to have been this time forcibly prevented. On hearing of his having turned back the first time from Ventimiglia, Catharine wrote to him with some severity. She tells him that she could not have believed a full-grown man in Christ could act so. "Bad, dear father," she writes: "I thought you had cut your teeth, so that you could eat strong meat; but I see you are still a babe, only able to drink milk." She tells him he ought to have gone on, trusting in God, who was able to have delivered him out of the hands of assassins; that, if he could not travel openly as a papal nuncio, he ought to have walked barefoot over the mountains, disguised as a pilgrim, and begging his way, until he arrived in the presence of the King of France. She ardently desired now to go herself to Paris, but her failing health, and the importance of the events which were rapidly succeeding each other in Rome, made it impossible for her to realize this wish. She wrote, however, a long and powerful letter to Charles V., which was conveyed to him by the hand of a private messenger. She counsels him to consult the University of Paris on the subject of the schism.[1] "You have at hand the fount of science," she reminds him, and expresses confidence in the justice of the verdict of the Sorbonne on the validity of Urban's election. The University of Paris, (founded by Charlemagne in 791), was reputed at this time as "the mother and mistress of arts and learning." It included sixty-three colleges, the principal of these being the Sorbonne, which ultimately gave its name to the whole. It had acquired a great authority in the Church, its members having proved themselves above all considerations of party or of temporary interests, and able to give a wise and just judgment on controverted questions. This University had given its verdict at first strongly in favour of Urban. Charles V., however, leaned personally towards the Cardinal of Geneva, and the re-establishment of the Papacy at Avignon. He addressed an urgent letter to the University, which was read before the full assembly of learned doctors, urging them to consider how great a misfortune it would be if France were divided on this question. The sovereign, princes, and nobles, as well as the prelates of France, had unanimously

---

[1] Letter 187.

declared themselves for Clement, and these all now waited for the University of Paris to sanction and endorse their decision. Charles's letter was regarded almost as a command. The University deliberated for several weeks, and in a general assembly at the end of that time, voted, by a considerable majority, in favour of Clement. The weightiest members of the Sorbonne, however, adhered to Urban, and a letter was addressed by the University to both the elected Popes, admonishing them to come to an agreement at once for the abdication of one or the other, in order to restore the Church to unity, under one head.

The strong castle of St. Angelo at Rome still remained in the hands of the Clementines. Constant collisions took place between the Romans and the Breton and Gascon soldiers of the anti-Pope, who defended the castle. A brave knight of Romagna, Alberico di Barbiano, attached to the cause of Urban, had formed at this time an army of Italians, whom he subjected to strict moral discipline, and inspired with a patriotic devotion. They invoked St. George as their patron saint. "This company of St. George," says Sismondi, "became the great school of the Italian militia; it produced the distinguished generals of the succeeding century, and redeemed the military honour of Italy." "These brave troops," writes Capecelatro, "were successful in driving out from our beautiful land the accursed Ultramontane invaders. Germans, Bretons, Gascons, and English, all fled before Alberico and his stern warriors." The soldiers of Clement had encamped at Marino, in the neighbourhood of Rome and their presence was a continual menace to the city. Clement daily sent messengers to the French army in the castle of St. Angelo, and it became evident to the Romans that a concerted attack was meditated by the foe within and without the city. On the 29th of April the Romans, under Barbiano, made a furious attack upon the army of Clement, which yielded and finally took to flight. The castle of St. Angelo surrendered, after a day of desperate fighting, and the Romans were again masters of their own city. It was popularly believed that this great victory was due to the prayers of Catharine. "She lamented," says her biographers, "to see the Church reduced to such sore straits as to be obliged to resort to arms; and she never ceased to supplicate God that these tribulations might cease." She wrote an address to Barbiano and his captains on the occasion of this victory, which Cartier justly calls a "noble and chivalrous harangue." She congratulates them on their victory, counsels humility, and beseeches them to direct their soldiers in the way of virtue, that they might never combat for anything but the truth, and might learn to become valiant soldiers of Jesus Christ. "Take for the base and principle of all your actions the honour of God. . . . In your character as chiefs give to your followers first the example of a true and holy fear of God. . . . I pray you also to take great care to surround yourselves with good and wise counsels, and to choose as officers, courageous, faithful, and conscientious men; for good chiefs make good soldiers. . . . Acknowledge with gratitude, you and yours, the benefits you have received from God, and from the glorious knight of St. George, whose name you bear. May he defend you! Pardon me if I have importuned you with words. Love for the Church and desire for your salvation urge me thus to write. As for us, we do as Moses did; when the people of Israel combated, Moses prayed, and so long as he prayed Israel prevailed. We do the same. Read this letter, if it please you, to all the captains."

Catharine had spent the day of the battle in prayer, sustained by her companions of the community of Santa Chiara. She now added action to prayer. The French were still defending St. Angelo when the sun was about to set. Catharine went to the castle, and presented herself to Rostagno,[1] who commanded it, and by her earnestness succeeded in inducing him to avoid further bloodshed, by surrendering, on the conditions proposed by the venerable Roman senator Giovanni Cenci, with whom she had previously been in consultation. In a patriotic letter which she subsequently addressed to the gonfaloniers of the republic of Rome, she gently reproaches them for having left unacknowledged the solid and peaceful service rendered by Cenci: "I pray you show consideration towards those who have won for us this victory. Help them in their need; above all, the poor wounded. Be kindly and pacific, so that you may retain their confidence. This is necessary, my dear brothers, in order that we be not guilty of ingratitude; and also it is politic. It seems to me that you have acted a little ungratefully in respect to Giovanni Cenci. I know with what zeal and with what generosity of heart he laid aside every consideration except that of serving God and the republic, by saving us from the danger which continually threatened us from St. Angelo. He acted with great wisdom; and

---

1 Some of the chroniclers give the name of the governor of the castle as Guy de Provence.

now not only has no acknowledgment been made of his
services, but the vice of envy has arisen and stirred up
various calumnies against him. It is an evil thing that you
should act thus towards those who serve you. It is offen-
sive to God and hurtful to yourselves ; for the city has need
of wise, prudent, and conscientious men. For the love of
Christ crucified, act no more in this fashion. . . I speak
thus in your own interests, and not from any private feeling. You know very well that I am a stranger here. I
speak for your own happiness, which with all my heart I
desire. I trust that, as discreet and honourable men, you
will accept the purity of the motives which urge me to
address you, and will pardon my boldness."

The victory of Marino was gained on the 29th of April,
1379. The Roman soldiers coupled the names of "St.
George and Catharine" in their songs of triumph, and in
their mutual congratulations over the victory. Catharine
was constantly seen in the city, and her presence increased
for the moment the enthusiastic love and veneration felt
for her by the people and by the army of St. George.
Every morning she had, by their own desire, an audience
with the magistrates of the city. She visited the wounded
in the hospitals, and charged the sisters of her household to
take care of their souls and bodies.

The usual results of victory began to be manifested—
a tendency to vainglory, self-gratulation, and insolence.
"It was laid upon her heart to labour that the occasion of
this victory should be so made use of as to confirm the
Roman people in their allegiance to the true Pontiff, and
still more to raise their thoughts towards God in acknowledgment that it is he who governs the universe

and disposes events."[1] She found Pope Urban very willing to listen to the proposal which she brought before him, for a public thanksgiving. It does not seem clear, indeed, whether Urban did not himself first propose it. Since his election to the papacy, he had been obliged to live in a house near the church of Santa Maria in Trastevere, it being impossible to pass along the road to the Vatican without insult and menace from the Clementine soldiers in possession of the Mole of Hadrian. It was now agreed that the Pontiff of Trastevere should go in solemn procession from Santa Maria in Trastevere to St. Peter's, taking up his abode henceforward in the Vatican. But by the counsels and efforts of Catharine, the matter was so ordered that this event should not be a mere vain show, calculated to increase the pride of victory, but rather a humbling of themselves, on the part of the leaders and people, before God, in the confession of sin and in the invocation of his presence and blessing. The ceremony was as follows. All the clergy of Rome, walking humbly and barefooted, preceded the Pontiff; then followed Urban, also barefooted, and with no outward show, or insignia of earthly rank. The whole of the people of Rome followed the Pontiff, " silently, in recollection and in prayer." The procession thus advanced towards St. Peter's, where, without the usual ecclesiastical pomp, it appears, the Pontiff offered up to God prayers and thanksgiving, with confession of sin ; and the crowd who followed him responded. The people were awed and impressed. The adherents of Clement had been at work for many weeks circulating calumnies against Urban, of a nature

---

[1] Capecelatro, Lib. ix.

to deprive him of the confidence of the Roman people; hence it was esteemed a prudent measure on the part of the Pontiff to make himself thus one of the people, so to speak, in an unostentatious ceremonial, and to renew an act of humility which had been unheard of since Pope Stephen IV., in 769, went in solemn procession in like manner from the Church of St. John Lateran to St. Peter's. Catharine wrote, some days later, to Urban: "I rejoice from the depths of my heart, father, to have witnessed the good pleasure of God fulfilled in you by that act of humility, such as has not been seen for a very long time. The spirits of evil put forth all their efforts to mar it by some abuse from within or from without, but the holy angels restrained their malice." Fearing that the temper of the Pontiff would lead him into the habit of appealing to arms, and trusting in such defences, she adds: "God will act for you, and will give to you the needful wisdom and force to act in such a manner as to guide his bark with prudence. . . . Now it is his will that you should call around you the servants of God. . . . *These*, father, are the soldiers who will give you the true victory."

The army of Clement had been completely routed at Marino. "The anti-Pope, almost demented with fear,"[1] saved himself by flight, and took refuge in the castle of Spelonica, whence he sent messengers to Queen Joanna to beg of her an armed escort to conduct him to Naples. The Queen not only sent him immediate succour, but prepared to receive him with great honours. When the galley of Clement reached the rock on which stood the

---

[1] "Pene demens factus Antipapa."—WALSINGHAM, in "Hist. Ang."

romantic Castle dell' Uovo, the Queen and her Court, who were waiting for him, came forth to meet him. Joanna had commanded that a beautiful bridge should be constructed, and thrown across from the rock to the galley, that Clement might land the more easily. She herself conducted him into the castle, which was festively adorned with banners; and having seated him on a throne prepared for him, she and her husband, the Duke of Brunswick, prostrated themselves at his feet and craved his pontifical benediction. A crowd of courtiers, ladies and young damsels, gorgeously and gaily attired, waited upon and did honour to him. Clement and his cardinals remained for several days in the enchanted castle,[1] in the midst of feasting and convivialities alternated with luxurious repose. But at the very moment when these revelries were at their height, the predictions and warnings conveyed in Catharine's letters to the Queen began to be verified. The Neapolitans regarded with a sullen displeasure the favour shown by their sovereign to the pretender to the papacy, as they judged him, a man of foreign blood, and the opponent of a Pope who was a Neapolitan. They saw that the Schism was thus dangerously encouraged, to the scandal of Christendom, and to the risk of the peace of Naples. The secret festivities of the castle, and the adoring prostrations in public, disgusted the people, who continued to nurse their ill-humour in silence, until an incident occurred which called forth its expression in full southern Italian fury. An artisan had uttered some too free and light words one

---

[1] Froissart records that the Castle dell' Uovo was believed to have sprung up in a single night, by magic.

day, concerning Queen Joanna and her guest, Clement VII. He was reproved by a noble called Andrea Ravignano; but the artisan persisting in his remarks, Andrea rode his horse over him and pierced one of his eyes with his spear. This insult was sufficient to excite the Neapolitans, in heart strongly attached to Urban, to tumult and rebellion. A tailor called Brigante, nephew of the artisan whose eye had been put out, assembled a crowd of the lowest of the population, who armed themselves and raised the cry, "Viva Papa Urbano!" In a few hours Naples was in revolution. The Archbishop of Naples, Bossuti, an Urbanite, who had lived in concealment since the Queen had declared herself the partisan of Clement, was conducted forth by the people and reinstated in his own palace, while the schismatic Bernardo, who had been elected in his place by Clement, was ignominiously driven forth from the city. Clement felt himself scarcely secure within the walls of the enchanted castle while such a tempest raged without. He once more fled and took refuge at Gaeta. Not many days later he re-entered his galley and set sail, with his cardinals, for the coast of France. A few weeks later he had re-established himself, with his Court, at Avignon. Thus the ill-advised Queen became indirectly the cause of the expulsion from Italy of the infamous Cardinal Robert of Geneva, whom she had adored as Pope, and at the same time brought on a civil war in her own kingdom, which continued to be renewed at intervals until her own tragic death, already recorded.

Catharine had gathered around her in Rome many of her friends, men and women, strong in the faith, and ready to do and to suffer all things for the cause of God.

She had joined with them in the solemn public thanksgiving to God for recent benefits. "The holy Church and her Pontiff began to breathe a little, and Catharine of Siena enjoyed at last some consolation in their peace." But this peace was of brief duration; fresh and even graver causes of anxiety arose. Despite her unceasing efforts as a mediator and pacificator, Catharine observed, from day to day, that the people of Rome were increasingly disposed to find a cause of quarrel with Urban. The Pontiff's harshness of manner and unbending character constantly tended to widen the breach. The Clementines, even after their defeat, had continued secretly to spread reports injurious to Urban, and to undermine the loyalty of his subjects towards him. Several conspiracies against his life were discovered and thwarted. Catharine wrote to him, "I beseech you as much as possible to guard your person, inasmuch as we must not tempt God by neglecting the precautions suggested by prudence. I say this because I know that there are wicked men who are not asleep, and who are watching to lay traps for your life."[1] Disaffection and threatened rebellion forced the Pontiff to remain almost a prisoner in the Vatican. Disorders prevailed in the city, and crimes of violence were daily perpetrated. Catharine gave herself continually to prayer. She wrote some account to Raymond of the bitterness of that experience, and the travail of her soul over the misguided people, whom she loved and pitied too. She wrestled in prayer all night long for the Church and for the world, and for "this poor people of Rome." She cried, in her anguish,

---

[1] Urban died by poison ten years after this time.

"Oh, Eternal God, take my life! Receive this only sacrifice which I can make. Take it, and let it be an offering for thy Church's sake. I have nothing else to give except that which thou didst give for me—*life.* O suffer me to pour out my life for the reformation of thy Church!" She pleaded, "Spare this people, O Lord! Let thy judgments fall on me, but have mercy on *them.*" And her request was heard, for she did indeed offer up her life, in anguish and prayers, and tears and vigils, for the attainment of that which was the all-engrossing desire of her soul. While she prayed, her feeble frame was shaken as by a whirlwind. She said that "if the divine power had not encircled her members," she could not have continued to live and to pray; she would have "fallen under her own weight." Night after night she maintained this conflict with the mighty Angel of the Covenant who wrestled with Jacob of old. "Yield to me now, for I am faint." "I will not let thee go except thou bless me." Thus she cried; and when she ceased, and the morning dawned upon her soul, there sounded in her heart the marvellous words, "As a prince hast thou had power with God, and hast prevailed." Whilst she was even thus praying, the noise of many feet was heard in the streets of the city. Secret conspiracy had failed; now open rebellion was proclaimed. Urban could not, among his many faults, plead guilty to that of faint-heartedness. He remained in the Vatican, making no preparations for defence. A tumultuous armed mob marched to St. Peter's. The cry was heard, "To the Vatican!" and, storming the doors, the crowd rushed in with vociferations and violent gestures. The foremost among them were well-known assassins. The multitude outside pressed forward, so that in a moment the building was filled with the revolutionaries. Urban entered from the opposite side, holding aloft the cross. Attired in his pontifical robes, and with the triple mitre on his head, he ascended the papal throne, and sat silently facing the multitude, with a fearless, immovable countenance. The grandeur and composure of his mien, and the "sternness and solemn majesty of his countenance at this terrible moment," filled the rude multitude with amazement not unmixed with admiration. They were awestruck; they stood still and gazed at the Pontiff. He was alone and unarmed; they counted their numbers by hundreds, and were armed with swords, clubs, and firebrands. "Urban smote them with the terrible majesty of his frown;" while, in the words of Pope Boniface VIII. when similarly assailed, he asked, "Whom seek ye?" At these words the assassins dropped their arms, and the people, smitten with a sudden sense of shame and fear, fled from the Vatican, and Urban was left alone. Catharine was outside in the midst of the crowd. For three days she laboured among the malcontents, showing herself an able mediator between the people and the Pontiff. "Her prayers, her presence, and her sweet and ardent eloquence did what could not have been done by armed force." In a few days peace and quietness were restored to the city, the people returned to their homes, and many testified a sincere sorrow for the violence of which they had been guilty.

The bad news of the final verdict of the University of Paris had reached Rome. Catharine, disappointed at the failure of Raymond's attempted embassy to Charles V., presented a petition to Urban to be permitted, even now herself to go to Paris. Urban replied that her presence was essential in Rome, and that he was unwilling that she should go. Indeed, it may be truly said that Catharine ruled in Rome at this time. Her labours were almost super-human. Every morning she repaired to the Capitol, where the gonfaloniers of the republic awaited her. No measure of importance was adopted without her counsels. The interests of the Commonwealth seemed to depend upon her presence and activity. Urban bestowed upon her the fullest powers and authority to act for the good of the Church. Prominent citizens waited at her door every day for a brief interview, and for words of advice on matters of difficulty, private and public. The chiefs of the army sought her counsels, and the sick and the prisoners sighed for the return of the day and hour which brought her to their bedside, or to their cell. Every day she went to St. Peter's to offer up her prayers for the people; every evening she retired to her own room to pray and to intercede, through the long night. Her frame became daily more and more attenuated. The lamp of life was fast burning out. Her biographers tell us that " she walked the streets of Rome like one who had issued from the tomb," so emaciated was she. Her sufferings showed themselves outwardly to all eyes, but nothing that medical art could suggest gave her any relief. Day by day, that pale, slight, ghost-like figure was seen passing through the streets, to the Capitol, to the Vatican, to St. Peter's and to the humbler people's quarters in Trastevere, intent on the Master's work, and unwearying in ministrations. She ruled in Rome. She ruled by the force of her prayers, and the power of Christian love. Those who passed her in the streets of the city, paused,

and crossed themselves. Love, and awe, and pity filled the
heart of the beholder at the sight of her ever-ready smile
of greeting, bright and cheerful and sweet as ever, while
her wasted frame seemed only to be held together and
borne up as by a miracle. "Her cruel sufferings increased
daily, her skin adhered to her bones, and she was tormented with a continual thirst; she walked, prayed, and
worked without intermission; but those who saw her would
have believed her to be a phantom rather than a living
being; her body was visibly consumed, but her soul rose
joyfully and courageously above all."

CHAPTER IX.

CIVIL discord had ceased, for a time, in Rome, and quiet reigned in the city. Catharine, feeling that her bodily strength was failing fast, addressed her last counsels to Urban, in the following letter, in which she urges upon him, besides the reformation of the Church, the exercise of self-control in his words and acts, and the faithful fulfilment of his promises (for Urban was held to be rash in promising, and sometimes inexact in the performance of his promise):—"Most holy and beloved father in Christ, your unworthy daughter Catharine writes to you in the ardent desire to see you following in the steps of the great St. Gregory, acting with prudence, guided by the sweet light of truth, and governing the Church and your people with such wisdom that nothing which you ordain may be called in question. I am aware, holy father, of the insolent and violent reply given by the prefect to the Roman ambassadors.[1] A general meeting of the Council ought to be held concerning this matter, at which the chiefs of the quarters, and other distinguished citizens should be present. I pray you, father, to see these per-

---

[1] This prefect was Francesco di Vico, Signor of Viterbo, an enemy of Urban, who on some occasion had insulted the Roman ambassadors sent to him in a conciliatory spirit.

sons frequently, and to bind them to you with prudence, in bonds of affection and fidelity. I entreat also, that when the report is brought to you of the decision of the assembly, you will receive the messengers with all possible gentleness, explaining to them what to your Holiness seems most needful to be done. Pardon me if I say what I ought not to say ; but I desire that you should understand and consider well the character of your Roman subjects, who are far more easily won and held in allegiance by gentleness than by harsh words, and force. . . . I humbly beseech you also to be very prudent in never promising anything except what it is distinctly possible for you to fulfil, in order to avoid the shame, confusion, and evil which may result from the opposite course. Bear with me, kind father, when I say such things to you. I trust that your humility and your goodness will make you accept them without indignation or scorn, although they are spoken by so unworthy a woman. He who is really humble does not criticize the person who counsels, but thinks only of the truth and of the honour of God. Take courage, and do not be troubled about the effects of an insolent reply from this rebel (Francesco di Vico) ; God will overrule all, for he is the ruler and protector of the Church and of your Holiness. Be always calm, in a holy fear of God, always blameless in your words and in your conduct . . . I pray you, moreover, to provide for the adjustment of the affair of which Leon has spoken to you,[1] for the scandal is continually augmenting, on account of

---

[1] Leon is supposed to have been a disciple of Catharine. There had been some difference between the Pope and the ambassadors of Siena concerning the restitution to the Sienese of the fortress of Talamone, and other matters, induced in part by the roughness of Urban's temper.

the treatment which the ambassador of Siena met with, and other things which daily keep alive anger and irritation in the feeble hearts of men. You have no need of such a spirit now; you need men who will be peaceable and not combative. Even admitting that all was done from a praiseworthy zeal, and that it can be justified, yet there are people who act with such haste and anger that their manner at least cannot be justified. I pray your Holiness, then, to make allowance for human infirmity; for I warn you that if some remedy be not applied, the sore will deepen. Recall to your mind the ruin caused throughout the whole of Italy, through the delay in deposing wicked governors who destroy the Church of God. I know that you are not ignorant of this. Let your Holiness see then what is right to be done. I humbly ask your benediction." This is the last letter which she addressed to the Pontiff. In a previous one she had pleaded again and again, and at greater length, for the reformation for which she continually laboured. "When we live for the honour of God," she wrote, "without thinking of self, we receive light, power, constancy, and a *supernatural perseverance*, through which we never fail, but continue with courage to do our duty. I have prayed, and I pray continually to the Eternal Father, to bestow this constancy upon you, father, and upon all faithful Christians, for in our present circumstances we have an extreme need for it. For myself, I will never cease to work, so long as God gives me the grace. I wish to give my life for you and the Church, in tears and watchings, and in humble, persevering prayer. God will enable me to do it, for of myself I can do nothing; and I know that humble, persevering, and believing prayer, provided its demands are just, *is never refused.*"

The following extracts from the last letters which Catharine wrote to Father Raymond, as well as the last to Stephen Maconi, who, on account of personal and family affairs had remained in Siena, are more especially interesting, because, in addition to the Christian fervour which pervades them, and the useful counsels which they contain in common with her other letters, they manifest the yearning tenderness of the mother about to leave her beloved family, and the solicitude of the faithful friend, mindful not only of the spiritual needs, but of all the smaller and temporal concerns of those with whom she has walked life's pilgrimage, and to whom she believes she is shortly to speak her last adieu. For the nearer the soul approaches to the divine and eternal source of love, the more fully do the obligations of sacred human love reveal themselves, and the more keen is the self-reproach for the neglect even of the smallest of these. Those who have loved the most, and with the greatest fidelity, have ever been the first to confess in the moment of death, " I have not loved enough! in many things I have been unfaithful to love."

"My dear Father in Jesus Christ,—Catharine, the servant of his servants, writes to you in the desire of seeing you a pillar of the Church, and ever led forward on the right path, by the light which reveals to us the truth. It seems to me, according to what I understand from your letter, that you have been subject to many internal conflicts by the snares of the evil one and through your own weakness. It has seemed to you that the burden laid upon you was beyond your strength, and you have thought that I have judged you by too high a standard of my own. You have thought also that my affection for you had diminished; but you are mistaken; and by what you have written you have proved rather that charity in me is augmented, and in yourself has diminished. I love you as I love myself; and I have hoped that the goodness of God would also make your affection perfect; but it has not been so, for you have been looking about to see whether you could cast off from you the burden which oppressed you, and have fallen back into weakness and unfaithfulness. I have seen this very clearly; and I wish that I had been the only one who remarked it. In pointing it out to you, have I not proved to you that my affection has increased instead of diminishing? But how is it that you have entertained the very least of these fears? How is it that you can ever have believed that I desire any other thing than the life of your soul? Where is the faith and the confidence which you ought always to possess? What has become of that assurance which you once had that all which happens to us is allowed and decided by God, not only in great events, but in the smallest circumstances? If you had remained faithful, father, you would not now have been vacillating and fearful before God and towards me, but, as an obedient and zealous son, you would have gone forward! If you had not been able to walk upright, you would have crept upon your hands and knees! If you had not been able to travel as a papal messenger, you would have travelled as a pilgrim! If you had had no money, you would have begged! Such boldness and obedience would have advanced our cause before God and in the hearts of man more than all worldly prudence and all human precaution. It is through my own shortcomings that I now fail to see this perfection in you. I know very well, however, that, although you have shown weakness, you are always possessed with a direct and holy desire to fulfil the will of God. I had, however, greatly wished that you had not stopped on your way, but that you had pursued your enemy to the death. For myself, I was at that time occupied night and day with the things of God, and with many affairs which have not succeeded on account of the want of zeal in those who undertook them, and, above all, through my own sins and imperfections. Alas! we see around us offences increasing and inundating us! In the kingdom of Naples we see the last state of things to be worse than the first! I shall have much to tell you on all these matters, unless, indeed, before I see you again I shall have received the favour of leaving this life. Yes, yes! I do assure you that I would have given all the world for you to have continued on your route! I will not, however, vex myself about it, because I am persuaded that nothing happens without some secret purpose of God. My conscience is at rest, for I have done all I could to further this embassy to the King of France. May the Holy Spirit accomplish that which we bad workers have failed to accomplish.

"As for the embassy to the King of Hungary, it appeared to be very acceptable to the Sovereign Pontiff, and he had decided that you and your companions should be charged to undertake it. I do not know what has caused him to change his mind. He now wishes that you should remain where you are, and do all the good you possibly can. I beseech you, put away all uneasiness.

"Devote yourself wholly to God, my father. Do not reckon too much on spiritual consolations. Hope and pray continually for these dead and dying, that the hand of Eternal Justice may be held back by our continual prayer. If you thus act, nothing will ever seem to you impossible, nor will you calculate concerning the difficulties or the results of what you undertake; but you will see, by the light of faith, that in Christ Jesus, and in him crucified, all things are possible, and that God never lays upon us any burden which is beyond our strength. I tell you, dearest father, that, whether we will it or not, the times in which we live invite us to die for the world. Let us willingly give ourselves as a sacrifice. . . . You ask me to entreat of the Divine Goodness that you may be filled with the ardour of St. Vincent, of St. Lawrence, of the great St. Paul, and of the beloved Disciple, and you tell me that you will then do great things, which will cause me to rejoice. I thank God for this; for without this ardour you will do nothing, either great things or little, and you will *not* be my joy and crown. It is in thinking so much of these things that I could wish that you were near me, in order that I could have shown you better all I desire to say. In being faithful you will do great things for God, and will bring to a happy conclusion the business which he confides to your care; or, if it does not succeed perfectly, it will not be your fault.

" You write to me that the Schismatics are seeking daily to arrest you : but you cannot doubt that God is strong enough to remove from them the power of accomplishing this desire. You ought also to consider, father, that you are not yet worthy of the great happiness of martyrdom, and you should consequently be without fear. Take care that that does not happen to you which happened to the Abbot of St. Antimius. Through fear, and under the excuse of not tempting providence, he fled from Siena to Rome, believing he should thus escape imprisonment and be safe ; but he was put in prison here, and he has suffered that which you know. Thus are pusillanimous hearts deceived. Be courageous, then, and face death. I ask your blessing."

"My dear father in Christ,—I write to you again, in the desire that no adversity and no persecution may turn you aside. Think of those glorious workers who have sacrificed their lives, and have watered the soil of the Church with their blood. Take example from them, that I may no more see you timid, and fearing your own shadow, but a valiant soldier of the Lord. Oh, my father, I wish that I could reveal to you the great mysteries of God which I have seen ! I will speak of them as briefly as I can, and in so far as human language will permit. I also will tell you what I wish you to do after my death. But do not be sorrowful on account of what I say, for I know not whether the Divine Goodness will recall me now, or leave me longer on earth. My father, God has shown me great things, which it is impossible for me to describe." [She then speaks of the Sunday of Sexagesima, on which she met with an accident which occasioned much suffering to the last hour of her life.] "I do not understand how I could ever get over such an accident. The pain in my heart was so great that my garment was torn by it. I fell, and remained in the chapel in great agony. On Monday evening I felt pressed in spirit to write to the Sovereign Pontiff and to three cardinals. My friends supported me, and I went to my cell; but when I had finished the letter to the Pontiff it became impossible for me to write another word, so great was the agony which I suffered. A little while afterwards a terrible spiritual conflict was permitted —an attack of the enemy of souls which almost overcame me. It seemed as if he were furious against me, as if he conceived that it had been I, who am but a frail vessel of clay, who had torn from his grasp that of which he has for so long a time retained possession in the holy Church. The terror of soul which was then added to my bodily sufferings was such that I felt impelled to fly from my cell, which I did, and went to the chapel, as if my cell had been the cause of my sufferings." [She then tells Raymond how she fell again and again, fainting, and at last, unable to speak or to move, she lay as if dead, but with her spiritual vision clear, and her powers of mind in full activity.] "My memory recalled all the circumstances and needs of the Church and of all Christian people. I was admitted to the presence of God. I cried to him in his presence, and with great confidence, taking the kingdom of heaven by violence, and offering up to him as my plea the blood of the Lamb and all the sufferings which he endured. It was permitted to me to plead with such urgency that I could no longer doubt that he granted my request. I then prayed for you all, beseeching him to accomplish in you his will and my own ardent desires. Last, I prayed for myself, that he would save me from eternal death. Thus I remained so long a time that our community wept for me as if I were dead. The spiritual terror was gone, and the Lord Jesus drew near to me, promising to receive my prayers and grant me my desires, and accept-

ing the offering which I had made of my poor life as a
sacrifice to his Church. Then he who is the Truth showed
me things which it is not possible to express in words. I
began to recover." [But again and again the spiritual
terror and conflict returned, such as it passes the imagination to conceive of, and she vainly attempts to speak of it.]
" Two days and two nights passed in these fierce tempests,
but the aim and desire of my soul changed not; it remained united to the object of its affection, while my body
seemed reduced to nothing. . . . . I can take no nourishment, not even a drop of water; my life holds by a thread;
and now I know not what the Divine Goodness wills to do
with me. He will fix a term to my miseries and anguish,
and cause them to cease, or he will, through ordinary means,
restore health to my body. I pray him only to accomplish
his will in me, and not to leave you orphans—you and the
others—but to direct you ever in the way of the truth. I
am persuaded he will do so.

" I was able to set myself again to toil for the tempest-
tossed vessel of the Church. I went to St. Peter's. I did
not wish to leave the place, night or day, until I saw
the people who were in revolt, again at peace with the
Sovereign Pontiff."[1] After some general counsels, she
adds: " I would ask of you also to gather together the
books and the other writings of mine which you will find—
you and Friar Bartholomew, Friar Thomas Caffarini and
the Master, (Giovanni Tantucci)—and to do with them

---

[1] This refers to the occasion when the populace, who had entered
the Vatican, retired in awe before Urban. The sudden calm, and
suppression of the revolt were attributed by all to the efforts and
prayers of Catharine.

whatever seems to you most useful and for the honour of God. I confide to you also this my poor family, that you may be to them, as much as you can, a pastor and father. Hold them together in the bonds of mutual charity, that they be not scattered as sheep having no shepherd. . . . . Pardon me if I have ever written anything to give you pain. I never wish to give you pain, but I wish to have fulfilled my duty, for I know not what God wills to do with me. Do not be grieved because we are separated; your presence would certainly have been a great consolation to me, but I have a still greater consolation, a still higher joy—that of seeing the good you are doing in the Church; and I pray you to work ever with a yet greater zeal, and never to yield before any persecutions. May you ever rest in the blessing of Christ Jesus.—CATHARINE. Rome, March, 1380."

"To Stephen di Corrado Maconi. Rome, January, 1380, —My very dear son in Christ Jesus,—I, Catharine, write to thee in the desire of seeing thee a mirror of all virtue, by the example of thy life, the teaching of thy words, and thy humble and continual prayers; that so thou mayest become an instrument in the hands of God to bring souls to Christ. Oh, how great is the strength we derive from prayer offered up in solitude and in self-knowledge! . . . . . Yesterday I received one of your letters, to which I reply in a few words. As for the favours I had promised you, I reply that you must never expect any more services from me unless you come yourself to claim them. I do not say that I shall ever refuse to help you in all your spiritual wants; for never have I more earnestly wished than now to instruct you in the things which God puts into my heart; and perhaps you never needed them more than now. You say that you are dissatisfied with your state of mind. When you are thoroughly so, I perceive that you will leave it for a better state. I hope that, as you have begun to remove the veil from your eyes, you will soon be able to take it away entirely. In reply to what you tell me of Master Matthew, I am exceedingly grieved for the trouble and annoyance which he has had on account of my negligence and ignorance. (Ask him to send me again a note of what it is which he requires, for I had indeed forgotten it.) I will do all I possibly can to remove the effect of my carelessness. Tell him that his trouble is still more my own. If this letter, &c. Have patience with me, &c. . . . [1] I have received a letter from the Abbot, who speaks of some new members of his community, among whom he hopes to reckon you. It is a great joy to me to see that you wish to advance in the religious life, but I am surprised that you should have made any engagement of this kind without letting us know. There is some mystery about it. I pray God that he will do with you what is most for his honour and for the good of your soul. I have much to say to you, but I cannot and will not write more. Neri is at Naples, where he has been well received by the Abbot Lisolo. He would have written to you, but he has been sick and nigh to death. Encourage all my children, and, above all, Peter. Recall me to him; and, in doing so, tell him from me that God loves few words and many good deeds. I do not, however,

---

[1] It is evident that this letter was written in great suffering. There are breaks and unfinished sentences. The writer begs Stephen to have patience with her, and apologizes for having lost or forgotten, in her extreme failure of health, some letter written to her.

impose silence upon him, and I do not forbid him to speak
or to write to me, if it will be a consolation to him to do so.
Indeed, I have sometimes been surprised that he has not
written. Lisa and all our family commend themselves to
you. There are here enclosed other letters, sealed. Give
them in this state to Mistress Catharine di Giovanni; she
will distribute them. Dwell ever in the remembrance of
the Holy Jesus."

Most of Catharine's published prayers bear the date of
the years 1379-80, and were written at Rome. They are
full of affection and of longings for the salvation of all. In
general she begins with the larger requests, for blessing on
all mankind; next she prays for the Church; and finally
concludes with a petition for her dear and intimate friends:
"O Eternal Love, I commend to thee, with all the strength
of my desires, those whom thou hast given me to love.
Thou didst confide them to me in order that I might continually awaken and revive them; and yet I have slept.
Do thou thyself revive them, gracious Father and God, so
that their eyes may be ever fixed on thee. I have sinned,
Saviour, I have sinned. Have pity on me. Lord, make
haste to help me. Amen."

"O Ineffable Love, how royally do those advance who
have no will except thy will. Those also learn with ease
thy doctrine. O, Eternal Saviour, what is thy doctrine,
and by what way shall we approach the Father? I know
of no other way save that which thou hast traced with thy
precious blood, and which thou revealest by the light of
thy ardent love. This day, then, I implore thy mercy,
that I may have the grace to follow thy teaching with simplicity of heart. . . . (She speaks, in her prayer, of the

many and varied means by which the Father draws erring souls to himself.) "Thy mercy, Lord, has shown to me—me most unworthy and sinful—that we must not judge our reasonable fellow-creatures, whom thou leadest by ways so many and so different. Jesus crucified is the one way; yet hast thou many means by which thou guidest sinners into this way. I give thanks to thee for this."

"Lord God, I offer my life to thee, now and for ever. Use it for thy glory. I supplicate thee, O Christ, by the merits of thy Passion, to purify thy Church from all its vileness, and to cut away the dead branches from the living vine. Delay not, O my Lord, I beseech thee. I know that thou canst, by thy power, slowly and gradually correct the deformed branches and re-plant thy vine; yet make haste, O Lord; make no long tarrying, O my God. Since thou hast power to create all things out of nothing, it is easy for thee to make use of that which already exists, in extirpating evil. I commend to thee my children, those whom thou hast committed to my affection and particular care. O that they may be enlightened by thy bright rays, that they may be purified from their sins and become active labourers in the field which thou hast assigned to them. Rebuke and visit upon *me*, O Lord, their errors and their weakness, for it is I who am answerable for them. I have sinned, Lord; have mercy on me."

The following is the last prayer which she recorded in writing. Rome, February, 1380:—

"Eternal God and Master, who didst form the vessel of the body out of the dust of the earth; who didst create the body so humble a thing, and then fill it with so great a

treasure—the soul, made in thine own image, O Eternal.
Thou, Lord, art the Great Master who canst create and re-
create, who canst break and bring to nought this fragile vase
as thou wilt.   O Father, I offer again to thee myself—my
life for thy Church. . . . . I commend to thee thy Church.
Eternal God, I commend to thee also my beloved children,
and if it be thy merciful will to take me away from earth, I
pray thee leave them not orphaned and comfortless; but
visit them by thy grace, and make them to live in the perfect light.   Unite them to each other in the bonds of love.
I beseech thee, Lord, that none of them may be lost; that I
may not be robbed of any one of them.   Forgive my sins,
my ignorance, and my negligence towards them, inasmuch
as I have not done all that I could and ought to have done
for them.   I have sinned, Saviour; have pity on me.   I
offer to thee, and cast upon thee my loved ones, for they are
my own soul.   If it be thy will, for their sakes, to let me remain in the body, Physician Supreme, then heal this body;
repair it; for it is all broken to pieces.   Grant us, Eternal
Father, O grant us thy heavenly benediction.   Amen."

It is from the young Secretary, Barduccio, that we have
the account of Catharine's last days.   The following letter
to his sister, containing that account, is given in a con-
densed form as to certain portions of it, and in the precise
words used by him in those parts of the narrative with
which we are most concerned.

Letter of Sgr. Barduccio di Canigiani to his sister, Maria
Petriboni, at the Convent of San Pietro di Monticelli, near
Florence:—In the name of Jesus Christ. . . . . I received
your letter, and communicated its contents to my afflicted
friends.   They thank you from the depths of their hearts.

You desire to become acquainted with the details of the last days of blessed Catharine. I can but very inadequately perform the duty you require of me. I will, however, relate what my eyes witnessed, and what my poor soul was able to comprehend. From the first days of January, 1380, a great change was perceived in her. She conceived a kind of horror of all nourishment; she could not even drink a single drop of water to quench her burning thirst, though her throat was continually so parched that she felt as if she was breathing fire. Her life appeared to hang by a thread. Nevertheless she seemed to be sustained by a secret, ineffable joy, and continued to be as active and gay as usual until about the 6th of March. On Sexagesima Sunday, at the hour of vespers, she met with an accident so grave that from that moment she never recovered her wonted health, nor was ever free from pain." [The nature of the accident referred to here, and in Catharine's letter to Raymond, can only be guessed. There are allusions to her having fallen upon the steps of St. Peter's, when entering the church to pray. It is not improbable that, after a day of unusual fatigue, she may have fainted at the portal, or, striking her foot on some obstacle, her weakness may have caused her to fall upon the hard pavement, thus giving some wrench to the muscles and nerves, which would account in part for the terrible sufferings of the weeks which followed.] "She was carried home," continues Barduccio. "She suffered much that night and the following Monday, when towards evening she revived a little. That night, while dictating a letter to me, she had so violent a crisis that we mourned her as dead. She fainted, and remained a long time without any signs of life. Yet afterwards she arose, and appeared unchanged and cheerful as ever. From that Sunday, however, new and extraordinary bodily sufferings afflicted her. During Lent, every morning after communion, her companions were obliged to raise her from the floor, and carry her to bed as if she were dead. Yet in the evening of each day she would revive, and arise and walk to St. Peter's, a mile distant; and having remained for vespers, she would return quite exhausted. Thus she continued until the third Sunday in Lent. She then bowed beneath the weight of sufferings which overwhelmed her, and the anguish which rent her soul in view of the sins which were daily committed against God, and of the perils and evils of the Church. She was consumed by pain, physical and mental. In the midst of this martyrdom, she said, 'These pains are *physical*, but they are not *natural*. God allows the evil one to torment me thus.' We believed that what she thus said was indeed the fact, for her sufferings were inconceivable. It is not possible to give you any idea of her patience. I will merely say that at each renewal of the torture she joyfully raised her eyes and hands to God, saying, 'Thanks be to thee, O ever-living Spouse of my soul, who dost continually crown thy poor handmaid with these new proofs of thy favour.'"

Here a portion of the deposition already cited of Friar Bartholomew of Siena may with advantage be inserted. This Bartholomew was the friend of her youth, who said, " When I first made her acquaintance she was young, and always wore a smiling countenance; I was also young, but I never experienced any trouble in her society." "When she was attacked by her last illness," he writes, "I was prior of a convent of Siena. The Provincial of my Order sent me on business to Rome. On my arrival there I hastened to her residence, being utterly ignorant of her state. I found her extended on planks, surrounded on every side by other planks, so that she seemed to be in a coffin. She was so emaciated that her bones could be easily counted. She appeared withered, and her face worn and sunk, and it no longer presented the same beauty as formerly. The sight broke my heart, and I asked her, amidst my tears, 'Mother, how is it with you?' When she recognized me, she was anxious to testify her joy, but she could not speak. I placed my ear close to her mouth, to be able to hear her reply; she said, 'All is well, thanks to our beloved Saviour.' I then told her of the motive of my journey, and said to her, 'To-morrow will be the Passover of our Lord, and I should like to celebrate it here, so as to give the Eucharist to you and your spiritual children.' She replied, 'Oh, would that our dear Saviour would permit me to partake of it!' I left her, and on the following day I returned to fulfil my promise. No one hoped to see her able to go to Communion, for she had been for some days incapable of making any movement. As we were preparing, however, she arose suddenly, to the great joy of all, and advanced towards the altar, where she remained till the conclusion. She was then carried back by the sisters to her bed, where she lay motionless as before. I was, however, permitted daily to converse with her during the few days I remained in Rome. She prayed with unabated ardour for the reformation and peace of the Church. 'Be assured,' she said, 'if I die' (and this she repeated to many others around her), 'the cause of my death is the zeal which burns and consumes me for the Church. I suffer gladly, and am ready to die for her, if need be.' The business which brought me to Rome was concluded, but I constantly resisted when pressed to return to Siena. I told this to Catharine, and she said I must go back. 'How can I go, and leave you in this extremity?' I asked; 'if I were far away, and were told of your condition, I would leave all and make haste to come to you. No, I cannot go without seeing you somewhat recovered, or at least without having some better hope of your recovery.' Catharine said, 'My son, you know very well what a consolation it is to me to see the faces of those whom God has given me, and whom I love in the truth. It would be a great happiness to me if God would grant me Father Raymond's presence as well as yours; but it is not his intention to grant me this; and I desire not my will, but his. You must go. You know that at Cologne there will soon be a Chapter of your Order for the election of a General Master. Father Raymond will be nominated; I wish you to be there with him, and to be obedient and useful to him. I command you this, as far as I have power.' I assured her that I would do whatever she commanded, but added, 'If it is God's will that I go, ask him to give you better health before my departure.' She promised me to do so, and when I returned on the following day, I found her so calm and cheerful, that I drew near to her, full of hope. She, who had hitherto remained so immovable, now stretched her arms towards me and embraced me so affectionately that I could not help shedding tears of joy. She then exhorted me to depart in peace. I left Rome. A short time after I had returned to Siena, a letter informed me that Catharine had quitted this life."

Barduccio thus proceeds : " She continued to be thus consumed by suffering until the Sunday before Ascension Day. Her body was then reduced to the state in which painters represent death ; her limbs seemed to be those of a mere skeleton covered with a transparent skin.   Her strength was so annihilated that she could not turn herself from one side to the other.   Her countenance however was beaming with joy and angelic devotion.   On Saturday night, about two hours before dawn, she became so much worse that we believed she was on the verge of her last moments.   She then called all her family and friends around her. . . She was reclining on the shoulder of Alessia ; she tried to rise, and with a little help remained in a sitting posture, though still supported by Alessia.   Someone had placed before her a little table on which were some relics of saints, but she did not look at them.   Her gaze was fixed upon the Cross. Then she accused herself, before him who died there, of all her sins.   ' Yes, I have sinned, O Eternal, I have miserably offended thee by my negligence and ignorance and ingratitude.   Thou didst command me to seek thee in all things, and to labour continually for thy honour and the good of man ; but I have avoided fatigue and labour. . . I have sought my own consolation . . . Alas ! thou didst charge me with the care of souls, thou didst give me children whom I was bound to love in a special manner, and lead them to thee in the way of life.   I have been weak towards them.   I have failed in solicitude for their interests ; I have not succoured them as I ought by continual prayer or by giving them a holy example and wise counsels.   Ah me ! with how little respect have I received all thy benefits, and the charge thou didst commit to me ; I did not gather

x

them with that desire and love which thou didst feel in sending them to me. Thou, Lord, didst, in thine infinite goodness, choose me in my tender infancy for thy spouse; but I have not been faithful enough to thee; my memory has not always been filled with thee, and with thy countless benefits; my understanding has not been solely directed to comprehend thee, and my will has not been bent towards loving thee with all my soul and strength.'

"After this, she asked pardon of us all. 'My beloved,' she said, 'I have indeed hungered and thirsted for your salvation. I dare not say the contrary. Nevertheless, I may have been wanting to you in many things; not only have I not set before you the highest example, but in regard to all your temporal wants, I have not been so faithful and attentive as I ought to have been. I therefore implore of you all, in general, pardon and indulgence, and I ask this also of each one of you in particular. I entreat you most humbly and earnestly to pursue to the end the path of virtue, that you may be, as I have told you before, my joy and my crown.' The grief which inundated my soul, (continues Barduccio), as she spoke these words, hindered me from hearing all she said; her voice, moreover, was feeble, and her sufferings so keen that she pronounced her words with great pain and difficulty. She then addressed a few words to Lucio, then to another, and to myself."

St. Antoninus adds to this: "Catharine, finding her end approaching, pronounced a discourse to her spiritual sons and daughters, exhorting them to brotherly love, and giving them also certain rules for advancing in the way of the Lord. And, first (she told them), that anyone who desired to be truly the servant of God, and wished really to possess him, must strip his heart of all selfish love of human creatures, and with a simple and entire heart must approach God. Secondly, that no soul can arrive at such a state without the medium of prayer, founded on humility ; that no one should have any confidence in his own works, but acknowledging himself to be nothing, should commit himself entirely to the keeping and leading of God. She asserted that through prayer all virtues progress and are invigorated, whilst without it they are weakened. Thirdly, that in order to attain to purity of conscience, it is necessary to abstain from all rash judgments and evil speaking against our neighbours ; that we must neither condemn nor despise any creature, even if it be the case of one whom we know to be guilty and vile, but to bear with him, and pray for him, because there is no one, however sinful, who may not amend his life. Fourthly, that we must exercise a perfect trust in the providence of God, knowing that all things that happen to us, through his divine providence, spring, not from his ill will to his creatures, but from his infinite love for them."

Catharine had just ceased speaking, when Stephen entered the room. He had been detained at Siena. One evening, he narrates, as he was praying in the Oratory of the Hospice della Scala, he heard a voice which said, "Make haste, and go to Rome. She, to whom you owe your soul, is dying." He dared not resist the impression thus made on him, and in all haste set out for Rome. When Catharine saw him, she said, "My Stephen, I thank God that you have come. His mercy will guide *you* also in the way of salvation." She then indicated to him her wish that he should, after her death, enter the Order of the Carthusians. She gave several other particular instructions to those around her. The friars who were present she recommended to place themselves under the direction of Father Raymond, as being a prudent and single-hearted man. "Apply to him," she said, "in your difficulties, and tell him, from me, never to be remiss, and never to fear, whatever may befall him." She appointed Alessia to be her successor over the household of the Mantellatas, who were so endeared to her by companionship in all her past labours. Lastly she turned to her beloved mother, who, bent with age and grief, stood motionless on one side by the pillow of her child, while Alessia on the other side supported her drooping head. Catharine asked Lapa to stoop down and kiss her, entreating her to give her her blessing. "Pardon my faults towards yourself, my best beloved," she said, "and give me your blessing." Barduccio continues, " I would that you had seen with what respect and humility she repeatedly asked the benediction of her aged mother, while that mother in return commended herself to the prayers of her daughter, and besought her to obtain for her the grace not to offend God by the bitterness of her grief. Catharine again prayed aloud for us all, and so tender and humble were her words, that we thought our hearts would cleave asunder."

But this was not yet the end. The extraordinary vitality she possessed was manifested by the sudden and almost incredible exertions she made from time to time, and almost to the last; and it now seemed to resist all the torture, and natural exhaustion of her worn-out frame. She lingered yet a few days. Again, in the early morning of a day in the last week of April, her little remaining strength seemed suddenly and altogether to forsake her. She lay perfectly motionless, giving no perceptible sign of life, and it was believed for a time that her spirit had fled at last. "It was, therefore, deemed expedient," says Barduccio, "to give her extreme unction, and the Abbot of St. Antimius hastened to administer it, as she seemed already bereft of all consciousness. After the application of this sacrament, a change came over her, and it now seemed, by the expression of her countenance and the movements of her arms, that she was sustaining a terrible assault from Satan." Several witnesses record this last sore conflict. When Catharine woke up from this temporary trance, a fever flush was on her face, and her mind was wandering. The poor brain was haunted with dark images, and the humble soul was plunged in deep darkness. She was to drink of that mysterious cup of anguish which is sometimes held to the lips of God's most faithful servants at the very moment when they are about to enter the valley of the shadow of death; a cup so bitter that many a trembling heart, looking forward to that hour, and knowing the cruelty of the enemy of souls, has cried out: "If it be possible, let it pass from me." Those around her looked on in silent awe, wholly unable to bring her any help or comfort; for she heard nothing that was spoken by human lips. She seemed to be listening with terror to some dark and horrible accusation. The nature and agony of that conflict, which lasted several hours, could only be guessed by her words and gestures. Sometimes she maintained silence, as if intently listening; sometimes she replied, but with a wild and wandering and troubled utterance. Sometimes, by a great effort, she raised herself a little, and seemed to answer back with scorn what she had heard. She gesticulated, as if pleading in agony her own cause ; sometimes her look became defiant ; then again she would smile, and again seemed to be filled with indignation.   That countenance which her companions had been used to see lit up with loving smiles, and full of serenity and holy joy, was now disfigured with the terror and anguish of that conflict which tests to the utmost the spiritual fibre of the human being—even of the holiest—when summoned to wrestle in the final death-grip with the spirit of evil, "the accuser of the brethren." Then, after maintaining a longer silence, she smiled and said distinctly, "No, never! never for vain-glory, but for the honour and glory of God."   One of the accusations heard by her soul in that conflict seems to have been that she had sought her own glory and had loved the praise of men. "Many persons," wrote Raymond, on receiving this account, "believed that she had courted praise, or at least enjoyed it, and for this reason took a pleasure in appearing in public. Some said, 'She ought to remain in her house, if she desires to serve God.' And this was her response, when she was dying, to those reproaches, the echoes of which tormented her fevered brain when thus laid low: 'No, never for vain-glory, but for the honour and glory of God.'"

Barduccio continues : "Catharine then began to repeat the words, 'Peccavi, Domine, miserere mei' (Lord, I have sinned; have mercy on me). She repeated them fifty or sixty times, raising her wasted right hand, which each time dropped suddenly again through weakness. Looking around her, she would say also, 'Saints of God, have pity on me !' After a time, as we were watching her, the expression of her countenance suddenly changed and became radiant like that of a seraph. Her eyes, which had been obscured with tears, were now lighted up with an inexpressible joy. She seemed to come forth, transfigured, from a profound abyss of darkness ; and that sight lightened the heavy burden of grief which had weighed upon us. She then again offered up prayer for those whom God had given her to love in a special manner, making use of the words of our Lord, when he commended his disciples to his Father : ' I pray for them whom thou hast given me ; for they are thine. And now I am no more in the world ; but these are in the world, and I come to thee. Holy, father, keep through thine own name those whom thou hast given me, that they may be one. I pray not that thou shouldest take them out of the world, but that thou shouldest keep them from the evil. Sanctify them through thy truth ; thy word is truth.' Finally, she blessed us all, and hailed that supreme moment of life which she had so much desired, pronouncing these words : " Yes, Lord, thou callest me, and I go to thee ; *I go—not on account of my merits, but solely on account of thy mercies*, and that mercy I implore in the name, O Jesus, of thy precious blood.' She breathed forth several times the words, 'O precious Saviour, O precious blood !' She then said, 'Father, into thy hands I commend my spirit,' and with a countenance radiant as an angel's, she bowed her head and died."

Catharine died at six o'clock on the evening of Sunday, the 29th of April, 1380, at the age of thirty-three years. It was the festival of St. Peter Martyr, the courageous Dominican, who, after a long apostolic career, fell under the blows of assassins, and when dying wrote upon the ground with the blood that flowed from his wounds, the first words of the *Credo*, "I believe in God."

A Roman lady of high rank, called Semia, had a vision, it was said, on the night after Catharine's death. She saw her ascending a golden staircase into heaven, and the Son of Man approaching to greet her by name. She did not know that Catharine was dead ; but, full of this vision, she ran early the next morning to the house in the street of Santa Chiara, and knocked at the door ; but no one answered. "The neighbours informed her that Catharine had been visiting the churches, and that there was no one there ; for those within, who were mourning her, concealed her death, being desirous that the rumour should not get abroad too soon, as they would not be able tranquilly to discuss what was best to be done. It was decided that on the morrow the body of Catharine should be carried to the church of the Preaching Friars, called the church of the Minerva." Stephen says, evidently with an affectionate pride mingling with his reverence for his beloved mistress, " I carried her body with my own hands to the church of the Minerva, where it was deposited in a coffin or chest of cypress wood." As soon as the corpse of Catherine had been borne to the church, the whole city of Rome became aware of her death, and a multitude collected from every side. "The populace moved forward like turbulent waves, hoping to be allowed to touch her garments." Her disciples, fearing for the safety of the beloved body, placed it behind the grate of the chapel of St. Dominic. She lay with her hands crossed on her breast, and a smile of infinite peace on her face. She was clothed in a new white robe and veil, and the dear old, worn Dominican cloak was wrapped around her. Her followers by turns kept vigil night and day around her. Semia, the Roman lady just mentioned, seeing the vast crowd, asked its cause, and when she knew that Catharine was dead, she forced her way, sobbing, to the place. She said to the friends around, " How cruel of you to conceal from me the death of my spiritual mother whom I loved so much! Why did you not summon me ? " While they were making their excuses she inquired at what time Catharine died. " About the sixth hour," they replied, " she gave up her soul to her Creator." " I saw her, I saw her ! " cried Semia ; and she recounted the vision to the Mantellatas, who were shielding the corpse by their presence.

So great a crowd pressed daily into the church during the three days that the body remained there, that it was necessary to place guards and. sentinels around and inside the building. On the third day a celebrated Doctor of Theology ascended the pulpit, intending to preach her funeral sermon ; but it was impossible to obtain sufficient calm to allow him to proceed. At last he pronounced, as audibly as he could, the words, " This holy one has no need of *our* preaching and eulogy ; she herself speaks, and her life is her eulogy ;" and he came down from the pulpit, not even having begun his discourse. Friar William of England left his retreat at Lecceto to go to Siena when the news of Catharine's death had reached that city, and preached a sermon to a great multitude who held her name in honour. " It is with hymns of joy," he said, " and not with tears, that we should celebrate the death of Catharine." " Some days after her death," says Bartholomew of Siena, in his deposition, "a man of exalted piety, named John of Pisa, came very early in the morning and knocked at my door. I opened it, and he said to me, 'Catharine of Siena is coming.' 'How can she come?' I asked, 'for she is dead.' 'You will see her,' he replied, and vanished so quickly that I could not call him back. One Sunday after this, after having recited the midnight office, I lay down to take a little repose, when, towards daylight, I saw, in a cloudless sky, a multitude of blessed spirits advancing in procession. They were clothed in white, and they sang sacred hymns, the *Kyrie Eleison* and *Gloria in Excelsis.* In the centre of the procession was Catharine. She was clad like the angels, and she resembled the Saviour. In her hand she bore a palm-branch, her head was inclined, and her eyes cast down. I prayed that God would send me the comfort of beholding her countenance. I was heard; she raised her head and looked at me with the ineffable smile which always expressed the joy of her soul. The procession then resumed its onward march, continuing the heavenly chants."

The republic of Siena having expressed, by a deputation of its citizens to the Roman Pontiff, its jealousy of the honour of the possession of the body of the saint, and its desire to establish a monument to her in her native city, the Pope ordained the "pious mutilation," which cannot be contemplated without a feeling of pain. The head of the poor saint was severed from the body, and with great ceremony was presented in a coffer to the ambassadors of the city of Siena. It was a year after her death that the coveted relic was conveyed to her native city.

Two monks of the church of the Minerva carried the treasure. The entrance into Siena resembled a popular triumph. The Bishop had ordained that a solemn procession should leave the city and go forward a mile on the road towards Rome, in order to meet those who bore the relic. The streets of Catharine's native city, so far from having the appearance of mourning, were decked as if for a festival. It was the month of May, and the city gates were adorned with arches of flowers; flowers also were strewn in the streets; the whole population, joyous and in holiday attire, stood waiting on the ramparts and the slopes leading down from the city; the houses were hung with scarves and banners, and leafy garlands; the bells of the churches rang out as if for a holiday. The procession was headed by the different guilds and associations of workmen. Then followed the representatives of the different monastic orders, singing psalms of praise; after this came the clergy, carrying tapers. The head of the procession, having encountered the messengers bearing the relic on the road from Rome, turned with them, and the long procession re-entered the city. Close around the sacred remains walked the relations and disciples of Catharine. First among the former was seen the venerable Lapa, now in her eightieth year. (Lapa died at the age of ninety.) She leaned upon the arm of Alessia. As she passed, the people saluted her—sometimes with tears, sometimes with joyful words of congratulation. "How happy art thou!" they said, "to witness thus the recognition by the Republic of thy sainted daughter." But Lapa wept. It was then that she repeated her regret at having survived so many of her loved ones. "It is only I," she said, "who cannot die. It seems as if

God had riveted my soul to my body." The magistrates and gonfaloniers of the city followed the clergy in the procession, and, finally, the flower of the nobility of Tuscany closed the rear of this *cortége* of honour. The procession having reached the gates of the old church of St. Dominic, so endeared to Catharine in her childhood and youth, Stephen, Father Raymond, and the brothers and sisters of St. Dominic who were waiting there, received the precious relic and placed it in the church. The people continued during the day to commemorate her by religious services and social assemblies.

The custom has been maintained to the present day of having an annual festival in the month of May on the feast of St. Catharine, at which a banquet is prepared for the poor and needy of the city and its neighbourhood. It was at first a commemoration of a religious character, concluded by an address given by an appointed speaker upon the life and virtues of the saint ; but the custom has degenerated into a mere feast, at which very little real appreciation of the character of Catharine is observable. Efforts have been made, however, within the last twenty years in Italy to revive the memory of her in a rational and useful manner, so that the facts of her life and the excellence of her character may be made prominent, in place of those childish traditions and superstitions connected with her name which are now current.

We may follow briefly the history of a few of the friends of Catharine of whom we know anything after her death.

Barduccio, whom she specially loved on account of the singular purity of his character, was attacked a few weeks after her death with disease of the lungs. It was evident

that he would never recover; and Alessia and others counselled him to leave Rome, as the climate was hurtful to
him. He went to Siena, where he died in a few months,
at the age of twenty-three.

Stephen entered the Order of the Carthusians, and became prior of a large convent at Milan, and the active
visitor of other convents of his order. In his old age he
retired to Pontignano, at the foot of his beloved hills of
Siena. He transcribed the life of Catharine in Latin and
Italian. Several copies of these biographies were made.
One was sent by request to the King of Hungary, another
to the King of England; others to various potentates.

One of his last acts was to write the appendix, already
quoted, to the record of Father Raymond, at the time when
the question arose of Catharine's canonization. He thus concludes his testimony: "Here, then, is my testimony to the
life of Catharine of Siena. I have written it without research, and in the simplicity of my heart, though oppressed
with physical sufferings and numerous occupations. You required of me to be truthful in all that I should advance, and
I affirm in sincerity and quietness of conscience that I have
added nothing to the truth. I know that a false tongue slays
the soul, and that God has no need of our exaggerations. I
know also that it is not permitted to do evil that good may
come. Be persuaded, therefore, that I have told the truth.
I attest it in the presence of the Omniscient, to whom be all
praise and glory for ever and ever. This declaration has
been written by two notaries in the presence of numerous
witnesses. We have appended to it the great seal of our
convent in order to satisfy your request." Stephen died in
1424. It is said of him, that when he was an aged man it

was his constant delight, in his walks with his friars, to speak of Catharine. "He recalled the smallest details of her life; and on one occasion, at the sudden remembrance of some little thing illustrative of her loving kindness and her sufferings, he burst into tears. It seemed as if his heart would break; the brothers were obliged to support the old man to a seat, in an open meadow, where a soft wind was blowing. He here recovered his equanimity after a time."[1]

The young nobleman, Neri di Landoccio, Catharine's ambassador to Naples, did not return to Rome before her death. He afterwards wrote out Catharine's book, and collected her letters. He gave up all his wealth and possessions, and retired to a life of seclusion and study.

Alessia only survived her beloved friend and mistress a year or two, leaving the guardianship of the mystic family to Lisa, the sister of Catharine.

Certain French writers have attributed the scandalous division in the Church to Catharine's influence. It was she who persuaded Gregory XI. to return to Rome, and the Schism, they assert, was a consequence of that return. It is easy, however, to see that the Schism was the natural consequence of the long voluntary expatriation of the Popes, and their residence at Avignon. These were, as we have already seen, the causes to a great extent of the political and social miseries of Italy in the fourteenth century. The cardinals, almost all French, never ceased after the election of Urban VI. to long for the return to their native land, and resented the efforts of the newly elected Italian Pope to reform the morals of the clergy.

---

[1] Bollandus, p. 971.

Their last resource, as we have also seen, was the election of a rival Pope, a Frenchman, and one who would restore to them the delights of Avignon. The Schism lasted until the Council of Constance in 1417. The restoration of the unity of the Church was at that time achieved in a great measure through the magnanimity of Gregory XII. and the efforts of the Cardinal of Ragusa. Angelo Corrario who was afterwards elected by the Roman Church as Gregory XII., was Archbishop of Venice and Patriarch of Constantinople at the time of the election of Urban VI. He was an intimate friend and ally of Catharine.[1] She wrote to him urgently on the great subject she had at heart—the reformation of the Church—beseeching him to elect as pastors only men of pure and honourable lives, and to be fearless in rebuking vice. He held her in such veneration that, on receiving the news of her death, he sent a messenger to Rome to beg to be allowed the possession of some relic of her. This was granted to him, and the relic was found after his death suspended round his neck. It is not unnatural to suppose that her ardent counsels to him concerning contempt for this world and its honours, dwelt in his mind, and that his magnanimous action at the time of the Council of Constance may to some extent have been due to her living influence and the memory of her advice. The Cardinal of Ragusa had also been a friend of Catharine. He frequently sought her counsels. He and others of her disciples never ceased to labour for the destruction of the Schism.

Gregory XII., according to all historians a learned and

----

[1] See Letter No. 341, edition Gigli.

pious man, voluntarily resigned the Papacy in 1415, so that there might again be only one Pope. An Italian Pope was elected, and it was agreed by the French supporters of the Papacy of Avignon, that that city should henceforth be abandoned by the Papal Court, which should be permanently re-established at Rome. Thus discord ceased, and unity was restored to the Church. But a mere outward unity, such as this, would have failed to satisfy Catharine, had she lived to see it realized. The true "unity of the spirit, in the bond of peace and righteousness of life," a unity based upon a living and fruitful faith in Christ crucified, is what she would have desired and laboured for with the unceasing activity and fervour which characterized her through life ; and more eagerly than ever, in the midst of increasing corruptions in faith and practice, would she have looked onward to that reformation of which she spoke to her friends at Pisa, when she foretold : "After these tribulations God will purify his Church by means unknown to man ; he will revive the souls of his elect, and the reformation of the Church will be so beautiful that the prospect of it fills my soul with joy."

One word concerning some of the contemporaries of Catharine who were not distinguished as those just mentioned for virtue or piety. John Hawkwood, the warlike chieftain, whose fame as a soldier lives to this day, died in Tuscany in 1394 of malaria fever, worn out by campaigning and exposure. The Florentine republic, which he had continued to serve, caused him to be buried with honours in the cathedral of Santa Maria del Fiore, and an equestrian statue, which they elevated to his honour, may there be seen to this day.

Bernabos Visconti, the cruel and detested Duke of Milan, and tyrant of Lombardy, continued successfully in his course of rapacity and self-aggrandizement until the year 1385. He had thirty-three children, of whom all but five were bastards. He continued to enrich himself by extortions and intolerable taxes imposed on his subjects. " His brutal pride, his transports of anger, his cruelties and his profligacy, had brought upon him the universal contempt and hatred of the Italian people." He found himself more secure in his dominions, and more at peace outwardly with neighbouring states in this year than he had ever been in the course of his life. But he was shortly to be called to judgment. John Galeazzo Visconti, his nephew, was as ambitious and unscrupulous as himself. He had determined to possess himself of his uncle's vast estates and wealth. In order to carry out his plan, artifice was necessary. Galeazzo suddenly appeared before the world in a new character. Having been till now a soldier and a worldling, he seemed to become a penitent and a fanatic; he frequented the shrines and churches all day long; he wore a coarse penitential garment, and walked with his eyes cast down. He was surrounded with a numerous guard, all wearing the aspect of penitents, his pretext for this being that he was afflicted with a nervous fear of assassination. He affected great timidity and a superstitious dread of death, and would start at every sound. His uncle regarded all this with scorn, and spoke of his nephew as a lunatic whose worldly career must now be regarded as closed. Galeazzo then had it proclaimed that he intended to visit a miraculous image of the Virgin at Varese on Lago Maggiore. He set out from his ducal palace at Pavia, with a numerous escort, on this pious pilgrimage. On the evening of the 6th of May the troop approached Milan. Bernabos came forth to greet his nephew; he rode out from the Vercellina gate, on a mule, unaccompanied. He had been warned by a physician of Milan that treachery awaited him; but he replied to the warning with the scorn of one who has passed a long life of unchecked and successful villany. "But the time had come when God was about to call to account this detestable man, laden with so many crimes."[1] His nephew approached and embraced him tenderly, and then turning to his followers, he suddenly threw off the mask of the meek pilgrim, and pronounced, in the rude German which was at that time the military language of all Europe, the one word, "Arrest!" In a moment Bernabos was surrounded by armed men; one seized the bridle of his mule, another cut the belt of his sword, and another bound his hands behind his back. In vain the betrayed man cried out against the treachery of Galeazzo to his own kinsman, his own flesh and blood. Galeazzo marched into Milan and took possession. Not a voice was raised on behalf of Bernabos, who was conducted, bound and blindfolded, to the dungeon of the castle of Trezzo, which he himself had built, and in which many victims of his cruelty had died a violent or a lingering death. The sons of Bernabos failed to bring him any aid. No one arose for his defence. The world was glad to forget him; his own relations even ceased to mention his name. "He had leisure," says Muratori, "for meditation, in the prison of

---

[1] Muratori, Lib. xii., p. 667.

Trezzo, on the instability of human greatness." Three times, at intervals, poison was administered to him ; but his robust frame resisted its effects to such a degree that it did not prove fatal, but only produced the most insupportable bodily anguish. Thus, for seven months, he lived, or rather died, a long, lingering, and horrible death, alone, with no one to minister to the wants of his tortured body, or to speak to him a word of hope in God. Catharine had written to him, a few years before, faithful and earnest letters, full of love and pity for the sinner whom she addressed, and whose evil doing she rebuked with horror. " Do not suppose," she wrote, " that because we see no sign in this life that God's eye is upon us, he will not one day visit our offences. When the soul is leaving the body, it will then be fully proved that God has seen all. . . . The Sovereign Judge never leaves unpunished the injustices of man, which are visited in the place and at the time appointed by him ; above all at the moment of death, when the veil which shrouds our vision is torn asunder— then all is clearly seen." She concluded her stern rebukes and warnings with words of pleading and charity : " O ! resist not the Spirit of God which is calling you. Think, O, think that the blood and tears of the Divine Son are able to cleanse you from head to foot. Despise not this offer of grace. Behold how God loves you ! No tongue can tell, no heart can conceive, the mercy and grace which will be granted to you, if you will but dispose yourself to rid your soul of mortal sin. Humble yourself under the mighty hand of God, and believe in Jesus crucified for you." It was believed that the miserable man retained in his heart some echo of these words, written by one whose hope and pity for sinners were known to be illimitable, and whose name had then been, for five years, revered as that of a prophet acquainted with the secrets of God. For it was told of him at the last, and to the surprise of all, "Behold he prayeth!" Worn out and dying, unclean and uncared for, the forlorn creature dragged himself and his chains, day by day, from his pallet to the grating of his cell, where a dim ray from without fell upon his unshorn and haggard face; and clutching, with foul and bony fingers the bars of his window, he remained, hour after hour, and day after day, gasping forth in his agony, without ceasing, the words, " Cor contritum et humiliatum, Deus non despicies"—" A broken and a contrite heart, O God, thou wilt not despise."[1] He died on the 18th of December, 1385, at the age of sixty-four.

In the course of this narrative, the letters of Catharine, which have been quoted in order to illustrate her public career, are for the most part those addressed to great people, princes and potentates, ecclesiastical and temporal. It must not be supposed, however, that her correspondence was wholly, or even chiefly, with persons of high rank or authority; the greater number of them are addressed to humbler persons. Many are written to members of her own family, which was a very large one; a great number to men and women at the heads of convents or religious societies; others are addressed to persons without name, who were in some kind of trouble and greatly in need of a friend. The following list will give some idea of the extent and variety of her correspondence :—

---

[1] Muratori, Lib. xii., p. 669 ; and notes of P. Burlamacchi on the " Letters of St. Catharine."

Twenty-four letters to Master Pipino, a tailor of Florence, and Agnesa his wife. (These were probably the honourable citizens who sheltered her during the revolution, when it was deemed unsafe by others to receive her into their houses). A letter to the keeper of the prisons (*stinche*) at Florence. To a harness-maker of Lucca. To the Elders of Lucca. To Master Francis, physician to the Pope. Five letters to Peter Gambiacorti, Signore of Pisa, and his family. To Master Cristofero Gana, who had asked her to help him to choose a wife. Many letters to Alessia dei Sarracini, her most dear and intimate friend. To Laurencio di Pino, Jurisconsult and Professor of Law at the University of Bologna. To her three brothers settled as wool-dyers at Florence. (In one of these letters she begs them to be more loving to their mother, Lapa, and to repay to her some money which she had lent them). Many letters to Stephen, and to Neri di Landoccio. To a linen-weaver at Florence. To a currier named Perotti and to Lippa his wife, at Lucca. To Sabri, a goldsmith at Siena. To an abominably profligate man, name not mentioned. To several prisoners at Siena. To the Jew Consiglio, a usurer, who had settled in Siena and made so large a fortune that the magistrates of the city thought it right to institute an inquiry into the means by which he had amassed it. Many letters addressed to the magistrates of Siena and of Lucca ; to the gonfaloniers of Perugia, of Florence, and of Rome. To various citizens of Siena, thirty-four letters. To Brothers of St. Dominic, and to Mantellatas, fifty-five letters. A letter to her little niece Jenny ; one to a great prelate not named ; and one to a " Lady who was always murmuring." One of the most remarkable of her letters, in respect of dignity of style, is that which she addressed to the magistrates of Siena when they complained of the length of her visit to the aristocratic family of the Salimbeni, in the neighbourhood of that city. She writes: "In reply, dear Brothers and Signors, to the letter which Thomas di Guelfuccio has brought me from you, I desire to thank you for the kindness which you manifest towards your fellow-citizens, and towards myself in particular, who am so little worthy. You desire my return. I do not act on my own impulse, but I leave it to God to order my ways; and so soon as the Holy Spirit permits me to obey your orders, I will bow my head, and go wherever it is your good pleasure that I should go; but I shall always consider the will of God before that of men. At the present moment I see it not to be possible for me to return, because it is necessary that I should conclude an important business concerning the convent of St. Agnes, and that I should confer with the nephews of Monsignore Spinello, in order to bring about the reconciliation of the sons of Lorenzo. A long time has elapsed since you yourselves took up this affair, and as yet nothing has been accomplished. I do not wish that, through any negligence of mine, or through my sudden departure, the matter should be postponed. I should fear thus to displease God. Be assured I will return as soon as God's work is completed. Have patience, therefore, gentlemen—you and my other fellow-citizens. Do not open your hearts to all the fancies suggested by the evil one, who only desires to hinder every good work for the honour of God, the salvation of souls, and your own peace. I regret the trouble which my fellow-citizens give themselves in their judgments of me. It appears as though they had no better occupation in life than to speak ill of me and my companions. For myself they are right, for I have faults enough ; but for those who are with me, they are wrong. We shall conquer, however, by patience. Patience is never conquered ; she is always victorious, and ever remains at last mistress of the position. What really grieves me is that the darts flung after us fall back again upon those who fling them. No more. May you rest in the holy remembrance of God. —CATHARINE." One more citation only shall be given, as characteristic of her tender and liberal nature. Fra Giusto, prior of the convent of Montoliveto, had had scruples about receiving into his community a certain gentle young friend of Catharine, because he was the illegitimate and disowned son of a dissolute man. Catharine writes : " I pray you, dear father, never to regard anyone in the light of any outward circumstances, or of any greatness or baseness of birth which he may possess. Question not if such an one be legitimately or illegitimately born. The Son of God, in whose steps you are bound to follow, never discarded anyone on account of his outward condition, were he a just man or a criminal ; but every reasonable creature desiring to flee from sin was and is acceptable to him. . . . . Let this youth be born as he may, God no more despises the soul of one born in sin, than he does the soul of one born in wedlock. It is good and sincere desires alone which are regarded by our God ; and, therefore, I pray and demand that you receive kindly this tender plant who desires to be planted in your garden, for he has a good will and holy desires. . . . I have wondered exceedingly at your refusal of him. Perhaps he who brought the message made some mistake. But now I pray you, in the name of Christ crucified, to dispose yourself to receive him heartily, for he is a good boy; if he had not been so, I would not have sent him to you." On another occasion she wrote to an Abbot of Montoliveto, beseeching, or rather commanding, him to receive again a young monk who had run away, and now penitently desired to return.

It must not be supposed that the many letters addressed by her to persons in a humble sphere of life were such as we, in modern times, may write very many of in a day, on common matters of business. The letters to her friends who were artisans or tradesmen of Florence and Siena are in general very long and earnest arguments upon the Christian life, and full of affectionate counsels concerning the state and condition of the individual addressed, and of his family. She wrote to them in the same terms as she wrote to Kings, Cardinals, and Popes—with reverence and considerateness, combined with courageous truthfulness, and, when necessary, with severity, and addressing them alike as " most dear and honoured father in Christ." She was a true republican, in the sense that in her dealings with men as fellow-sinners and fellow-Christians she recognized no differences of rank.

It is not difficult to imagine what were the faults in Catharine's character, and the natural tendencies against which she, most probably all her life, had to contend. Her zeal and fire would naturally carry her on to impatience; and it must have been difficult for her to bear with equanimity the delays and checks induced by the stumblings and errors of others which so often postponed or injured the work she had at heart. It is evident also that her genius for command may have tempted her to exercise an imperious self-will, and to rule in too despotic a manner. Again, there are evidences that at times, when the strong claims of active duty were relaxed, she incurred a danger of being carried away by excess of feeling, in the exaltation of her spirit, and the intense communion of her soul with the unseen. This latter danger was controlled, however, by the deep, strong, human affection which ever impelled her to impart to others all that she had received of God, and to see in every human being who needed help the image of him whom her soul adored. Impatience and impetuosity of will were corrected—as indeed every other fault of character can alone be corrected—by the constant exercise of the virtues which balanced and controlled them, hope, patience, faith, and the renunciation of self. Towards the end of her life it is observable that she dwelt very strongly and constantly on the virtue of patience—that virtue of which no doubt she had felt the deficiency in herself, and which she had resolutely striven to possess. Patience, she thought, was the great lesson, above all others, which God is always teaching his children. She calls it the " touchstone of all the virtues."

The canonization of Catharine took place in 1461. The proceedings had first been instituted, and witnesses had begun to be questioned, in 1402, by Gregory XII. But the troubles of his times in connection with the Schism obliged him to postpone these preliminaries; and it fell to the lot of Eneas Silvius, a Sienese, who was elevated to the papacy as Pius II., to place her name on the calendar of the saints. There is a touch of nature in the otherwise formal Bull of Canonization published by him. "This affair has been deferred," he says, "until our time, and the canonization of our countrywoman has been referred to us. The sanctity of the virgin of Siena shall be proclaimed by a native of Siena; and we confess that in this we experience a sensible consolation. We should have contemplated in any case with joy the virtues, the genius, the greatness of soul, the strength and fortitude of this blessed Catharine; but we do so all the more because she, like ourselves, first saw the light in the city of Siena."

Cardinal Ximenes caused the letters of Catharine to be translated into Spanish about the year 1450, Spain having, up to that time, refused, in its partisanship for Clement, to recognize the merits of the champion of Urban VI.

Catharine's letters only very rarely contain any allusions to her own outward history, although they reveal abundantly the character of her mind. They are for the most part purely spiritual; and when she refers to any contemporary event, it is from the lofty view of the Christian, who regards more the spirit than the external movements of the times in which she is placed. It is with difficulty that we are able to trace in them any clear outline even of her own outward relations with the Church and with her personal friends and contemporaries, though we see in them clearly the travail of her soul for all these, and her indefatigable zeal in labouring to win men to Christ.

I have accomplished my task, of writing the story of the life of Catharine of Siena. Very imperfectly, I am too well aware, has it been done; yet I conclude with the hope that the record may carry a message to the hearts of many who read it, and may be the means of reviving the strong and loving influence of this woman, who lived five hundred years ago, so that it may be said concerning her, even now, "she being dead, yet speaketh." It is no easy task, looking back through the mists of ages, to discover athwart the medium of the apotheoses of the saint which are presented to us by Catholic writers as biography, the real woman, such as she was in her true character. The greatest of the saints were flesh and blood like ourselves; yet not so, by any means, are they represented by the mediæval hagiologist. The memoir by Father Raymond gives us the internal life of Catharine as faithfully as he was able to render it; but her wonderful outward life and public career are almost entirely left out of his record. When he mentions any part of these, he does so only parenthetically, and in order to illustrate the several virtues which formed, as he says, "her aureole." The formality of style usual in his time leads him to head his various chapters according to the different graces in which she excelled. One is headed "Her Patience;" another "Her Austerities;" another "Her Sighs for Death," &c. A more wearisome and uninteresting memoir could hardly be imagined of a very original and highly gifted person, whose life was like a beautiful drama, ever widening, and increasing in solemnity and fulness of incident to the end. And yet conscience reproaches me for a species of ingratitude in pronouncing this judgment of Raymond's work; for to him, above all others, are we indebted for the *key* to both her inward and outward life; and from him alone, her intimate friend and companion, do we gather some of the most touching incidents and the most characteristic traits. He rarely condescends, however, to give a plain statement of any of the facts of her life. For example, he never states historically that she went to Florence, or why. He merely says, in different parts of his book, " When we were at Florence, she did or said so and so;" and then calls upon the reader to admire the great humility or the superhuman patience of the saint. He very rarely gives a date. There are, it may be said, three dates in the whole course of the book, which come to the eager student of her active life with a sense of surprise and relief, as a sign-post would to a traveller after a hundred miles of vague wandering through a country without roads. All the other early biographies of Catharine are based upon that of Raymond, with little variation. It may be truly said that these biographers unconsciously represented Catharine in a form which as nearly resembled the real woman as the figures on the painted windows of old churches resemble the flesh and blood originals. To describe human enthusiasm in high and passionate action requires a gift which few writers have possessed. Instead of the high and beautiful humanity, the old biographers of the saints give us only a superhumanity which leaves us with an unsatisfied longing to possess the real portrait instead. Fully appreciating the difficulty of the task, and foreseeing the necessarily most imperfect result, I set it as my aim to endeavour, by steady and honest study, to bring out truthfully, as far as was possible, the real woman, Catharine of Siena. At the best, the picture must be defective. Owing to the omissions in the biographies of Raymond and his imitators, it has been necessary to search for side lights upon her character and career, in many of the annalists and chroniclers of her time, lay and ecclesiastical. Some of these have afforded considerable help towards eliciting the humanness of the person portrayed, and the reality and activity of her life. Although in most of these her name is cited with a tender reverence, yet this is not always the case. The adverse testimonies are not without their value. Some speak of her as one "reputed to be wise," but having no knowledge of the world, of public questions, or of diplomacy. The French historians of the Schism who espoused the cause of Clement VII. seldom speak well of her. This is not unnatural, considering the prominent part she took in upholding the Italian Pope. Indeed, her reputation in France, until a very recent date, has suffered from the blackening touches given to the portrait of her character by the Clementines, in the same way that the character of Joan of Arc remained in England so long under the slur cast upon her by our own Shakespeare and his contemporaries. M. Bouchon, the translator into French of Machiavelli's "History of Florence," made the following comment upon the notice there given of Catharine and her mission to Florence: "Pius II. on his death-bed repented bitterly of three things: of having written the book of 'The two Lovers;' of having preached a crusade; and of having canonized that sovereignly contemptible woman, Catharine of Siena."[1] Sismondi remarks, with a touch of the peculiar nineteenth century scorn of women: "It was not to be expected that they (the Eight of War) should

---

[1] It may be worthy of remark, that Maimbourg, a historian of the period of the Schism, who was an ardent Clementine, invariably speaks with respect of Catharine.

be biassed by the advice of a well-meaning but enthusiastic woman, in matters of importance to the State;" and we have occasional notices of her, of this character, either contemptuously patronizing or positively hostile, down to a few words of the present day, written by the Rev. Andrew Reed, who speaks of her as the "Dominican Pythoness," who was "said to have visions of Christ."[1]

There is, however, a certain value, real of its kind, in the early biographies, pale and unlife-like, and abounding in puerilities as they are. The writers at least believed what they wrote, and their affection for the subject of their biographies led them undoubtedly to put down the substance of the truth concerning her, however enveloped that substance may be with clouds of incense and mists of superstitious reverence. Tedious and disappointing as they are, they will yet appear to many readers far more satisfactory than sketches of her life, or poems in her honour written by persons full of enthusiasm for the genius and power of the human being, full of poetic appreciation of the beauty of the life of self-devotion (or as it is now the fashion to call it, altruism), but utterly rejecting the faith of which that life was the outcome and product. Alike inquisitive and critical concerning the ecstasies, exaltations, and trances of the mystic, while dwelling with artistic delight on the beauty of this noble apparition on the stage of history, the modern sceptic throws himself for the moment on his face before her, and worships "he knows not what;" he

---

[1] "The Story of Christianity, from the Apostles to the Present Day," p. 287.

then goes his way, never having truly known what manner of person she was, unbelieving as ever in regard to the common inheritance which the poorest and most miserable struggler after Christ shares with the highest and holiest of the saints, and ignorant as before of that eternal source and fount of life whence the most noble and gifted, as well as the meanest of the children of men must needs draw the life through which alone they are transformed into saints of God.

There is no need to call upon any to admire the genius of Catharine. There are many who will be able to draw philosophical deductions, infinitely better than I can, from the facts of such a life and such a character as have been depicted. There are many who will be interested in regarding Catharine as a typical character, or the representative of much that was the best and strongest in the era in which she lived; as a person who could only by any possibility have been born and nurtured under the sunny skies of Italy, who could only have proceeded from such a simple and hardy race as that of the artisans of Siena, and who could only have reached what she attained to under the combined and strongly-contrasted influences of Roman Catholicism and Republicanism. In all these respects Catharine stands, as it were, apart from us, and at a distance. We have no share in the circumstances above named, which may have contributed more or less to her greatness. In concluding, therefore, I had rather draw attention to what we in England, and in the nineteenth century, have in common with her—what, indeed, every human being shares or may share with her.

In common with her, we possess much that is external to us; the priceless inheritance claimed and striven for by all who have been truly great in the sense of bringing blessing to humanity. We have one Father, the Eternal, the Just One, the ever Faithful, whose name is Love. We have one Saviour, he who is the Word, who was with God from the beginning, and who was made flesh and lived among us, died, and rose again for our salvation. We have one Source, approachable by us all, of undying spiritual life—the Holy Spirit, whom that Saviour poured forth upon his waiting disciples on the day of Pentecost, and who now waits each moment at the door of every heart, to be admitted and to bring light, life, and peace. We have, in common with the saint whose life we have followed, an ever-free access to the Father, by prayer. That path of prayer which she firmly and unwearyingly trod is open to every one of us. If her life illustrates one truth more forcibly than another, it is that of the efficacy and power of prayer, and the fidelity of God in answering the petitions of those who wait on him. We have, in common with her, not only all this, which is external to ourselves, but we have each one of us within us the power to look upward, to pray, to turn our faces resolutely to the light, and to urge ourselves onwards towards that light. It requires no mighty genius to become strong in faith and in prayer. It needs not the hand of a giant to lay hold upon the hand of the All-powerful and All-loving. The hand of a child can equally well grasp that hand, and, in so doing, out of weakness be made strong. We have the power to cultivate the human affection within us, until, freeing itself from all littleness and egotism, it embraces humanity, and, liberated from the thraldom of restless passion and excess, it becomes a chastened, ever-burning, and unquenchable love towards our fellows, ever ready to weep with those who weep, and to rejoice with those who rejoice, to believe all things, to hope all things, and to endure all things.

We all have the power, God helping us, to become honest, truthful, courageous, just, patient, self-denying, and kind. We can all learn to oppose persistently and with courage what we know to be evil, and to speak each one to his neighbour, faithfully and in love, what we believe to be the truth.

Every truly great man or woman who can justly be called *blessed* as well as great, learned at first to be faithful n a few things, and in that which was least, before being called to control and to act in the midst of great things; and for each of us it is possible to begin from this moment to perform every act of our daily life with an upright intention and a pure conscience before God and man; and in so doing we shall have already advanced not a few steps along that path of humble glory which the blessed great have trodden before us. No truer meed of praise could be given to any man than that which Lord Cobham gave to Wycliffe: "As for that virtuous man Wycliffe, I shall say, of my part, both before God and man, that before I knew that despised doctrine of his I never abstained from sin. But since I learned therein to fear my Lord God, it hath otherwise, I trust, been with me. So much grace could I never find before in any instructions of the Church." There were hundreds who might have said this of Catharine of Siena. What can one human being do better for another than this—so to tell him the truth of Christ as to win him from sin and weakness, and set him on the path to heaven? This again, then, we have in common with Catharine—the wonderful power with which God has endowed us, as social and sympathetic beings, to impart what we know and love, to pass on from hand to hand the torch we bear, be it of a blazing brightness or as yet but dimly burning. But first we must ourselves possess the light.

Look well, then, reader, at this poor saint, at all the saints, at the good and noble, the great cloud of witnesses who have gone before, and are going. For as they were and are, so you may be. But, turning from these, look higher still. Turn your eyes towards him who is the Light of the World, the Saviour, to whom I pray that he will bless this poor work, and make it fruitful of blessing in the hearts of those who are able to read the lesson of a holy life through all the imperfections which mar the record.

THE END.